The Best
AMERICAN
SHORT
STORIES
1995

GUEST EDITORS OF
THE BEST AMERICAN SHORT STORIES

The Best
AMERICAN
SHORT
STORIES
1995

Selected from
U.S. and Canadian Magazines
by JANE SMILEY
with KATRINA KENISON

With an Introduction by Jane Smiley

HOUGHTON MIFFLIN COMPANY
BOSTON • NEW YORK

ISSN 0067-6233
ISBN 0-395-71180-0
ISBN 0-395-71179-7 (PBK.)

Printed in the United States of America

QUM 10 9 8 7 6 5 4 3

Contents

Foreword

ANYONE WHO HAS ever thrown a party knows the queasiness of the last hour: everything is ready, and you are alone. What if no one comes? I feel a similar apprehension each spring as I plant my garden. It's a long week spent hauling compost and peat moss, weeding and tilling, and, finally, dropping impossibly tiny seeds into furrows of earth. After all this, I can't help but think, What if nothing comes up? Each winter, as I clean out my old short story files and pack up the past year's journals and magazines, I'm left with the same mixture of anticipation and anxiety. With last year's stories selected, it is time to begin the whole process of reading and choosing again. But I worry. What if there are no dazzling stories this year? What if no one shows up?

Of course, the guests always arrive; it is human nature to want to be included. And, of course, the garden plot soon bristles with green nubs, for even the tiniest seed harbors within it a destiny — give it half a chance and it grows. Yet when I harvest a fist-size tomato four months later — from a plant that began as a seed flake in my palm and is now taller than I — it seems nothing short of miraculous.

And yes, at the end of the year there are always more than enough exceptional stories to fill an annual collection like *The Best American Short Stories*. I may marvel at a weighty Better Boy, but I am visited by an even greater sense of wonder when confronted by a fully realized short story. Year after year, writers, too, fulfill their own destinies, defying the obstacles and distractions of daily life in order to get words onto the page and out into the world. Invariably, as the year draws to a close, my file folders bulge with stories that have worked some sort of special magic on me. The harvest is always good, but it is far less predictable than the tomatoes. There are generally prize specimens by beloved authors, but there are many strange fruits as well. Each one is unique, each the result of a tiny seed of inspiration planted deep within a particular psyche and allowed to flourish there.

The contributors' essays at the back of this volume offer fascinating glimpses into the myriad ways short stories come to life. In many cases, the origins of a story are no more substantial than the tiny seed which, nevertheless, harbors within itself the possibility of astonishing abundance. The images that gave rise to these stories are as varied as the stories themselves: a face on a billboard, a child asleep in a car seat, a shattered knee, a woman reading a man's palm by the light of her dashboard, a mural in Belfast, a dead body. The stories that grew out of these seemingly inconsequential images are as remarkable as any wonder of the natural world: the slow-ripened fruits of their creators' long labors. Perhaps, as the years roll on, I will begin to take more for granted — the garden's annual production, the annual crop of short stories. But I suspect that, like me, readers of this anthology will continue to be astonished at the seemingly infinite human capacity to create.

Jane Smiley, this year's guest editor, says she found herself drawn to stories with a "sharp and exotic flavor." Her final selections attest to the diversity of this year's short stories — the harvest was plentiful and diffuse. Still, the stories she chose coalesced almost instantly into an organic whole, without any behind-the-scenes tugging and pulling for shape and balance. Jane Smiley brought both a keen appetite and a refined palate to her task. The result is a collection that, once assembled, seemed inevitable. We are grateful for her time and, even more, for the enthusiasm and good judgment with which she read.

The stories chosen for this anthology were originally published in magazines issued between January 1994 and January 1995. The qualifications for selections are (1) original publication in nationally distributed American or Canadian periodicals; (2) publication in English by writers who are American or Canadian, or who have made the United States or Canada their home; (3) publication as short stories (novel excerpts are not knowingly considered). A list of magazines consulted for this volume appears at the back of the book. Publications that want to assure that their fiction is considered each year should include the series editor on their subscription list (Katrina Kenison, *The Best American Short Stories,* Houghton Mifflin Company, 222 Berkeley Street, Boston, Massachusetts 02116-3764).

K.K.

Introduction

I AM NOT a good reader. I am slow and not very determined. I never make myself read a book to the end if I get bored in the middle. I am not especially forgiving — there are whole oeuvres of important and profound writers that I haven't read because I was put off by some quirk in the author's style. I like murder mysteries and magazine pieces about the five types of relationships that will never go anywhere. When magazines about horses and others about important social and political issues arrive the same day, I always read the horse magazines first. I read Tina Brown's *New Yorker* more eagerly than I used to read William Shawn's *New Yorker.*

More important, for the purposes of this collection, I always read the short story in any magazine last rather than first, and often with reluctance. The short story is the most demanding piece in the magazine because it has the strongest voice. Rather than the shared voice of standard prose, like the voice of the journalism and the essays and the ads, it is a voice idiosyncratic enough to be a little threatening, a little difficult. A novel gives a reader time to orient herself to that private voice, but with a short story, it's there and then gone, almost too much to take.

For that reason, that I am too slow and selfish a reader to keep up with contemporary short fiction, I was delighted to be asked to read for this collection and choose my favorites. I had no idea what to expect and was too busy to think about it anyway, so my first response on receiving the stories was to count them and to calculate how many I had to read each day in order to meet my

deadline. That calculation was two. It was late October, a good time
to begin a serious reading regime. I read at bedtime and in the
early morning, in the bathtub and in front of *Barney*, on airplanes
and car trips, in the middle of the night in the middle of St.
Petersburg, Russia, in Boston, Massachusetts, in Pasadena, California, and in rural North Carolina.

And it turned out that reading these authors heightened my
sense of all the other authors, dead and alive, whose spirits and
manuscripts and first editions are carefully preserved in places like
the Dostoevsky and Akhmatova museums in Russia and the Hunt-
ington Library in California. All the authors that I was reading and
thinking about seemed to enter into a lively dialogue with one
another, and to fertilize my inner life in a pleasing and invigorating
way, so that when I met my deadline and all the stories were read,
I was sorry rather than glad.

So I offer these twenty stories with both sorrow and gladness.
While they are the twenty that I preferred of the hundred and
twenty that I read, the pleasure that I had in reading the other
hundred certainly swelled, and in part created, the pleasure I felt
in reading these. The reader of this volume is in somewhat the
same position as the listener to an opera-highlights recording —
the music is thrilling and beautiful, but not as satisfying as the
whole production.

The order of the stories is neither alphabetical nor hierarchical,
but, I hope, artful, in the way that a Chinese meal is artful — designed so that the flavors enhance one another as the feast pro-
gresses. There are many sharp and exotic flavors here, but they are
flavors of different varieties. I hope that each story serves to make
the reader hunger for the next one.

The short story is an elusive, paradoxical form, not easily mastered, yet some of the best are written by beginning writers. While
the arc of a novelist's career is frequently easy to predict — complexity and wisdom that arise from more mature experience replace an early freshness of subject and approach — things are more
problematic for the short story writer. Myriad beginnings and
endings and subjects and characters seem to call for more and
more inventiveness. The familiarity that soothes in the novel can
seem repetitive in a series of short stories.

The form itself is difficult — *longueur* is fatal to a story, but suddenness can be damaging, too. Fitting the size of the subject to the size of the form is horribly difficult — too much detail fails to evoke feeling, but so does too little; the small incident can seem trivial, the dramatic incident melodramatic. Then there is the question of that last lonely criterion, taste. Not long ago, I contributed to an anthology of the favorite short stories, both famous and obscure, of some of today's well-thought-of writers. Writers of discrimination and authority, whose work and literary opinions I've long respected, chose stories, in some cases by acknowledged masters, that left me completely cold. No accounting for that.

A long reading project, such as choosing these stories has been for me, finally asserts its own terms. Whatever the reader thinks she prefers or knows about writing and reading eventually falls away, and finally all that is left is appetite — one story both piques and satisfies the appetite, but another, while worthy, does not. I read these stories blind, and for the most part, when I thought I might have guessed the identity of the writer, I subsequently discovered I was wrong. Looking over the list I have chosen tells me more about my taste than I ever knew. I've chosen almost half women, half men authors. I've chosen some rank beginners and many established writers, but no "elder statesmen." In many cases, I've preferred a peppery flavor of the strange or exotic, but in some cases the rich savor of the familiar seen with clarity and wisdom. Always I've been attracted to wit and almost always to a vigorous story line, as close as we come, or perhaps want to come in these times, to a plot.

My favorite reading pleasure is frustration, but frustration of a very particular kind, compounded of eagerness to get on with the story and an equally strong longing to linger over and savor the author's style and technique. I always think that when I am poised on that cusp, pulled equally in both directions, I am most fully responding to what a piece of fiction is, a made artifact but also a human relationship between writer and reader inside of which is nested another human relationship between characters.

When I am reading, I marvel at both miraculous moments — the moment when the print seems to disappear, overwhelmed by the pictures I am making in my imagination of the scenes I am reading, but also the moment when the print reappears and I am me again, rereading an especially delicious passage, trying to figure out just how the author came up with *that* and how different *that* is from anything I've read before or could come up with myself. The following stories offer many instances of such pleasure.

Almost all these stories, but particularly Thom Jones's "Way Down Deep in the Jungle," Andrea Barrett's "The Behavior of the Hawkweeds," and Jennifer Cornell's "Undertow," share a quality I love in a story — the sense of an effortlessly unfolding world so thoroughly imagined that it mimics the complexity of the world around us. The authors are patient and self-confident. They don't try to impress us from the first with everything they know, or even the most interesting thing they know; instead they allow not only the story line and the characters, but the theme, the style, and the setting to express themselves bit by bit.

In the Jones story, for example, the two new doctors who enter about halfway into the narrative neatly distinguish themselves from each other by both what they have to say and how they say it. In a few pages of dialogue, Jones evokes two lives, two points of view, and much of the two worlds that the young doctors have just left, but he does not call attention to his feat or allow the two young doctors to distract the reader from the main issues of the story. All the characters — Koestler, the head doctor, Johnson (his cook), Babbitt (the baboon), Hartman (the pilot), and the two new men — bring knowledge, opinion, attitude, desire, and fate, too, to their exotic encounter. The result is fascinating.

Andrea Barrett's world, in "The Behavior of the Hawkweeds," couldn't be more different — not the least foreign, an apparently familiar academic marriage in which the wife has willingly supported the husband's career, with the added irony that new research has superseded much of his expertise. But into this marriage she has brought a very specific treasure. The story explores the way she has both cherished her treasure and betrayed herself through it. Barrett's measured tone gives full weight to the moral dilemma the narrator must explore.

"Undertow" is perhaps not as finished a story as the other two, but it is deliciously rich. The simple opening is deceptive, because the characters soon blossom with understated eccentricity — Cornell's tone is transparent, perfect for the revelations to come.

Another thing I love in a story is to be tricked. There is nothing so attractive in some authors as deviousness, and for that we have Stephen Dobyns's "So I Guess You Know What I Told Him." Already in the first sentence there's a tick, a "Floyd," and cruelty. I'm sure I know where I am, which is in the American countryside, Gothic region. But no, the author, moral trickster, shows me something else entirely than what I thought I knew, thought I expected. And yet, Dobyns is never a sentimentalist. Floyd remains an ambiguous figure, but the layers of irony multiply, leaving the reader nicely defenseless.

Edward Delaney and Edward Falco practice trickery of a more traditional kind, mistaken identity being a feature of the plot of "The Drowning," and mistaken moral identity of the plot of "The Artist." These, one rural and Irish, one urban and American, are perhaps the most straightforward "tales" to be found in the collection, sturdy examples of mystery and suspense that fully satisfy the reader's eagerness to get on with the action, to know what happens next. Both remind us, in contradiction to current theory, that modern experience can be fashioned into stories, retold, and understood. These are satisfying pieces.

Every piece of fiction is in some degree also a how-to manual. Narrative is interested in the relationship between character and action, which is always expressed by *how* a character chooses to act, *how* a character meshes with circumstances. Why and what it means come later. Avner Mandelman's edgy "Pity," Don DeLillo's beautifully accomplished "The Angel Esmeralda," and Melanie Rae Thon's "First, Body" appeal to our desire to get inside the "how" of extremity.

Mandelman brazenly asserts that his characters perform assassinations for the Mossad, Israeli secret intelligence. The narrator's gossipy, flat tone makes us feel like inside dopesters. But the job goes tragically wrong. How it is meant to go and how the assassins fail quietly evoke the deep sadness that lies at the heart of evil and retribution.

"The Angel Esmeralda" brings a miracle into the heart of the South Bronx, into the lives of people we readily recognize — a nun of the old school, a younger, more practical nun, a mysterious local godfather figure, and an abandoned, terrified, and possibly crazy twelve-year-old. The local scenery is a chaos of burned-out cars and buildings, ailanthus trees, billboards, housing projects, graffiti. A tour bus goes by, its European passengers eager to stare out at the ruins. Into this fallen world comes grace, through the agency of the headlights of a passing commuter train. Of course it becomes an instant spectacle. But DeLillo never stops asking "how" all the way to the last line, so he never stops drawing meaning upon meaning from what becomes, in the end, a profound and exhilarating situation.

The opening sentence of "First, Body" is irresistible — "Two nurses with scissors could make a man naked in eleven seconds." Surely this must be true; if not, then why eleven and not ten? And with this sentence we are in the how-to world of hospitals and emergency rooms. Something is going to happen, and we are going to find out not only what, but how. For a long time in the story Thon holds her fire, pretending that she has not promised something special. When the climax does come, it is satisfyingly unusual, satisfyingly appropriate to a region of irony and injury and the will to survive.

The drama of some situations simply cannot be shrugged off, is always fascinating, which is probably why there are so many more murderers and their victims in literature than in real life. I found myself compelled, in different ways, by the drama of Kate Braverman's "Pagan Night," a disturbing and moving story that I cannot talk about without giving away, about two drug abusers and their infant, and Joy Williams's "Honored Guest," in which a teenage girl endures the slow death of her mother from cancer. The subtle play of the girl's mingled feelings of fear, embarrassment, grief, and self-absorption brilliantly evokes the sort of suffering that must shape an entire life, yet Williams's style is so economical that the reader is left feeling that a short story, and not an especially lengthy one, is the perfect form for this experience.

Drama of a chronic rather than an acute sort forms the subject of Andrew Cozine's first published story, "Hand Jive," the drama of a self at war with itself. "Hand Jive" uses the unique ability of fiction to privilege the inner life over the life of appearance to explore the dilemma of a young man who is powerfully compelled to make wild gestures with his hands and arms all the time that he knows this compulsion is separating him more and more from the rest of the world. Cozine's skill is in the clarity and wit of his tone and his unabashed willingness to go as deeply as necessary into the subject to make it understandable to the reader. After each of these three stories, I felt that I had learned something new, felt something true that I could not have imagined myself.

One conclusion I draw from my reading is that there aren't

enough humorous short stories being written. Almost no one wants to raise a laugh these days. Three welcome examples of the delicious play of wit over the page are Gish Jen's "Birthmates," Stephen Polansky's "Leg," and Daniel Orozco's "Orientation." None of these stories is comic, but all are funny. They have no other similarities with one another.

Gish Jen's story is one of the ironic accumulation of tiny circumstances during a day in the life of Art Woo, software salesman, who can't afford even the room with the view of the cooling towers at the conference center and has to put up at a much more suspect lodging. The way that circumstances come together, you could almost say that they conspire, but they don't, not really. Jen's superlative wit is in the way she keeps the ball rolling, the half-rueful, half-hopeful tone of Art's state of mind.

"Orientation" begins as a story any writer might be amazed she herself had never thought of. That first morning on the job, the tour of the office with the new colleague who's been assigned to show you the ropes. What a perfect premise for a story. But "Orientation" quickly declares its idiosyncrasy. The stylized form, with its implied second-person point of view and its reiterated verbal tics, builds with a sort of damped-down exuberance. "Orientation" is simultaneously sinister and fun, impersonal and human, very sly, very cool.

By contrast, "Leg" is very warm. Its world, of softball games, friendly pastors, family life, is a comforting one. Love, familial and friendly, is a significant factor in Polansky's story. The reader intuits early on that protagonist Dave Long's situation is becoming a dire one, yet the light, rueful, making-the-best-of-things narrative tone never flags. On the one hand, Dave ponders religious doctrine, on the other he suffers, but every moment what he does is done in the context of softball, TV, Neosporin, Metallica, and the other daily details of modern American life. I found "Leg" a lovely story.

There are some stories that you just want to be with, the way you want to be with some people. Plot and narrative strategy, however well worked out artistically, become secondary to a quality rather like charm. In the case of Jaimy Gordon's story, "A Night's Work," the attractive qualities are energy and invention, tethered in the night world of the small-time horse track, but too lively to be contained there. As soon as Nurse Pigeon finds Kidstuff, her significant other, dead on the road in "his fancy-man clothes," the chase begins. Nurse Pigeon's reaction to Kidstuff's death is as strange and wonderful as the milieu the reader explores in her company while she's ferreting out the cause of Kidstuff's demise and working through her response to it. The pizzazz of Gordon's style is invigorating.

In "Chiromancy" by poet Max Garland, the charm is quieter, more subtle. The story's premise is far more mainstream — a man and a woman who live in the same town meet, share a ride, and later ponder, separately, the meaning of a possible affair with each other. The point of view shifts between them, first in the car, then later, when they have retired to their own houses. It is a slight, even mundane situation that is given not only weight but also allure by the sheer appeal of Garland's language. He seems to enter fully into both inner lives, as well as into the passage of moments that could easily go by unfelt, unconsidered. While some stories in this collection remind the reader of the pleasures of drama, "Chiromancy" reminds us of the pleasures of careful thought and sensitive attention.

The charm of an attractive first-person narrative voice is the initial pleasure of Peter Ho Davies's first published story, "The Ugliest House in the World." Davies's narrator introduces what later turns out to be a profound and even fearsome situation as if he is just chatting. The tone is informative but casual, the subject the apparently trivial jokes everyone makes about various types of otherness — old age, illness, Welshness. All the characters seem well disposed toward one another, even fond, and so the jokes are a social rite, the affectionate side of teasing. It is only an unexpected but possibly preventable accident that hardens the teasing into antagonism, potential connection into irrevocable separation. "The Ugliest House in the World" has many layers, all subtly presented, all growing, with apparent ease and naturalness, out of what seems to be a casual style, what seems to be a conversational tone.

I save for last two stories of childhood by two established writers. Ellen Gilchrist's "The Stucco House" and Jamaica Kincaid's "Xuela," while entirely different from each other, both exhibit what seems to be effortless mastery of the form, effortless entry into the minds of children. Teddy, the protagonist of "The Stucco House," is clearly and quickly characterized on the first page of the story — a vulnerable and slightly immature but bright seven-year-old who is at the mercy of almost everyone in his family as well as ghosts, vampires, and bad dreams. Gilchrist neatly uses Teddy's point of view — equally limited by age and anxiety — to unfold the larger tale of Teddy's irresponsible mother, strict but loving grandparents, and indulgent stepfather. All of this is spaciously set in place — New Orleans, the bayou countryside. The characters do the best they can, but Gilchrist makes it sharply clear that the best may not be good enough, may not be enough to save Teddy and furnish him with what he needs. In the end, the child is more poignantly grateful than a seven-year-old ought to be for small reprieves and temporary stability.

The eponymous character of Jamaica Kincaid's "Xuela" is that staple and mythic character of short fiction, the orphan whose mother has died in childbirth. She announces herself immediately as thoughtful and serious, as well as a tough and unforgiving judge of those around her. Not for Xuela the desire to please, except as a survival tactic. Her story is the story of someone who, over the years of childhood, must learn to rely on herself, to please herself, yet who knows what softness and love she is missing and how the loss has shaped her. Xuela's is a brave and admirable voice, but not a charming one. The world she inhabits is rich and hard, full of stimulation but unkind and even dangerous. "Xuela" possesses in full measure the riveting exotic power that characterizes Kincaid's earlier work.

Certain words reappear in my descriptions of these stories — "strange," "exotic," "rich," "charming." Finally, the thing that all good short stories offer is a sudden and ineluctable experience of something not ourselves, a character, an incident, a place more or less distant from who and where we are that is, for a few minutes, so much more alluring than what we know that we give ourselves up to it. Every one of these stories gave me that exquisite experience. I offer the same to you.

JANE SMILEY

DANIEL OROZCO

Orientation

FROM THE SEATTLE REVIEW

THOSE ARE THE OFFICES and these are the cubicles. That's my cubicle there, and this is your cubicle. This is your phone. Never answer your phone. Let the Voicemail System answer it. This is your Voicemail System Manual. There are no personal phone calls allowed. We do, however, allow for emergencies. If you must make an emergency phone call, ask your supervisor first. If you can't find your supervisor, ask Phillip Spiers, who sits over there. He'll check with Clarissa Nicks, who sits over there. If you make an emergency phone call without asking, you may be let go.

These are your IN and OUT boxes. All the forms in your IN box must be logged in by the date shown in the upper left-hand corner, initialed by you in the upper right-hand corner, and distributed to the Processing Analyst whose name is numerically coded in the lower left-hand corner. The lower right-hand corner is left blank. Here's your Processing Analyst Numerical Code Index. And here's your Forms Processing Procedures Manual.

You must pace your work. What do I mean? I'm glad you asked that. We pace our work according to the eight-hour workday. If you have twelve hours of work in your IN box, for example, you must compress that work into the eight-hour day. If you have one hour of work in your IN box, you must expand that work to fill the eight-hour day. That was a good question. Feel free to ask questions. Ask too many questions, however, and you may be let go.

That is our receptionist. She is a temp. We go through receptionists here. They quit with alarming frequency. Be polite and civil to the temps. Learn their names, and invite them to lunch occasionally. But don't get close to them, as it only makes it more difficult when they leave. And they always leave. You can be sure of that.

The men's room is over there. The women's room is over there. John LaFountaine, who sits over there, uses the women's room occasionally. He says it is accidental. We know better, but we let it pass. John LaFountaine is harmless, his forays into the forbidden territory of the women's room simply a benign thrill, a faint blip on the dull flat line of his life.

Russell Nash, who sits in the cubicle to your left, is in love with Amanda Pierce, who sits in the cubicle to your right. They ride the same bus together after work. For Amanda Pierce, it is just a tedious bus ride made less tedious by the idle nattering of Russell Nash. But for Russell Nash, it is the highlight of his day. It is the highlight of his life. Russell Nash has put on forty pounds, and grows fatter with each passing month, nibbling on chips and cookies while peeking glumly over the partitions at Amanda Pierce, and gorging himself at home on cold pizza and ice cream while watching adult videos on TV.

Amanda Pierce, in the cubicle to your right, has a six-year-old son named Jamie, who is autistic. Her cubicle is plastered from top to bottom with the boy's crayon artwork — sheet after sheet of precisely drawn concentric circles and ellipses, in black and yellow. She rotates them every other Friday. Be sure to comment on them. Amanda Pierce also has a husband, who is a lawyer. He subjects her to an escalating array of painful and humiliating sex games, to which Amanda Pierce reluctantly submits. She comes to work exhausted and freshly wounded each morning, wincing from the abrasions on her breasts, or the bruises on her abdomen, or the second-degree burns on the backs of her thighs.

But we're not supposed to know any of this. Do not let on. If you let on, you may be let go.

Amanda Pierce, who tolerates Russell Nash, is in love with Albert Bosch, whose office is over there. Albert Bosch, who only dimly registers Amanda Pierce's existence, has eyes only for Ellie Tapper, who sits over there. Ellie Tapper, who hates Albert Bosch, would walk through fire for Curtis Lance. But Curtis Lance hates Ellie Tapper. Isn't the world a funny place? Not in the ha-ha sense, of course.

Anika Bloom sits in that cubicle. Last year, while reviewing quarterly reports in a meeting with Barry Hacker, Anika Bloom's left palm began to bleed. She fell into a trance, stared into her hand, and told Barry Hacker when and how his wife would die. We laughed it off. She was, after all, a new employee. But Barry Hacker's wife is dead. So unless you want to know exactly when and how you'll die, never talk to Anika Bloom.

Colin Heavey sits in that cubicle over there. He was new once, just like you. We warned him about Anika Bloom. But at last year's Christmas Potluck, he felt sorry for her when he saw that no one was talking to her. Colin Heavey brought her a drink. He hasn't been himself since. Colin Heavey is doomed. There's nothing he can do about it, and we are powerless to help him. Stay away from Colin Heavey. Never give any of your work to him. If he asks to do something, tell him you have to check with me. If he asks again, tell him I haven't gotten back to you.

This is the Fire Exit. There are several on this floor, and they are marked accordingly. We have a Floor Evacuation Review every three months, and an Escape Route Quiz once a month. We have our Biannual Fire Drill twice a year, and our Annual Earthquake Drill once a year. These are precautions only. These things never happen.

For your information, we have a comprehensive health plan. Any catastrophic illness, any unforeseen tragedy is completely covered. All dependents are completely covered. Larry Bagdikian, who sits over there, has six daughters. If anything were to happen to any of his girls, or to all of them, if all six were to simultaneously fall victim to illness or injury — stricken with a hideous degenerative muscle disease or some rare toxic blood disorder, sprayed with semiautomatic gunfire while on a class field trip, or attacked in their bunk beds by some prowling nocturnal lunatic — if any of this were to pass, Larry's girls would all be taken care of. Larry Bagdikian would not have to pay one dime. He would have nothing to worry about.

We also have a generous vacation and sick leave policy. We have an excellent disability insurance plan. We have a stable and profitable pension fund. We get group discounts for the symphony, and block seating at the ballpark. We get commuter ticket books for the bridge. We have Direct Deposit. We are all members of Costco.

This is our kitchenette. And this, this is our Mr. Coffee. We have a coffee pool, into which we each pay two dollars a week for coffee, filters, sugar, and CoffeeMate. If you prefer Cremora or half-and-half to CoffeeMate, there is a special pool for three dollars a week. If you prefer Sweet'n Low to sugar, there is a special pool for two-fifty a week. We do not do decaf. You are allowed to join the coffee pool of your choice, but you are not allowed to touch the Mr. Coffee.

This is the microwave oven. You are allowed to *heat* food in the microwave oven. You are not, however, allowed to *cook* food in the microwave oven.

We get one hour for lunch. We also get one fifteen-minute break in the morning, and one fifteen-minute break in the afternoon. Always take your breaks. If you skip a break, it is gone forever. For your information, your break is a privilege, not a right. If you abuse the break policy, we are authorized to rescind your breaks. Lunch, however, is a right, not a privilege. If you abuse the lunch policy, our hands will be tied, and we will be forced to look the other way. We will not enjoy that.

This is the refrigerator. You may put your lunch in it. Barry Hacker, who sits over there, steals food from this refrigerator. His petty theft is an outlet for his grief. Last New Year's Eve, while kissing his wife, a blood vessel burst in her brain. Barry Hacker's wife was two months pregnant at the time, and lingered in a coma for half a year before dying. It was a tragic loss for Barry Hacker. He hasn't been himself since. Barry Hacker's wife was a beautiful woman. She was also completely covered. Barry Hacker did not have to pay one dime. But his dead wife haunts him. She haunts all of us. We have seen her, reflected in the monitors of our computers, moving past our cubicles. We have seen the dim shadow of her face in our photocopies. She pencils herself in in the receptionist's appointment book, with the notation: To see Barry Hacker. She has left messages in the receptionist's Voicemail box, messages garbled by the electronic chirrups and buzzes in the phone line, her voice echoing from an immense distance within the ambient hum. But the voice is hers. And beneath her voice, beneath the tidal *whoosh* of static and hiss, the gurgling and crying of a baby can be heard.

In any case, if you bring a lunch, put a little something extra in the bag for Barry Hacker. We have four Barrys in this office. Isn't that a coincidence?

This is Matthew Payne's office. He is our Unit Manager, and his door is always closed. We have never seen him, and you will never see him. But he is here. You can be sure of that. He is all around us.

This is the Custodian's Closet. You have no business in the Custodian's Closet.

And this, this is our Supplies Cabinet. If you need supplies, see Curtis Lance. He will log you in on the Supplies Cabinet Authorization Log, then give you a Supplies Authorization Slip. Present your pink copy of the Supplies Authorization Slip to Ellie Tapper. She will log you in on the Supplies Cabinet Key Log, then give you the key. Because the Supplies Cabinet is located outside the Unit Manager's office, you must be very quiet. Gather your supplies quietly. The Supplies Cabinet is divided into four sections. Section One contains letterhead stationery, blank paper and envelopes, memo and note pads, and so on. Section Two contains pens and pencils and typewriter and printer ribbons, and the like. In Section Three we have erasers, correction fluids, transparent tapes, glue sticks, et cetera. And in Section Four we have paper clips and push pins and scissors and razor blades. And here are the spare blades for the shredder. Do not touch the shredder, which is located over there. The shredder is of no concern to you.

Gwendolyn Stich sits in that office there. She is crazy about penguins, and collects penguin knickknacks: penguin posters and coffee mugs and stationery, penguin stuffed animals, penguin jewelry, penguin sweaters and T-shirts and socks. She has a pair of penguin fuzzy slippers she wears when working late at the office. She has a tape cassette of penguin sounds which she listens to for relaxation. Her favorite colors are black and white. She has personalized license plates that read PEN GWEN. Every morning, she passes through all the cubicles to wish each of us a *good* morning. She brings Danish on Wednesdays for Hump Day morning break, and doughnuts on Fridays for TGIF afternoon break. She organizes the Annual Christmas Potluck, and is in charge of the Birthday List. Gwendolyn Stich's door is always open to all of us. She will always lend an ear, and put in a good word for you; she will always give you a hand, or the shirt off her back, or a shoulder to cry on. Because her door is always open, she hides and cries in a stall in the women's room. And John LaFountaine — who, enthralled when a woman enters, sits quietly in his stall with his knees to his chest — John LaFountaine has heard her vomiting in there. We have come upon Gwendolyn Stich huddled in the stairwell, shivering in the updraft, sipping a Diet Mr. Pibb and hugging her knees. She does not let any of this interfere with her work. If it interfered with her work, she might have to be let go.

Kevin Howard sits in that cubicle over there. He is a serial killer, the one they call the Carpet Cutter, responsible for the mutilations across town. We're not supposed to know that, so do not let on. Don't worry. His compulsion inflicts itself on strangers only, and the routine established is elaborate and unwavering. The victim must be a white male, a young adult no older than thirty, heavyset, with dark hair and eyes, and the like. The victim must be chosen at random, before sunset, from a public place; the victim is followed home, and must put up a struggle; et cetera. The carnage inflicted is precise: the angle and direction of the incisions; the layering of skin and muscle tissue; the rearrangement of the visceral organs; and so on. Kevin Howard does not let any of this interfere with his work. He is, in fact, our fastest typist. He types as if he were on fire. He has a secret crush on Gwendolyn Stich, and leaves a red-foil-wrapped Hershey's Kiss on her desk every afternoon. But he hates Anika Bloom, and keeps well away from her. In his presence, she has uncontrollable fits of shaking and trembling. Her left palm does not stop bleeding.

In any case, when Kevin Howard gets caught, act surprised. Say that he seemed like a nice person, a bit of a loner, perhaps, but always quiet and polite.

This is the photocopier room. And this, this is our view. It faces southwest. West is down there, toward the water. North is back there. Because we are on the seventeenth floor, we are afforded a magnificent view. Isn't it beautiful? It overlooks the park, where the tops of those trees are. You can see a segment of the bay between those two buildings there. You can see the sun set in the gap between those two buildings over there. You can see this building reflected in the glass panels of that building across the way. There. See? That's you, waving. And look there. There's Anika Bloom in the kitchenette, waving back.

Enjoy this view while photocopying. If you have problems with the photocopier, see Russell Nash. If you have any questions, ask your supervisor. If you can't find your supervisor, ask Phillip Spiers. He sits over there. He'll check with Clarissa Nicks. She sits over there. If you can't find them, feel free to ask me. That's my cubicle. I sit in there.

THOM JONES

Way Down Deep in the Jungle

FROM THE NEW YORKER

DR. KOESTLER'S BABOON, George Babbitt, liked to sit near the
foot of the table when the physician took his evening meal and eat
a paste the doctor had made consisting of ripe bananas and Canadian Mist whiskey. Koestler was careful to give him only a little, but
one scorching afternoon when the generators were down and the
air-conditioners out, Koestler and Babbitt sat under the gazebo out
near the baobab tree that was the ersatz town square of the Global
Aid Mission and got blasted. It was the coolest spot you could find,
short of going into the bush. The baboon and the man were waiting
for a late supper, since the ovens were out, too. Cornelius Johnson,
the Mission cook, was barbecuing chickens out in the side yard —
not the typical, scrawny African chickens, but plump, succulent
ones that Johnson made fat with sacks of maize that the generous
donors to Global Aid had intended for the undernourished peo-
ples of the region.

It had been a gruelling day, and Koestler was drinking warm
whiskey on an empty stomach. At first, he was impatient for a meal,
then resigned to waiting, then half smashed and glad to wait, and
he began offering Babbitt straight shots of booze. When he saw the
look of sheer ecstasy that came over Babbitt's Lincolnesque face, he
let the simian drink on, convinced that the animal was undergoing
something holy. And perhaps he was, but after the initial rush of
intoxication, Babbitt made the inevitable novice drinker's mistake
of trying to amplify heaven. He snatched the whole bottle of Canadian Mist and scampered off into the bush like a drunken Hunch-
back of Notre Dame. Koestler had to laugh; it seemed so comical —

the large Anubis baboon was unwilling to share the last of the amber nectar with his master. Well, there was always more where it came from, but suddenly Koestler wondered about the rapidity with which Babbitt had been slamming it down. He was afraid Babbitt would poison himself. Koestler took off into the bush after the animal, and he was instantly worried when he did not find Babbitt in any of his favorite trees. But Babbitt, who was perched higher than usual, announced his presence by launching the empty bottle down at Koestler like a bomb, just missing him. It was a calculated attempt at mayhem, Koestler realized as Babbitt began to rant and rave at him with an astonishing repertoire of hostile invective which not only puzzled Koestler but wounded him to the core. Koestler had been Babbitt's champion and staunchest defender. Virtually no one on the compound had any use for the large and powerful baboon. As Sister Doris, the chief nurse, liked to say, Babbitt was aggressive, noisy, a biter, a thief, and a horrendous mess-maker with no redeeming quality except the fact that he was one of God's creatures. Father Stuart quickly pointed out that crocodiles were God's creatures, too, but that didn't mean you had to let them move in with you. Almost every day someone would come up to Koestler and besiege him with complaints about the animal. Only Father Stuart had the nerve to confront Babbitt directly, once using a bird gun to shoot Babbitt's red ass with a load of rock salt, an incident that caused the priest and the doctor to cease speaking to each other, except through third parties. Koestler and the priest had become so estranged that Koestler refused to dine with the rest of the staff, and this suited him fine, since he no longer had to sit through the sham of hymns, prayers, and all the folderol that surrounded meals in the lodge.

Koestler was a loner, and preferred his own company to that of anyone else after long, hard days of bonhomie with the junior physicians and the in-your-face contact with patients — patients not only deprived of basic necessities but lacking such amenities as soap, mouthwash, and deodorant. Koestler found that it was useful, and even necessary, to remain remote — to cultivate the image of the chief — since an aspect of tribalism invaded the compound in spite of the artificial structure of the church, which was imposed on it and which never seemed to take very well in the bush. The newfangled wet blanket of civilization was thrown over ancient customs to almost no avail. But there were ways to get things done out here, and Koestler embodied those most notable characteristics of the New Zealander: resourcefulness, individualism, and self-reliance. In fact, Koestler carried self-containment to a high art. He had a lust for the rough-and-tumble, and preferred the hardships of Africa to the pleasant climate and easygoing customs of his homeland. As Koestler was fond of thinking, if Sir Edmund Hillary had a mountain to conquer when he climbed Everest in 1953 and breathed the rarefied air there, Koestler had baboons to tame and tropical diseases to vanquish in the here and now of Zaire. Koestler modestly considered himself New Zealand's gift to equatorial Africa.

Now Babbitt was high up another tree, raising so much hell that the majority of the Africans — workers and convalescents — had assembled to watch. Babbitt scrambled back and forth along a limb with a pencil-size twig in his fingers, mimicking the manner in which Koestler smoked his Dunhill menthols à la Franklin Delano Roosevelt. Babbitt's imitation was so precise that it seemed uncannily human. Then, having established his character, he did something far worse: he imitated the way Koestler sat on the toilet during his bowel movements, which were excruciatingly painful because of Koestler's piles.

This was all much to the delight of the Africans, who roared and fell to the ground and pounded it or simply held their sides and hooted hysterically. Babbitt, who was so often reviled, feared, and despised, now gave the Africans enormous pleasure. They roared anew each time Babbitt bared his teeth and shook his fist like evil incarnate, once nearly toppling from his limb before abruptly grabbing hold of it again. Babbitt's flair for the dramatic had roused the Africans to a fever pitch. Some of the natives began to dance as if invaded by unseen spirits, and this frightened Koestler marginally, as it had during his first days in Africa. Koestler thought that when the Africans were dancing — especially when they got out the drums and palm wine — they were as mesmerized by unreason as the mobs who once clamored to hear the irrational, primitive, but dangerously soul-satisfying ravings of Hitler and other megalomaniacs and Antichrists of his ilk.

The doctor retained his composure throughout the episode and, speaking to his pet in reasonable tones, attempted to persuade him to come down. Koestler knew that baboons did not climb trees as a rule, and while Babbitt was not an ordinary baboon, he was very unsteady up in a tree, even when sober. But the more sweetly Koestler coaxed, the more Babbitt raged at him. Koestler instructed Johnson — the only African who was not holding his sides with laughter — to run back to the compound and obtain a stretcher to use as a safety net in case Babbitt passed out and fell from the tree, but as the doctor was intently giving Johnson these instructions, a wedge of smile cracked the African's face and he fell to howling as well.

"So, Cornelius, this is how it is with you," Koestler said with a certain amount of amusement. "You have betrayed me as well." As the others continued to hoot and wail, Koestler remembered that his friend, Jules Hartman, the bush pilot, would be flying a pair of new American docs in later that day, and considered what a marvellous story this would make. He wanted to join in the fun, but as Babbitt began to masturbate, Koestler's impulse to laugh and give in to the moment was quickly vanquished by feelings of shame, anger, and real concern at the possibility of Babbitt's falling. Furthermore, it was his job to see that things didn't get out of control. An inch freely given around here quickly became the proverbial mile. The doctor raised his voice just slightly, insisting that the audience make a pile of leaves underneath the tree to break Babbitt's fall, which seemed all but inevitable. "*Mister* Johnson, see that this is done immediately," Koestler said. "I had better see heel-clicking service, do you hear me?"

Johnson wiped the smile from his face and began abusing the Africans. Soon a formidable pile of leaves had been gathered, but then Koestler, who was plotting the trajectory of the possible fall, was distracted when a small boy charged onto the scene and summoned the doctor to the clinic. A child had been bitten by a snake and was dying, the boy said. Koestler hastened back, the heavily laden pockets of his bush shorts jingling against his legs as he trotted alongside the young messenger, trying to get the boy to identify the type of snake responsible for the bite so he would be able to respond immediately with the appropriate dosage of antivenin, based on the victim's body weight, the bite pattern and location, the amount of edema present, and a number of other factors, including the possibility of shock. His alcohol-benumbed mind was soon clicking like a computer.

The child's father, tall, lean but regal in a pair of ragged khaki shorts — his ebony skin shiny with oily beads of perspiration and covered with a number of pinkish-white keloid scars — stood impassively outside the clinic with a hoe in one hand and a dead cobra in the other. The man muttered something about how the snake had killed his cow, how quickly the animal had fallen stone dead. In fact, he seemed more concerned about the dead animal than about his child, which, after all, was only a girl.

Inside the surgery, Sister Doris was already at work on the girl, who had been bitten twice on the left leg. Koestler assumed that the snake had deposited most of its neurotoxic venom in the cow; if the girl had not been bitten second she would have been as dead as the cow, since the snake was large and the girl was small and frail.

Koestler cautiously administered a moderate dose of antivenin, antibiotics, and Demerol for pain. Then he auscultated the child's chest. Her lungs sounded fine, but since the natives were enamored of hypodermic needles, he gave her a B_{12} shot — the magic bullet he used on himself to relieve hangovers. Before long the child's color improved, and only then did Koestler's thoughts return to Babbitt's latest caper. It seemed like an event that had happened in the distant past.

Mopping perspiration from his face, Koestler stepped outside and told the girl's father that his daughter was very strong, that the bite had been one of the worst Koestler had ever seen, and that the daughter was very special to have survived it. Actually, the little girl would probably have survived with no intervention whatever. But to survive a serious snakebite gave the victim unique status among the natives. Koestler hoped the father would now see his child in a new light, and that she would in fact have a better life from here on in. Sister Doris picked up on this and embellished the story until the crowd that had gone to witness Babbitt's debauchery had gathered outside the surgery to examine the dead snake and catch a glimpse of the young girl who would have unspecified powers and privileges for the rest of her life.

Koestler returned to the office in his small brick duplex — a mere hundred square feet cluttered with a large desk, five filing cabinets, books, whiskey bottles, medical paraphernalia, ashtrays, and a tricolored, fully assembled human skeleton. Koestler shook the last

Dunhill from his pack and lit it. How long had it been since he had eaten last? He had a full-blown hangover now, and the cigarette, which tasted like Vicks VapoRub and cardboard, practically wasted him. He heard Johnson's feet flip-flopping along in an oversized pair of Clarks which Koestler had handed down to him, and looked out to see Johnson rushing toward the office, anxiously followed by a couple of boys who were carrying Babbitt toward the gazebo on a stretcher.

Koestler was not pleased. In the first place, Johnson had let the chickens burn in all the excitement, and now Koestler's fears about Babbitt were realized as he listened to the story of how the baboon had passed out and dropped from the tree with his arms tucked to his sides. He pictured the monkey falling like a black leaden weight, an oversized version of the Maltese Falcon. He would not tell Hartman of the incident, after all, since if he did he would never hear the end of the pilot's ridicule about Koestler's misplaced love for the absurd animal. Absurdity was a very big part of his life, even as he strove to attain a kind of nobility in spite of it. Koestler became completely fed up with Babbitt as Johnson explained that the animal was basically unhurt. Koestler wondered if he should get himself a dog for a pet, since every other creature on the planet seemed inclined to shun him. It must be some vibe he gave off, he thought. Beyond superficial relationships, he was alone. Even Hartman, once you got past the fun and games, did not really care one whit about him. Not really. My God, he felt vile! Koestler suddenly realized how his devotion to the monkey must have seemed to the staff: as inexplicable as he had found Philip Carey's pathetic masochistic attachment to Mildred, the green-skinned waitress in *Of Human Bondage,* a book he had read many years ago as a kid in Auckland, the very book that had pushed him into medicine and off to faraway tropical climes.

To be this much alone offered a vantage point from which he might look into the pit of his soul, but what good was that? How much truth could you bear to look at? Particularly if it left you a drunken sot. Koestler forked down a can of pink salmon; then, to clear his palate of fish, he chewed on stale twists of fried bread dusted with cinnamon and sugar while from his window he watched Johnson and the boys lift Babbitt onto the veranda of the gazebo, out of the sun. In a moment, Johnson was back in Koestler's office in his floppy pair of Clarks, so large on him they were like clown shoes.

"Him falling hard. Missing the falling nest altogether," Johnson exclaimed.

"Well," Koestler said with satisfaction, "you know how it is — God looks out after drunks and such. Maybe it will teach the bugger a lesson." Koestler fixed a Cuba libre and asked Johnson to salvage some of the overroasted chicken or run over to the kitchen and rustle up something else, depending on what the staff had been eating. According to Johnson, it had been hartebeest, which Koestler, as a rule, found too stringy. He told Johnson to smother some of it in horseradish and bring it anyway. That was about all you could do. There was a tinned rum cake he had been saving since Christmas. He could have that for dessert.

Koestler looked out his window as the sun flared on the horizon and sank behind a curtain of black clouds, plunging the landscape into darkness just as his generator kicked in and the bright lights in his office came on and his powerful air-conditioner began to churn lugubriously. He took a long pull on his drink, found another pack of cigarettes and lit one with a wooden match, and waited for the liquor to do its job. Johnson was slow on the draw. An African glacier. It was just as well. Koestler would have time to eradicate his hangover and establish a pleasant alcoholic glow by the time Johnson returned with the food. In the meantime, he got busy with paperwork — stuff that was so dull it could only be done under the influence. Hartman and the green docs were already overdue, and he knew he would be tied up with them once they got in. In the beginning, new physicians were always more trouble than they were worth, and then, when they finally knew what they were doing, they lost heart and returned to lucrative practices back home. The altruism of most volunteers, Koestler thought, was pretty thin. Those who stayed seemed to do so for reasons that were buried deep in the soul.

Koestler woke up at dawn feeling very fit, while Babbitt spent the morning in abject misery. He would retreat to the corner of the doctor's office and hold his head in his hands; then he would approach Koestler (who was busy at his desk), pull on the doctor's pant leg, and implore him for help. Koestler cheerfully abused the animal by uttering such clichés as "If you want to dance, Georgie, you have to pay the fiddler. Now stop pestering me," and "You've sold your soul to the Devil, and there's not a thing I can do for you! Are you happy with yourself now?"

When Koestler finished his paperwork, he showed the baboon some Polaroids he had taken of it vomiting in the night. "Look at you," he said. "This is utterly disgraceful. What would your mother think of this? I've got a good mind to send them to her."

Babbitt abruptly left the room to guzzle water from a rain puddle but quickly returned when some Africans outside, who had witnessed the folly of the previous afternoon, began laughing derisively. He fled to his corner and held his head and, to Koestler's amazement, he was still there when the doctor came back to the room for a wash before dinner. The animal presented himself to Koestler like the prodigal son.

"I could fix it all with a shot, George, but then you'll never learn, will you? Zip-a-Dee-Doo-Dah and out drunk again."

Babbitt buried his head in his hands and groaned mournfully.

Koestler finally took pity on him and gave him a B_{12} injection with five milligrams of amphetamine sulfate. In a half hour, Babbitt seemed as good as new, apart from a sore neck. The doctor took care of this by fixing Babbitt up with a small cervical collar cinched with Velcro. Koestler expected Babbitt to rip it off, but the animal was glad for the relief it provided. Koestler watched as Babbitt retreated to a hammock that hung in the gazebo under the baobab tree. In almost no time, he was sleeping peacefully. At the sight of Babbitt snoring in the absurd cervical collar, Koestler began to laugh, and he forgave his pet for most of the nonsense he had pulled during his drunken spree.

After Johnson served breakfast, Koestler took a stroll around the compound, barking orders at everyone in sight. The Africans ducked their heads submissively in his presence. Good, he had them cowed. He would ride them hard for a few weeks to reëstablish his absolute power. If he had given them their inch, he would get a yard back from them. When he stuck his head into the mission school for a minute, Brother Cole, who was demonstrating to the children how to write the letter "e" in cursive, took one look at the doctor and dropped his chalk. Koestler imagined that he saw the man's knees buckle. No doubt Father Stuart, with all his carping, had blown

Koestler up into a bogeyman. He rarely showed himself at the school. The children whipped their heads around, and when they caught sight of the "big boss," their heads just as quickly whirled back. Koestler tersely barked, "Good morning, please continue. I'm just checking on things. Don't mind me." Ha! Feared by all. By the time Koestler completed his Gestapo stroll, the compound was as quiet as a ghost town. He went into the clinic at nine, and with the help of the nurses completed over forty-five procedures by four-thirty. No record by any means, but a good day's work.

Late that afternoon, Koestler took his dinner on the gazebo as usual and got drunk with Hartman and the two new young docs, who had spent the greater part of the day with the mission's administrator. Both Americans were shocked by the heat, the long flight, and, no doubt, by the interminable introductions to the staff and the singsong ramblings of that repetitive bore Father Stuart, who delighted in giving visitors a guided tour of the compound. The doctors seemed happy to be knocking back high-proof alcohol, and when Koestler fixed the usual bowl of banana mash and Canadian Mist before bridge, a number of rhesus monkeys rushed in from the jungle to accept the magical paste and soon were drunk and rushing around the compound fighting and copulating. Babbitt, who had ditched his cervical collar, was having none of the paste. The baboon seemed chastened and wiser. Koestler noted this with satisfaction and felt completely reconciled with his pet.

One of the newbies, a wide-eyed young doctor from Hammond, Indiana, said, "I see that the whole fabri of the social structure breaks down when they drink. It's like some grotesque parody of humans, but with none of the subtleties — just the elementals."

"It doesn't take Jane Goodall to see that," said Hartman. He had flown the Americans in that morning, and had got a head start on the Canadian Mist that afternoon. To Koestler's eye, the pilot appeared to be on the road to a mean, brooding drunk, rather than the more typical Hartman drunk — that of merriment, cricket talk, vaudeville routines, and bawdy songs. Koestler had recently run some blood work on his friend and knew that Hartman's liver was getting a little funny, but he could only bring himself to give Hartman a perfunctory warning and a bottle of B vitamins, since Koestler liked to match Hartman drink for drink when he made his twice-weekly drops at the mission and, as Koestler told Hartman, chastising him would seem like a ridiculous instance of the pot calling the kettle black. Like himself, Hartman was an old hand in Africa, and while he was not a Kiwi, he was close, having been raised in Launceston, Tasmania. Those pretentious types from mainland Australia looked down their noses on Taz, as they did on New Zealand — the poor sisters.

While Hartman had the typical apple cheeks and large ears that made Tasmanians look almost inbred, he liked to claim that he was Welsh. "May the Welsh rule the world!" he often said, but at other times he admitted that a year in Wales, with forays into much detested England, had been the most boring of his life. Whenever the subject came up, whether he was drunk or sober, the English were "Those bloody Pommy bastards!"

From the moment Babbitt had refused the alcohol mash, the doctor had been in a good mood, and now he began to pontificate. "As a rule, a baboon will only get drunk once, a monkey every day. Incredible animals, really, are baboons. Very smart. Did you know they can see in color? Actually, their visual powers are astounding."

"What happened to its neck?" the young doctor from Hammond, Indiana, asked. "It keeps rubbing its neck."

"It's a long story," Koestler replied. His cheerful countenance turned sour for a moment. "George Babbitt is a long-term experiment. He's come from the heart of darkness to the sunshine of Main Street. My goal is to turn him into a full Cleveland."

"What's a full Cleveland?" Indiana asked.

"A full Cleveland is a polyester leisure suit, white-on-white tie, white belt, white patent-leather shoes, razor burn on all three chins, and membership in the Rotary Club and the Episcopal church."

"You forgot the quadruple bypass," the other newbie, who was from Chicago, said.

"Well, he's got a running start there," said Koestler.

The baboon had stationed himself between Hartman and Koestler. Hartman held the stump of a wet cigar in his hand and seemed poised to relight it. Babbitt was intent on his every move.

"Georgie smokes a half a pack of cigarettes a day," Hartman said.

"*Used* to smoke —"

"Still does," Hartman said. "Whatever he can mooch from the Africans."

"Well, I'll soon put an end to that," said Koestler. "He's getting fat and short-winded. His cholesterol is up there. How long has he been smoking this time, the bloody bugger? He'll end up with emphysema, too. And how come I didn't know about this? I used to know everything that went on around here! I've got to cut back on the juice."

"Dain bramage," said Hartman.

"It's not funny," Koestler said.

"What's the normal cholesterol for a baboon?" Indiana asked. His cherubic face made him seem impossibly young.

"One-twenty or thereabouts," Koestler replied. "I couldn't even get a reading on his triglycerides — his blood congeals like cocoa butter."

Indiana began to giggle. "Jeez, I still can't believe that I'm in . . . Africa."

"Tomorrow you will believe," said Koestler. "You will voice regrets."

"I mean, I *know* I'm in Africa. I knew that when Mr. Hartman landed that DC-3. Talk about a postage-stamp runway — and those soldiers! Are those guns *loaded*?"

"That runway is a piece of cake," Hartman said. "More than adequate. And the guns *are* loaded. The political situation is very uptight these days. Not that we can't handle that; it's just that it's getting impossible to make a decent wage. I've got a good mind to sell the plane and head back to Oz. I'm getting too old for this caca."

"You won't last a week in Australia and you know it," Koestler said. "All the oppression of civilization. Sydney's getting almost as bad as Los Angeles. Every other bloody car is a Rolls or Jaguar. Not for you, my friend. You'll have to put on a fucking necktie to take in the morning paper."

"Darwin's not so bad," Hartman said, punching at a large black fly. "In Darwin an eccentric can thrive. Colorful characters. Crocodile Dundee and that sort of thing. I can make milk runs to New Guinea, do something —"

Suddenly Hartman seemed drunk, and he glowered at Indiana. "If you think this runway was crude, sonny boy, you've got a fuckin' long way to go." He sailed the half-empty bowl of banana mash into the wisteria bushes, and a few of the monkeys went after it, scrapping over the paste.

"Well, it wasn't exactly O'Hare International," Indiana said. "And how come the Africans sandbagged the tires?"

"To stop the hyenas from eating them," Koestler said. "It's hell to procure tires in these parts."

"Eating tires?" Indiana said. "You're shitting me!"

"The object of our little get-together is to ease you into your new reality," Koestler said. "If you get hit with everything too fast, it can overwhelm. Tomorrow will be soon enough. The leper colony — a rude awakening."

"What kind of scene is that?" the young doctor from Chicago asked. He was a dark man, with a hawk nose and a thick head of hair as black and shiny as anthracite; he was short, muscular, and had copious body hair. Koestler took him to be about thirty.

"It's a bit smelly. Poor buggers. Pretty much Old Testament, if you know what I mean. Your leper is still the ultimate pariah. In the beginning, there's 'gloves and stockings' anesthesia, and in the end, if we can't interrupt the course of the disease, a great deal of pain. They only believe in needles — they love needles. So use disposables and destroy them. That's the first rule. The second rule is this — if you have a patient who requires one unit of blood, do not give it to him. If he requires two units of blood, do not give it to him. If he requires three units of blood, you will have to give it to him, but remember that that blood will most likely be contaminated with H.I.V., hepatitis B, and God knows what all, despite the assurances from above."

"AIDS — slim," Hartman said evenly. "The only safe sex is no sex. Do not even accept a hand job."

"I've heard that they take great offense if you don't eat with them," Indiana said. "I've heard they'll put the evil eye on you if you don't eat with them."

"It's true," Koestler said.

"So you eat with them?"

"Hell no! I don't get involved with them on a personal level. You cannot let your feelings get in your way. If you do, you will be useless. Move. Triage. Speed is the rule. You'll see the nurses doing things that your trauma docs can't handle back in the States. Hell, you'll see aides doing some very complicated work. It comes down to medical managing. The numbers defeat you."

Johnson came out to the gazebo bearing a tray of chilled coconut puddings. He set a dish next to each of the men and then began to light the Coleman lanterns and mosquito coils as the sun did its orange flare and fast fade into the horizon. As it disappeared,

Koestler said, "Thank God. Gadzooks! Sometimes too hot the eye of heaven shines, huh boys? Especially when you're smack-dab on the equator."

The new men said nothing but watched as, one by one, Johnson picked up the last of the drunken rhesus monkeys by their tails and flung them as far as he could before padding back to the kitchen.

Indiana looked out at the monkeys staggering in circles. "They don't know what to do — come back for more or go into the jungle."

"Those that make for the bush the leopard gets. It's one way to eradicate the bastards," said Koestler darkly.

"I see — method behind the madness," Chicago said.

"Johnson's been using his skin bleach again," Hartman observed. "He's gone from redbone to high yellow in a week. Wearing shoes, yet. The Eagle Flies on Friday Skin Pomade for some Sat'day-night fun."

"It's not only Saturdays," Koestler said. "He goes through two dozen condoms a week. His hut is littered with the wrappers. He's insatiable."

"Well, at least you got that part through to him. Use a rubber."

"Johnson is no dummy, Jules. He knows the score, believe me. He's very germ conscious. That's one thing. A compulsive hand-washer. I trust him with my food absolutely."

As Indiana spooned down the pudding, he looked nervously at Hartman, who was a bulky man, and was glowering at him. "What's this 'redbone, high yellow' stuff?" Indiana said.

Hartman said nothing and continued to stare at the young doctor. Indiana looked at the other men and then laughed, "Hey! What's with this guy?"

Chicago picked up his pudding and began to eat. "And now for something completely different," he said. "The evil eye."

Hartman's face brightened. He relaxed his shoulders and laughed softly. "I remember a doctor — an American, tropical medic — didn't believe in the superstitions, and in the course of things he humiliated a witch doctor. The old boy put a curse on this hotshot, and it wasn't more than a week before the American stepped on a snake. I had to fly him to Jo'burg, since he was really messed up, was this chap. A year, fourteen months later he's back, forty pounds lighter, and a rabid animal bites him on the second day in. It took us three weeks to get rabies vaccine, and it came from a dubious source. He took the full treatment, but came down with the disease anyhow. Bitten on the face. Travels to the brain faster. Funny thing about rabies — makes a bloke restless. Nothing to do for it, either. Dr. Koestler, Johnson, and I had to lock him up in one of those chain-link-fenced compartments in the warehouse."

"Excessive scanning," Koestler said. "Hypervigilance. You could see the whites of his eyes —"

"From top to bottom," Hartman said. "Very paranoid, drinking in every sight and sound."

"What made it worse," Koestler said, "was the fact that he knew his prognosis."

"Yeahrr," said Hartman. "The paranoiac isn't necessarily wrong about things — he just sees too much. Take your hare, for instance. Your hare is a very paranoid animal. Your hare has basically been placed on the planet as food. He doesn't have a life. When you are an instant meal, you are always on the lookout. So, paranoid. Well, our friend was a lion, which all doctors are, present company included — they're tin gods from Day One — and, while it may work in America, it doesn't cut any ice down here; he humiliated this old witch doctor, so there wasn't any way out. No need to go around asking for trouble in this life, is there? The hare sees too much, the lion not enough — and there's the difference between happiness and hell, provided you are a real and true lion, not some bloody fool who is misinformed."

Hartman had the fleshy, broken nose of a pug, and as he spoke he kept brushing at it with his thumb. He sneezed three times in rapid succession.

"The curious thing," Koestler said, "is that the stupid bleeder died professing belief in science. He had a little slate and a piece of chalk, and when we finally went in to remove the body, I read his last words: *Amor fati!* 'Love your fate.' A stubborn bloody fool."

"Wow," Indiana said. "What did you do for the guy? Did he just die?"

"Of course he died. 'Slathered like a mad dog' is no mere cliché, let me tell you. I was inexperienced back then and had to play it by ear. All you had to do was say the word 'water' and he had esophageal spasms. You try to anticipate the symptoms and treat them, but we just aren't equipped here. The brain swells, you see, and there's no place for it to go."

Koestler accidentally bumped his pudding onto the floor with his elbow, and Babbitt quickly stepped forward and scooped it up in neat little handfuls.

Indiana picked up his dessert and tasted another spoonful. "This is good."

"Good for a case of the shits. Did you boys bring in any paregoric?"

"Lomotil," Chicago said. "Easier to —"

"Transport," Hartman said, picking up a greasy deck of cards and dealing them out for bridge.

"Mix it with Dilaudid and it will definitely cure diarrhea," Koestler said.

"You got some cholera in these parts?" Chicago said. He was beginning to sound like an old hand already.

"No," Koestler said vacantly. "Just the routine shits." He picked up his cards and fanned through them.

As Indiana finished his pudding, Johnson padded back out to the gazebo with a bowl of ice, another quart of Canadian Mist, and four cans of Coke Classic.

"I had this patient call me up at three in the morning," Indiana said.

"Called the doctor, woke him up," Chicago recited.

Indiana said, "Hypochondriac. Right. She's got lower GI pain. Diarrhea. Gas. The thing is — she's switched from Jell-O pudding to Royal pudding."

"Doctor, what can I take?" Chicago sang.

"I said, 'Delilah, remember how you — Delilah, I don't think you have a ruptured appendix. Delilah! Remember when you switched from RC Cola to Pepsi?'"

"Doctor — to relieve this bellyache," Chicago sang.

"I said, 'Put the lime in the coconut. Yeah, it does sound kind of *nutty.* That's good. Now, haven't you got a lime? You've got lime juice. One of those little green plastic lime things? O.K., that's good, now listen closely — *You put de lime in de coconut an' shake it all up; put de lime in de coconut and you drink it all down.* Trust me, Delilah, an' call me in de morning.'"

"And she never called back," Hartman said soberly. "Very clever."

"Let me get this straight," Koestler said. "You put de lime in de coconut?"

"Yeahrrr," said Hartman. "Jolly good."

"It's not bad, but that's his only routine," Chicago said. "I've spent seventy-two hours with the man, and that's it. That's his one trick. Plus, he's a fuckin' Cubs fan."

"Hey," Indiana said. "Long live Ernie Banks! Speaking of weird, we brought in three cases of sardines," Indiana said. "What's with all the sardines?"

"They are an essential out in the bush," Koestler said, removing a can of King Oscar sardines from his pocket and shucking the red cellophane wrapping. "Look at that, a peel-back can. No more bloody key. It's about time."

Hartman said, "They've only been canning sardines for ninety years."

Koestler jerked the lid back and helped himself to a half-dozen fish, his fingers dripping with oil. "Why, Jules, don't take personal offense. I'm sure His Majesty has enough on his mind without worrying about zip-open cans." Koestler offered the tin around, and when everyone refused, he gave the rest of the fish to Babbitt. "King Oscar sardines are worth more than Marlboro cigarettes in Africa," he declared.

"King Oscar, the nonpareil sardine," Chicago said.

Indiana filled his bourbon glass with Coke, Canadian Mist, and a handful of ice cubes, which melted almost instantly.

Hartman fixed his hard stare on young Indiana. "What exactly brought you to Africa, sonny boy?"

"I came to serve humanity, and already I'm filled with a sense of the inexplicable. I can't believe I'm in Africa. And fuck you very much."

"Speak up. You sound like a bloody poof — 'I came to serve humanity,'" Hartman said.

"And you sound like a major asshole. Why don't you try a little anger-management training?"

"Bloody poof, I knew it. Nancy girl!"

"Fuck!" Indiana said. "You're drunk. I'm not even talking to you."

"Won't last a week. Mark my words," Hartman said.

"Tomorrow you will believe," Koestler said. "The leper colony."

"Separates the men from the boys," said Hartman.

"Way down deep in the jungle," said Chicago, "we have the leper colony. We have Hansen's disease. That which we call leprosy by any other name would smell just as sweet: indeterminate leprosy, tuberculoid leprosy, lepromatous leprosy, dimorphous leprosy. 'What's in a name?'"

To Koestler's astonishment, Chicago pulled out a fat joint and torched it up. He took a long drag and passed it to the other American.

"I did a rotation at the leprosarium in Carville, Louisiana, when I was in the Navy," Chicago said. "I learned how to understand the prevailing mentality of the patient suffering from Hansen's disease."

"Put yourself in their 'prosthetic' shoes, did you?" Hartman said.

"The kid's right," Chicago said. "You're a hostile person. A real live turd. Shut up and listen. I mean, these patients are in denial until a white coat gives it to them straight. Zombie denial, man. You should see the look on their face. It's not a look like you've got cancer, which is a good one, instant shock. The you've-got-Hansen's look is more like, 'I have of late — but wherefore I know not — lost all my mirth —'"

"I know that look," Koestler said. "I see it every morning whilst I shave. Jules, the man knows Shakespeare."

"I suppose a leper colony in Africa is a hut made out of buffalo shit —"

"In your leper colony over there in the States," Hartman said, "are all the lepers bloody nigs?"

"You really are a racist, aren't you?" Indiana said.

Koestler attempted to deflect this inquiry. "I believe the current phraseology is 'African-American,' Jules, or, if you must, 'black.'"

"Some are black. Some are white. Some are Hispanic," Chicago said. "That word of yours is not in my vocabulary, and if you say it again —"

"You'll what?"

"Jules, please," said Koestler. "Don't be bloody uncouth."

Hartman pitched his head forward and pretended to sob over his cards. "I'm an uncouth ruffian, I won't deny it." He gulped down some whiskey and said, "When that faggot over there wants to fly home for ballet lessons, it won't be in my plane."

"Aryan Brotherhood," Indiana said.

Koestler raised his hand to silence the doctor while he turned to Chicago. "Where on earth did you score that joint?" he asked. "Did you give it to them, Jules?"

"Actually, it was your man, Johnson," Indiana said. "God, am I ever high. Everything is so . . . surreal."

"Johnson? That bugger!" Koestler said. "He's got his hand in everything."

Koestler put the wet end of the joint to his lips and took a tentative puff. As he did, Chicago pulled out another and lit it.

"Fuck," Koestler said. He took another hit. A much bigger one.

Chicago handed the new joint to Koestler's baboon, who greedily inhaled the smoke, and for the next few moments the whole curious party sat around the table attempting to suppress coughs.

"I'm so fucking high," Indiana said. "Jesus."

"A minute ago *I* was drunk; now *you* can't tie your shoelaces," Hartman said. "Poofter!"

"Let's have a little music," said Koestler. He flipped on the shortwave and fiddled with the dial. "I have got nothing but bloody Radio Ireland recently, half Gaelic, and then an hour of bird calls! Needs a new battery." He slapped at the radio and then, with Dixieland accompaniment, an Irish tenor was singing, *"I've flown around the world in a plane —"*

Koestler joined in. *"I've settled revolutions in Spain —"*

He flipped the dial and slapped the set until he hooked into American Armed Forces Radio. After an announcer listed the major-league ball scores, Jimi Hendrix came on blaring "Red House."

The men sat back and listened to the music. Koestler popped up to turn up the volume, his weather-beaten face collapsing inward as he took in another draught of marijuana smoke, closed his eyes, tossed his head back, and got into the song. He was soon snaking about the duckboard floor of the gazebo, playing air guitar to the music, his face frozen in a look of mock ecstasy.

"Hey, if Father Stuart could only see us now," Hartman said.

"Father Stuart *can* see you now!" The priest flipped on an electric torch and stepped out of the darkness up onto the gazebo. "This is a hospital, not a fraternity house! Kindly remember that. People are trying to sleep. Can't you think of others for a change?" He turned to the new doctors. "I'm glad to see that you two lads are off to an auspicious beginning."

The priest, dressed in a bathrobe and flip-flops, picked up the shortwave, switched it off, slung it under his arm, and clopped back toward the lodge. The beam of his flashlight, which was tucked between his shoulder and chin, panned the wisteria bushes, the ground, the sky, and the buildings of the compound as he attempted to push down the telescopic antenna on the radio. For a moment, the men sat in stunned silence. This was followed by an explosion of laughter.

Koestler started up as if to go after the priest, but then thought better of it and sat down at the table. He reached into his bush shirt and removed another can of sardines, handing them to Babbitt, who quickly tore off the lid, ate the fish, and then licked the olive oil from the inside of the can. "You might not believe it, but Georgie can open a can of sardines even with a key," Koestler said proudly. "Fuck, he's got the munchies," Indiana said, as he fell into a paroxysm of laughter.

Chicago studied the red sardine jacket, giggling as he read: "Add variety and zest to hot or cold meatless main dishes. . . . By special royal permission. Finest Norway brisling sardines."

"Brisling?"

"It's that advertising thing," Chicago said. "Brisling is Norwegian for 'sprat,' which means small marine fish. Not each and every small fish you pull in is certifiably a herring; some other small fish get picked up by the school. No false advertising this way."

"Wow," Indiana said sardonically. "Are you Norwegian or something?"

"Lebanese," Chicago said. "I already told you that."

Indiana said, "Who runs that country, anyhow? I was there, and I don't know that much. All I remember is that they won't even give you the time of day."

"No way," Chicago said. "The people are friendly as hell. The government of Norway is a hereditary constitutional monarchy, a parliamentary democracy, and the king is endowed with a certain amount of executive power. In reality, however, the king is limited in the exercise of power."

"He's a Norway freak!" Indiana said.

"More likely he's got a photographic memory," Hartman said.

"Touché, Mr. Hartman," Chicago said.

"I still can't believe I'm in Africa," Indiana said. "Heavy. Fourteen-year-old kids with machine guns — and, my God, look at the stars. There are so many of them."

"Stop acting so fucking incredulous," Hartman said. "You're really getting on my nerves."

"Watch Sister Doris," Koestler said. "She's forgotten more about jungle medicine than I'll ever know."

"Doris? Man, she's unattractive. She's ugly, man," Indiana said.

"She'll be looking pretty good in about five months; that is, if you last that long," Hartman said. "You'll be having some pretty intensive fantasies about that woman. Are you going to last, sonny boy?"

"Fuck off. I got through a residency at Bellevue. I guess I can hack Africa."

"The thing about Doris," Koestler said, slicing the air with the edge of his hand, "is that she's what we call an A-teamer. The A-team takes all of this business seriously. Tight-asses. Father Stuart is A-team beaucoup. There are B-teamers, who take a more casual approach. You will line up with one of these factions. Personally, if the political thing doesn't ease up a bit, I'm going to boogie out of this hellhole. I've no desire to have my throat slit. Stuart and Doris will stay until the last dog is hung."

"Go back to Kiwiland and listen to them harp about All Blacks rugby and that bloody yacht trophy," Hartman said. "Family's gone. Africa's your home, man."

"I've got a few cousins left in Auckland, and I do miss New Zealand beer, rather," Koestler said. "I'm not going to hang around and get my throat cut. I'd rather try a little lawn bowling."

"The natives are restless?" Indiana said.

"Yes, Percy le Poof," Hartman said. "The natives are restless."

"Politics as usual. So far, it hasn't filtered down to the villages," Koestler said. "It's a lot safer here than in Newark, New Jersey, I would imagine."

Suddenly the men fell silent and examined their cards. A swarm of insects buzzed around the gazebo like a wall of sound.

Despite the mosquito coils, the insects attacked ferociously. Hartman was the first to hop up, and he moved with a quickness that startled the others. With no warning, he roughly grabbed Indiana's head in the crook of his muscular forearm and savagely rubbed his knuckles over the top of the young doctor's head. His feet shuffled adroitly, like those of a fat but graceful tap dancer, as he yanked the doctor in various directions, never letting him set himself for balance. Hartman ran his knuckles back and forth over the young man's crew cut, crying, "*Haji Baba!* Hey, hey! *Haji Baba!* Hey, hey!"

"Ouch, God damn!" Indiana shouted. He was tall, with a basketball-player's build, and he finally wrested himself out of Hartman's powerful grip. He stood his ground, assuming a boxer's pose. Both he and Hartman were suddenly drenched with sweat. "You fucker! Shit!"

Hartman threw his hands in the air, his palms open in a gesture of peace. As soon as Indiana dropped his guard, Hartman waded in throwing roundhouse punches. One of these connected, and a chip of tooth pankled off a can of Coke Classic on the table. Indiana pulled Hartman forward, going with the older man's momentum. At the same time, he kicked Hartman's feet out from under him, and the two men rolled off the gazebo, and Indiana rode astride Hartman's broad back like a cowboy. Indiana had Hartman's arm pulled up in a chicken wing with one hand while he felt for his missing front tooth with the other.

"You son of a bitch!" Indiana said. "Fat bastard." He pounded Hartman's large ears with the meaty side of his fist. "I'll show you who's a faggot. How do you like it?"

He continued to cuff the pilot and cranked the arm up higher until Hartman cried, "Oh God, stop!"

"Had enough? Had enough?"

"God, yes. God, yes. I give!"

Indiana released his grip and got up. He was covered with black dirt. He was studying an abrasion on his knee when Hartman leaped atop him pickaback and began clawing at his face.

Hartman cried, "Son of a bitch, I'll kill you!" Once again the two men began rolling about in the dirt. This time Hartman emerged on top, and his punches rained down on the younger man until Chicago and Koestler each snatched him by one of his arms and dragged him off and flung him back into his chair. He started to get up, but Koestler shoved him back down with both hands and then pointed a finger in his face.

"You're drunk. Knock this shit off immediately!"

Hartman clutched his chest and panted frantically, wheezing. Rivulets of sweat coated with black dust rolled down off his face and dropped on his lap like oily pearls. Koestler poured out a large glass of whiskey and handed it to Hartman, who said, "Oh, fuck!"

Indiana stood over the man as if he were contemplating taking a swing at him. Hartman seemed unconcerned.

"Just having a bit of fun is all," Hartman said agreeably. "Didn't mean anything by it." Indiana drew away from Hartman, who managed the entire glass of whiskey in three gulps. "I believe all that marijuana got me going. No offense intended. Apologies all around."

Hartman took a mashed cigar out of his pocket, twisted off the broken end, and lighted it. He puffed rapidly without inhaling and wafted the smoke in front of his face to clear away the mosquitoes. Then he pulled himself up, set his glass on the table, and said, "It's been a long day, and here I am, shitfaced again. Good night, all."

Hartman hastily made his way up the path toward the sleeping quarters beyond the surgery. As he went, he laughed again and repeated the famous Monty Python litany, "And now for something completely different — sawing logs. Ah, zzzzz! Ah, zzzzz! Ah, zzzzz!" Indiana turned to Koestler. "What is with that guy?" "Don't mind Jules. He's a jolly good fellow. You'll grow to love him. And he won't remember a thing about tonight. Blackout drunk, this — presumably. I might not remember any of it, either."

From the distance, an elephant blared, a big cat roared, the hyenas began their freakishly human wailing, and the whole cacophony of jungle sounds took over the night.

Was it a minute or an hour later that Babbitt hopped on Hartman's empty chair and seemed to beseech the card players to deal him in? The men had drifted off into their separate thoughts. Babbitt grabbed the bottle of Canadian Mist from the card table and, brandishing sharp canine teeth that shone like ivory in the glow of the Coleman lanterns, caused both the young doctors to duck to the floor before he quickly sprang off into the black jungle. Even Koestler hit the deck, wrenching his knee. When he got up, he brushed himself off and said, "That settles it, I'm getting myself a dog."

"Christ, that's one mean son of a bitch!" said Chicago. "And I thought you said a baboon will only get drunk once. Here I thought he was poised to go for that goat-shit cigar. I mean, so much for your full Cleveland."

"Georgie is not your average baboon," Koestler said with a shrug. "Especially when he's stoned. When you've got a stoned baboon, all bets are off."

Indiana looked at Koestler. "What are we going to do? Are we going after him?"

"Not likely — anyhow, you need to clean up. Put something on those scratches. They can go septic overnight in this climate."

"But the leopard."

"Not to worry. I'll send Johnson and some of the men out with flashlights and shotguns. I'm absolutely fried from that joint. I'm not going out there — although we have to do something about that cat. He's getting altogether too bold, and we have children about. I'm going to have to roust Johnson. Anyhow, welcome to the B-team, gentlemen — Har har! Try to get some sleep. Tomorrow is going to be a rather difficult . . . a rather gruesome . . . well, shall I say, it won't be your typical day at the office? Up at dawn and that sort of thing." Koestler tossed back the last of his drink. "Rude awakening, the leper colony. Not for the faint of heart."

The young doctors grimly nodded an affirmation as Koestler made a pretense of cleaning up around the card table. He watched the two men stumble back to their rooms in the dorm, and when they were out of sight, he picked up one of the fat roaches that were left over from their party. He lit it with his Ronson and managed to get three good tokes off it. He heard the leopard out in the bush. Who was it? Stanley? Was it Sir Henry Morton Stanley who had been attacked by a lion, shaken into shock, and who later reported that he had felt a numbness that was a kind of bliss — a natural blessing for those creatures who were eaten alive? Not a bad way to go. Of course, leopards were smaller. Slashers.

Koestler picked up Indiana's drink, which was filled to the brim; it was warm, and the Coke in it had gone flat. It didn't matter. There seemed to be a perfect rightness to everything. That was the marijuana. Well, what difference did it make? It was his current reality. When he finished the whiskey, Koestler got up and clicked on his small chrome-plated penlight and followed its narrow beam into the bush. The beam was just long enough to allow him to put one foot in front of the other. Finding Babbitt would be almost impossible. *Amor fati.* Choose the right time to die. Well, there was no need to overdramatize; he was just taking a little midnight stroll. The leopard, unless it was crazy, would run from his very smell.

As soon as Koestler got under the jungle canopy, the air temperature fell ten degrees. The bush smelled damp and rotten. Yet, for the first time in thirty years, Koestler felt at one with the jungle. A little T-Bone Walker blues beamed in from some remote area of the brain: *They call it Stormy Monday, but Tuesday's just as bad.*

At the sound of Koestler's heavy boots, the nocturnal rustlings of the bush grew still. Koestler could then hear drums from the nearby village. There had been an elephant kill. Somehow his peripheral awareness had picked up on that news at some point during this most incredible day. Elephant kill. House of meat. Cause for celebration. The doctor proceeded into the darkness. The penlight seemed to dim; were the batteries low? Beneath the sound of the drumbeats, Koestler heard a branch snap. He stood stock-still in the middle of it all. He flipped his penlight right and left, and in a low, piping voice, said, "Georgie, Georgie? Where are you, my little pal? Why don't you come on back home? Come back home to Daddykins."

ELLEN GILCHRIST

The Stucco House

FROM THE ATLANTIC MONTHLY

TEDDY WAS ASLEEP in his second-floor bedroom. It was a square, high-ceilinged room with cobalt blue walls and a bright yellow rug. The closet doors were painted red. The private bath had striped wallpaper and a ceiling fan from which hung mobiles from the Museum of Modern Art. In the shuttered window hung a mobile of small silver airplanes. A poet had given it to Teddy when he came to visit. Then the poet had gone home and killed himself. Teddy was not supposed to know about that, but of course he did. Teddy could read really well. Teddy could read like a house afire. The reason he could read so well was that when his mother had married Eric and moved to New Orleans from across the lake in Mandeville, he had been behind and had had to be tutored. He was tutored every afternoon for a whole summer, and when second grade started, he could read really well. He was still the youngest child in the second grade at Newman School, but at least he could read.

He was sleeping with four stuffed toys lined up between him and the wall and four more on the other side. They were there to keep his big brothers from beating him up. They were there to keep ghosts from getting him. They were there to keep vampires out. This night they were working. If Teddy dreamed at all that night, the dreams were like Technicolor clouds. On the floor beside the bed were Coke bottles and potato-chip containers and a half-eaten pizza from the evening before. Teddy's mother had gone off at suppertime and not come back, so Eric had let him do anything he liked before he went to bed. He had played around in Eric's dark-room for a while. Then he had let the springer spaniels in the house, and then he had ordered a pizza and Eric had paid for it. Eric was reading a book about a man who climbed a mountain in the snow. He couldn't put it down. He didn't care what Teddy did as long as he was quiet.

Eric was really nice to Teddy. Teddy was always glad when he and Eric were alone in the house. If his big brothers were gone and his mother was off with her friends, the stucco house was nice. This month was the best month of all. Both his brothers were away at Camp Carolina. They wouldn't be back until August.

Teddy slept happily in his bed, his stuffed animals all around him, his brothers gone, his dreams as soft as dawn.

Outside his house the heat of July pressed down upon New Orleans. It pressed people's souls together until they grated like chalk on brick. It pressed people's brains against their skulls. Only sugar and whiskey made people feel better. Sugar and coffee and whiskey. Beignets and café au lait and taffy and Cokes and snowballs made with shaved ice and sugar and colored flavors. Gin and wine and vodka, whiskey and beer. It was too hot, too humid. The blood wouldn't move without some sugar.

Teddy had been asleep since eleven-thirty the night before. Eric came into his room just before dawn and woke him up. "I need you to help me," he said. "We have to find your mother." Teddy got sleepily out of bed, and Eric helped him put on his shorts and shirt and sandals. Then Eric led him down the hall and out the front door and down the concrete steps, and opened the car door and helped him into the car. "I want a Coke," Teddy said. "I'm thirsty."

"Okay," Eric answered. "I'll get you one." Eric went back into the house and reappeared carrying a frosty bottle of Coke with the top off. The Coke was so cool it was smoking in the soft, humid air.

Light was showing from the direction of the lake. In New Orleans in summer the sun rises from the lake and sets behind the river. It was rising now. Faint pink shadows were beginning to penetrate the mist.

Eric drove down Nashville Avenue to Chestnut Street and turned and went two blocks and came to a stop before a duplex shrouded by tall green shrubs. "Come on," he said. "I think she's here." He led Teddy by the hand around the side of the house to a set of wooden stairs leading to an apartment. Halfway up the stairs Teddy's mother was lying on a landing. She had on a pair of pantyhose and that was all. Over her naked body someone had thrown a seer-sucker jacket. It was completely still on the stairs, in the yard.

"Come on," Eric said. "Help me wake her up. She fell down and we have to get her home. Come on, Teddy, help me as much as you can."

"Why doesn't she have any clothes on? What happened to her clothes?"

"I don't know. She called and told me to come and get her. That's all I know." Eric was half carrying and half dragging Teddy's mother down the stairs. Teddy watched while Eric managed to get her down the stairs and across the yard. "Open the car door," he said. "Hold it open."

Together they got his mother into the car. Then Teddy got in the backseat and they drove to the stucco house and got her out and dragged her around to the side door and took her into the downstairs hall and into Malcolm's room and laid her down on Malcolm's waterbed. "You watch her," Eric said. "I'm going to call the doctor."

Teddy sat down on the floor beside the waterbed and began to look at Malcolm's books. *Playing to Win, The Hobbit, The Big Green Book.* Teddy took down *The Big Green Book* and started reading it. It was about a little boy whose parents died and he had to go and live with his aunt and uncle. They weren't very nice to him, but he liked it there. One day he went up to the attic and found a big green book of magic spells. He learned all the spells. Then he could change himself into animals. He could make himself invisible. He could do anything he wanted to do.

Teddy leaned back against the edge of the waterbed. His mother had not moved. Her legs were lying side by side. Her mouth was open. Her breasts fell away to either side of her chest. Her pearl necklace was falling on one breast. Teddy got up and looked down at her. She isn't dead, he decided. She's just sick or something. I guess she fell down those stairs. She shouldn't have been outside at night with no clothes on. She'd kill me if I did that.

He went around to the other side of the waterbed and climbed up on it. Malcolm never let him get on the waterbed. He never even let Teddy come into the room. Well, he was in here now. He opened *The Big Green Book* and found his place and went on reading. Outside in the hall Eric was talking to people on the phone. Eric was nice. He was so good to them. He had already taken Teddy snorkeling and skiing, and next year he was going to take him to New York to see the dinosaurs in the museum. He was a swell guy. He was the best person his mother had ever married. Living with Eric was great. It was better than anyplace Teddy had ever been. Better than living with his real daddy, who wasn't any fun, and lots better than being at his grandfather's house. His grandfather yelled at them and made them make their beds and ride the stupid horses and hitch up the pony cart, and if they didn't do what he said, he hit them with a belt. Teddy hated being there, even if he did have ten cousins near him in Mandeville and they came over all the time. They liked to be there even if their grandfather did make them mind. There was a fort in the woods and secret paths for riding the ponies, and the help cooked for them morning, noon, and night.

Teddy laid *The Big Green Book* down on his lap and reached over and patted his mother's shoulder. "You'll be okay," he said out loud. "Maybe you're just hung over."

Eric came in and sat beside him on the waterbed. "The doctor's coming. He'll see about her. You know, Dr. Paine, who comes to dinner. She'll be all right. She just fell down."

"Maybe she's hung over." Teddy leaned over his mother and touched her face. She moaned. "See, she isn't dead."

"Teddy, maybe you better go up to your room and play until the doctor leaves. Geneva will be here in a minute. Get her to make you some pancakes or something."

"Then what will we do?"

"Like what?"

"I mean all day. You want to go to the lake or something?"

"I don't know, Ted. We'll have to wait and see." Eric took his mother's hand and held it. He looked so worried. He looked terrible. She was always driving him crazy, but he never got mad at her. He just thought up some more things to do.

"I'll go see if Geneva's here. Can I have a Coke?"

"May I have a Coke." Eric smiled and reached over and patted his arm. "Say it."

"May I have a Coke, please?"

"Yes, you may." They smiled. Teddy got up and left the room.

The worst thing of all happened the next day. Eric decided to send him across the lake for a few days. To his grandmother and grandfather's house. "They boss me around all the time," Teddy said. "I won't be in the way. I'll be good. All I'm going to do is stay here and read books and work on my stamp collection." He looked pleadingly up at his stepfather. Usually reading a book could get him anything he wanted with Eric, but today it wasn't working.

"We have to keep your mother quiet. She'll worry about you if you're here. It won't be for long. Just a day or so. Until Monday. I'll come get you Monday afternoon."

"How will I get over there?"

"I'll get Big George to take you." Big George was the gardener. He had a blue pickup truck. Teddy had ridden with him before. Getting to go with Big George was a plus, even if his grandfather might hit him with a belt if he didn't make his bed.

"Can I see Momma now?"

"May."

"May I see Momma now?"

"Yeah. Go on in, but she's pretty dopey. They gave her some pills."

His mother was in her own bed now, lying flat down without any pillows. She was barely awake. "Teddy," she said. "Oh, baby, oh, my precious baby. Eric tried to kill me. He pushed me down the stairs."

"No, he didn't." Teddy withdrew from her side. She was going to start acting crazy. He didn't put up with that. "He didn't do anything to you. I went with him. Why didn't you have any clothes on?"

"Because I was asleep when he came and made me leave. He pushed me and I fell down the stairs."

"You probably had a hangover. I'm going to Mandeville. Well, I'll see you later." He started backing away from the bed. Backing toward the door. He was good at backing. Sometimes he backed home from school as soon as he was out of sight of the other kids.

"Teddy, come here to me. You have to do something for me. Tell Granddaddy and Uncle Ingersol that Eric is trying to kill me. Tell them, will you, my darling? Tell them for me." She was getting sleepy again. Her voice was sounding funny. She reached out a hand to him and he went back to the bed and held out his arm and she stroked it. "Be sure and tell them. Tell them to call the President." She stopped touching him. Her eyes were closed. Her mouth fell open. She still looked pretty. Even when she was drunk, she looked really pretty. Now that she was asleep, he moved nearer and looked at her. She looked okay. She sure wasn't bleeding. She had a cover on the bed that was decorated all over with little Austrian flowers. They were sewn on like little real flowers. You could hardly tell they were made of thread. He looked at one for a minute. Then he picked up her purse and took a twenty-dollar bill out of her billfold and put it in his pocket. He needed to buy some film. She didn't care. She gave him anything he asked for.

"What are you doing?" It was Eric at the door. "You better be getting ready, Teddy. Big George will be here in a minute."

"I got some money out of her purse. I need to get some film to take with me."

"What camera are you going to take? I've got some film for the Olympus in the darkroom. You want a roll of black-and-white? Go get the camera and I'll fill it for you."

"She said you tried to kill her." Teddy took Eric's hand and they started down the hall to the darkroom. "Why does she say stuff like that, Eric? I wish she wouldn't say stuff like that when she gets mad."

"It's a fantasy, Teddy. She never had anyone do anything bad to her in her life, and when she wants some excitement, she just makes it up. It's okay. I'm sorry she fell down the stairs. I was trying to help her. You know that, don't you?"

"Yes. Listen, can I buy Big George some lunch before we cross the Causeway? I took twenty dollars. Will that be enough to get us lunch?"

"Sure. That would be great, Teddy. I bet he'd like that. He likes you so much. Everybody likes you. You're such a swell little boy. Come on, let's arm that camera. Where is it?"

Teddy ran back to his room and got the camera. He was a scrawny, towheaded little boy who would grow up to be a magnificent man. But for now he was seven and a half years old and liked to take photographs of people in the park and of dogs. He liked to read books and pretend he lived in Narnia. He liked to get down on his knees at the Episcopal church and ask God not to let his momma divorce Eric. If God didn't answer, then he would pretend he was his grandfather and threaten God. Okay, you son of a bitch, he would say, his little head down on his chest, kneeling like a saint at the prayer rail. If she divorces Eric, I won't leave anyway. I'll stay here with him and we can be bachelors. She can just go anywhere she likes. I'm not leaving. I'm going right on living here by the park in my room. I'm not going back to Mandeville and ride those damned old horses.

*

Big George came in the front door and stood, filling up the hall. He was six feet five inches tall and wide and strong. His family had worked for Eric's family for fifty years. He had six sons and one daughter who was a singer. He liked Eric, and he liked the scrawny little kid that Eric's wife had brought along with the big mean other ones. "Hey, Teddy," Big George said, "where's your bag?"

"You want to go to lunch?" Teddy said. "I got twenty dollars. We can stop at the Camellia Grill before we cross the bridge. You want to do that?"

"Sure thing. Twenty dollars. What you do to get twenty dollars, Teddy?"

"Nothing. I was going to buy some film, but Eric gave me some so I don't have to. Come on, let's go." He hauled his small leather suitcase across the parquet floor and Big George leaned down and took it from him. Eric came into the hall and talked to Big George a minute, and they both looked real serious and Big George shook his head, and then Eric kissed Teddy on the cheek and Big George and Teddy went on out and got into the truck and drove off.

Eric stood watching them until the truck turned onto Saint Charles Avenue. Then he went back into the house and into his wife's workroom and looked around at the half-finished watercolors, which were her latest obsession, and the mess and the clothes on the floor and the unemptied wastebaskets, and he sat down at her desk and opened the daybook she left out for him, to see if there were any new men since the last time she made a scene.

June 29, Willis will be here from Colorado. Show him the new poems. HERE IS WHAT WE MUST ADMIT. Here is what we know. What happened then is what happens now. Over and over again. How to break the pattern. Perhaps all I can do is avoid or understand the pattern. The pattern holds for all we do. I discovered in a dream that I am not in love with R. Only with what he can do for my career. How sad that is. The importance of dreams is that they may contain feelings we are not aware of. FEELINGS WE ARE NOT AWARE OF. The idea of counterphobia fascinates me. That you could climb mountains because you are afraid of heights. Seek out dangers because the danger holds such fear for you. What if I seek out men because I want to fight with them. Hate and fear them and want to have a fight. To replay my life with my brothers. Love to fight. My masculine persona.

Well, I'll see Willis tonight and show him the watercolors too, maybe. I'll never be a painter. Who am I fooling? All I am is a mother and a wife. That's that. Two unruly teenagers and a little morbid kid who likes Eric better than he likes me. I think it's stunting his growth to stay in that darkroom all the time . . .

Eric sighed and closed the daybook. He picked up a watercolor of a spray of lilies. She was good. She was talented. He hadn't been wrong about that. He laid it carefully down on the portfolio and went into her bedroom and watched her sleep. He could think of nothing to do. He could not be either in or out; he could not make either good or bad decisions. He was locked into this terrible marriage and into its terrible rage and fear and sadness. No one was mean to me, he decided. Why am I here? Why am I living here? For Teddy, he decided, seeing the little boy's skinny arms splashing photographs in and out of trays, grooming the dogs, swimming in the river, paddling a canoe. I love that little boy, Eric decided. He's just like I was at that age. I have to keep the marriage together if I can. I can't stand for him to be taken from me.

Eric began to cry, deep within his heart at first, then right there in the sunlight, at twelve o'clock on a Saturday morning, into his own hands, his own deep, salty, endless, heartfelt tears.

Big George had stopped at the Camellia Grill, and he and Teddy were seated on stools at the counter eating sliced-turkey sandwiches and drinking chocolate freezes. "So, what's wrong with your momma?" Big George asked.

"She fell down some stairs. We had to go and get her and bring her home. She got drunk, I guess."

"Don't worry about it. Grown folks do stuff like that. You got to overlook it."

"I just don't want to go to Mandeville. Granddaddy will make me ride the damned old horses. I hate horses."

"Horses are nice."

"I hate them. I have better things to do. He thinks I want to show them, but I don't. Malcolm and Jimmy like to do it. I wish they were home from camp. Then he'd have them."

"Don't worry about it. Eat your sandwich." Big George bit into his. The boy imitated him, opened his mouth as wide as Big George's, heartily ate his food, smilingly let the world go by. It took an hour to get to Mandeville. He wasn't there yet. He looked up above the cash register to where the Camellia Grill sweatshirts were displayed — white, with a huge pink camellia in the center. He might get one for Big George for Christmas or he might not wait that long. He had sixty-five dollars in the bank account Eric made for him. He could take some of it out and buy the sweatshirt now. "I like that sweatshirt," he said out loud. "I think it looks real good, don't you?"

"Looks hot," Big George said, "but I guess you'd like it in the winter."

Teddy slept all the way across the Causeway, soothed by the motion of the truck and Big George beside him, driving and humming some song he was making up as he drove. Eric's a fool for that woman, George was thinking. Well, he's never had a woman before, just his momma and his sisters. Guess he's got to put up with it 'cause he likes the little boy so much. He's the sweetest little kid I ever did see. I like him too. Paying for my lunch with a twenty-dollar bill. Did anybody ever see the like? He won't be scrawny long. Not with them big mean brothers he's got. The daddy was a big man too, I heard them say. No, he won't stay little. They never do, do they?

Teddy slept and snored. His allergies had started acting up, but he didn't pay any attention to them. If he was caught blowing his nose, he'd be taken to the doctor, so he only blew it when he was in the bathroom. The rest of the time he ignored it. Now he snored away on the seat beside Big George, and the big blue truck moved along at a steady sixty miles an hour, cruising along across the lake.

At his grandparents' house in Mandeville his grandmother and grandfather were getting ready for Teddy. His grandmother was making a caramel cake and pimento cheese and carrot sticks and Jell-O. His grandfather was in the barn dusting off the saddles and straightening the tackle. Maybe Teddy would want to ride down along the bayou with him. Maybe they'd just go fishing. Sweet little old boy. They had thought Rhoda was finished having children and then she gave them one last little boy. Well, he was a tender little chicken, but he'd toughen. He'd make a man. Couldn't help it. Had a man for a father even if he was a chickenshit. He'd turn into a man even if he did live in New Orleans and spend his life riding on the streetcar.

Teddy's grandfather finished up in the barn and walked back to the house to get a glass of tea and sit out on the porch and wait for the boy. "I might set him up an archery target in the pasture," he told his wife. "Where'd you put the bows the big boys used to use?"

"They're in the storage bin. Don't go getting that stuff out, Dudley. He doesn't need to be out in the pasture in this heat."

"You feed him. I'll find him things to do."

"Leave him alone. You don't have to make them learn things every minute. It's summer. Let him be a child."

"What's wrong with her? Why's she sick again?"

"She fell down. I don't want to talk about it. Get some tea and sit down and cool off, Dudley. Don't go getting out archery things until you ask him if he wants to. I mean that. You leave that child alone. You just plague him following him around. He doesn't even like to come over here anymore. You drive people crazy, Dudley. You really do." She poured tea into a glass and handed it to him. They looked each other in the eye. They had been married thirty-eight years. Everything in the world had happened to them and kept on happening. They didn't care. They liked it that way.

Teddy's uncle Ingersol was five years younger than Teddy's mother. He was a lighthearted man, tall and rangy and spoiled. Teddy's grandmother had spoiled him because he looked like her side of the family. Her daddy had died one year and Ingersol had been born the next. Reincarnation. Ingersol looked like a Texan and dressed like an English lord. He was a cross between a Texan and an English lord. His full name was Alfred Theodore Ingersol Manning. Teddy was named for him but his real father had forbidden his mother to call him Ingersol. "I want him to be a man," his father had said, "not a spoiled-rotten socialite like your brothers."

"My brothers are not socialites," Teddy's mother had answered, "just because they like to dance and have some fun occasionally, which is more than I can say for you." Teddy always believed he heard that conversation. He had heard his mother tell it so many times that he thought he could remember it. In this naming story he saw himself sitting on the stairs watching them as they argued over him. "He's my son," his mother was saying. "I'm the one who risked my life having him. I'll call him anything I damn well please."

Teddy's vision of grown people was very astute. He envisioned them as large, very high-strung children who never sat still or finished what they started. Let me finish this first, they were always saying. I'll be done in a minute. Except for Eric. Many times Eric just smiled when he came in and put down whatever he was doing and took Teddy to get a snowball or to walk the springer spaniels or just sit and play cards or Global Pursuit or talk about things. Eric was the best grown person Teddy had ever known, although he also liked his uncle Ingersol and was always glad when he showed up.

All his mother's brothers were full of surprises when they showed up, but only Uncle Ingersol liked to go out to the amusement park and ride the Big Zephyr.

Ingersol showed up this day almost as soon as Big George and Teddy arrived in the truck. Big George was still sitting on the porch drinking iced tea and talking to Teddy's grandfather about fishing when Ingersol came driving up in his Porsche and got out and joined them. "I heard you were coming over, namesake. How you been? What's been going on?"

"Momma fell down some stairs and me and Eric had to bring her home."

"Eric and I."

"I forgot."

"How'd she do that?"

"She said Eric tried to kill her. She always says things like that when she's hung over. She said to tell you Eric tried to kill her." There, he had done it. He had done what she told him to do. "If she divorces Eric, I'm going to live with him. I'm staying right there. Eric said I could."

His grandfather pulled his lips in. It looked like his grandfather was hardly breathing. Big George looked down at the ground. Ingersol sat in his porch chair and began to rub his chin with his hand. "You better go see about her, son," his grandfather said. "Go on over there. I'll go with you."

"No, I'll go alone. Where is she now, Teddy?"

"She's in bed. The doctor came to see her. He gave her some pills. She's asleep."

"Okay. Big George, you know about this?"

"Just said to bring the boy over here to his granddaddy. That's all they told me. Eric wouldn't hurt a flea. I've known him since he was born. He'll cry if his dog dies."

"Go on, son. Call when you get there." His grandfather had

unpursed his mouth. His uncle Ingersol bent down and patted Teddy's head. Then he got back into his Porsche and drove away.

"I'm going to stay with Eric," Teddy said. "I don't care what she does. He said I could stay with him forever."

Ingersol drove across the Causeway toward New Orleans thinking about his sister. She could mess up anything. Anytime they got her settled down, she started messing up again. Well, she was theirs and they had to take care of her. I wish he *had* thrown her down the stairs, Ingersol decided. It's about time somebody did something with her.

Teddy's mother was crying. She was lying in her bed and crying bitterly because her head hurt and her poems had not been accepted by *White Buffalo* and she would never be anything but a wife and a mother. And all she was mother to was three wild children who barely passed at school and weren't motivated and didn't even love her. She had failed on every front.

She got out of bed and went into the bathroom and looked at how horrible she looked. She combed her hair and put on makeup and changed into a different negligee and went to look for Eric. He was in the den reading a book. "I'm sorry," she said. "I got drunk and fell asleep. I didn't mean to. It just happened. *White Buffalo* turned my poems down again. The bastards. Why do I let that egomaniac judge my work? Tell me that."

"Are you feeling better?"

"I feel fine. I think I'll get dressed. You want to go out to dinner?"

"In a while. You ought to read this book. It's awfully good." He held it out. It was *The Snow Leopard,* by Peter Matthiessen.

"Has the mail come?"

"It's on the table. There are some cards from the boys. Malcolm won a swimming match."

"I wasn't sleeping with him, Eric. I went over there to meet a poet from Lafayette. It got out of hand."

Eric closed the book and laid it on the table by the chair. "I'm immobilized," he said at last. "All this is beyond me. I took Teddy with me to bring you home. For an alibi if you said I pushed you down the stairs. I can't think about anything else. I took that seven-year-old boy to see his mother passed out on the stairs in her pantyhose. I don't care what you did, Rhoda. It doesn't matter to me. All I care about is what I did. What I was driven to. I feel like I'm in quicksand. This is pulling me in. Then I sent him to Mandeville to your parents. He didn't want to go. You don't know how scared he is — of us, of you, of everything. I think I'll go get him now." Eric got up and walked out of the room. He got his car keys off the dining room table and walked out into the lovely hot afternoon and left her there. He got into his car and drove off to get his stepson. I'll take him somewhere, he decided. Maybe I'll take him to Disney World.

Teddy was sitting on an unused tractor watching his grandfather cut the grass along the edge of the pond. His grandfather was astride a small red tractor pulling a bush hog back and forth across a dirt embankment on the low side. His grandfather nearly always ran the bush hog into the water. Then the men had to come haul it out and his grandfather would joke about it and be in a good mood for hours trying to make up for being stupid.

Teddy put his feet up on the steering wheel and watched intently as his grandfather ran the bush hog nearer and nearer to the water's edge. If his grandfather managed to get it in the water, they wouldn't have time to ride the horses before supper. That's what Teddy was counting on. Just a little closer, just a little bit more. One time his grandfather had turned the tractor over in the water and had to swim out. It would be nice if that could happen again, but getting it stuck in the mud would do. The day was turning out all right. His uncle Ingersol had gone over to New Orleans to get drunk with his mother, and his cousins would be coming over later, and maybe Eric and his mother wouldn't get a divorce, and if they did, it might not be too bad. He and Eric could go to Disney World like they'd been wanting to without his mother saying it was tacky.

His grandfather took the tractor back across the dam on a seventy-degree angle. It was about to happen. At any minute the tractor would be upside down in the water and the day would be saved.

That was how things happened, Teddy decided. That was how God ran his game. He sat up there and thought of mean things to do and then changed his mind. You had to wait. You had to go on and do what they told you, and pretty soon life got better.

Teddy turned toward the road that led to the highway. The Kentucky Gate swung open, and Eric's car came driving through. He came to get me, Teddy thought, and his heart swung open too. Swung as wide as the gate. He got down off the tractor and went running to meet the car. Eric got out of the car and walked to meet him. Crazy little boy, he was thinking. Little friend of mine.

JAIMY GORDON

A Night's Work

FROM THE MICHIGAN QUARTERLY REVIEW

NURSE PIGEON found Kidstuff dead in the dirt road a little after midnight. She squatted down and laid two fingers on his wrist and held up a piece of bottleglass from the road in front of his mouth, but already she knew he was dead by the way two snails of moonlight turned in the whites of his half-cocked eyes. He had on his best lizard paddock boots and a new turquoise dress shirt with a white bottle print that turned out when you looked up close to resemble tiny naked girls. His dove gray, seventy-five-dollar cowboy hat was lying in the ditch.

Nurse Pigeon could tell from his fancy-man clothes that he hadn't thought about dying or even being sick when he left. She found that hard. Death ought not to sneak up on a thoughtful person like Kidstuff. In life you wished to see what was coming to you, which had nothing to do with where you were going. You weren't going anywhere. Nurse Pigeon didn't hold with that churchy philosophy. She had had a scientific education and knew when you were dead you were dead.

It was a Saturday night in late May and the weather had been unusually fine. Kidstuff must have taken sick at the racetrack and tried to make it home to Nurse Pigeon, who had finally gone down the lane to see why the dogs were barking. It touched her deeply that he had made it home, even if the long walk had finished him, even if his body had ended up lying in Little Rockcamp Run, county road 80, and only his fingers touching the post with the late Weems Pigeon's blue mailbox on it.

Kidstuff was a blacksmith by trade, with arms knotted like rope and a leathery hide from working all year long in the weather on the dirt strip between shedrows. A kid-sized man with a slow, tilted smile, he had always been liked, and not only by women. A blacksmith is one of the few at the track in business for himself alone. Kidstuff made nor man nor woman feel like a two-bit flop, though there were plenty in Charles Town who met that description, and people said he could even work for Frances Blinky Cornford without ruining his good name, for a hood needs a decent blacksmith the same as anybody else. Kidstuff always had all the work he wanted, but as far as work went, he never was trying to corner the market. He was out there in the sun and wind almost every day with his farrier's box and tools, but why, he would ask, add ten more horses to his rounds when he couldn't hold on to a dollar with a pair of fire tongs?

That he was not jealous of every sawbuck added to Kidstuff's popularity, especially since he did not think himself too good to gamble. Plenty of times he worked on the cuff, for nothing at all in front until a horseman's luck changed, and now and then he found out this jeff was trying to win with some old stalwart he'd been saving away, finally running him where he belonged. "Going to let my mama here run tomorrow?" Kidstuff would smile, hammer in hand, from the shadow under the long dark belly. "She got a shot if she don't come up lame." The one in the porkpie hat might shrug coyly. But from time to time the horseman said, "She'll win, that's from me to you, cowboy," and the next evening Kidstuff would stand at the post parade and try to make out from the lilt in her feet if she had been properly medicated. Just because a trainer told you he had sincerely decided to win didn't mean he would win, and plenty of times Kidstuff went down with him.

Kidstuff hadn't been looking well lately, but the idea there was no life left in his agile body came to Nurse Pigeon as a shock. She had loved Kidstuff a long time, even after he confessed she was no longer everything to him as she once had been, and he would start, he could not help himself, chasing other women. Ruth Pigeon had always been a big girl, and now, it was true, she was plain fat. She wore loose flowered dusters without belts, or white uniform tops shaped like pillowcases over pants with elastic waistbands. As for how she looked anymore, she had decided a few years ago to put it out of her mind, and she had. She reminded herself that for some of those terrible midlife diseases you had a better chance if you saw them coming and had some padding on you. And anyway she didn't care to take diet pills at her age. It wasn't restful.

Nurse Pigeon had enjoyed her share of Kidstuff's company all the same. She took care of him when he was sick, or pie-eyed on bootleg whiskey and goofers, or tapped out. Sometimes he slept on the foldout sofa in her living room, though by the time he showed up at night he might be in no shape to unfold it. When he did come into a roll, he made sure Nurse Pigeon had her stake — maybe two or three times a year.

They were true friends, though now she was sorry she had let him borrow away the last grand of the three-thousand-dollar savings account she had started up for the two of them in 1956 from what was left of Weems Pigeon's death benefit, one dizzy summer when there were seventeen-year locusts and they almost got married. She regretted handing it over even to save Kidstuff from having his pretty nose and jaw broke for a bad debt, because, after all, he was going to die in a week anyhow. But how could she have known he would die, though it's true his eyes had a yellowish cast and for months he hadn't eat anything but boiled eggs and toast and fifteen-cent racetrack pizza? She had seen that small wiry type of hard-drinking gambler last for years and years without taking in any type of solid nourishment whatsoever. Sure he'd have been mad if she'd said no, but she knew him so well she could bear by now to have Kidstuff mad at her for a week, even if it was his last week.

Nurse Pigeon had worked like a man all her life. She had ended up in a woman's profession, but it was always the hard cases the county sent her to — that bricklayer who had a tumor growing on his brain that gave him the idea he was flying off his bed and out the window. And half a dozen other big laboring men who had taken sick all of a sudden and had to be lifted on and off the pot like babies, and of course some of them didn't like it and would wrassle her like a gorilla.

She had always figured that when Kidstuff finally passed, she would comfort herself with a trip to a faraway place with palm trees. Palm trees were a thing she had never seen. She would put a wide line, not black, but broken diamondy white like sunshine through palm trees, between this life and that. She wouldn't even swim, she had heard the South Seas were warm as a bathtub and full of sharks.

Moreover, swimming wasn't restful. For two weeks she would lie in a hammock between two palm trees and comely brown boys would fan her and wait on her hand and foot. Then she could go on alone.

But now it turned out that, speaking strictly of money, Kidstuff would be no more good to her dead than he ever was alive. This was hard, very hard, and when she gazed at Kidstuff lying there on the bone white dirt he seemed to be shrinking from the meanness of it. To be worth nothing to an old friend in the end was too low: for Nurse Pigeon to go right on working like she always had was too cold to his memory. Right then she saw the correct thing to do.

But first she went through his pockets, for he hadn't definitely told her he'd gotten around to straightening that old debt with her thousand, and even if he had she wouldn't put it past him to hold out a few yards on Two-Tie or anyone else if something good was running.

And sure enough, she found a dispiriting thing — a one-inch-high bundle of fifty-dollar parimutuel tickets from Thursday's fifth race at Pocono Downs, the pink stack wrapped in a rubber band, and a stub from a round-trip Greyhound ticket to Scranton, PA. She threw them in the ditch in disgust. The rubber band busted and they blew about the bottom of the culvert and lost themselves in the tangled suckers on its bank.

Whereupon she really had to wonder, though Kidstuff hadn't been looking well lately, though last month he had wandered to the kitchen door and puked into the dark garden with a terrible silky ease as though he didn't even feel it, all the same she had to ask herself if she could be one hundred percent sure this death was due to natural causes or if some discontented creditor had not helped him out of this life. She reflected on Two-Tie Samuels, who had the reputation of being a square dealer, though certainly he had to keep a little low-grade muscle on call in his line of work. Two-Tie might be seriously out of patience with Kidstuff, who had seemed in a deep hole of late, even apart from what he owed. Of late he'd be sitting at Nurse Pigeon's kitchen table at two in the morning with the *Telegraph* spread out over his cold greasy toast that had one little half-moon bit out of it. Night after night he had combed the racing cards of dinky tracks and county fairs in Ohio and Pennsylvania for a sure thing he could horn in on. "I hear Blinky's got an old stakes horse from Cucaracha Downs or somewhere. They're hiding him on a farm back of Middleway, going to drop him in for nothing one day when nobody's looking. But I'm looking." "It ain't healthy to bust into somebody else's game," Nurse Pigeon had warned him. For that could make a person hot. But hot enough to kill? Nurse Pigeon knelt down and examined her dear one for a sign of foul play. He did not look banged around. He did not even look scared. It was something about the way the wild honey eyes just floated, fixed in one place: he looked cut loose, and satisfied to be so.

You can't keep a-hold of ten dollars? Three weeks ago she had asked Kidstuff to pick her up a sack of chicken and a six-pack on his way home from the track, and tried to hand him a ten-dollar bill, but he wouldn't take her money. *I'm a-going down the drain,* he had said, and he had. *If it wasn't for the half in hock, I wouldn't be here at all.* Of course if he had taken her money, he would have had to come home to Nurse Pigeon with the chicken. Kidstuff did not always intend on coming home to Little Rockcamp Run anymore. His favorite dolly lived in the Horseman's Motel just to the south of the backside fence. His second-best girl lived in town. He had never had any trouble locating women who would take an interest in his welfare. He still looked like a handsome youth who had fallen in a tanner's vat, not much different in death than in the contrary condition. His skin was red-brown like a chestnut and drawn tight over the bones — you could say he was baby-faced right down to the skeleton. He had always struck Nurse Pigeon as refined, even delicate, at least compared to her, and she could easily have leaned down and kissed his parted lips and the white teeth winking through them. He was a man who had never had a bad smell about him, and somehow even after falling on his face one night down a complete flight of stairs in the old building of the Horseman's Motel, and once, on the gravel service road between the two tracks, getting hit from behind by a lady in a station wagon who had lost big, he still had all his pretty teeth.

She might have kissed him, but instead she took hold of his fancy paddock boots and carefully drug his legs out into the road. She sank down in the dirt next to him, slung his head and chest like a baby over her shoulder, and clawed her way back up the post with the Pigeon family mailbox on it. He was a clumsy bundle more than a heavy one: his sharp little bones pressed into her like springs from bad upholstery. She winced but shuffled all the way up the lane with him and unrolled him into the backseat of the rusted-out Grand Prix before she remembered about the muffler — all that racket would not do — then grasped once more the purple lizard boot-heels, a little less patiently and tenderly this time, so that his head bounced from the running board into the blue-rocked lane, and his eyes appeared to roll up half in his head like a broken baby-doll's. "Jesus lead me to the cross," she muttered, trying to maintain a certain respect. But it was better to realize Kidstuff was nothing but a busted suitcase by now, empty but proof of his hard traveling.

In the other car, the little Volkswagen, she had nowhere to stuff him where she could hope to get him out again by herself except for the seat beside her: so she stood on the driver's seat and, with her back braced against the roof of the car, placed her two hands on the top of his head and pressed down as hard as she could, till his knees popped forward and the skull full of sweet black curls sank down out of sight.

And then she took the old logger's road that came down into Charles Town the back way, over Bushrod Hill, where no other car would venture at this hour. She went slow, you had no choice but to go slow down the slick-ditched red clay roadbed, so that she wouldn't reach the service drive between the motel and the two racetracks until at least three o'clock in the morning. She knew from Kidstuff that Rose Dewglass crawled under the fence from the backside of Shenandoah Downs around eleven, opened up a bottle of Portagee red, and at midnight went down like a rock sinker, you could not wake her with a fire horn, till three-thirty when she sat up in the bedclothes with her wide-open blue bottleglass eyes staring at the snowy TV screen. Then you could talk sense to her, Kidstuff said. *I bet you was talking sense into her,* Nurse Pigeon remarked. Kidstuff said that wasn't the point. The point was you could wager your last dollar on this routine, which he would have liked to do, but since Nurse Pigeon would not take the bet and there was nobody else to whom he would divulge a ladyfriend's secrets, he never could figure out a way. Whyever do you tell me this, Nurse Pigeon had thought but not said. Alas, there was nothing he might not tell her, his true friend, that last sorry and dwindling year.

Rose Dewglass had the one-room-plus-dinette clear at the tail end of the new prefab motel block, spitting distance from the racetrack fence. So Nurse Pigeon knew what to do: she backed up the Volkswagen into the thicket of piss-elm and serviceberry that grew along the fence, reached across Kidstuff to open his door, and then planted her pink moccasins against his side and pushed with her stout calves until his shoulders tilted north out of the car and his right arm caught in the bushes. Whereupon she hurried around the car and, hooking his limp arm around her neck, half dragged, half shoved him on her hip through the damp weeds. "Damn you, Eugene, pick up them feet," she stage-whispered, in case an insomniac was spying on them from the darkness behind a pair of gray-glowing drapes. She wondered where she had got the name Eugene; she didn't know a single person named Eugene.

At last they arrived at a little quilted metal door that reminded Nurse Pigeon of the toilet in a Greyhound. She managed to twist the knob and knee the sticky door across the yellow cat-pee-smelling shag rug, and just as she unloaded Kidstuff through the opening with a swing of her hip, she heard a *boing* and a squeeze of soap opera music went off in her chest. But it was only four foot of metal stripping waving over her head like a magic wand. The pointy toe of Kidstuff's lizard boot had forked sideways and caught in the sardine-can door jamb, and the rest of him unrolled like a camp mattress into the living room, except his head, which came down in the dinette in a pile of Super Shoppers, still rolled up with the red rubberbands around their middles.

Nurse Pigeon was out of breath from hauling Kidstuff even this far, and now that he was lying facedown on loopy wall-to-wall carpeting, she couldn't make him slide. She locked his head, or rather his skinny neck, under one arm with the round knob of his skull sticking out frontwards, and pushed off like a mule, letting her whole weight fall forward. That pulled his boots over the threshold. At last she was able to close the door behind them. The electric clock on the stove said three-twenty-four. Of course stove clocks were always out of whack, it might even be slow, she realized, and her heart began to pound. She and Kidstuff might not make it to the bedroom — but then she happened to see a pair of ball-bearing roller skates sticking out of a box of galoshes and other junk. She parked the two flattened bug-looking things side by side next to Kidstuff's hind end and, rolling him over half at a time, like making a bed with the patient still in it, managed to set the skates under him and drag him bit by bit through the goldy loops of the rug. The skates cut tracks that she couldn't quite rub out with her moccasins. Cheap gold carpet fluff was sticking all over his trousers. Nurse Pigeon considered these things only a moment. Rose Dewglass was not the observant type. She wouldn't think it strange if Kidstuff's head was twisted around backwards, which by now it halfway was.

Finally they arrived at the bed and Nurse Pigeon drew a breath. Rose lay naked except for pink nylon underpants, spread-eagled on her back down a trench in the rotten mattress. Seeing the ponygirl in this position with her breasts pooling sideways like lily pads and soft red-gold hairs peeking out of the legbands of her panties, she knew why Kidstuff had spent so many evenings over here. She was pretty, pretty like a cream rose, and if she was less than brainy, at least she was not trying to outsmart anybody. She was a regular ponygirl. She would get up on any horse, but she had no morals. She took money and dope from her boyfriends if they had any, but half the time she gave it away, the stuff and herself too. Even Kidstuff said that on her own back, not a horse's, was Rose's natural position. But oh she was pretty. Nurse Pigeon refused to be sad about how pretty she was: tonight, heck, the prettier the better. And Nurse Pigeon got down on the floor, tunneled under Kidstuff, and with a huge grunt bucked him up onto the bed. Then she stood up, knees crackling, and regarded him disconsolately. There were blue marks on his forehead and neck. A pinkish liquor had leaked from his nose and some kind of grit or gravel was sticking to it. One of his eyelids was rolled back almost all the way open, with a little yellow carpet lint glued to the corner. The other was half closed. From both all the light had drained out. They looked dusty. When she had found him in Little Rockcamp Road, he had seemed pretty much the old Kidstuff whose smiling face was always squinted to one side as if trying to see around corners, which he was. But now his upper lip was curled back in an expression of mild disgust. She spit on one finger and rubbed the dirt off his front teeth. Even Rose Dewglass might notice that. And still he didn't look right.

Nurse Pigeon tried to make herself get out of the room. She could feel her heart beating in her ears. Any minute now Rose Dewglass would sit bolt upright and take in Nurse Pigeon between her and the TV set. Suddenly Nurse Pigeon realized that, even drunk, Kidstuff, who was always a gentleman, would have pulled off his boots before lying down in a lady's bed, and probably his britches too. She bent over and pried, cursing, at the fancy purple boots until she remembered the cunning brass zippers on their heels and the boots plopped to the floor. And she had worked his jeans down to the backs of his sad-faced kneecaps when Rose Dewglass hiccupped once and Nurse Pigeon bolted for the exit.

When her hands stopped shaking on the doorknob, she knocked politely. In a minute or two Rose Dewglass came. She had put on a green chenille wrapper, which was falling apart like those bathrobes always did, and with one fingernail she scratched sleepily in the V of the neckline.

"Is that Ruthie? What you want, Ruthie?" And her clear pale eyes, through which even in the dark you could practically see out the back of her skull to her thoughts falling through a hole into empty space, told Nurse Pigeon she hadn't taken any notice of Kidstuff in her bed — not yet.

Nurse Pigeon said: "I want my husband."

"Who?"

"Kidstuff."

"I ain't got him," Rose said and yawned. "He never come, not all week." Then she blinked quizzically. "Your husband? Say, y'all never really got married, did you, Ruthie?"

"I wouldn't call him my husband if we was not legally married." Nurse Pigeon lied with dignity.

"Gee," said Rose. "I thought you was just old friends."

Nurse Pigeon nodded. "I have reason to believe he come here tonight. I am not sore about it, only he wasn't looking too good this week, and I am here to take him home and nurse him."

"He ain't here," Rose repeated.

Should she have seen this coming? Nurse Pigeon decided to steamroll right over it. "Also, he was carrying quite a large roll of cash money," she continued calmly, "which he happened to have borrowed it from me."

Rose just stood there in her green thready robe, shaking her red-gold, permanent-waved head. She was embarrassed. She was not the mercenary kind, Nurse Pigeon knew that already. Now Nurse Pigeon had to think of a way to get Rose back into the bedroom where she would see Kidstuff, without actually telling her to do this. To take up time she told Rose:

"He off-ten told me he loved you best of all his girls," though this wasn't quite true.

"Yeah?" Rose smiled shyly. "I seen him at the track tonight," she admitted. "I won't say I didn't, but he didn't want no parts of me. I seen him up the clubhouse hanging around that bleach blond woman of Blinky's. I hope he don't have a case for that tart."

"I believe it was a passing thing," Nurse Pigeon said.

"Somebody oughta tell him."

"He's gone on to other foolishness, I believe."

"I bet he's over there right now."

Nurse Pigeon shrugged, but inwardly she was perplexed. What had Kidstuff been doing all week?

"Y'all could use my telephone if you want to," Rose offered. "Call the bitch."

Nurse Pigeon hesitated. "I don't care to step foot in your room," she said. "I get a funny feeling just thinking about it. However, maybe you would do me the favor to dial the woman and ask if she seen Kidstuff? Kidstuff looking the sorry way he was and all." What was that Boston floozy's name? There was no time to worry about such refinements. Nurse Pigeon made a number up. Rose padded off toward the bedroom. Nurse Pigeon sat down on the curb of the concrete apron around the motel and clamped her teeth. It wasn't a shriek when it came, more like a cat yodel, but you could hear it. Rose came flapping back in her green bathrobe.

"I swear to my god, Ruthie," she panted, "I never seen him come in."

"I ain't sore," Nurse Pigeon said. "I just come to take him home."

"He ain't decent," Rose said.

"I'll sit in my car till he comes out."

Rose's fingernails dug into the soft part of Nurse Pigeon's hand. "I think he's dead, Ruthie. He looks dead." She was crying.

The two of them hurried through the kitchenette into the bedroom. Nurse Pigeon winced: the end of the bed was like a scene in a blue movie, where the man lies on his back and his pants dangle with dowdy obscenity from his ankles to the floor. It was hard to look at his bluish peter flopped sideways out of its scrubby nest in the way a peter can look dead even when it's alive; it was hard to look and it was hard not to look. Kidstuff's face was gray, the *O* of his lips gone ragged at the bottom, and by now even the rows of pretty teeth looked outsize for his mouth like cheap dentures. On this

side of the bed, Nurse Pigeon spotted the ball-bearing roller skates.
She nudged one under the bed frame with her toe.

"We never did nothing, not tonight," Rose squeaked, "I swear."

Nurse Pigeon said: "I tried to fix it so's he'd die in his own bed,
but it was not to be."

"Ain't you going to pull his pants up?" Rose suddenly pleaded.

"Why should I do so?" Nurse Pigeon said. "I seen him naked
plenty of times before." She made as if to back out of the room.

"You ain't going to leave him here with me?"

"Why, whatever else?"

"He's your husband." Rose was shocked.

"You was the one he loved," Nurse Pigeon replied.

"He always come home to you," Rose argued.

Nurse Pigeon said with sudden bitterness: "He took my last one
thousand dollars and blew it in the Poconos Thursday. Now I don't
even have money to bury his carcass."

"Oh Ruthie."

"You can explain to people what kilt him."

Rose's eyes went big. "I don't know what kilt him."

Nurse Pigeon shrugged. "They'll find out."

"Kidstuff said he was spending this week with you," Rose cried,
and burst into loud sobs. Nurse Pigeon eyed her, trying to see if it
was true.

"Well, he didn't," Nurse Pigeon said. Something peculiar here,
she was thinking, for Kidstuff didn't lie to women for the fun of it.
Lying was too much work.

"I never took no money from him, Ruthie," Rose said.

"I know that," said Nurse Pigeon, feeling sorry for her now. "But
you didn't need no money from Kidstuff, everybody knows that too."

"What do you mean?"

Nurse Pigeon shrugged. Rose on her pony escorted jumpy horses
from the barn to the track, and sometimes, if they weren't too sore,
even jogged them around it, and for this she made peanuts. But she
had more boyfriends than Nurse Pigeon had ever dreamed of, not
all of them no-accounts either, though two out of three wouldn't
work in a pie factory.

"I never been alone with a dead person."

"It's only Kidstuff. You was always good to him. A dead body is
nothing but meat. Science tells you that."

Rose began to cry again and Nurse Pigeon sighed. She had had the only scientific education in her small circle of friends. Often she felt like a freak on account of her opinions.

Rose went to the doorway and barred the way with her arms sticking straight out. "You can't leave me here with a dead person."

"All that about ghosts is so much business," Nurse Pigeon said.

"Put him in your car and take him home with you," Rose begged.

"That wouldn't be one bit right," Nurse Pigeon said, and, being the bigger woman, began to push past her.

"Ruthie! Wait!" Rose ducked behind the counter of the kitchenette and came up again holding a peanut butter jar full of curly bills. Nurse Pigeon, her hand on the doorknob, was careful not to stare straight at it.

"Lookit. I got money. You can take as much as you want if you'll only carry him out of here."

Nurse Pigeon stopped in the doorway as if turned to stone by this idea, and Rose caught up with her and took her hand by the wrist and stuffed it into the jar. The green bills had that cool, sharp-cornered, hardly used feeling of fifties or better — and sure enough, when Nurse Pigeon pulled out her hand, it had three fifties and two hundreds woven between the fingers. And the jar was empty. She held a fifty out to Rose. After all, the girl had to eat. But Rose pushed her hand away. "Take it," she said, "I don't want it." Young and foolish, Nurse Pigeon thought. They stood looking at each other. "You done the fair thing by Kidstuff," Nurse Pigeon said. "Don't tell nobody," Rose said.

Now Nurse Pigeon asked, in a practical voice: "How am I going to get him in the car?" For it would show a certain lack of mother wit to advertise how she could drag Kidstuff around all by herself. Together they went into the bedroom and at once Nurse Pigeon knew she had made a mistake. "Stand backwards to him," she ordered Rose, "and take up his feet. And don't look." Rose did as she was told, but they got only as far as the concrete strip around the cheap new part of the Horseman's Motel before her hands were shaking so bad that she dropped Kidstuff onto his heels. She turned and looked down at what she had been holding: his two feet in striped stockings. A bruise-colored second toe, long and jointed like a peanut, poked through each sock. In the eerie white light of the last sodium lamp on the racetrack side, they saw more: his pants, which Nurse Pigeon had yanked up but in her haste neglected to button, had bunched at his hips; this gave him a disrespected, manhandled look. His face hardly resembled Kidstuff at all in this light. And on his white stomach, purple threads raked the skin like the cheap tattoos that used to come in Cracker Jack boxes. He looked ransacked. Even Nurse Pigeon gasped a little.

"Lookit, Ruthie," Rose whispered. "You can't tell me his soul ain't quit him. How can I go back in that trailer?"

"Aw go on to bed," Nurse Pigeon said, picking Kidstuff up and packing him down firmly into the passenger seat of the Volkswagen all by herself. "The sweet falsehood has gone out of him, that's all."

But when she drove off from the Horseman's Motel parking lot, the small hairs were moving on the back of her neck. And she caught sight of Rose Dewglass in her rearview mirror, crawling under the fence to hole up in some tackroom on the backside.

Kidstuff's other dolly was of a stripe that the late Weems Pigeon liked to call a diamond hussy. Shirley O'Reedy, Nurse Pigeon recalled, or was it O'Rooney? It went without saying that she came from somewhere else — seven or eight years ago Blinky had brought her in from Suffolk Downs, or Scarborough or Rockingham Park or one of those bullrings up north. You saw her in spikes and spangles in the clubhouse every night, not so often with Blinky nowadays, but when approached by some neon shirtfront full of mucty-muck and flashing a fat roll that he hadn't had time to lose again yet, she could ice the chump with a single glance. Nurse Pigeon had a grudging respect for women in the sex profession, so long as they managed to practice their arts without keepers. At first when Kidstuff took up with Blinky's concubine, even his yesterday concubine, Nurse Pigeon naturally feared for his health, and yet nothing untoward had occurred. But now Kidstuff had no more health to protect.

Nurse Pigeon drove up in front of a low brick house on Berryville Street, a half-pint but classy-looking place, its white porch deep in glossy bushes, an oval window over the front door and one of those metal signs in the garden that said Dolley Madison popped a garter there or something on the way to her wedding. A lantern poured light like honey over a porch swing. At first Nurse Pigeon tried to prop Kidstuff lifelike in a corner of the swing, but the sight of that

Dolley Madison plate had shortened her patience, who did that Boston Irish think she was, and so Nurse Pigeon pushed the bell, MISS SHIRLEY O'RICKEY it read, and squeezed herself on the swing beside Kidstuff and the chains creaked and the slats groaned and pretty soon the door opened.

"Great Jesus, lemme call my doctor," Miss Shirley O'Rickey said. Around her neck she clutched a silky robe whose collar of feathers shuddered like white tarantulas. She was around forty, maybe, and to Nurse Pigeon's mind had always had slightly piggy charms, puffy lips, pink cheeks, big round breasts, but now her face looked waterlogged and oyster white under the platinum hair, like too much hooch over too many Miltown. "He don't need a doctor," Nurse Pigeon informed her.

"Is he gone?"

Nurse Pigeon let the matter speak for itself.

"Shouldn't I call somebody to make sure?"

"I am a licensed practical nurse."

"Well, shit," Miss Shirley O'Rickey said. She held on to a porch post as if her knees were weak. "He told me he was all through. He said he was going home to his nurse and I laughed at him. He didn't look any worse than usual. What did he die of?"

"Fast women," Nurse Pigeon tried, but it sounded so foolish she had to add: "And red eye. His liver give out I think."

"The liquor sounds right. I always thought pussy kept Kidstuff going."

"I wouldn't say that much," Nurse Pigeon pointed out icily.

"How far'd he get last night?"

"You was the last to talk to Kidstuff."

Miss Shirley O'Rickey laughed unpleasantly. "You wouldn't be trying to sucker me?"

"And don't pretend you wasn't jazzing him."

"That was over. We had business. He took care of a little matter out of town for me, strictly business. In business matters your sweetie and me always saw eye to eye."

It dawned on Nurse Pigeon what sort of business was alluded to and her blood pressure whirled up like a chain saw. "I heard you rolled high, but you didn't need to drag my husband in," she said, standing up in Miss Shirley O'Rickey's face.

"I know he wasn't your hubby," Miss O'Rickey said sweetly.

"Kidstuff worked hard for his nut."

"You know what I liked about your sweetie?" Miss O'Rickey recalled. "When he was sweet on me Kidstuff never gave me a goddamn thing. Well, maybe he brought me over a pizza now and then."

"A pizza is better than nothing," Nurse Pigeon declared, glaring at her. "It so happens he borrowed heavy from me and I don't even have the loot to put him in the ground proper. Where was he all week?"

Miss O'Rickey touched her pinky to the corner of her mouth and blinked her glued-on eyelashes genteelly at Nurse Pigeon. "I believe my partnership in this last deal went down all right for Kidstuff. Didn't he come home to you?"

"That's correct," Nurse Pigeon said, not without pride.

"I mean, girlfriend, you had to checked his pockets, that's the type you are." Automatically, both of them glanced at Kidstuff's pockets, hanging out like tongues, pale and obscene, from his undone, wrenched-up pants. "So what are you trying to get out of me?" All at once Miss Shirley O'Rickey's summing-up tone was hard as a jackhammer, and she was eyeballing Nurse Pigeon in a manner like to freeze her hair at the roots. Something about that face convinced Nurse Pigeon it was time to back out quietly, taking Kidstuff with her. Miss O'Rickey had powerful friends.

"I mean to send the finest flowers you ever saw," Miss O'Rickey added. "A nickel wortha white roses and that's a promise, to Kidstuff not to you. He was good for it."

"Why, that would be princely, more than ever I hoped," Nurse Pigeon exclaimed sincerely, just as Miss Shirley O'Rickey slammed the door in her face.

In the watery first light Nurse Pigeon drove Kidstuff down Charles Town Avenue, as she had done on a thousand less weighty occasions. Kidstuff had not driven an automobile since 1955, for as soon as he found himself behind a steering wheel he suffered from a panicky notion that his luck had run out and some berserk motorist would plow into him at any moment. Often Nurse Pigeon had dropped him at the track in the morning when she was on her way to pick up charts at the Jefferson County Department of Health. She had even chauffeured him to Two-Tie's after-hours card game now and then, when they were both flush and in good humor.

Once he had won four hundred dollars at Two-Tie's and they had driven fifty-two miles straight to Baltimore, stayed in the McKeldin Suite of the Sheraton Belvedere Hotel and sent out for bottle beer and steamed crabs. That was before middle age overtook them and Kidstuff's health went into decline and Nurse Pigeon's weight rose over 170 pounds. They couldn't indulge that way in front of each other anymore without one of them getting worried and sad and picking a fight. And once she had driven him into town on the Fourth of July because he had a pain deep in his nose. He had been dizzy for two days; suddenly they had each other talked into thinking it was cancer of the brain. Nurse Pigeon used her little bit of pull with the Charles Town medical establishment to get him seen on the Fourth. Dr. Lois Pettiman had been giving a barbecue, and examined Kidstuff up in her own bedroom. After a few minutes she came to the window and threw up the sash and stood there hollering down at Nurse Pigeon in her car in the driveway, that it was just sinus and she ought to be ashamed of herself, a trained nurse like she was. But that had been two years gone. When he was really dying, Kidstuff never complained at all.

Now Nurse Pigeon pulled up in front of Two-Tie's storefront on Charles Town Avenue and peered into the blacked-out window light from the curb. Way in the back she saw a tiny flicker: light from the backroom was leaking through a hole in the door where the doorknob had been removed, and people were moving in front of it, which meant they were still back there playing cards. Satisfied, she zigzagged over alleys and parking lots until she was in a dead-end court, her bumper almost touching a fifty-gallon drum outside Two-Tie's back door. She got out of the Volkswagen and stood on tiptoe to see to the bottom of it — sweepings of sawdust and cigarette butts, old *Morning Telegraph*s, bent up flat pizza boxes and greasy paper napkins, unopened junk mail. The drum was about half full, loosely packed.

This time Nurse Pigeon tried fishing Kidstuff up from the seat by the collar of his turquoise dress shirt, but she had forgotten that the shirt with the tiny naked girls on it closed with snaps instead of buttons, and just as she had him up in the air, the snaps popped open one after the other, his arms flew out like heavy wings and he sank back down with his knees sideways under the dashboard. Something starless and black as stove iron settled on her then. She knew it for a kind of doom. She had come to a place where even Kidstuff would stick and say no, but she would ignore his imploring voice. *Naturally you do not have as much to say about it as you did once,* she heard herself explain, *but you will be taken care of.* And in a hurry now she clutched Kidstuff around the middle and plunged him head-first into the trash barrel. Above the rim his feet in their two striped stockings pointed outwards like nautical flags. Nurse Pigeon studied this sight for only a moment. Then she drove the Volkswagen from alley to alley until she was back on Charles Town Avenue, and this time she parked in front and banged on Two-Tie's office door.

The clock on the Farmers and Merchants Bank said five-o-three. Through a scratch in the window blacking she saw Two-Tie himself barge through the doorknobless door from the backroom. He was hunched over a big, bluish, bona fide–looking pistol, but as soon as he cracked the entry and saw who it was, he let the thing hang down by his side.

"It's Ruth Pigeon," he called to the back, "Kidstuff's woman." With one hand he fumbled a gray padlock back onto the front door. "What's on your mind, dear?"

Two-Tie Samuels was so called because he had the sartorial peculiarity of wearing two bow ties at once, one black, one striped, every day of his life. He had a high, mild peep of a voice that seemed to have been squeezed down to nearly nothing by the short fat neck and its redundant haberdashery. Even so she could tell he was worried to see her here by herself at this hour. It couldn't mean anything good.

"Where's my husband?" she asked.

Two-Tie placed a hand on her elbow to steer her toward the backroom. Like the one on the gun, it was hairless and white and dimpled like a girl's. "Frankly, Ruth," he piped in his small voice, "I was about to ask you the same question."

"I ain't seen him all week," Nurse Pigeon said.

Two-Tie's upper lip nested in his lower lip and he nodded thoughtfully, for he was a thoughtful sort of businessman. He had been ruled off the backside long ago for alleged conflicts of interest and unsavory associations, but racetrack people, down to the lowliest one-man, one-horse gyp-rope operation, or down-and-out hotwalker, or toothless groom living in a tackroom on a two-dollar dose of King Kong liquor per day, still required his services from time to time. What services were these? Usually a loan — cash in front for a set of teeth, cash to pay the feed man, cash to straighten a traffic ticket or buy a new starter to get the truck back on the road. And once Kidstuff, having almost lost his pretty front teeth to a spooked filly he was shoeing in the packed dirt between two barns, had seized the fat and snot-encrusted kid who had come clattering through for the fourth time on his training wheels, and shaken him till his wad of pink bubblegum popped out like a cork. And the boy had turned out to be the son of a cousin of Blinky Cornford, the kind of hood who unlike civilized Two-Tie had people snuffed — but Kidstuff called Two-Tie, and Two-Tie cooled things down. In exchange for such services, Two-Tie naturally expected a consideration. But from racetrackers he sometimes asked no interest at all — just the pleasure, as he would say, of doing business with a sportsman who had an insider's view of life on the backstretch.

Through the back doorway Nurse Pigeon recognized a couple of sour-faced, wrinkled jockeys from the Charles Town tracks, and an old lady trainer named Sal. Nurse Pigeon followed Two-Tie into a shabby den fragrant with delicacies: on a dusty desktop in the shadows, next to a big gray adding machine, lay half-stripped carcasses of take-out barbecue chicken, open bottles of Carling's Black Label, and yawning pizza boxes with a coagulated wedge or two sticking among pearly orange polka dots of oil. From all this, though it was getting to be breakfast time, Nurse Pigeon turned her face the other way.

"I ain't seen Kidstuff for a week," she repeated, "and it ain't like him."

"You been looking?"

"I have not exactly had time to look," said Nurse Pigeon. "I am a full-duty licensed practical nurse."

Two-Tie nodded. "Well, I been looking high and low for Kidstuff," he said, "and I still ain't seen him. I hear he flashes through the clubhouse tonight but he's gone before my boys can pull his coat. So if you should run into him before I do, I want you to tell him this for Two-Tie. Two-Tie wants the whole story. He'll know what I mean. For if that is his regular plan on how to act at the racetrack, it don't matter how good a blacksmith he is, that sucker is out of work and nobody won't do business with him. Tell him that, will ya?"

Nurse Pigeon, ears hot, said she would tell him.

"He'll turn up. Now how about a cold beer, Ruth?" Two-Tie held out a bottle. Nurse Pigeon shook her head. Her back was up against the doorknobless door, as if she was edging out the way she came in, toward the blacked-out storefront.

"And Ruth — puh-leese bear it in mind — always use the back door." Two-Tie waved a hand and a humpbacked jockey named Archibald, if she remembered right, held open the steel alley door for Nurse Pigeon. "I can't have people banging on my office door at this hour of night, attracting god knows what order of riffraff," Two-Tie went on. "Come any time, dear, but always, always, come to the back."

Nurse Pigeon had to decide whether to work up a scream or play it more natural. She was not the screaming kind; to utter a noise at the sight of a dead body was contrary to both her temperament and her scientific training. However, since this company hardly knew her, she felt that a scream would be to the point, and put the least strain on their understanding. She screamed. The steel door behind her was still coming to the end of its hydraulic gasp. She focused on Kidstuff's striped feet sticking up out of the trash and screamed raggedly and as loud as she could, while behind her the heavy door swung back open.

"You kilt him," she hollered.

From behind her came Two-Tie's high small voice. "Yank him out of there. Is it the blacksmith?"

Archibald and the other jockey each took hold of an ankle and they pulled Kidstuff free of the trash barrel.

"Gar," said Archibald. "It's him."

They dropped him on the ground and Nurse Pigeon, tired of screaming, assumed a dazed and stony expression. Some sort of dark oil from the bottom of the barrel had made Kidstuff's hair clump together in front, and a white wadded-up napkin had got stuck in the open hole of his mouth.

"Jesus Mary Joseph," creaked old Sal, with a half-scared, half-compassionate glance at Nurse Pigeon. "God will punish them what done such a thing."

"You kilt him," Nurse Pigeon whispered.

"I ain't seen him in a week," Two-Tie said patiently.

"What kind of hood leaves a stiff in his own garbage can?" Archibald argued, reasonably but with too much relish. Nurse Pigeon peered at him with hatred.

"The kid looks terrible," Two-Tie observed. "He looked terrible all week."

"You said you ain't seen him in a week," old Sal said suspiciously.

"I mean last week."

"He could have a eensy little bullet hole under his clothes," said Archibald. "I seen that before, where it took the doc two hours to find the hole and meanwhile the joker kicks."

"Shut up," Two-Tie said. He cleared his throat. Nurse Pigeon could see he was getting ready to explain something to her. Ladies in her condition, when left unreconciled to the facts, had been known to talk to the authorities. On the other hand he did not know the facts, not all the facts; he hadn't seen her coming. Still, he knew something.

"Say a blacksmith got a flash," he began, "that somebody was schooling a broke-down old stakes horse from Mexicali with the worst paper you ever see to win his first time out after two years on the farm. Now this was highly classified poop. But the blacksmith somehow got this flash, maybe from the owner's girlfriend, and passed it on to a professor of such flashes for a consideration. The owner would kill if he knew! But I am surely not going to show my own face at that fifty-dollar window in the Poconos, so what could he do? Nutting without he knew my source."

"Now they tell me my source — would you believe it — my source strolls up to the window himself! Kidstuff! And lays down the whole roll, just as the numbers change embarrassingly from 50 to 1 to 5 to 1, and then the pathetic nag goes off at even money. . . . How do you explain such reckless disregard for his own safety, to say nutting of mine?"

"A thousand dollars," Nurse Pigeon said faintly.

"One grand, three grand, five grand, a lot of cabbage. My beard didn't look over Kidstuff's shoulder and count it. Which reminds me of a curious fact," Two-Tie added. "You know in the past such considerations with Kidstuff was seldom monetary. He had too much class for that. However on this occasion he had to have a dime in cold cash and, interestingly, Ruth, your name come up."

Nurse Pigeon stood blinking.

"Kidstuff said it was for you."

"Maybe he was meaning to pay me back," Nurse Pigeon murmured.

Two-Tie looked doubtful. "I see them go daffy like that before," he said. "Throwing borrowed dough around, getting on important people's nerves like they was trying to buy it at a discount." He shook his head. "What he did with all that money?" he asked rhetorically.

Nurse Pigeon said: "That was my last thousand dollars which he lost."

"Lost?" said Two-Tie. "He win. Señor Solaz win by seven lengths going away. The dumb fans like to lynch the jockeys and meanwhile Blinky Cornford posts several goons by the parimutuel windows because he would like to talk private with Kidstuff, but they are still waiting for Kidstuff to show himself when the track closes. In short the blacksmith vanished into air and nobody ain't seen him since."

"Somebody caught up with him," Archibald remarked.

Two-Tie solemnly shrugged. "I know nutting," he said. He made a little motion with his pointer finger, and Archibald and the other jockey picked up Kidstuff by the elbows and propped him against the brick wall in the blindest angle of the alley, where in the thinning shadow of dawn he appeared to be lost in desolate thought. "Bring your car around, Ruth," he said, "and get him out of here."

The tears Nurse Pigeon began to shed now were genuine, and for herself alone. Two-Tie bowed from deep in his neck, slowly and ponderously, like an oil rig on a hillside in Mineral County, and said: "Who knows what got him? I know nutting." But then he drew out a money clip and peeled off fifties until there was a loose nest of them, and pressed this poke into her hand.

"He did win," he explained.

Nurse Pigeon nodded.

"Buy him nutting but the best."

Nurse Pigeon said she would.

She had heaved the tickets into the ditch with such force that the rubber band had busted and they flew about like flower petals at a wedding, some sticking awhile to the overgrown bank, some to the road, some to the curd of gray leaves in the ditch bottom. But the spring had been so very fine that the ditch was dry. Her own car, with Kidstuff in it when she first drove off into the night, had floated some into the woods forever, and others were probably lining the new nests of flycatchers and phoebes by now. A mild May wind breathed over those few that were left, lifting their edges. Nurse Pigeon walked up and down the dirt lane in the cool dawn, picking up what she could find and blowing the grit off. In the end she had seven.

She ached to think of all the ones — a pink block of fifty-dollar tickets as tall as a joint of your finger, with a rubber band around it — that were gone, but she had to, for Kidstuff's sake. Kidstuff would have sent her to the Isle of Tahiti. She was going maybe to Ocean City instead, but at least she was going. She had toted up her night's work on the dusty windshield of the Volkswagen: after she went to Pennsylvania to cash her tickets she would have their honeymoon roll back, hers and Kidstuff's, with a few yards to spare. Through the finger smears on the windshield, through the clear numbers written in opaque dust, she could make out Kidstuff's upright head, his yanked-back cheeks the color of gritty pavement now, and that grin. To think there went the most beautiful boy that ever was, and now it was all over, she had saved him, and everybody had done right by him, and both of them might rest.

AVNER MANDELMAN

Pity

FROM ZYZZYVA

WE'VE BEEN WATCHING him for two weeks, Léon and I, from inside a shop across the avenue Foch. It belonged to a local Jew who helped the *Mossad* every now and then, and didn't ask any questions. This time he closed his shop for us — I didn't ask how much it was costing him. It was a posh boutique, with chinchilla and astrakhan coats hanging under Tiffany lamps, and mink jackets in the corners, and Léon and I made ourselves at home, taking turns at the Zeiss monoscope behind the curtain. We watched the second-floor apartment across the avenue, where the man who called himself Charles LeGrand now lived.

Until the month before we weren't even sure it was he; but then the local Mossad *katsa* broke into the office of LeGrand's dentist in Neuilly, made copies of his x-rays and sent them to the archive of *Yad VaShem,* and after a week the answer came back that it was indeed he, Karl Joachim Gross, The Smiler himself. In forty-three, he had personally supervised the killing of five, maybe six thousand Jews in the Lodz ghetto, two thousand of them children, and who knows how many more in Maidanek. Not a very big fish, compared with Eichmann and Mengele, but a fish just the same. Took us five years to locate him, once it was decided to go one level down, since we had gotten all the ones above him already. The funny thing is, the HQ for catching Nazi fugitives was in Paris, and Gross was number three on our list, yet it took us that long to find him. We had looked for him in Rio, and La Paz, even in Santiago, and here he was all the time in avenue Foch, right between our legs, four hundred meters away from our own consul's apartment.

This Gross, he now owned a little newspaper by the name of *Vents Neufs,* New Winds, a liberal paper, supportive of Israel, culture, art, shit like that. Most probably as camouflage, because fuckers like him never change. It's in the blood, whatever it is. He was old now, more than seventy, though he carried himself as erect as if he were de Gaulle, or something, and he lived on the second floor of a gray apartment building on the good side of the avenue, the north side, with two poodles, a little girl (his granddaughter, maybe, or a niece), and a blond Swedish nurse or a nanny, whatever she was, that took care of the girl, maybe of him, too. We didn't care about her, or the girl. Only him. I especially. My grandparents went in the Lodz ghetto, also two uncles, three aunts, and all my cousins. Only my father escaped.

At first, after I had tracked Gross down in Paris, the *Memuneh,* the Mossad's chief, got cold feet and wanted to take me off the case. But then my father intervened and said I was a pro, he had trained me himself, I could handle it, they shouldn't insult me, this and that. So they let me continue, but they glued Léon Aboulafia to me, a Moroccan Jew from Casablanca, who knew Nazis only from the movies, from Tach'kemoni High School, and maybe also from Yad VaShem, but that's it. Eichmann, too, they had let only Moroccan Jews guard him. I mean, we are all good soldiers and obey orders, but why take chances.

So we had been watching this Gross for two weeks, pigging out on *boeuf en croûte* and croissants and fancy cheeses that the local shadowers who kept a backup team in a café nearby left us every morning at the back door, when we finally got the go-ahead, straight from the *Midrasha* in Tel Aviv. The embassy *bodel,* a short fat woman by the name of Varda, came by one evening and slid an envelope into the mail slot in the front door, just like that, with the code words *Sun in Giv'on,* which meant we could take him, and it was up to us how to do it.

The orders, when we had left Tel Aviv, were to take Gross alive, bring him to Yerushalayim for a trial, but if anything went wrong, not to think twice, to take him down immediately, silent or noisy, then scram to London via Calais, where two DST border guards were on our payroll.

It went without saying that taking down Gross would look bad for me, what with my father's intervention and the Memuneh breaking the rules for me, and everything. "But better this than headlines," my father said, when right after Léon and I had landed in Paris, I called him from a hookers' café in Pigalle, going through one of our Zurich lines. "If you got to take him down, do it."

"No, I'll bring him alive, don't worry," I said.

"But don't take chances. I don't want to see you with *tzitzes* on your back." Which meant, "I don't want to see you on the front cover of *Ha'Olam HaZeh.*"

Ha'Olam HaZeh is the yellow rag of Israel. The back pages show women with exposed tzitzes, the front cover exposes the political scandal of the day.

"Oh, don't worry," I said. "I'll bring him. Nobody'll know anything, until he's in the glass booth."

The glass booth was where Eichmann had sat for his trial, so a crazed survivor of some camp couldn't shoot him or something.

There was a little pause. All around me were hookers, cackling in argot.

"Don't worry," I said again. "He'll be there soon."

"With God's help," my father said. (He had become religious in his old age, after he had retired.) "With God's help."

"With, without, you get the cage ready," I said, "he'll be there."

This was two weeks before. Now it was Friday night. I had been watching the literary program *Apostrophes* on the small television, using the earphones, and Léon was at the 'scope, when the envelope slid in. We both knew what it was, even before Léon clicked open his katsa knife and slit it open.

It took him two minutes to decipher the message with his *Tzadi-Aleph.*

"Mother's cunt," Léon said to me in Hebrew after finishing the computation. "We go."

Usually we spoke French, in case someone heard voices inside. But I guess he got excited. Take-downs he had done already, two, maybe three, but this was his first abduction, and a Nazi, too.

I myself had done three abductions before, two of them in Europe, one in Cairo. None was a Nazi, but so what. Nazis, Arabs, they are all the same to me. Haters of Yisrael, destroyers of Ya'acov, as the Bible said, it is a mitzvah to persecute them, to exterminate them to the tenth generation, like King Shaul was supposed to do to the

Amalekite, by the order of God, when he foolishly took pity on his enemy and so lost his kingship. We learned about this, in the Midrasha, in the katsa course; about the dangers of having a soft heart. No pity or compassion for these fuckers. None.

Not that I had any fear, now, of this. If anything, it was just the opposite. I knew the stories as well as anyone, what the old hands said, that there was nothing like catching a Nazi — it's better than sex, getting your hands on one of them, a real live one, being part of God's own Sword of Vengeance, so to speak. Even experienced katsas sometimes went crazy, when they saw a Nazi up close. Six years ago in Buenos Aires, two katsas from *Eytanim* department, the Russian shadowers, with fifteen years' service between them, slit the throat of an old hag they were supposed to bring in, some Austrian nurse who was said to have helped Mengele do selections. Her trial in Yerushalayim was ready to begin, with documents stacked a meter high, Golda's speech to the Knesset already printed in large type, so she could read it to the TV cameras without glasses, the editors' committee already briefed, everything, when suddenly, the night before shipment, the Nazi hag said a few words to one of them, maybe spit in his face, something, and they slit her throat. Just like that, both of them, one after the other. They were not even Ashkenazi Jews, or anything. One a Moroccan, like Léon, the other a Jerusalemite, his parents originally from Turkey, both sets of grandparents still living, even; still they did her, not a second thought. Go learn why. Maybe it's in the genes, now, this hatred. Like men and snakes, forever and ever, with no forgiveness possible.

Later the two were demoted, of course, but after less than six months they both got their ranks back, after Golda personally intervened on their behalf with my father, who was the Memuneh then. Because who can say he would have behaved differently? she said. Who can say he would have stayed his hand? Orders are orders, but sometimes there's a limit.

A week in that furrier boutique, still waiting for the go-ahead, that's exactly what I had begun to feel. Ten days, and still nothing. By then I was really beginning to worry, because you never know, someone might have gotten it into his head to cancel. Who knows what goes on in the corridors in the *Q'irya*, in Tel Aviv, or in the Knesset committees, in Yerushalayim, with all these soft-hearted kibbutzniks. I even suggested to Léon, once, to do it before any orders arrived, then tell the Midrasha we were faced with FCRI, field-circumstances-requiring-initiative. But Léon said no. It was too this, it was too that, and I didn't argue with him too much, because, let's face it, I didn't want to make more of a mess than we had to, and also because of my father, and the Memuneh, and everything. But with every day that passed, my obedience was weakening, because I was getting sicker and sicker of seeing this Gross strolling down the avenue with the poodle leash in one hand, the little girl's hand in the other, the nurse behind. Every time I saw him ambling by, happy and smiling and pink, not more than five meters away, I had to stop myself from rushing out to stick a tape over his white smile, throw him in the VW van, then drive the parcel to the Israeli embassy and let the resident katsa take care of the rest. I mean, the consul would have *plotzed,* since it would have made him directly involved. But what the hell, we could, if we had to. In such matters we outranked him and he knew it.

Anyway, the orders came, so the only thing left to do, besides the actual job, was decide when and how to do it, and how to ship him over. Finally (it took three hours of arguing), we decided to bag Gross on Sunday. (Sunday mornings he went with his little granddaughter, or niece, or whatever she was, to La Madeleine, without the nurse.) We would then ship him out to Israel the very same night, no delay.

Now, normally, shipping him would have been an Aleph-Aleph problem, because after Switzerland, which is a complete police state, where the SSHD always knows when every foreigner farts, France is the worst place in Europe. In Switzerland they are at least polite to you, and also are honest and stay bribed, once you pay them off. But these French fuckers — everybody, flics, DST, SDECE, CRS — they'll all happily take whatever you slip them, stick it in their ass-pocket, then go and haul you in anyway and divide the loot with the boss. That's the national character. Whores from birth, is what they are. No wonder they all collaborated with the Nazis in the forties, helped them ship the Jews to the camps, also managed some of the local camps for them, from Vichy. Fucking bastards, the Nazis and the French both. I once saw the train station on the outskirts of Paris, near the Porte de Clignancourt, from where they had sent the Jews east — a crumbling structure and rusty rails, not even a sign of what had once happened there. Not a plaque, not a note, nothing. Sometimes I wish I had been born then, so I could fight the fuckers when they were still young, like my father did, after he got out of the Polish forests and roamed all over Europe with a pair of knives and a Luger, and a little notebook where he kept score in *Rashi* Hebrew script. But we can't all be lucky.

This time, though, it seemed we were: two of our missile boats were docked in Marseille, for installation of these new CW radars from Dassault, and Thomson CSF digital sonar, that Peres had bribed out of Giscard, and by chance I knew the captain of one of them — also a Tel Aviv boy, by the name of Amirav Feiglin, who had once been with me in Young Maccabi, and also later, in Flight Course, which we both flunked. Years before, in Wormaiza Street, he had once stolen my bike, and when I caught him I of course beat him up, but I also let him beat me back a little, and we remained friends. Saturday morning, Varda arrived for last-minute instructions. I asked her to send Ami a message in *Tzadi-Tzadi*, regular IDF MilCode, bypassing the embassy katsa, and ask him if he would take a live package with him on the boat to Haifa, in a large box, and also us, Léon and me, without passports.

Varda made a face when I asked her to bypass the embassy katsa, but she agreed, as I knew she would. I used to fuck her, two years before, when she was new in the Paris station and not yet so fat from all this Parisian butter. I was stationed in Paris then for a series of take-downs of some local PLO *shawishes*, who had helped blow up two El Al offices, and she was the decoy, masquerading as a hooker. Old business this, doesn't matter. The main thing is, she agreed to give Ami the message, and also help drive the van.

"You need anything else?" she asked, after I had finished telling her what I wanted.

She had entered the boutique via the side door, and now sat in the purple armchair of the furrier's customers, rubbing her cheek on a white astrakhan coat that cost maybe 200,000 francs, maybe more. Her freckled face, under the thick makeup, was still pretty, also her tits were still upright; only her flanks had begun to go flabby and her ankles had thickened, maybe from all this walking, trailing people, eating on the run. Also, two years ago, she was told to put on weight, because Arabs like them fat, and now it was

probably hard to take it off. It's not the healthiest thing, being a
junior embassy katsa. But what do you want, there are worse things
than giving your youth to your people. At least there's still a people
to give it to.

"Yes," said Léon, "syringes, tapes, sack, everything."

He, too, had fucked her once or twice. I am sure, for form's sake,
when he had arrived in Paris. But of course it was no big deal. In the
Mossad, fucking is like a handshake. It's a greeting to a colleague.
It's even sort of encouraged, so you don't have people falling in
love with each other, screwing up the operational chain of command. If everyone screws everyone, it doesn't matter anymore, and
you can direct your mind to more important stuff. Anyway, that's
the theory. I remember how after fucking Varda exclusively for
more than a year, I was told several times to look around, there were
more women in the Mossad, a new crop every year coming from the
Midrasha, what did I get stuck on this fat broad for. (She wasn't that
fat, then.) Finally, I got the hint and stopped it; or maybe she did, I
can't remember. Maybe she got the hint, too. This was just after the
business with the PLO shawishes. Anyway, it was a long while back.

She said now, "Maybe you need more people?"

I saw she was eager to get in on the thing, not just to drive.
Catching a live Nazi, it doesn't come up every day.

"No," I said. "Léon and I are enough, for this."

"Sure," Léon said. "It's a small job."

His first abduction, already an expert.

"No, I can help, too," Varda said. "Really."

I saw she didn't get it, so I said, "You are also a Polack, a Bilavsky,
they won't let you."

Couldn't she see it? The orders were to bring him alive, that's
why there were only two of us, in a job that required four at least. To
minimize the chances of a repeat of the Buenos Aires fuckup.

"Only on my father's side," Varda said. "My mother was from
Greece."

"Same thing."

The Nazis had also killed half the Jews of Greece, and sent the
other half to Auschwitz. I was once in Salonika with a small backup
team from *Kardomm*, on a take-down job of a PLO mechanic. On
my day off I went to the local Jewish cemetery. It was so full of
headstones, you could hardly walk. If Tito hadn't stopped them in
Yugoslavia, and Montgomery in El Alamein, these fuckers would

have done the same in Tel Aviv, brought down the Third Temple. Touch and go, it was. Touch and go.

Varda said, "No, I got my Authorization last month. Really."

"Congratulations," Léon drawled. "Commander."

The Authorization is a permission to kill without having your life or the life of a colleague threatened, based on FCRI. It's roughly equivalent to an officer's commission in the Army.

Varda's nose turned red. "No, really. So if you need someone."

I began to say it was okay by me, but Léon said quickly it was not something he wanted to take on. Maybe because she was half a Polack, or maybe because he did not want a woman on the job. Moroccans are like that. Women for them are good only for one thing, babies. Maybe for fucking, too, but even for this they prefer each other.

"Authorization, shmauthorization," Léon said. "You want to help drive, fine, drive, but this thing, Mickey and I do it."

He said it as if he was giving the order all of a sudden, and I got mad. I said if she wanted to help, let her help, why not? Maybe we could use a woman.

"Like how, use?" Léon said. "We don't need anybody else. Two is enough, for this, mother's cunt, an old man and a little girl!"

I said, "But if, I don't know, the little girl shouts, or something."

"So what? Mother's cunt! She shouts, he shouts, anyone shouts, it's the same thing. Anything goes wrong, we take him down, ten seconds, we are gone."

"You or me?" I said. "Who will do him? If we have to."

Léon got all red in the neck. He knew very well that the one who took down Gross would have it on his file forever. The Panicker, the one who had screwed up The Smiler's trial. But if he now said I should do it, if we had to, it would be like admitting he didn't have the stomach for it.

Varda looked at me with professional admiration, at how I had hemmed Léon in. But I didn't give a shit about that, now. "So who would do him?" I asked again.

"We won't have to," Léon said at last, his voice sandy.

"And if he fights?"

I don't know why I was so mad at Léon, all of a sudden.

"So he fights!" Léon snarled. "So he fights! Lift some weights tonight, so you can bend his arm!"

Varda said pacifically, "This Swedish nurse, she could make trouble, if she comes, or the girl, what do I know."

Léon snapped at her that he would ask for her opinion if he wanted it.

"Fuck you," Varda snapped back at him. "Fuck you, ya Aboulafia, you speak nicely or I'll take off your left ball."

I liked her again, now. That's the way.

"It's too big for you," Léon said.

"An olive, I bet," Varda said, which was nice of her, too, implying she had never seen it.

There was a short silence while we regrouped, so to speak, picking at the cheese, pouring Chambertin, passing napkins.

Finally, Léon said the nurse never came on Sundays. The shadowers had told us so.

I said nothing. Both he and I knew that this did not mean a thing. The shadowers fucked up half the time. A bunch of Yemenite boys good for nothing. Only because of the coalition agreement did they take them in at all.

"Yeah," I said at last, not wishing to restart anything. It would all go on our report anyway, every word of this, from the tape recorder, which we had to leave open by standing orders.

"But I can take care of her," Varda said, not making clear whether she had meant the nurse, if she came, or the girl.

"No, no," Léon said. "Mickey and I will do it. It'll be a breeze."

"So anyway, if you need me."

"Fine, fine," Léon snapped. "We heard you."

But of course it wasn't a breeze.

I had the first inkling of this the next morning, when we parked the VW van on rue Blé, a quiet side street forking off the north end of avenue Foch, waiting for Gross to appear.

Half an hour and he hadn't come yet.

"Abort," I said to Léon. "He's late. Late! Something is wrong. Abort, Léon, abort!"

Taking down Gross, each one of us could decide on his own, and justify later. But aborting on lateness, for this we needed a consensus.

"Nah," Léon said. "Don't be a *yachne*. He had a diarrhea, from too much cheese, or maybe a hangover. Something."

Fifteen minutes more. Still nothing.

"Abort!" I said.

"You want to veto?" Léon said. "On your head."

I thought about it. Aborting on a hunch was permissible, but if it came out later it was nothing, I would be a yachne forever. An old woman. Not in my file, but where it counts. In the Midrasha's cafeteria, in the Sayeret's summer camp, in the hotel safe rooms.

"It's a Nazi," Varda said. Her face had become puffy, as if air was blowing through it, from within. "A fucking Nazi. You won't wait for him a half hour?"

"All right," I said at last. "For a Nazi I'll wait."

Ten minutes more. Fifty minutes late.

"Relax," Léon said to me. "It's still quiet."

Indeed, rue Blé was deserted. Even avenue Foch had almost no cars. Maybe a cab or two going to Neuilly.

"Yeah," I said grudgingly. "It's quiet."

Maybe it would still be all right.

But when Gross finally came around the corner, embalmed in a black suit and sporting a dark Tyrolean hat, it was plain for all to see that it was an Aleph-Aleph fuckup.

He was holding the girl in one hand, the Swedish nurse in the other, and behind the nurse, all holding hands, were a bunch of little girls all dressed in black, squeaking and chirping like blackbirds. (Later we learned it was the niece's birthday, and her school friends had all come along, for church.)

"Shit in yogurt!" Varda said in Hebrew.

I said nothing, but it was obviously a disaster.

Without looking at me, Léon said we should abort. "Just let him go, we'll come back next week."

But now I, all of a sudden, was hot to trot. Maybe because, I don't know, I saw him now before me. The bright smile, the upturned old nose, the soft white hands.

"No," I said to Léon. "Let's get him."

Léon, crouching near his own eyehole, at the van door, shook his head, so I grabbed his shoulders and said the missile boats were leaving Marseille the next day. If we postponed, we'd have to wait another week, dump Gross in the embassy, to be sent on El Al as diplomatic cargo, in a box, then he might die en route, there'd be no trial, nothing, only bureaucratic shit forever and ever. "You want Bleiman telexing Glilot for the next hundred years?"

Yoram Bleiman was our consul in Paris — his daughter was married to the PM's younger son, the one who avoided military service by going to a yeshiva. I knew for a fact the PM could stand neither one of the three; but did I want my fuckups coming up at Friday evening meals at the PM's table for the next five years? Also, I could see my own father giving me that pained look, across our own Friday table. (After my mother died I went to live with him, in our old apartment, on Wormaiza Street.)

"So he'll telex," Léon said. "Let him telex."

"All right, sure," I said. "Let's go back, have one more croissant, wait another week, maybe they'll send another team, an experienced one. Maybe a bunch of Yemenites they'd pull off some tail-job, in Cyprus."

Léon got all white around the nose. For a brief moment I thought he would punch me. Then he got up from the floor. "All right, fuck it, let's go."

Even this late on a Sunday morning, perhaps ten o'clock already, rue Blé was still deserted as a lane in Yerushalayim on Yom Kippur. The café-tabacs were all shuttered, the lottery office closed, not even pigeons on the sidewalks. Aside from the squealing little girls, it was calm and quiet. We might even have had the required thirty seconds to do it — rush out when he was passing the *pâtisserie*, grab him, inject him, and throw him in, all in one movement (a dozen times we had practiced this, before we left Tel Aviv), but because we had hesitated and argued, Gross had already passed us by. So when we finally jumped out, clanging the van door open in our haste, he turned and stared at us. His cheeks got all tight and military — he knew on the instant — and then his face fell apart and he screamed. It was a scream the likes of which I had never heard before, worse than if someone had slit his throat open.

And then everything got fucked up all to hell.

The Swedish nurse, as if she had practiced this before, bashed Léon on the back of the head with both fists, twice, and he fell as if he was made of wood, straight forward, mashing his nose on the pavement: there was a loud crack, like a piece of lumber breaking, and blood squirted out of his face as though a faucet had burst.

All the little girls began to scream, the whole lot of them, and scurry about like crazed mice, and by that time Gross was running down rue Blé — seventy-two years old, but loping ahead like a deer towards avenue Foch. Then the Swedish nurse threw herself on me, tugging at the roots of my hair, spitting and hissing, in Swedish and German and French.

For a full minute I battled with her, first punching her ample solar plexus, then between her legs, all the while trying to inject her in various parts, when all at once she tore away from me and threw herself upon Varda, who was for some reason struggling with the little girl.

"My angel!" the nurse screeched in German. "No one is going to take you if I —"

Varda let go of the girl and grabbed the nurse by the hair, and in a second had her on the sidewalk in a reverse nelson. I wanted to shout at her, to tell her to go easy, but I had no time to talk, because right then two little girls in lace-trimmed black dresses raced past me, screeching, and as one tripped, both of them fell upon each other and somehow got tangled between my legs, just as I was trying to hoist Léon on my shoulder.

I was knocked down again, with Léon on top of me; and as I kept trying to peer from between the skinny white socks dancing and scampering before my eyes, with Léon's blood dripping on my eyebrows, I saw the nurse lying on the sidewalk, like a large blond chicken with her neck bent sideways, oddly elongated.

Varda's pink face swam into my view. "I had to!" she screeched. "I had to!"

"Get into the van and let's go!" I said, struggling again to my feet, feeling Léon's blood dripping on my neck.

But Varda was already gone, racing toward avenue Foch, Gross's little girl dragging behind her, legs akimbo.

"Mathilde!" I hollered. (This was Varda's code name.) "Mathilde! Let's go!"

But she kept running, dragging the girl behind her.

"*Halt!*" she shouted at Gross in German, and I saw that she had grabbed his little niece by the throat, with her own katsa knife under the little ear. "Come back, you fucker!"

Madness!

Through Léon's blood I saw Varda jerking the little girl's head back, the white neck arching upwards.

Madness! Madness! One look at the Nazi, and we forgot every-thing. Everything!

Then, as in a slow dream, I saw that the girl was not Gross's niece at all, but one of the other girls Varda had grabbed by mistake. The girl's eyes, frozen with terror, looked up into Varda's chin, as if something was growing out of it.

I wanted to shout, to tell Varda that she had got the wrong girl, that she had made a dreadful error, that The Smiler would never come back for a stranger, that the flics would be upon us in a second, but an invisible fist seemed to have been rammed down my throat and not a word came out.

"Halt!" Varda screamed across the avenue. *"Ha-a-lt!"*

Then, to my dull astonishment, as in a silent movie, I saw Gross halt in midstride.

He turned around, honking cars flowing to his right and left, like water unfurling before a reed growing in the Yarkon River, and for a brief second he looked at Varda, then at me, smiling crookedly.

"Haaalt!" Varda howled, in a voice like an animal's. "Come heeere!" *Madness!*

As I tugged my Beretta out of its plastic holster at the small of my back and hoisted it up, Gross kept staring at me with that peculiar little smile. Then his smile widened and softened and turned radiant. And as Varda's knife began to move, I felt my bladder loosen; and all at once, with my index finger already searching for the soft trigger spot, I found myself hoping that the man floating in the *V* of my gun sight would dash away from me, hoping beyond hope.

Leg

FROM THE NEW YORKER

WHEN Dave Long tagged up and tried for third, everyone had to laugh. A bone-head move, and, for Dave — typically a prudent guy — uncharacteristic. As he took off, Dave laughed, too, at his own folly. Church-league softball, one gone in the last inning, not a blessed thing on the line — the game was without meaning and out of reach — and he went on a shallow fly to left.

"Good Lord," his wife, Susan, said to the woman next to her. She was sitting in the aluminum bleachers with the rest of the Bethany Baptist bunch. She had arrived late — barely in time to see Dave reach second on an overthrow. He was surprised to see her. Susan Long was a busy, charitable woman. She worked half time keeping the books for Nuñez Chiropractic and gave her afternoons and evenings to business of the church, the school, the community. Before the game, Dave and his son, Randy, grabbed some food downtown — as they did two or three times a week. Given her responsibilities at the church, which included a leadership role in Christian education, her several Bible-studies and support groups, her involvement in such service arms as Member Care and Prayer Chain and Meals on Wheels, Susan had little time to prepare supper, or eat it. "What the heck is he doing?" she said.

Dave was trying for third. There was no question: he knew he should stay at second, he should not go, and he went. The left fielder, Pastor Jeff, of the Alliance Church, had a cannon. He looked at Dave as if Dave were pursued by demons. Pastor Jeff spoke to him. In shallow left field he was close enough to speak to Dave as he headed for third.

"Where are you going, Dave?" Pastor Jeff said. "You're dead, man." Dave smiled. He liked Pastor Jeff. On the street. He hadn't cared for his manner in the pulpit, the few times he'd heard him preach. Pastor Jeff was too tall — he was six feet nine — and his preaching posture was stooped and condescending. He was also too familiar and digressive for Dave, who had been raised in the cooler, straighter logic of the Episcopalians. But Pastor Jeff had the straight truth here: Dave *was* dead. To rights. Dave had been fast, but he was forty-four now, and he was too slow to pull this sort of stunt.

Dave's son, his only child, Randy, stood a way off, down the third-base line, behind the Cyclone fence. He was hanging from the fence as if tethered there, his arms stretched out above his head, his fingers laced through the wire, the toes of his sneakers wedged in the bottommost holes. He shook his head back and forth, almost violently. Randy was thirteen. He had not wanted to come watch his father play.

"God," he said when Dave tagged up. "Stupid. You're stupid."

Randy was a big, strong kid. He was, almost all the time now, angry at his father. He could tolerate his mother, but everything about Dave, who you would have thought the more approachable parent, enraged him.

Randy hated the way Dave dressed. He hated his whole wardrobe, in particular a blue down jacket Dave had had for years and wore when he drove Randy to school on winter mornings.

"You garbageman," Randy would say to him. "You look like a garbageman. You grunge monkey."

Dave liked this latter expression; he tried not to smile.

"Laugh," Randy said. "Laugh. The garbagemen dress better than you do."

Dave's beard, which he kept respectably trimmed, made Randy angry.

"No kisses, wolfman," Randy said, if Dave bent over his bed to kiss him good night. "You werewolf. You're scaring me, wolfman."

Randy spoke with stage disdain of Dave's friends. Dave's car, a Taurus wagon, was boring and dumb — for Randy, an emblem of all that was insufferable and pedestrian about his father. But the thing that really drove Randy wild was that Dave liked to read. Dave rose every morning at five so he could spend a quiet hour reading and thinking and praying. Which left him irredeemable in Randy's eyes. If Dave sent Randy to his room or otherwise disciplined him — this happened more often than Dave wanted — Randy would say, in his cruellest, most hateful voice, "Why don't you just go read a book, Mr. Reading Man. Mr. Vocabulary. Go pray, you praying mantis."

Watching Randy in his father's presence — the way his face went tight, the way his back stiffened — listening to the explosive, primitive noises he made in place of speech, you could see the boy's anger was beyond his control and understanding. It had sandbagged the kid, hit him blind side. It made Dave very sad. He missed the easy love of his son. He missed talking to Randy, he missed his companionship, and he felt sorry for him, because in the periodic rests between peals of rage, when he took breath, Randy was clearly dazed and spent and, himself, sad.

Sometimes it was hard for Dave to remember that this abrasive, scowling thing, always coming at him, was his own son. Randy would bump him or leer or growl, make some foul and belligerent gesture, and before he'd had time to set or check himself, Dave would have responded in kind. "You shut your mouth, punk, or I'll shut it for you," Dave might say. He would grab Randy's arm above the elbow and squeeze it hard, trying to hurt him, and he would fill with regret and shame.

Randy said, "Stupid. You're stupid," and Dave, slow but hellbent for third, heard him.

Shoot, Dave thought. Poor kid. What am I doing?

Pastor Jeff threw a rope to the third baseman, also named Jeff, who worked in the auto-salvage yard. This layman Jeff caught the ball and straddled the bag, waiting for Dave, who was still only halfway there.

"Dumb," Randy said. "You are stupid." He untangled himself from the fence and turned his back to the field.

The third-base coach, Pastor Rick, senior pastor at Bethany Baptist, was at a loss. When the ball left the bat, a weak fly, he had raised his hands, palms out, signalling Dave to stay put. "Hold up, Gomer," he shouted, but it was too late — Dave had committed himself.

Pastor Rick was Dave's age. They met downtown once a week for lunch to discuss Scripture and Dave's personal journey in faith. They had that day, over turkey melts and iced tea, considered Matthew 7:13–14, a familiar passage Dave had lately found compelling and vexing: "Enter through the narrow gate. For wide is the gate and broad is the road that leads to destruction, and many enter through it. But small is the gate and narrow the road that leads to life, and only a few find it." After a space of silent meditation, Pastor Rick asked Dave what he thought the Gospel writer might have meant by the word "narrow." They had their Bibles on the table before them.

"Apart from the obvious?" Dave said.

"Yes," said Pastor Rick.

"Are you asking because you know, or because you want to know?"

"The second," Pastor Rick said. "I don't know. How would I know?"

"You're Baptist."

"No shit," Pastor Rick said.

"If we knew what the Hebrew was," Dave said. "Or the Greek."

"Good question. I don't. So?"

Dave thought a moment.

"Maybe as in severe," he said. "I don't know. Narrow. As in pinched. It pinches you to go through. What's the word? Straits. Straitened. Maybe exclusive. Most people are excluded. They are left out. Unpopular. Maybe narrow as in simple. Sheer. Simple. Severe. Did I already say that?"

"Yes, you did."

"Yeah, well that's what I come up with."

"Good stuff," Pastor Rick said.

"What have you got?" Dave said.

"Half my sermon. Thanks."

A female fan on the Bethany side was yelling, "Slide, Dave, slide!" This was a joke, because no one slid in church league — the guys were too old, too sedate — and, besides, Dave was wearing shorts. Everyone laughed. Dave heard the call for him to slide, and he, too, found the proposition laughable.

Then he slid. He raised his right hand in a fist. He yelled, "Oh, mama!" And from six feet away, and at what was for him top speed, he slid into third. Under the tag. Around the tag, really. No one who watched could believe it. It was the best, the only hook slide anyone had ever seen in that church league.

The base paths were a hard, dry, gravelly dirt, and Dave tore up his leg. He stood up, called time, and limped off the bag. He looked down at his leg, the left, which was badly abraded from ankle to knee. Beneath a thin film of dirt, which Dave tried to wipe off with his hand, the leg was livid, strawberry, a crosshatch of cuts and gashes, bits of sand and gravel in the wounds.

Pastor Rick was beside him. He put his arm around Dave.

"Why did I do that?" Dave said. "Ouch."

"Wild man. You O.K.?" Pastor Rick said. "Nice slide."

"Thanks. I'm O.K. I think."

"Can you walk? You want a runner?"

"Nah," Dave said. "I'm fine."

"You sure?"

"Yeah," Dave said.

Pastor Rick patted Dave on the rump. "All right, then. Go get 'em."

Dave turned to the crowd. He smiled sheepishly and waved.

Susan stood up in the stands.

"I'm O.K.," he said.

"Big jerk," she said to herself as she sat down. Then, to the woman next to her, "I don't believe it." She took a magazine out of her purse and looked at the cover. She stood up. She shook the magazine at Dave. He pretended to cower, and the crowd laughed.

Randy, who had wheeled to watch the play from the left-field foul line, was embarrassed: that his father slid; that his father slid in shorts and hurt himself sliding; that the slide, in this context — a game for coots and feebs and wacko fundamentalists — was inordinately, ridiculously good; and, on top of it all, that his mother had got into this bad circus act. Randy began to drift in his father's direction, up the line. Dave watched his unwitting tack with gratitude and wonder. He looked at Randy, shrugged his shoulders, and smiled, a bit goofily.

It was only when Dave smiled at him that Randy realized he was moving toward his father. He wrenched himself away. Randy turned and headed for the parking lot.

Dave's leg looked bad, painful, but it didn't really begin to hurt until after the next batter, Lloyd Weeks, who worked for Dave at the cereal plant, tapped a ground ball to the pitcher, stranding Dave at third and rendering perfectly gratuitous his miracle slide.

Randy caught a ride with his mother, who left as soon as the game ended, taking time only to tell Dave to get home and clean up his leg. To give Randy some time for his anger, Dave stayed to help gather the equipment, then wound up going for a beer with Pastor Rick and a few of the men. His leg was stinging. He doused it with cold water from a spigot by the backstop. At Tiny's, he ordered a beer and a Scotch. He poured out the Scotch on his napkin and swabbed his leg.

"Shoot," Dave said. "That stings."

"That is one ugly leg," said Pastor Rick.

Pastor Jeff of the Alliance Church held up his diet Coke and waggled it. "Just for the record," he said. "And if anyone asks, I wasn't here."

"Who was?" said Pastor Rick.

"Great slide," said Pastor Jeff to Dave. "I had you nailed."

"Never in doubt," Dave said.

Dave nursed his beer, listening to Pastor Rick and Pastor Jeff disagree about glossolalia and about the dangers (Pastor Jeff) and the appeals (Pastor Rick) of ecumenism, and then commiserate about the unremitting demands of the lectionary.

"You write me this week's," said Pastor Rick. "I'll give you half the take."

"I'll do it for nothing," said Pastor Jeff. "You preach what I write."

"Sure, sure," said Pastor Rick. He looked over at Dave. "My guys couldn't handle it."

"Talk about speaking in tongues," Dave said.

Pastor Jeff laughed, then sat up very straight.

"I cast thee out, little feller," he said to Dave.

"I was just leaving," Dave said.

When Dave got home it was half past nine, and Susan was already asleep. Randy was closed up in his room listening to his music. Dave stood outside the door. Randy had the volume down, but Dave could still feel in his feet the pulse of the bass and the drum. It was a song he knew.

> They
> They betray
> I'm your only
> true friend now
> They
> They'll betray
> I'm forever there

He knew the song, he knew the CD. Metallica. Randy played it
often and loud, and Dave had listened to it several times, on his
own, when Randy wasn't around.

> Hate
> I'm your hate
> I'm your hate
> when you want love

The boy had taste. This music was virtuoso stuff, and Dave thought
it might lead him to other forms. But the lyrics, which seemed to
speak to Randy so nearly — the spirit, pitch-dark and bereft, to
which Randy vibrated with such sympathy — made Dave unhappy
and fearful. He'd told Randy, once, that he liked the music.

Randy needed no time to work into his rage. "You don't like it.
You don't know anything about it. You've never even heard it."

"I've heard it," Dave said, backing off. "I think it's good. Forget it."

"You don't know anything," Randy said. "Keep out of my room.
Don't touch my stuff."

Dave showered, and dabbed his leg with a soapy washcloth. The
injury was worse than he'd thought. There was almost no skin left
on the wound, which covered a sizable portion of the leg, from the
ankle to the knee. It looked as if someone had gone at his leg with a
cheese grater. The tissue around the lesions was pink and swollen.
When they were clean, they would not stop bleeding. The blood
didn't flow so much as pool up, and he used a roll of toilet paper
trying to stanch it. When it still would not stop, he wrapped his
lower leg tightly in some gauze bandage he dug out of the vanity
drawer and fastened that with adhesive tape. Almost at once, his leg
began to throb. It felt hot. It was already infected, he figured. He lay
down on the living-room couch and elevated his leg with a cushion.
After a few minutes the blood had seeped through the gauze, and
Dave gingerly removed it. There would be no way to stitch the thing
— the surface area was far too large and irregular. He thought
about going over to the emergency room. Instead, he boiled some
water in a pot. He soaked a fresh dish towel in the water, lifted it out
with salad tongs, and, thinking to cauterize the wound, applied it to
his leg. It scalded him. He cried out but held the towel to his leg as
long as he could bear to.

Then he sat down on the kitchen floor, his left leg stretched out
before him, and prayed.

His praying was rarely premeditated or formal. Most often it was a phototropic sort of turn, a moment in which he gave thanks or stilled himself to listen for guidance. He shied from petitionary prayer. With all he had, it felt scurvy — scriptural commendation notwithstanding — to ask for more. This night, his leg hurting to the bone, he permitted himself a request.

"Father," he said quietly, "please help me to see what I can do for Randy. He is in great pain. I love him. If it is your will, show me what I might do to bring him peace."

Dave looked up. Randy was watching him from the bottom of the stairs.

"Amen," Dave said. He smiled. "Hey, bud."

Randy said nothing. He stood looking at Dave.

Dave got to his feet.

"Man, this sucker hurts," he said. "What are you up to?"

"You screamed," Randy said. He did not move from his spot on the stairs.

"I burned myself," Dave said.

"I came down."

"Thanks," Dave said. "I'm O.K."

Randy snorted. He shook his head and went back upstairs.

The doctor used the word "suppuration." Despite Dave's home-spun palliatives, the wound had begun to form and discharge pus. So much that by the end of the next day, when Dave came home from work and called the doctor, the pants he'd worn to the plant were sodden and glued to his leg.

"You'd better come in and let me look at it," the doctor said. "Can you come in sometime tomorrow?"

"I can't," Dave said. "I can't get away. What do I do for it on my own?"

"You keep it clean," the doctor said. "You use a topical dressing. Bacitracin. Neosporin. I'll tell you this: if it's as infected as it sounds, you'll need a course of oral antibiotics. Perhaps even intramuscular."

"Or what?" Dave said.

"What are you asking?"

"I'm asking what might happen."

"That's not a question," the doctor said. "All sorts of things *might* happen. Which is why we don't fool around. Staph. Strep. Massive swelling. You want more? Gangrene. Sepsis. Work at it, you could lose your leg. Does that scare you?"

"Yes," Dave said.

"Good," the doctor said. "Because we're not negotiating. You come in. Day after tomorrow."

"If I can," Dave said.

"No, no. Not if you can. You come in."

The leg continued to weep. After several days, the pain was so bad, so deep, he could not put any weight on it. Though he tried keeping it clean, it had begun to smell. At night he removed the dressing and left the wound open to the air.

"Randy gone?" Susan said. She was on her way to Nuñez Chiropractic and stopped in the kitchen to sit with Dave for a minute while he ate breakfast.

"He's gone," Dave said.

"How did he go?"

"He was peaceful," Dave said. "I don't know — light. He seemed lighter. I said goodbye. Then he said goodbye. No agony. No outbursts. We had ourselves a remarkable morning."

"What's your day like?" Susan said.

"Good," he said. "The same. The usual. What about yours? You busy?"

"The usual," she said. "Listen a minute. I'm concerned about you. About your leg."

"Don't be," he said.

"It's bad."

"Not too bad," he said. "It's better today."

"I've thrown away two pairs of your pants," she said. "And I can see. You can't walk. How can you say it's better?"

"It is. I'll be fine."

"Why don't you go to the doctor? Did you call him?"

"I did call," Dave said. "He told me what to do for it. I've got an ointment. What about dinner? We in or out?"

"I'll make something," Susan said. "Dinner. You tell me now. What's going on?"

"What?" he said.

"Tell me what you're doing. Because I'm concerned. I'm worried. And I've got to go. Please. What are you doing?"

"Nothing."

"Nothing," she said.

"Hacking around. Whatever. You know me."

"I know you," she said. "We're talking about your leg."

"It will be fine," he said.

Dave did not go to work. Without crutches or a cane he could not make it to the car. He phoned his secretary and told her he'd be out of town for several days, maybe a week. He devised, halfheartedly, a story about his mother, who suddenly needed tending to. His secretary was confused by the story, but she did not question him. He would call her again, that afternoon, he said, to fill her in. Could she handle things for a while in his absence?

He spent the morning stretched out on the couch, the living-room curtains drawn, in prayer. At one point he woke from a near trance to find his heart wildly beating, as if he'd just run a set of wind sprints. He was not flushed or dizzy or short of breath. He felt calm and relaxed, except for the steady thrum of pain in his leg and his heart thumping away. The strangeness of it made him laugh. He took a few deep breaths and closed his eyes.

In the afternoon, just before Randy got home from school, the doctor called.

"I called your office," the doctor said. "You weren't there."

"I'm here," Dave said. He was, by then, on the cool kitchen floor, supine, three crocheted hot pads beneath his head, his left leg raised slightly, the foot resting on a cookie tin.

"Your secretary said you were out of town."

"I haven't left yet," Dave said.

"I want to know how your leg is, David, and why you didn't come in as I asked."

"The leg is fine," Dave said. "I put that ointment on it. It's looking good."

"No more discharge?"

"None."

"It's healing?" the doctor said. "The pain is subsiding?"

"Seems to be," Dave said.

"So. Good. That's good. You're lucky. These things can turn nasty if they're not attended to. You got lucky. The next time I tell you to come in I want you to come in."

"I will," Dave said. "Thanks for calling."

Dave was on the kitchen floor when Randy came home from school. He thought about getting to his feet, but he had found a comfortable, if somewhat ludicrous, position and was unwilling, even for Randy, to suffer the pain that would attend trying to stand up. Randy came into the kitchen for his snack. He looked at Dave lying on the floor and stepped over him on his way to the refrigerator.

"Thanks for not stomping me," Dave said.

Randy got out the milk and poured himself a glass. "What are you doing?" he said.

"It's cool down here. I'm having a little trouble standing."

"What is it?" Randy said, without looking at him. "Your leg again?"

This was the first mention Randy had made of Dave's leg, though Dave could see, in the way Randy had behaved the past few days — restrained, even equable — that he'd been aware of it.

"How was school?"

"O.K.," Randy said.

"Any trouble?"

"No."

"Have you got homework?"

"No. A little."

"Get yourself something to eat," Dave said.

"I am," Randy said, and he began probing the refrigerator. He took out packages of Muenster cheese and sliced ham and a jar of mayonnaise. "Where's Mom?"

"Out," Dave said. "What do you need?"

"Nothing. Where are we going for dinner?"

"Here," Dave said.

Randy made himself a sandwich.

"You hungry?" Dave said. A question he regretted as soon as he had asked it. It was the sort of question — nervous and dumb and self-evidently posed to fill the uneasy space between him and his son — that invariably caused in Randy a detonation.

"Starving," Randy said.

"Well, leave some room for dinner."

"I am," Randy said.

Sunday afternoon was hot, and Pastor Rick came by the house, in cutoff jeans, tank top, baseball cap, and flip-flops, to see Dave.

Susan had put him up to it. She'd lingered in the narthex after the
service to talk to him. Pastor Rick had begun to worry about Dave
on his own. He hadn't heard from him in nearly a week, and, seeing
Susan at church alone that morning, he thought something might
be wrong. Dave was as steadfast a parishioner as Pastor Rick had.
Susan was undisguisedly afraid. She said the whole thing was inexplicable. Dave could no longer walk at all. No matter how tenderly
she urged, no matter how forcefully she insisted, he would not go to
the doctor. He claimed it was simply a matter of keeping off the leg
for a few more days. But, so far as she could see, it was worse. She
admitted that he seemed calm and reasonable and in amazingly
good spirits, but he could not get off the couch, and spent his time
now in the living room.

"Where is that gimp?" Pastor Rick said, loudly enough for Dave to
hear. Susan had gone to the door to let him in. "Why is this room so
dark? What is this thing on the couch? Can't we open the curtains?"

"It's cooler like this," Dave said. He was glad to see Pastor Rick.
"Sit down. Relax. You're not in charge here. This is my house, bud."

"Tough guy," Pastor Rick said as he sat in a cane rocker opposite
Dave, who, to receive his friend, had worked himself up to a sitting
position.

"What's with you?" Pastor Rick said.

"Not much."

"Where you been?"

"Here and there. Mostly here."

"You missed a game. Susan, you got anything to drink?"

"What would you like?" She was standing at the entrance to the
living room.

"You got a beer?"

"We do," she said.

"Cold?"

She nodded.

"Bring it on," he said. "You want one, Dave?"

"I'm fine," Dave said.

The two men talked for about an hour in the darkened room.
Susan delivered the beer, then left them alone. They talked, first,
about baseball. At one point Pastor Rick turned on the TV, and they
watched the last two innings of a game. They talked about their
children, their faith. Pastor Rick had been chafing under denomi-

national expectations, these having especially to do, as he described it to Dave, with his maverick preference for the indicative Gospel over the imperative, for the good news over the dos and don'ts. There were, likewise, the expectations of the particular body of believers at Bethany Baptist, which he divided roughly into two camps. Those with what he called a "mature" faith were at ease with a theology and homiletics less than prescriptive. The others, new to the faith, or unable to push beyond a relatively simplistic version of it, were skittish without a neatly packaged set of rules and admonishments.

"I think you got it backward," Dave said.

"Oh, yeah? How's that?"

"It's we mature ones who need the hard line. We don't know what to do with grace once we've got it. It's too much for us. It's too much. We don't know how to behave. And so we behave as we always did, grace or no. I've been thinking about this."

"I see that," said Pastor Rick.

"I have. We're sloppy. We're slack. We're smug. We're just flat-out disappointing. You got to whip us into shape, or we embarrass ourselves. And each other."

"Be careful what you ask for," Pastor Rick said.

Just before he left, he turned the conversation directly to the question of Dave's leg.

"You don't need to do this," he said. "It isn't called for."

"I know," Dave said.

"It's crazy."

"What do I say?"

"You don't say anything," Pastor Rick said. "You go to the doctor, is what you do."

"Maybe I will."

"Don't, and I'll be back to take you myself."

The family had supper that night in the living room — Dave ate on the couch, Susan on the cane rocker from a tray, and Randy on the floor in front of the television. Susan fixed a light salad and made fresh lemonade; it was too hot to eat much else, though Randy asked for a grilled-cheese sandwich. It was a quiet meal. Dave and Susan hardly spoke. Randy watched a sports-magazine show; he was subdued, well-mannered. Dave, who was light-headed and running a low-grade fever, was happy. After supper he fell asleep on the couch. He was not aware of Susan and Randy going up to bed.

At two in the morning, he woke when Randy came down the stairs. Dave turned on the table lamp behind his head, and when his eyes got used to the light, he could see that Randy was crying. He was standing at the foot of the couch, a plaid cotton blanket draped shawl-like over his shoulders. He was wearing boxer shorts and nothing else, and he was weeping. Dave looked at him for a moment, certifying that he was neither dream nor delirium.

"Randy," Dave said. "You O.K.? What time is it?"

"I don't know," the boy said. "Two. I'm O.K."

"What's wrong?"

"I came down."

"Have you been asleep?"

"No."

"I was out cold," Dave said. "What's going on?"

"Nothing," Randy said.

"You're crying."

"I'm not crying," Randy said. "I came down because I want to say something. Go to the doctor. That's all I came down for."

"Hold a minute," Dave said. "Let me get up here."

Without thinking, Dave swung his feet off the couch and tried to stand up. He wanted to touch Randy. To make some sort of physical contact with his son. To comfort him, put his arm around his shoulder, hold him. Dave's left foot touched the floor, and the pain in his leg was astonishing. It knocked him flat on the couch.

"Whoa," Dave said. "Hold the doors. Good Christ."

"Do you see?" Randy said. "For shit's sake, Dad. Do you see? Are you nuts? What are you doing?"

"I'm not sure," Dave said. "I'm really not sure."

"Oh, man. Oh, man. What are you doing? Go to the doctor."

It was, by then, too late. He would lose the leg.

"That's not a bad idea," Dave said. "I will."

PETER HO DAVIES

The Ugliest House in the World

FROM THE ANTIOCH REVIEW

Ash Cash

RELLIES ARE RELATIVES. Grumblies are patients. Gerries are geri-
atrics. Ash cash is the money you get when you sign a cremation
form.

A full house is when someone comes into Accident and Emergency with every bone in their arms and legs broken. I once saw a
woman with a full house. She'd been fighting with her husband in
the car and told him to stop. When he wouldn't she opened the
door and jumped out.

Accident and Emergency is called A and E. I did my last job in A
and E, but I couldn't afford it, so now I'm working on a gerry ward.
Gerries are the grumbliest grumblies of them all, but the ash cash
from a job on gerries keeps me in food and drink all week which
means I can keep up the payments on my student loan. You don't
get any money when they bury a patient, because if they have any
doubts about the cause of death they can dig the body up again. But
with cremation someone has to take responsibility. That's what they
pay you for. Fortunately, cremation is more popular with gerries by
a ratio of three to one.

A taff is a Welshman. Everyone in the doctor's mess calls me taff
or taffy. Mr. Swain, the mortuary attendant, calls me boyo, especially during the rugby season when Wales loses badly. Last winter
when Wales was touring Australia and losing each game by world-

record scores I'd order a lager in the mess and everyone would shout, "Make mine a Fosters, mate." Once, Mr. Swain actually welcomed me into the morgue wearing a bush hat with corks dangling around the rim. Last winter I had to visit the mortuary almost daily to fill out crem forms.

I'm not really Welsh. I don't speak Welsh. I've never lived in Wales. But my father is Welsh and since he was laid off last year he's moved back there and bought a cottage with his golden handshake. He was fulfilling a promise he made to himself when my mother died. The cottage was three miles from the place he was born and ten miles from the chapel where they married. When I said I wasn't happy about it and that I'd been hoping to see more of him, he said, "It can't be helped. I've been promising myself this for twelve years. It's not as if you haven't had a warning. I always kept my promises to you. Now I'm going to keep one to myself."

A golden handshake is what they give you when you've been working for the same company for thirty-five years and they lay you off with a month's notice and before your pension comes due. "Golden handshake!" he said. "Makes me feel like King Midas." My father's handshake was worth twenty-five thousand pounds, and he spent it all on his cottage. I told him he could have had it for less.

"What about the Welsh nationalists?" I said. "What if they start another arson campaign against holiday homes?"

"So?" he said. "I'm not a tourist. This is my home."

"But what if you want to sell? This is a holiday home. It's too small for a family. You could only ever sell it to tourists. If they start burning holiday homes again you'll never get twenty-five thousand back for it."

"I won't be selling," he said. "This is my home. This is where I plan to live from now on."

He certainly could have had the cottage for less, but he liked the idea of spending the whole sum on it. He liked the neatness of that. I think he could have knocked them down a couple of thousand on what they were asking. A couple of thousand would pay off about half my debt. A couple of thousand is about six months of ash cash on gerries, and about a year on any other ward.

When I go into the morgue to sign the form for Mrs. Patel, Mr. Swain is there as usual, sitting at his desk in the bright windowless room. He's reading a thing in the paper about Neil Kinnock, the leader of the Labour party and a Welshman. "Dr. Williams," he calls out when he sees me. "Have you read this?"

"I don't have time to read papers, Mr. Swain."

"It says here that if Kinno wins the election he's going to do to the country what your people have been doing to sheep for centuries."

Mrs. Patel is so pale I hardly recognize her. She'd been one of our best patients — quiet, clean, and uncomplaining. The staff would have been quite sorry to lose her if it wasn't for her rellies, who were so demanding and suspicious of the hospital that everyone was glad to see the back of them. I sign the form and hand it to Swain.

"I hope you don't mind a joke, doctor," he says as he passes the receipt across.

"No," I say. "As a matter of fact, I'm going to Wales this weekend."

"Ah, a romantic getaway?"

"A funeral."

And Swain, who lays out bodies every day and talks to them and reads to them from his paper, blushes. The roll of fat at his neck goes bright red against the collar of his white coat.

"I'm so sorry," he says.

My Father Fishes with His Bare Hands

On the morning of the funeral, I look out the window of my father's cottage and see him up to his ankles in the waters of the stream. He is crouching over rocks and encircling them in his arms. From this distance it looks as if he is trying to get a grip and heave them out of the streambed, but I know he's just running his fingers around them, feeling for trout. I watch him for ten minutes as he moves from rock to rock, wading unsteadily through the water. Then I pull an anorak over my robe and push my bare feet into my shoes and go out to fetch him.

He is tickling for trout, as he calls it. It's an old poacher's method. "No rod, no line, no nets, no hooks. No incriminating evidence," as he says.

I don't want to go all the way down the field, but I don't want to shout to him. It is too early and I don't want to hear my voice ringing off the stone walls and slate roofs of the village. Besides, he'll accuse me of scaring off the fish. Everything I do always scares off the fish. Standing on the bank my shadow on the water scares them off. Running along the bank as a child, my footsteps scared them off. Little grains of earth rolled down the bank and alerted them. "My setting foot in Wales scares them off," I tell him.

"You'll catch your death," he says when I get close. He doesn't turn around. He has his head cocked, looking away into the distance, concentrating on his fingertips under the surface. I look at his feet in the water. They are so white they shine. I wonder what kind of feeling he can have in his fingers. He closes his hands and draws them out empty and dripping.

"Look who's talking. You better come in. It's time to get ready."

"Another ten minutes," he says. "You used to be able to pull them out of here in a bucket. But I know there's at least one bugger left. I saw him with the boy."

He looks back at the stream, choosing another rock.

"Come on. I'm freezing my bollocks off here." He begins to bend down. I look around and go over to the nearest mole hill and scoop up two handfuls of loose earth and throw them in the water upstream from him.

"What the bloody hell are you doing?"

"Out," I say. "Now." I clap my hands together and the dirt flies off them.

"You're worse than your mother," he says, but he wades to the bank and I give him my hand.

"You're a sight." Standing on the bank with his old trousers rolled up past his knees and his shirtsleeves pushed up past his elbows, he looks like a child who's grown out of his clothes.

"You can talk." I pass him his shoes and socks and let him lean on my shoulder to pull them on. I put an arm round his waist to steady him, but he shakes it off.

"I can manage."

"Fine."

I don't want to start anything this morning. The night before, I arrived and heard the kettle whistling from the street. When I went inside it was glowing red-hot and the whole cottage was full of steam. I ran through all the rooms thinking he'd had a stroke, and then I found him sitting on the wall out back looking down towards the stream. "It's only a kettle," he said innocently and I said, "The last time it was only a microwave."

I start back towards the cottage, picking my way around the piles of sheep droppings scattered everywhere. "I'll never understand why you let their sheep in here. We could repair the wall in an afternoon."

"They keep the grass down."

"They fertilize it so it grows more. Sheep aren't as dumb as they look."

"Your grandmother used to pick up horse droppings in her handkerchief and bring them back in her handbag for her roses."

I stop and put my arm on his shoulder. "Don't give yourself any ideas."

The Ugliest House in the World

THE UGLIEST HOUSE IN THE WORLD — 100 YARDS is a sign on the road just before you reach my father's village. The story of the ugliest house is that there was once a law in Wales that if you could build a house in a day and sleep a night in it, an acre of land around it was yours. The house had to be stone just to make things a little harder. That's why the ugliest house is so ugly. It's little more than eight feet high, with higgledy-piggledy walls of granite and slate. The walls were originally dry stone, which means they were built without cement. Stones were just balanced one upon the other, with smaller rocks wedged between them to stop them rocking.

Six years ago, Mr. Watkins, the farmer who owns the ugliest house, decided to open it to the public in the hope that he could make some money from tourists. The name came from his daughter, Kate. She called it that when she was a little girl. The farmer had to pay to put a new corrugated iron roof on it, and the council made him pour wavy lines of concrete between some of the looser rocks. The effect was to make the house even uglier.

There is a plaque inside and a single light bulb by which to read it, since the ugliest house has only one small window. The plaque tells the story with a few embellishments. No one actually lived there except for that one night required by law. The family who built the place had a perfectly good home in the village and they just wanted the land for grazing. In bad weather, their sheep were penned in the house. Between the wars it was used as a shelter for tramps, and the plaque mentions a rumor that George Orwell spent a night there researching *Down and Out in Paris and London*.

Since then, the house has been a shelter for climbers in the area and then from 1955 to 1966 a bus shelter for the White Star line. Farmer Watkins hoped that the ugliest house would provide an income for Kate when she came back from Liverpool, pregnant at the age of sixteen. She learned the plaque off by heart and sat at the door with her child for a whole summer to charge admission, but the takings from that first season weren't even enough to pay for the roof. The farmer made one last attempt to have HOME OF THE UGLIEST HOUSE IN THE WORLD added to the name signs at either end of the village, but the council refused to even put it to a vote.

Mr. Watkins stood up in the meeting and shouted, "Fascists! Communists! Tin-pot dictators!" But the leader of the council shouted him down: "This meeting does not have time for frivolous notions and will eject any time-wasters from these proceedings. Sit down, Arwyn, you bloody idiot." Kate went to a technical college in Caernarfon instead, and learned hairdressing, and Mr. Watkins abandoned his front room to the smells of ammonia and peroxide.

The Watkinses are my father's nearest neighbors. Their farm has several acres of land turned over to sheep. The ugliest house lies between the two properties and they share the stream in which my father fishes. The name of the village is Carmel and on the hillside above it are others called Bethel and Bethesda — all named from the Old Testament.

The Second Ugliest House in the World

Before walking up the street to the chapel, I polish my father's black shoes and help him on with them. His feet in his socks are as cold and smooth as stone and I rub them hard before I slip the shoes on. They feel like they've been worn down by the stream. He sips his tea and looks out the window while I rub. Afterwards, he looks at himself in the mirror while I brush the dandruff off his shoulders.

When we step outside, I can see mourners emerging from all the houses of the village, making their way to the chapel. Kate and her father are being helped up their path and I tell Father to wait. We hang around in front of the cottage, stamping our feet and blowing on our hands.

I call my father's cottage the second ugliest house in the world.

Inside, it is bright and cozy, but outside it is finished in pebble-dash. Pebble-dash is a traditional style of decoration in North Wales. It is literally what it says it is. When the plaster on the outside walls is still wet, handfuls of tiny pebbles — gravel really — are thrown at it. I suppose it gives added insulation. In general, the style calls for the walls to be whitewashed and then the effect can be quite pleasing. Unfortunately, the tourists who owned the house before my father had the bright idea of redoing the pebble-dash with multicolored gravel, like you find at the bottom of fish tanks. They let the field grow over with heather and long grass, and the moles undermine it; they let the boundary walls collapse and the gate rust; but they did over the house.

Every time I visit my father, I offer to whitewash the whole house. He always says, "I'll get to it. What's the rush? I'm a retired gentleman now." Since I found out he was living off sausages and baked beans I always bring a couple of bags of groceries when I come to visit him, but once I set four tins of paint on the kitchen table. He got angry and said, "I'll do it. I don't need your bloody help. Your heart's not in it, anyway." He means that I don't approve of him moving here. He's right.

"Why do you come then?" he asks me whenever I bring it up.

"Because I want to spend some time with you. Is that a crime?"

Kate says it best: "The average age in North Wales is fifty-three. Unemployment is at thirty-nine percent. The population has fallen faster than the population of any other region in Britain in the last ten years." Kate puts copies of the *Economist* and the *New Statesman* on the table in her kitchen when she wants to turn it into a waiting room for her customers. She offered a skinhead cut, dyed red at half price during the last election. She charges girls to pierce their ears, but she offers one free ear to boys. She calls Wales "the land of the dead, an old folk's home the size of a country."

Kate hates it here. She tells me how much she envies my life. "Why?" I say. "Because you're not stuck here," she says. "You're not stuck," I tell her. "Oh no," she says. "Not at all. A twenty-two-year-old hairdresser with a six-year-old son. I'm very mobile. I'm so light and flighty I'm surprised I don't just float away."

Gareth, Kate's son, had a lot to do with the success of her business. The old ladies who came to her most often never opened one of her magazines. They spent all their time gazing at Gareth. They used to leave a separate little something for him after they'd tip Kate.

Ian Rush Walks on Water

Gareth was a six-year-old Liverpool fan when my father moved in next to the ugliest house in the world. He wore his red team shirt everywhere and, when Kate wanted it to wash, he kept pestering her for the away-team strip. In the end, his grandfather bought it for him. "Forty quid those shirts cost," Kate told me. "And he grows out of them every year. We spoil him rotten."

Kate hated Gareth's being a Liverpool fan. It reminded her of his father. "He was a wanker," she once told me. "But he was a way out of this dump. I wouldn't have minded if he'd just left me. I could have made do. I could have found someone else. But when he left me with Gareth, where else could I go?"

Gareth and my father used to play football in the garden of the cottage. They moved two stones from the top of the dry stone wall marking the boundary between the two properties and used them for goal posts. I used to watch them, sometimes with Kate. Gareth was too small to shoot from a long way out. He had to get close to the goal before he could kick it far enough to take a shot, but then my father would come charging out like an old bear and bundle him over and take the ball. He'd hold him off with one arm until Gareth got tired trying to run around him. They would both be laughing and panting. When the boy began to kick his shins my father would drop-kick the ball into a far corner of the field. He used to find that funny. He didn't like it when I called him a cheat. "If I didn't cheat," he said, "I couldn't play with him."

"He loves you," Kate said.

"Did you used to cheat like that when you played with me?"

"I honestly can't remember."

"As your doctor, I'm telling you, you should take it easy out there."

As Gareth got closer you could always hear him talking to himself breathlessly. At first it was just mumbling, but as he got closer you would hear this running commentary on his own game: "He passes to Rush. Rush beats one man. He beats two. Still Rush. He turns. Shoots. Scores!"

Ian Rush is Liverpool's star striker and a Welshman. Kate told me that Gareth was once sent home from Sunday school for carving graffiti into the desks. He carved LIVERPOOL AFC and YOU'LL NEVER WALK ALONE and IAN RUSH WALKS ON WATER.

I was a big disappointment to Gareth, I think. He would run up to me where I leaned on the gate with his mother and try to pull me away.

"Why don't you play?" he'd ask.

"I don't think so, Gareth. I've got a bad knee."

"But you're a doctor."

"Doctors get hurt too."

"But you can make yourself better."

"I'm on holiday. I don't even make myself better on holiday."

Another time, he said to me, "Why don't you live here? Your dad lives here. If you lived here your knee might get better and you could play football with us."

Another time, he said, "If you have a little boy he'd want you to play with him."

"Gareth, I'm not even married."

"So? Do you have a girlfriend?"

"Gareth, don't you have anyone your own age to play with?"

"No."

The first time I met Gareth, he scored a goal and threw himself to his knees the way he had seen the players do on TV. Unfortunately, my father's field wasn't Anfield and he slid into a half-buried rock. He began to wail. His mother came rushing out of their house, and my father ran to the boy.

"It's okay," my father kept saying.

"What happened?" Kate said.

They called me to have a look at him, but I just smiled and waved. My father came over.

"What's wrong with you?" he said. "Come and look at the boy. He's got hurt playing with me and his mother's worried. What kind of a doctor are you?"

"He's fine," I said. "You can see it from here. Look at him rolling around. If he has that much movement in the knee there's no damage. All he wants is sympathy, which you're much better at giving."

"Don't be childish. At least put the mother's mind at rest."

Kate looked over at us at that moment. She had that hard stare of hers, the one that says, "I don't care, but make your mind up." It's the one she has when she stands behind her customers as they look in the mirror and try and tell her how they want their hair. Anyway, it made me go over.

"Hold still, Gareth. I can't help if you don't let me look at it." He stopped for a moment and looked at me and I lifted his leg and felt around the knee. "Does that hurt? That?" I looked thoughtful for a moment. I flexed his leg. "Well, Gareth, I would have to say that in my carefully considered opinion what we've got here" — I paused for effect — "is a bad knee." He didn't get it, but Kate did. She laughed out loud. She couldn't stop. She told me later it wasn't that funny. She was just so relieved. Gareth looked at her in amazement, but it made him forget his knee. She tried to say she was sorry, but when she saw his face she went off again.

"You better lay off football for a while," I said and that's when my father promised he'd teach him how to fish and they marched off down to the stream leaving me alone with Kate.

Perspective in Renaissance Painting

We sit at the back of the chapel. The coffin has been placed end on to the aisle rather than side on, and from here it is hard to tell how long it really is. It looks about the size I'm used to. The discovery reminds me of perspective in Renaissance painting.

The coffin is closed, but the minister talks about Gareth's love of football and of Liverpool and I imagine him lying there in the red shirt he was always so proud of, with Ian Rush's number nine on the back.

Kate and her father are sitting in the front row. Her head is bowed, but her shoulders are still and I am sure she is dry eyed. My father leans over and whispers in my ear, "I only wish we could have caught one fish. I promised him we'd get one." I shake my head. My father was supposed to take the boy fishing last week. He forgot when they were meeting and he was out shopping when Gareth came for him. The boy went to play in our drive while he waited. He was swinging on the stone gate post when it toppled over on him. It was solid slate. It's still lying to one side of the drive and I will offer to help carry it out of the way sometime. It will take two of us, although my father hurled it there by himself when he found the boy. Not that it made any difference.

There are only four pallbearers. The coffin rides on their shoulders but each with his free hand holds it in place as if it were so light it might just float away.

No one has said anything to us at the chapel, but when we get up to leave, two men slide into the pew on either side of us. I recognize the one next to me as the local grocer. He once told me that my father had bought a bar of soap off him every day for a week. Sure enough, under the sink at the cottage I found bar after bar after bar, but when I asked Father if he had some he said, "No, I think I must have run out."

"Sorry," the grocer says. "The family would prefer if you don't come to the grave."

Father hangs his head and looks at his hands.

"My father wants to pay his respects," I say. I'm watching people file out.

"The family would prefer if he stayed away."

"Did Kate say that?"

"The family."

The man next to my father says something to him in Welsh.

"What did he say? What did you say to my father? What did he say to you?"

No one answers.

"Take your father home," the grocer says.

"What did he say? I'm not going anywhere until I know what he said."

"He said, 'Are you satisfied?'"

"What the bloody hell does that mean?" I say. "It was an accident."

The grocer waits until the last person leaves and the four of us are alone in the chapel.

"A lot of people are saying it was negligence. They're saying it wouldn't have happened if your place had been properly kept up."

I get my father to his feet. The grocer puts his foot up on the pew in front to block the way. His leg is straight and if he leaves it there I will stamp down and break it at the knee.

"Get out of my way. I'm taking him home." He lets us by.

"You do that," the grocer shouts after me. "Take him home. Take him back to England."

Kate Hops from Foot to Foot

Kate and I used to make love in the ugliest house. I would stand in the darkness beside the wall and when I heard the rattle of the chain holding the door shut I would step out. She brought blankets from her house and I brought a torch from my car. It was always too cold to undress. She would push my trousers down and I would lift her skirt. When I touched her breasts she would shy away and make me rub my hands together to warm them. She would hop from foot to foot while she waited for me to be warm enough to touch her.

Once I asked her if her father knew where she was going on the weekends when I was visiting. "I'm sure," she said. "But he knows better than to ask." I wondered, then, if she went out every weekend.

"Doesn't your father know?" she asked me back.

"I don't know," I said. "I don't think about it. He never brings it up."

"What would you do if he did?"

"I'd lie. I already lie. I tell him I come to see him."

"That's not a lie," she said. "Why else would you come?"

"I can't imagine."

"I'm serious."

"I come to see you."

"That's what you tell your father when you're lying. Why should I believe you?"

I lay on my back and looked up at the rough walls above me and thought of the people who built them. I wondered how they felt sleeping beneath them on that first night with all that precariously balanced weight around them. Did they have confidence in their balancing act? Maybe they drew lots.

Conversations with Kate were like a balancing act.

Another time she said to me, "If you're worried about your father being able to look after himself up here you should take him away. I don't want to stop you doing what's right."

"You're not stopping me."

"I try to look in on him as often as I can."

"I appreciate that."

Grandfather's Dog

When we get home I tell my father I've decided to take him home with me the next morning. He says he's staying.

"Didn't you hear them? They think you're responsible. I'm not leaving you here."

"I am responsible. They're right. Who else's fault is it?"

"It doesn't have to be anybody's fault."

"I promised him. He was here because I promised him."

"You promised him you'd catch him a fish," I shout. "Don't be stupid. You're not responsible for his death. It was an accident. No one's responsible."

"This is my home," he says. "I can't leave."

"This is where you live. It's not your home. It hasn't been your home for forty years."

"Rubbish." He stands at the window and points. "My father lived over that hill and my uncle over that one. Did I ever tell you about them?"

"Yes," I say. "Lots of times."

It's a story about the time my grandfather's dog had a big litter and he told the family that they were not to sell any of the pups. His brother disobeyed him and told him the dogs had died. When my grandfather found out he'd sold them he never spoke to him again as long as he lived. My father says his uncle was the one who met him at the station when he came back from Germany to see Grandfather before he died. Even then the old man wouldn't see his brother. When I was a child I always thought it was a story about greed or about telling the truth, but that isn't it. It's not a story about my uncle. It's a story about my grandfather.

"Why weren't the puppies to be sold?" I say now.

"I can't remember," my father says. "It doesn't matter."

"Then what's the point of the story?"

"I don't know. Something about seeing things through."

"You're talking like a bloody idiot. You're as bad as these people. I'm not leaving here without you. You will be in that car tomorrow if I have to carry you."

The Dam

In the late afternoon, my father goes down the field to the stream. He's still in his black suit, with a spade on his shoulder, but I haven't the energy to fight with him. I'm sitting on our wall, watching Kate's house. I keep my eyes on the net curtains of her kitchen as I hear him splashing his way into the stream. The lights come on in her house; someone, not Kate or her father, comes out and pushes through the sheep who are clustered around the house for warmth. Whoever they are they stride up the path and vanish.

I hear him splashing and cursing behind me. If there is a fish in there still, it is too quick for him. I remember when we used to come up here on holiday and he would catch a dozen or more. He'd string grass stems through their gills and let me carry them in the door, although I never caught a single one. All he let me do at the riverbank was sit and touch the caught fish. I learned that they started out slick and became sticky as the afternoon wore on. Somewhere between the two states they died. He said that if I played with them and got used to the feel of them I'd learn how to catch them. He was wrong. It wasn't the feel of the fish I was afraid of. It was the feel of the unknown when I slid my fingers into the water. He probably couldn't have cured me, but he didn't try that hard — as long as I sat still and let him enjoy himself reliving his boyhood.

I see the door to the house open and shut again, and in the yellow light I see Kate. I assume she is making for the ugliest house and I pick up my torch and move to meet her, but then I see she is heading for my father and I quicken my pace.

"How are you?" I ask her gently.

"I just want to see your father," she says.

"Why?"

"I hear you had some trouble in the chapel and I wanted to say I'm sorry for it."

"They said it was his fault. You don't think that, do you?"

"It's all our faults," she says. "If you'd taken him home when you should have. If I hadn't given you a reason for letting him stay here."

"That's insane." She's talking like a relly. "It was an accident. A random accident. No one's to blame. No one's responsible. The gate was just loose."

I put my hand on her arm but she shrugs it off and strides on towards him. I follow, shaking my head.

She stands on the bank with her hands on her hips and looks down at him in the water. In the dusk the water is black except for where it bubbles white around his calves. She just looks at him for a long moment. I'm ready to put my hand over her mouth and carry her kicking and biting back to her father's house if necessary.

"Are there really fish in here still?" she says.

"I hope so," he says. "There always have been as long as I can remember."

"Show me how you catch them," she says, and he explains to her about trout tickling.

"Who taught you all that?"

"My father," he says. He turns and looks into the gloom. "Over there you could just see the road to our old house."

"You should come in," Kate says, and he smiles up at her tone and I almost think he is going to listen to her.

"Let me catch you a fish first." He winks at her.

"It's too dark, isn't it?"

"Not if you help me. This is my last chance. Will you?"

"What do you want me to do?"

"The surest way is to build a dam."

She takes the torch from me and holds it while he uses the spade to dig a narrow channel beside the stream. The stream is horseshoe-shaped at this point and he digs the trench from the start of the loop to the end of it. Lights are coming on in all the windows of the village on the hillside behind us.

"You're crazy," I say. "Both of you." But I take my own shoes and socks off and get down into the stream and begin moving rocks. I'm not having him manhandle them. The stream is so cold, I lose the feeling in my feet in minutes. It makes it hard to keep my footing, but I work faster thinking that even if I drop a rock on my toes I'll never feel it. I pile them up at the neck of the horseshoe and my father cuts the last yard of trench and water begins to rush down the channel. He lifts clumps of turf and throws them into the water to seal my dam and the water stops flowing into the horseshoe and begins to run out of it at the bottom. Kate stands at the other end beating the water, driving the fish back.

The level begins to drop slowly. The banks are revealed. Stones and gravel give way to mud.

"Shine the torch," my father says and I take it from Kate and move it back and forth across the remaining water. It is brown from the mud at the bottom. We wait for any movement.

"There," Kate cries. She points and in the light I see her arm is streaked with dirt. My father climbs down into the streambed and mud flecks his trouser legs. He crouches over the shallow pool left in the center of the stream and slides his hands in. He catches something and shouts, but looses his grip and his hands thrash in the water. It is as if he is washing them. Finally, he gets a grip and throws something up onto the bank. In the torch light I see it is an eel, black and shiny. It twists in the grass and I take the spade and chop it in two. I turn around and with the torch I see my father on his knees in the streambed. He has his hands deep in the mud. Kate is standing over him with her hand on his shoulder. He is shaking.

"I know," she says. "Oh, I know."

"What are you doing?" I say. The torch plays back and forth from one face to the other. "What are you doing? It was an accident. It's nobody's fault. What are you doing?"

Whitewash

When I take him out to the car in the morning, we see that the walls have been covered in red graffiti. I don't speak Welsh, but even I know what "Cymru am byth" means. It's a Nationalist slogan: "Wales forever."

I make my father sit in the car while I go and fetch the cans of whitewash from the shed. I wonder who did it. The grocer maybe. Maybe even Kate's father. I wonder if they were up here daubing it while we were down by the stream. It is nine o'clock on a Sunday morning and people are opening their curtains and fetching their newspapers. I imagine the whole hillside watching me as I paint over the slogan. Of course, I keep going. I've been wanting to do this for so long.

It takes me almost two hours to do the whole cottage and when I'm finished it shines in the bright morning light.

GISH JEN

Birthmates

FROM PLOUGHSHARES

THIS WAS what responsibility meant in a dinosaur industry, toward the end of yet another quarter of bad-to-worse news: You called the travel agent back, and even though there was indeed an economy room in the hotel where the conference was being held, a room overlooking the cooling towers, you asked if there wasn't something still cheaper. And when Marie the new girl came back with something amazingly cheap, you took it — only to discover, as Art Woo was discovering now, that the doors were locked after nine o'clock. The neighborhood had looked not great but not bad, and the building itself, regular enough. Brick, four stories, a rolled-up awning. A bright-lit hotel logo, with a raised-plastic, smiling sun. But there was a kind of crossbar rigged across the inside of the glass door, and that was not at all regular. A two-by-four, it appeared, wrapped in rust-colored carpet. Above this, inside the glass, hung a small gray sign. If the taxi had not left, Art might not have rung the buzzer, as per the instructions.

But the taxi had indeed left, and the longer Art huddled on the stoop in the clumpy December snow, the emptier and more poorly lit the street appeared. His buzz was answered by an enormous black man wearing a neck brace. The shoulder seams of the man's blue waffle-weave jacket were visibly straining; around the brace was tied a necktie, which reached only a third of the way down his chest. All the same, it was neatly fastened together with a hotel-logo tie tack about two inches from the bottom. The tie tack was smiling; the man was not. He held his smooth, round face perfectly expressionless, and he lowered his gaze at every opportunity — not so that it was rude, but so that it was clear he wasn't selling anything to anybody. Regulation tie, thought Art, regulation jacket. He wondered if the man would turn surly soon enough.

For Art had come to few conclusions about life in his thirty-eight years, but this was one of them — that men turned surly when their clothes didn't fit them. This man, though, belied the rule. He was courteous, almost formal in demeanor; and if the lobby seemed not only too small for him, like his jacket, but also too much like a bus station, what with its smoked mirror wall, and its linoleum, and its fake wood, and its vending machines, what did that matter to Art? The sitting area looked as though it was in the process of being cleaned — the sixties Scandinavian chairs and couch and coffee table were pulled every which way, as if by someone hellbent on the dust balls. Still, Art proceeded with his check-in. He was going with his gut here. Here, as in any business situation, he was looking foremost at the personnel; and the man with the neck brace had put him at some ease. It wasn't until after Art had taken his credit card back that he noticed, above the check-out desk, a wooden plaque from a neighborhood association. He squinted at its brass face plate: FEWEST CUSTOMER INJURIES, 1972–73.

What about the years since '73? Had the hotel gotten more dangerous since then, or had other hotels gotten safer? Maybe neither. For all he knew, the neighborhood association had dissolved and was no longer distributing plaques. Art reminded himself that in life, some signs were no signs. It's what he used to tell his ex-wife, Lisa — Lisa who loved to read everything into everything; Lisa who was attuned. She left him on a day when she saw a tree get split by lightning. Of course, that was an extraordinary thing to see. An event of a lifetime. Lisa said the tree had sizzled. He wished he had seen it, too. But what did it mean, except that the tree had been the tallest in the neighborhood, and was no longer? It meant nothing; ditto with the plaque. Art made his decision, which perhaps was not the right decision. Perhaps he should have looked for another hotel.

But it was late — on the way out, his plane had sat on the runway, just sat and sat, as if it were never going to take off — and God only knew what he would have ended up paying if he had relied on a cabbie to simply bring him somewhere else. Forget twice — it could have been three, four times what he would have paid for that room with the view of the cooling towers, easy. At this hour, after all, and that was a conference rate.

So he double-locked his door instead. He checked behind the hollow-core doors of the closet, and under the steel-frame bed, and also in the swirly green shower-stall unit. He checked behind the seascapes, to be sure there weren't any peepholes. That *Psycho* — how he wished he'd never seen that movie. Why hadn't anyone ever told him that movies could come back to haunt you? No one had warned him. The window opened onto a fire escape; not much he could do about that except check the window locks, big help that those were — a sure deterrent for the subset of all burglars that was burglars too skittish to break glass. Which was what percent of intruders, probably? Ten percent? Fifteen? He closed the drapes, then decided he would be more comfortable with the drapes open. He wanted to be able to see what approached, if anything did. He unplugged the handset of his phone from the rest, a calculated risk. On the one hand, he wouldn't be able to call the police if there was an intruder. On the other, he would be armed. He had read somewhere a story about a woman who threw the handset of her phone at an attacker, and killed him. Needless to say, there had been some luck involved in that eventuality. Still, Art thought (a) surely he could throw as hard as that woman, and (b) even without the luck, his throw would most likely be hard enough to at least slow up an intruder. Especially since this was an old handset, the hefty kind that made you feel the seriousness of human communication. In a newer hotel, he probably would have had a new phone, with lots of buttons he would never use but which would make him feel he had many resources at his disposal. In the hotel where the conference was, there were probably buttons for the health club, and for the concierge, and for the three restaurants, and for room service. He tried not to think about this as he went to sleep, clutching the handset.

He did not sleep well.

In the morning he debated whether to take the handset with him into the elevator. Again he wished he hadn't seen so many movies. It was movies that made him think, that made him imagine things like, *What if in the elevator?* Of course, a handset was an awkward thing to hide. It wasn't like a knife, say, that could be whipped out of nowhere. Even a pistol at least fit in a guy's pocket. Whereas a telephone handset did not. All the same, he brought it with him. He tried to carry it casually, as if he were going out for a run and using it for a hand weight, or as if he were in the telephone business.

He strode down the hall. Victims shuffled; that's what everybody said. A lot of mugging had to do with nonverbal cues, which is why Lisa used to walk tall after dark, sending vibes. For this he used to tease her. If she was so worried, she should lift weights and run, the way he did; that, he maintained, was the substantive way of helping oneself. She had agreed. For a while they had met after work at the gym. That was before she dropped a weight on her toe and decided she preferred to sip piña coladas and watch. Naturally, he grunted on. But to what avail? Who could appreciate his pectorals through his suit and overcoat? Pectorals had no deterrent value, that was what he was thinking now. And he was, though not short, not tall. He continued striding. Sending vibes. He was definitely going to eat in the dining room of the hotel where the conference was being held, he decided. What's more, he was going to have a full American breakfast, with bacon and eggs, none of this Continental breakfast bullshit.

In truth, he had always considered the sight of men eating croissants slightly ridiculous, especially at the beginning, when for the first bite they had to maneuver the point of the crescent into their mouths. No matter what a person did, he ended up with an asymmetrical mouthful of pastry, which he then had to relocate with his tongue to a more central location, and this made him look less purposive than he might. Also, croissants were more apt than other breakfast foods to spray little flakes all over one's clean dark suit. Art himself had accordingly never ordered a croissant in any working situation, and he believed that attention to this sort of detail was how it was that he had not lost his job like so many of his colleagues.

This was, in other words, how it was that he was still working in his fitfully dying industry, and was now carrying a telephone handset with him into the elevator. Art braced himself as the elevator doors opened slowly, jerkily, in the low-gear manner of elevator doors in the Third World. He strode in, and was surrounded by, of all things, children. Down in the lobby, too, there were children, and here and there, women he knew to be mothers by their looks of dogged exasperation. A welfare hotel! He laughed out loud. Almost everyone was black, the white children stood out like little missed oppor-

tunities of the type that made Art's boss throw his tennis racket
across the room. Of course, the racket was always in its padded
protective cover and not in much danger of getting injured, though
the person in whose vicinity it was aimed sometimes was. Art once
suffered what he rather hoped would turn out to be a broken nose,
but was only a bone bruise with so little skin discoloration that
people had a hard time believing the incident had actually taken
place. Yet it had. *Don't talk to me about fault, bottom line it's you Japs
who are responsible for this whole fucking mess,* his boss had said — this
though what was the matter with minicomputers, really, was personal computers. A wholly American phenomenon. And of course,
Art could have sued over this incident if he could have proved that
it had happened. Some people, most notably Lisa, thought he
certainly ought to have at least quit.

But he didn't sue and he didn't quit. He took his tennis racket on
the nose, so to speak, and when the next day his boss apologized for
losing control, Art said he understood. And when his boss said that
Art shouldn't take what he said personally, in fact he knew Art was
not a Jap, but a Chink, plus he had called someone else a lazy wop
just that morning, it was just his style, Art said again that he understood. And then Art said that he hoped his boss would remember
Art's great understanding come promotion time. Which his boss
did, to Art's satisfaction. In Art's view, this was a victory. In Art's
view, he had perceived leverage where others would only perceive
affront. He had maintained a certain perspective.

But this certain perspective was, in addition to the tree, why Lisa
left him. He thought of that now, the children underfoot, his handset in hand. So many children. It was as if he were seeing before
him all the children he would never have. He stood a moment,
paralyzed; his heart lost its muscle. A child in a red running suit ran
by, almost grabbed the handset out of Art's grasp; then another, in
a brown jacket with a hood. He looked up to see a group of grade-
school boys arrayed about the seating area, watching. Already he
had become the object of a dare, apparently — there was so little
else in the way of diversion in the lobby — and realizing this, he felt
renewed enough to want to laugh again. When a particularly small
child swung by in his turn — a child of maybe five or six, small
enough to be wearing snowpants — Art almost tossed the handset
to him, but thought better of the idea. Who wanted to be charged
for a missing phone?

As it was, Art wondered if he shouldn't put the handset back in his room rather than carry it around all day. For what was he going to do at the hotel where the conference was, check it? He imagined himself running into Billy Shore — that was his counterpart at Info-Edge, his competitor in the insurance market. A man with no management ability, and no technical background either. But he could offer customers a personal computer option, which Art could not; and what's more, Billy had been a quarterback in college. This meant he strutted around as though it still mattered that he had connected with his tight end in the final minutes of what Art could not help but think of as the Wilde-Beastie game. And it meant that Billy was sure to ask him, *What are you doing with a phone in your hand? Talking to yourself again?* Making everyone around them laugh.

Billy was that kind of guy. He had come up through sales, and was always cracking a certain type of joke — about drinking, or sex, or how much the wife shopped. Of course, he never used those words. He never called things by their plain names. He always talked in terms of knocking back some brewskis, or running the triple option, or doing some damage. He made assumptions as though it were a basic bodily function: of course his knowledge was the common knowledge. Of course people understood what it was that he was referring to so delicately. *Listen, champ,* he said, putting his arm around you. If he was smug, it was in an affable kind of way. *So what do you think the poor people are doing tonight?* Billy not only spoke what Art called Mainstreamese, he spoke such a pure dialect of it that Art once asked him if he realized that he was a pollster's delight. He spoke the thoughts of thousands, Art told him, he breathed their very words. Naturally, Billy did not respond, except to say, *What's that?* and turn away. He rubbed his torso as he turned, as if ruffling his chest hairs through the long-staple cotton. Primate behavior, Lisa used to call this. It was her belief that neckties evolved in order to check this very motion, uncivilized as it was. She also believed that this was the sort of thing you never saw Asian men do — at least not if they were brought up properly.

Was that true? Art wasn't so sure. Lisa had grown up on the West Coast, she was full of Asian consciousness; whereas all he knew was that no one had so much as smiled politely at his pollster remark. On the other hand, the first time Art was introduced to Billy, and Billy said, *Art Woo, how's that for a nice Pole-ack name,* everyone broke right up in great rolling guffaws. Of course, they laughed the way people laughed at conferences, which was not because something was really funny, but because it was part of being a good guy, and because they didn't want to appear to have missed their cue.

The phone, the phone. If only Art could fit it in his briefcase! But his briefcase was overstuffed; it was always overstuffed; really, it was too bad he had the slim silhouette type, and hard-side besides. Italian. That was Lisa's doing, she thought the fatter kind made him look like a salesman. Not that there was really anything the matter with that, in his view. Billy Shore notwithstanding, sales were important. But she was the liberal arts type, Lisa was, the type who did not like to think about money, but only about her feelings. Money was not money to her, but support, and then a means of support much inferior to hand-holding or other forms of finger play. She did not believe in a modern-day economy, in which everyone played a part in a large and complex whole that introduced efficiencies that at least theoretically raised everyone's standard of living. She believed in expressing herself. Also in taking classes, and in knitting. There was nothing, she believed, like taking a walk in the autumn woods wearing a hand-knit sweater. Of course, she did look beautiful in them, especially the violet ones. That was her color — Asians are winters, she always said — and sometimes she liked to wear the smallest smidgeon of matching violet eyeliner, even though it was, as she put it, less than organic to wear eyeliner on a hike.

Little Snowpants ran at Art again, going for the knees — *a tackle,* thought Art, as he went down; Red Running Suit snatched away the handset and went sprinting off, triumphant. Teamwork! The children chortled together; how could Art not smile a little, even if they had gotten his overcoat dirty? He brushed himself off, ambled over.

"Hey, guys," he said. "That was some move back there."

"Ching chang polly wolly wing wong," said Little Snowpants.

"Now, now, that's no way to talk," said Art.

"Go to hell!" Brown Jacket pulled at the corners of his eyes to make them slanty.

"Listen up," said Art. "I'll make you a deal." Really he only meant to get the handset back, so as to avoid getting charged for it.

But the next thing he knew, something had hit his head with a crack, and he was out.

*

Lisa had left in a more or less amicable way. She had not called a
lawyer, or a mover; she had simply pressed his hands with both of
hers and, in her most California voice, said, *Let's be nice*. And then
she had asked him if he wouldn't help her move her boxes, at least
the heavy ones that really were too much for her. He had helped.
He had carried the heavy boxes, and also the less heavy ones. Being
a weight lifter, after all. He had sorted books and rolled glasses into
pieces of newspaper, feeling all the while like a statistic. A member
of the modern age, a story for their friends to rake over, and all
because he had not gone with Lisa to her grieving group. Or at least
that was the official beginning of the trouble; probably the real
beginning had been when Lisa — no, *they* — had trouble getting
pregnant. When they decided to, as the saying went, do infertility.
Or had he done the deciding, as Lisa later maintained? He had
thought it was a joint decision, though it was true that he had done
the analysis that led to the joint decision. He had been the one to
figure the odds, to do the projections. He had drawn the decision
tree, according to whose branches they had nothing to lose by
going ahead.

Neither one of them had realized then how much would be
involved — the tests, the procedures, the drugs, the ultrasounds.
Lisa's arms were black and blue from having her blood drawn every
day, and before long he was giving practice shots to an orange, that
he might prick her some more. He was telling her to take a breath
so that on the exhale he could poke her in the buttocks. This was
no longer practice, and neither was it like poking an orange. The
first time, he broke out in such a sweat that his vision blurred and
he had to blink, with the result that he pulled the needle out slowly
and crookedly, occasioning a most unorangelike cry. The second
time, he wore a sweatband. Later he jabbed her like nothing; her
ovaries swelled to the point where he could feel them through her
jeans.

He still had the used syringes — snapped in half and stored, as
per their doctor's recommendation, in plastic soda bottles. She had
left him those. Bottles of medical waste, to be disposed of responsi-
bly, meaning that he was probably stuck with them, ha-ha, for the
rest of his life. A little souvenir of this stage of their marriage, his
equivalent of the pile of knit goods she had to show for the ordeal;
for through it all, she had knit, as if to gently demonstrate an

alternative use of needles. Sweaters, sweaters, but also baby blankets, mostly to give away, only one or two to keep. She couldn't help herself. There was anesthesia, and egg harvesting, and anesthesia and implanting, until she finally did get pregnant, twice, and then a third time she went to four and a half months before they found a problem. On the amnio, it showed up, brittle bone disease — a genetic abnormality such as could happen to anyone.

He steeled himself for another attempt; she grieved. And this was the difference between them, that he saw hope still, some feeble, skeletal hope, where she saw loss. She called the fetus her baby, though it was not a baby, just a baby-to-be, as he tried to say; as even the grieving-group facilitator tried to say. She said he didn't understand, couldn't possibly understand, it was something you understood with your body, and it was not his body but hers that knew the baby, loved the baby, lost the baby. In the grieving class the women agreed. They commiserated. They bonded, subtly affirming their common biology by doing 85 percent of the talking. The room was painted mauve — a feminine color that seemed to support them in their process. At times it seemed that the potted palms were female, too, nodding, nodding, though really their sympathy was just rising air from the heating vents. Other husbands started missing sessions — they never talked, anyway, you hardly noticed their absence — and finally he missed some also. One, maybe two, for real reasons, nothing cooked up. But the truth was, as Lisa sensed, that he thought she had lost perspective. They could try again, after all. What did it help to despair? Look, they knew they could get pregnant and, what's more, sustain the pregnancy. That was progress. But she was like an island in her grief, a retreating island, if there was such a thing, receding to the horizon of their marriage, and then to its vanishing point.

Of course, he had missed her terribly at first; now he missed her still, but more sporadically. At odd moments, for example now, waking up in a strange room with ice on his head. He was lying on an unmade bed just like the bed in his room, except that everywhere around it were heaps of what looked to be blankets and clothes. The only clothes on a hanger were his jacket and overcoat; these hung neatly, side by side, in the otherwise empty closet. There was also an extra table in this room, with a two-burner hot plate, a pan on top of that, and a pile of dishes. A brown cube refrigerator. The drapes were closed; a chair had been pulled up close to him; the bedside light was on. A woman was leaning into its circle, mopping his brow. *Don't you move, now.* She was the shade of black Lisa used to call mochaccino, and she was wearing a blue flowered apron. Kind eyes, and a long face — the kind of face where you could see the muscles of the jaw working alongside the cheekbone. An upper lip like an archery bow, and a graying Afro, shortish. She smelled of smoke. Nothing unusual except that she was so very thin, about the thinnest person he had ever seen, and yet she was cooking something — burning something, it smelled like, though maybe it was just a hair fallen onto the heating element. She stood up to tend the pan. The acrid smell faded. He saw powder on the table. It was white, a plastic bagful. His eyes widened. He sank back, trying to figure out what to do. His head pulsed. Tylenol, he needed, two. Lisa always took one because she was convinced the dosages recommended were based on large male specimens; and though she had never said that she thought he ought to keep it to one also, not being so tall, he was adamant about taking two. Two, two, two. He wanted his drugs, he wanted them now. And his own drugs, that was, not somebody else's.

"Those kids kind of rough," said the woman. "They getting to that age. I told them one of these days somebody gonna get hurt, and sure enough, they knocked you right out. You might as well been hit with a bowling ball. I never saw anything like it. We called the man, but they got other things on their mind besides to come see about trouble here. Nobody shot, so they went on down to the Dunkin' Donuts. They know they can count on a ruckus there." She winked. "How you feeling? That egg hurt?"

He felt his head. A lump sat right on top of it, incongruous as something left by a glacier. What were those called, those stray boulders you saw perched in hair-raising positions? On cliffs?

"I feel like I died and came back to life head-first," he said.

"I'm going make you something nice. Make you feel a whole lot better."

"Uh," said Art. "If you don't mind, I'd rather just have a Tylenol. You got any Tylenol? I had some in my briefcase. If I still have my briefcase."

"Your what?"

"My briefcase," said Art again, with a panicky feeling. "Do you know what happened to my briefcase?"

"Oh, it's right by the door. I'll get it, don't move."

And then there it was, his briefcase, its familiar hard-sided, Italian slenderness resting right on his stomach. He clutched it. "Thank you," he whispered.

"You need help with that thing?"

"No," said Art, but when he opened the case, it slid, and everything spilled out — his notes, his files, his papers. All that figuring — how strange his concerns looked here, on this brown shag carpet.

"Here," said the woman, and again — "I'll get it, don't move" — as gently, beautifully, she gathered up all the folders and put them in the case. There was an odd, almost practiced finesse to her movements; the files could have been cards in a card dealer's hands. "I used to be a nurse," she explained, as if reading his mind. "I picked up a few folders in my time. Here's the Tylenol."

"I'll have two."

"Course you will," she said. "Two Tylenol and some hot milk with honey. Hope you don't mind the powdered, we just got moved here, we don't have no supplies. I used to be a nurse, but I don't got no milk and I don't got no Tylenol, my guests got to bring their own. How you like that."

Art laughed as much as he could. "You got honey, though, how's that?"

"I don't know, it got left here by somebody," said the nurse. "Hope there's nothing growing in it."

Art laughed again, then let her help him sit up to take his pills. The nurse — her name was Cindy — plumped his pillows. She administered his milk. Then she sat — very close to him, it seemed — and chatted amiably about this and that. How she wasn't going to be staying at the hotel for too long, how her kids had had to switch schools, how she wasn't afraid to take in a strange, injured man. After all, she grew up in the projects, she could take care of herself. She showed him her switchblade, which had somebody's initials carved on it, she didn't know whose. She had never used it, she said, somebody gave it to her. And that somebody didn't know whose initials those were, either, she said, at least so far as she knew. Then she lit a cigarette and smoked while he told her first about his conference and then about how he had ended up at the hotel by mistake. He told her the latter with some hesitation, hoping he wasn't offending her. But she wasn't offended. She laughed with a cough, emitting a series of smoke puffs.

"Sure must've been a shock," she said. "Land up in a place like this. This no place for a nice boy like you."

That stung a little. *Boy!* But more than the stinging, he felt something else. "What about you? It's no place for you, either, you and your kids."

"Maybe so," she said. "But that's how the Almighty planned it, right? You folk rise up while we set and watch." She said this with so little rancor, with something so like intimacy, that it almost seemed an invitation of sorts.

But maybe he was kidding himself. Maybe he was assuming things, just like Billy Shore, just like men throughout the ages. Projecting desire where there was none, assigning and imagining, and in juicy detail. Being Asian didn't exempt him from that. *You folk.* Art was late, but it didn't much matter. This conference was being held in conjunction with a much larger conference, the real draw; the idea being that maybe between workshops and on breaks, the conferees would drift down and see what minicomputers could do for them. That mostly meant lunch.

In the meantime, things were totally dead, allowing Art to appreciate just how much the trade show floor had shrunk — down to a fraction of what it had been in previous years, and the booths were not what they had been, either. It used to be that the floor was crammed with the fanciest booths on the market; Art's used to be twenty by twenty. It took days to put together. Now you saw blank spots on the floor where exhibitors didn't even bother to show up, and those weren't even as demoralizing as some of the makeshift jobbies — exhibit booths that looked like high school science fair projects. They might as well have been made out of cardboard and Magic Marker. Art himself had a booth you could buy from an airplane catalog, the kind that rolled up into cordura bags. And people were stingy with brochures now, too. Gone were the twelve-page, four-color affairs; now the pamphlets were four-page, two-color, with extra bold graphics for attempted pizzazz, and not everybody got one, only people who were serious.

Art set up. Then, even though he should have been manning his spot, he drifted from booth to booth, saying hello to people he should have seen at breakfast. They were happy to see him, to talk shop, to pop some grapes off the old grapevine. Really, if he weren't staying in a welfare hotel, he would have felt downright respected. *You folk.* What folk did Cindy mean? Maybe she was just being matter-of-fact, keeping her perspective. Although how could anyone be so matter-of-fact about something so bitter? He wondered this even as he took his imaginative liberties with her. These began with a knock on her door and coursed through some hot times but ended (what a good boy he was) with him rescuing her and her children (he wondered how many there were) from their dead-end life. What was the matter with him, that he could not imagine mating without legal sanction? His libido was not what it should be, clearly, or at least it was not what Billy Shore's was. Art tried to think *game plan,* but in truth he could not even identify what a triple option would be in this case. All he knew was that, assuming, to begin with, that she was willing, he couldn't sleep with a woman like Cindy and then leave her flat. She could *you folk* him, he could never *us folk* her.

He played with some software at a neighboring booth; it appeared interesting enough but kept crashing so he couldn't tell too much. Then he dutifully returned to his own booth, where he was visited by a number of people he knew, people with whom he was friendly enough. The sort of people to whom he might have shown pictures of his children. He considered telling one or two of them about the events of the morning. Not about the invitation that might not have been an invitation, but about finding himself in a welfare hotel and being beaned with his own telephone. Phrases drifted through his head. *Not so bad as you'd think. You'd be surprised how friendly the people are. Unpretentious. Though, of course, no health club.* But in the end the subject simply did not come up and did not come up until he realized that he was keeping it to himself, and that he was committing more resources to this task than he had readily available. He felt invaded — as if he had been infected by a self-replicating bug. Something that was iterating and iterating, growing and growing, crowding out everything else in the CPU. The secret was intolerable; it was bound to spill out of him sooner or later. He just hoped it wouldn't be sooner.

He just hoped it wouldn't be to Billy Shore, for whom he began to search, so as to be certain to avoid him.

Art had asked about Billy at the various booths, but no one had seen him; his absence was weird. It spooked Art. When finally some real live conferees stopped by to see his wares, he had trouble concentrating; everywhere in the conversation he was missing opportunities, he knew it. And all because his CPU was full of iterating nonsense. Not too long ago, in looking over some database software in which was loaded certain fun facts about people in the industry, Art had looked up Billy, and discovered that he had been born the same day Art was, only four years later. It just figured that Billy would be younger. That was irritating. But Art was happy for the information, too. He had made a note of it, so that when he ran into Billy at this conference, he would remember to kid him about their birthdays. Now, he rehearsed. *Have I got a surprise for you. I always knew you were a Leo. I believe this makes us birthmates.* Anything not to mention the welfare hotel and all that had happened to him there.

In the end, he did not run into Billy at all. In the end, he wondered about Billy all day, only to finally learn that Billy had moved on to a new job in the Valley, with a start-up. In personal computers, naturally. A good move, no matter what kind of beating he took on his house.

"Life is about the long term," said Ernie Ford, the informant. "And let's face it, there is no long term here."

Art agreed as warmly as he could. In one way, he was delighted that his competitor had left — if nothing else, that would mean a certain amount of disarray at Info-Edge. The insurance market was, unfortunately, some 40 percent of his business, and he could use any advantage he could get. Another bonus was that Art was never going to have to see Billy again. Billy his birthmate, with his jokes and his Mainstreamese. Still, Art felt depressed.

"We should all have gotten out before this," he said.

"Truer words were never spoke," said Ernie. Ernie had never been a particular friend of Art's, but somehow, talking about Billy was making him chummier. It was as if Billy were a force even in his absence. "I tell you, I'd have packed my bags by now if it weren't for the wife, the kids — they don't want to leave their friends, you know? Plus the oldest is a junior in high school, we can't afford for him to move now, he's got to stay put and make those nice grades so he can make a nice college. Meaning I've got to stay, if it means pushing McMuffins for Ronald McDonald. But now you . . ."

"Maybe I should go," said Art.

"Definitely, you should go," said Ernie. "What's keeping you?"

"Nothing," said Art. "I'm divorced now. And that's that, right? Sometimes people get undivorced, but you can't exactly count on it."

"Go," said Ernie. "Take my advice. If I hear of anything, I'll send it your way."

"Thanks," said Art.

But of course, he did not expect that Ernie would really turn anything up. It had been a long time since anyone had called him or anybody else he knew of; too many people had gotten stranded, and they were too desperate. Everybody knew it. Also, the survivors were looked upon with suspicion. Anybody who was any good had jumped ship early, that was the conventional wisdom. There was Art, struggling to hold on to his job, only to discover that there were times you didn't want to hold on to your job, times to maneuver for the golden parachute and jump. That was another thing no one had told him, that sometimes it spoke well of you to be fired. Who would have figured that? Sometimes it seemed to Art that he knew nothing at all, that he had dug his own grave and didn't even know to lie down in it, he was still trying to stand up.

A few more warm-blooded conferees at the end of the day — at least they were polite. Then, as he was packing up to go back to the hotel, a mega-surprise. A headhunter approached him, a friend of Ernest's, he said.

"Ernest?" said Art. "Oh, Ernie! Ford! Of course!"

The headhunter was a round, ruddy man with a ring of hair like St. Francis of Assisi, and sure enough, a handful of bread crumbs: A great opportunity, he said. Right now he had to run, but he knew just the guy Art had to meet, a guy who was coming in that evening. For something else, it happened, but he also needed someone like Art. Needed him yesterday, really. Should've been a priority, the guy realized that now, had said so the other day. It might just be a match. Maybe a quick breakfast in the A.M.? Could he call in an hour or so? Art said, *Of course.* And when St. Francis asked his room number, Art hesitated, but then gave the name of the welfare hotel. How would St. Francis know what kind of hotel it was? Art gave the name out confidently, making his manner count. He almost didn't make it to the conference at all, he said. Being so busy. It was only at the last minute that he realized he could do it — things moved around, he found an opening and figured what the hell. But it was too late to book the conference hotel, he explained. That was why he was staying elsewhere.

Success. All day Art's mind had been churning; suddenly it seemed to empty. He might as well have been Billy, born on the same day as Art was, but in another year, under different stars. How much simpler things seemed. He did not labor on two, three, six tasks at once, multiprocessing. He knew one thing at a time, and that thing just now was that the day was a victory. And all because he had kept his mouth shut. He had said nothing; he had kept his cool. He walked briskly back to the hotel. He crossed the lobby in a no-nonsense manner. An impervious man. He did not knock on Cindy's door. He was moving on, moving west. There would be a good job there, and a new life. Perhaps he would take up tennis. Perhaps he would own a Jacuzzi. Perhaps he would learn to like all those peculiar foods they ate out there, like jicama, and seaweed. Perhaps he would go macrobiotic.

It wasn't until he got to his room that he remembered that his telephone had no handset.

He sat on his bed. There was a noise at his window, followed, sure enough, by someone's shadow. He wasn't even surprised. Anyway, the fellow wasn't stopping at his room, at least not on this trip. That was luck. *You folk,* Cindy had said, taking back the ice bag. Art could see her perspective; she was right. He was luckier than she, by far. But just now, as the shadow crossed his window again, he thought mostly about how unarmed he was. If he had a telephone, he would probably call Lisa — that was how big a pool seemed to be forming around him, all of a sudden; an ocean, it seemed. Also, he would call the police. But first he would call Lisa, and see how she felt about his possibly moving west. *Quite possibly,* he would say, not wanting to make it sound as though he was calling her for nothing, not wanting to make it sound as though he was awash, at sea, perhaps drowning. He would not want to sound like a haunted man; he would not want to sound as though he was calling from a welfare hotel, years too late, to say, *Yes, that was a baby, it would have been a baby.* For he could not help now but recall the doctor explaining about that child, a boy, who had appeared so mysteriously perfect in the ultrasound. Transparent, he had looked, and gelatinous, all soft head and quick heart; but he would have, in being born, broken every bone in his body.

EDWARD J. DELANEY

The Drowning

FROM THE ATLANTIC MONTHLY

MY FATHER came from the old country in middle age, and to his last he instilled in me the peculiarities of his native tongue. Even now, at the age of seventy, I am left with his manners of speech, his inflections and growls. He left me with his sayings, and I recall one in particular, his favorite, a half-comic shout of equal parts exasperation and petition: "Help me, Father Alphonsus!"

Most often this was uttered in moments of high disgust. My father worked as a hod carrier until he was seventy, a job that condemned him through all those years to being eternally strong and eternally exhausted. At night, sitting in his chair in the parlor of our tenement, he would brood over the five of us, his children, as we bickered over one thing or another — the last scrap of the night's loaf, a new toy pilfered from a classmate — and he would take on the resigned look of a condemned man, and invoke the name of this priest, a man he had known long ago. And then, if my mother didn't rush from the kitchen to herd us from danger, my father would often hit one of us.

Even late in life he had ridged muscles along his chest and back. His face was etched with a sunburned and skeptical squint. When we were young, he hit hard. When he sat down again, walled in now by the wails of a child, he'd rub the sting from his cracked hands and fall into a black mood. "Forgive me, Father Alphonsus," he'd mumble. The meaning always seemed clear. My father was a man of weakness and vices, and he made no apologies. He prayed for strength in the face of us. Much later in life I found myself praying aloud to Father Alphonsus a time or two, such as when my own son stole a car. The matter was quietly settled in the office of a police-department captain, with the victim of the theft staring at me from across the table and my son quietly sobbing. Father Alphonsus, the faceless man of grace, hovered ethereally over the proceedings. Alphonsus, my father told us, was the most well-intentioned man he had ever known, "if such things should count for anything." Alphonsus was a near relation, the keeper of faith in Fenagh, the hamlet on Lough Ree where my father was born.

"He was a man who knew nothing but to offer the best he could," my father said. "I have neither his patience nor his benevolence." My father wasn't cruel, but he lived a life of bricks on his back, the stabbing workday sun, and day's-end liquor bought with the desire for the most liquid at the lowest negotiable rate. He'd drink and play our battered phonograph, closing his eyes and giving himself over to the crackling arias. Though he often invoked the name of his old village priest, he found no priest here to be worthy, and he fell away from the Church despite my mother's prodding. When I was seventeen and was offered a scholarship to Boston College, he complained bitterly that I could do better than to deal with Jesuits, insincere bastards that they were. I suspected that my father could have done much better than his dire life, but he seemed not to want to, couldn't fully engage in the way things were. It didn't seem unusual that a hod carrier would prize his books, his Greek classics and sweeping histories. He was Irish, and illegal. He could not become lace-curtain Irish, and my father had nothing good to say about those who were. He maintained through his life the sidelong glance he had learned when he first came off the boat, before he found my mother and married her.

This Father Alphonsus was one of the few people mentioned from my father's youth. I had no sense of what the man was like, his look or manner. At times I wondered if he was real. But one day, late in his life, my father came to feel a desperate need to tell me a story.

This would have been 1952. My father was about the same age as I am now, but he was much closer to death than I assume myself to be. A resolute smoker of filterless Camel cigarettes, he was in the advanced stages of cancer of the larynx, which at the time was virtually incurable. In the nursing home, in a wicker wheelchair, he talked compulsively despite the ongoing strangulation of his voice box. He'd take a deep breath and then release it in long, rattling phrases, and I would sit and listen to monologues about his job and friends and enemies and crooks and aces. Later, in his yellow-walled hospital room, he'd go on and on while I watched the rectangle of sunlight glide imperceptibly across the waxed floors and then fade and die. I sensed in all this talk a spiraling movement toward something central. He had, he told me, things he needed to say. Important things. What happened on Father Alphonsus's final day was one.

Alphonsus had been the youngest of six, born six weeks after his father's death by pneumonia, and from the moment of his birth his mother had unshakable plans for him. Alphonsus would be her last chance, and she was the kind of woman who felt that producing a priest was a fitting and necessary act of completion to her maternal career. From the earliest age Alphonsus was groomed for sacred duty. She made him tiny knitted vestments and pasteboard altars as playthings, enlisting his older brothers, rougher boys, to encourage Alphonsus to believe that he was different. Alphonsus's mother spoke to him nightly about the duties he would assume, bedtime tales about faith and good works. His oldest brother, Eamon, explained to him about celibacy, and none too charitably. But Alphonsus listened and nodded. The details Eamon so eagerly shared, using examples of his own sordid exploits as proof of what Alphonsus would miss, horrified the younger boy. Eamon waited then for a response. Alphonsus's nightly sessions with his mother allowed him to apply the appropriate word: "sacrifice." "Good lad," Eamon said. Alphonsus, even as a child, was looking forward to the priest's solitary life. His heroes were the Irish hermits of the Middle Ages. He read stories of their lives on the rocky islands off the west Irish coast, lives of gray skies and gray seas. These stories filled him with awe for the heroism embodied in shunning the world.

Sacrifice did not define the process of Alphonsus's rise to the priesthood. He slid through seminary and took up his works back at St. Enda's in Fenagh, his boyhood church. When his superior, the aged Father O'Donnell, passed away on the night after Christmas, 1906, the twenty-six-year-old Alphonsus became his village's spiritual leader.

Nights, standing in his bedroom as rain washed the windows of the drafty stone rectory, he thought that he didn't regret what he had become but that he wouldn't ultimately measure up. The feeling wasn't new. He had completed his studies with neither distinction nor exceptional difficulty. He had never considered himself brilliant, but he had enough intelligence to see his own utter lack of intuition. Could a priest, confronted with the fluid nature of reality, afford not to rely heavily on hunches and inspiration? In his small room in the seminary he prayed long and searchingly, believing that a sudden feeling of enlightenment or resolve might be transmitted from the Creator. But when he finished with his prayers, he felt nothing.

In the first dozen years or so after ordination things went relatively well. His posting to the village seemed clear notice that not much was expected of him from his superiors. Alphonsus presided over the reassuring cycle of dawn masses, funerals, and weddings; he taught catechism and organized a football team of the younger boys. These were the things Alphonsus had imagined himself doing effectively. He'd stand at the edge of a rain-softened field, the winds off the lough making the edges of his cassock snap and tighten around his legs, and he'd watch the boys, some playing barefoot, as they kicked the ball about. He felt like a giant then, affecting a sternness he recalled in O'Donnell. He hoped to instill in them the fear he'd held of the old man. But at the same time, he felt small and weak in the face of the unanticipated crisis. It had not yet happened, but he knew its inevitability, if not its form. He felt that these things could be seen by the shrewd among his parishioners: his stammering uncertainty when faced with the difficulty of a pregnant girl, Amanda Flynn, asking to be quietly married, even though half the town had already heard whispered dispatches of her condition. Or the town's thieves and adulterers and his sheeplike acceptance of them sitting in the front pews, their faces masks of haughty and false devotion. He would meet their eyes briefly and then look away.

One day, after years of this stoic service, Alphonsus awakened early to a knocking on the door. This tapping was light but relentless, on and on until he had let his eyes adjust and find the phosphorescent hands of his clock. It was three o'clock. An early riser, Alphonsus was surprised to be rolled out of bed, and the insistent softness of the knocks as he descended the stairs indicated to him a call for last rites, perhaps for the elder John Flanagan, who'd been kicked shoeing a horse and was not expected to recover. At the door he found a boy, perhaps ten years old, shivering.

"Father, you have to hear a confession," the boy said.

"Pardon?"

"A confession. You hear confessions, don't you?"

"Well, I thought you were . . ." Alphonsus felt a twinge of anger. "Of course I hear confessions. But I generally don't find children on my doorstep at odd hours. Now, get inside here. We'll do it in the study, and it had better be good."

"It's not I who needs to," the boy said. "The person is waiting inside the church."

What was this? Alphonsus made the boy stand in the entry while he ascended the stairs to change clothes. The oddity of this demanded confession made him suspicious. For a shaky moment he worried that this would be a robbery. He sat at the edge of the bed, still in his underclothing, his cassock across his knees. He tried to place the boy's face. The child was not one of his footballers; the face was reminiscent of the O'Neals, a family of beggars who lived in a beaten-down mud cottage outside the town, near the lough shore. Alphonsus heard the door below open and then shut. The thought of what might be afoot — being lured out by the boy and then thrashed for his pocket watch — made him wary. Alphonsus went to the bedroom window and looked out. The boy had left the house and now stood on the dark lawn with a man. They were shadowy forms, but he could see that they were looking up at him. The man raised his arm and waved. Alphonsus waved back and then held out a raised index finger: *one moment.* The man nodded.

When Alphonsus came out the door, he felt the glassy cold cutting through his sweater. The man and boy moved forward to meet him, in the steam from their own breathing. The man, his face hidden by the pulled-down front of his cap, was staring at the ground.

"The boy said you'd gone inside the church," Alphonsus said.

"No, Father. He's right inside the confessional."

They stayed in the yard while Alphonsus went in. He fumbled for a candle at the back of the nave, still half waiting for hands to seize at him from the dark. But in the weak light the church was still. He entered the confessional, snuffed the candle, and slid back his screen.

"Are you there?" Alphonsus said.

"Aye, Father."

"Then go ahead."

The voice began its mumbled recitations, and as he waited, Alphonsus rubbed his eyes of sleep and wondered about the elder John Flanagan and whether he had lived through the night. Alphonsus was feeling light and electric, not quite anchored in the dark. He realized that the man had stopped talking.

"Go ahead," Alphonsus said.

"Father, I've breached the Fifth Commandment."

Alphonsus was silent. He was sure the man was confused. "Do you mean adultery, then?" he said.

"No."

"Tell me the Fifth Commandment."

"Thou shalt not kill."

Alphonsus felt strangely calm. This was the first time he'd encountered such an infraction. A killer! He silently recalled the seminary lessons: *Forgiveness is the priest's task, punishment the law's.*

"Who?" Alphonsus said.

"I don't know his name."

"Who knows about this?"

"No one, Father."

"Not your friends outside?"

"Not even them. Only you."

"And where is the dead man?"

"In the woods near the lough."

"Is that where you killed him?"

"That's where I did him, Father."

Alphonsus leaned back against his bench. He told himself to go slow.

"And while you were standing over his body there in the woods, were you feeling remorse for your act?"

"I felt sorry I had to breach a commandment."

"Was it self-defense?"

"In a manner of speaking."

"What manner was that?"

"That we are all in danger, Father."

"Some men, to prove their remorse, might turn themselves in."

"Aye," the voice said. "Some might."

"And why not you?"

"Others will be involved. Others who don't deserve such troubles."

"How so? Troubles from whom?"

"From the Black and Tans."

"Oh, my," Alphonsus said. He ran his fingers along the starched smoothness of his collar. Matters had taken on a more troubling dimension. He now understood that the dead man was a policeman from the RIC, the Royal Irish Constabulary. Four years had passed since the Easter Rising in Dublin, and in this four years of undeclared civil war the RICs, seen by many as agents of British rule, had often been targets. The RICs were Irishmen, but more and more the younger men had left the ranks, some openly disavowing their ties, others simply slipping out, often to England. Those who remained were the older hands, who after years of service were not sure whether to be more afraid of the Irish Republican Army or of a lost pension. But with each new death of a constable came more recrimination and violence.

The Black and Tans, since they'd been brought in from England, had begun a policy of retribution that was as simple as it was vicious. When a policeman was killed, the Tans generally burned the village nearest the killing. Alphonsus did not need to calculate the distance to the shores of Lough Ree: as a sport fisherman, he knew the lough, a landlocked elbow of water a mile wide and eleven long.

"Father . . . ?"

"Yes."

"My penance?"

Good God! Was this how simple it should be? Alphonsus was speechless. Penance? He sat for a long time, thinking, wondering whether he could somehow find a way to consult with someone. What was the penance for such an act?

"I can grant no penance yet," Alphonsus said. "I want you to return here at the same time tomorrow night. I want you to do nothing except pray. Take no action. Now, where is this body?"

"Father, I don't know if . . ."

"Good Lord, man! Tell me where this poor lad is, so he can receive the sacrament due him!"

"Do you know the path to the rock formations on the east side of the lough?"

"I do."

"He's twenty or thirty yards north of the path, about a quarter mile up from the shore."

"How did he get there?"

"He was answering a call for help."

The man fell silent. Alphonsus could hear his breathing. "Father?" he said. "Father, I thought you had to grant penance."

"Not in the case of the Fifth Commandment," Alphonsus said. "Most people have no experience in this." He quivered at his own lie, but his voice remained firm.

As Alphonsus sat in the confessional, listening to the receding footsteps and then the slam of the church door, he rubbed his hands on his knees, trying to calm himself. Indeed, he was thinking of the town of Balbriggan, which had burned a few weeks before at the hands of the Black and Tans.

But, Alphonsus wondered, could this man who had spoken to him in the confessional truly be repentant, having known what his actions would lead to? Alphonsus thought not. But he had, from his training, clear guidelines: as much as he wanted this man to turn himself in, he could not require it. And doing so probably wouldn't help, once the dead man was discovered. The Black and Tans, so called because of their odd makeshift uniforms of khaki army trousers and black RIC tunics, were men in whom the cruelty of war had become ingrained. They were being paid ten shillings a day, good money, but still they often sought as payment the suffering of those they saw as enemies, which was nearly anyone Irish.

Alphonsus relit his candle. The movement of the shadows in the boxed closeness of the confessional made him think of the lick of flames. The Black and Tans' terror felt close at hand. Why should anyone be absolved?

In the morning he offered sunrise service to a handful of sleepy elders and then returned to the rectory for breakfast. The housekeeper, Mrs. Toole, had brought in a two-day-old copy of *The Irish Times,* and over his toast he went through it slowly, looking for news on the Troubles. In the village he had heard talk of how the Black and Tans had taken to roaring down Dublin streets on a lorry, wildly firing their weapons; in Kiltartan a woman was dead, hit by stray shots with a child in her arms. But in the *Times* he found no mention.

He changed into his gardening clothes. His flower beds faced the woods, and at the edge of the trees he had vegetables. He spent hours here, for the priesthood had not proved to be excessively demanding. Many days he stood at his fence, watching the movements of the drawn carts and of his parishioners, the cottiers coming from the clodded potato fields. Far off, on an open meadow, unfurled bolts of linen bleached in the sun, long white bars against the hard green. Today, in the garden, he contemplated the early-morning confession, and the meeting that night. He felt ludicrous standing here in the garden, but at the same time he wanted to be nowhere else, for he was alone.

Down the rutted lane that curved behind the near cottages he saw Sean Flynn, the retired schoolteacher, walking his dog. The animal, runty and of no clear breed, dug at a rabbit hole. Flynn, leaning on his cane and softly cursing the dog, saw Alphonsus, and ambled up.

"Father!"

"Mr. Flynn."

"Have we been fishing this week, Father?"

"I confess I haven't. But soon."

"Father, the weather's turning cold."

"I know, I know. It's pitiful that I haven't."

"Today, then."

"No, I have some matters."

"Father, clear your mind."

"Perhaps."

"You really should."

"I think I will, Mr. Flynn. Really."

"Today."

"Yes, today."

It would be his reason, then, to go to the lough. In the house, packing his equipment, he slipped in his stole and oils. He put on a clean cassock and adjusted his biretta, his priest's crown with its hard sides and pompon. Mrs. Toole was down below, dusting in the dining room, and he went to the kitchen to pack a jam sandwich.

"I'll be off fishing now," he said.

"Today?" she said.

"Why not?"

"With Mr. Flanagan on his deathbed from that horse kicking him?"

"Um, well, I'll be back by midafternoon. I heard he's doing better."

"Really? Who told you?"

"Mr. Flynn. We were just talking outside."

Mrs. Toole went back to dusting the china cabinet. "You and the fishing," she said.

"Every chance I get," Alphonsus said.

"Father?"

"Yes?"

"You're fishing dressed like that?"

"If anyone does need last rites, I don't want to do it in my fishing clothes. I shan't be long, anyway."

The row from his usual fishing spot to the shoreline edge of the path was longer than he was used to. After pulling his boat onto the rocks, he walked up and down the path several times, first making sure no one was near, and then beginning to scan the thick woods for any sign of the body. The killing had been in the dark, he assumed, so perhaps the instructions were confused. The day had become brilliantly crisp, and he couldn't see anything human amid the play of shadows and light. Alphonsus stepped off the path and walked broad circles, searching, pulling up the hem of the cassock so he wouldn't get muddy. He kept his eye on the path, too, in case someone came. He wouldn't have an answer if asked what he was doing.

After an hour he sat. He unfolded his sandwich from its greased paper and ate, thinking. He had, in his estimation, covered nearly every possible spot where a body might be. He wondered if this was a hoax. He was too exhausted and tense to fish, and the winds beyond the woods seemed to be picking up. Had he been fishing, he might have been in dangerous waters. He wished he didn't have to return to the village, to the confessional. Bad things were to happen, and he had no idea how to stop them. If he didn't find the body, someone else would: the absence of this constable would eventually become known. Though some constables deserted, slipping away to the north or across to Britain, Alphonsus reasoned that only proof of a desertion would curb the Black and Tans' impulse for destruction.

His calling was powerful, but an unwillingness to absolve the man in the confessional was stronger, a mixture of revenge and principle he couldn't shake free of. He didn't know if that man had been an O'Neal, but he was certain the man was like the O'Neals, someone embittered with his lot and perhaps too willing to blame everything on the British. But he had to absolve, to heed his vows. When his sandwich was gone, he walked down to the lough and drank at water's edge from cupped hands. Back up the path, but now not as far from shore, he plunged into the woods, again searching.

The body was half hidden with wet leaves, the accumulation on the windward side like dunes overtaking a pyramid. Alphonsus knelt, put his hand on the shoulder, and gently rolled the man on his back.

"Hello, Thomas," Alphonsus said.

He hadn't considered the possibility that he would know the deceased. The body was that of Thomas Shanahan, a royal constable stationed at the RIC barracks on the other side of the lough. Thomas had from time to time come to mass at Alphonsus's church. Alphonsus had made a point of welcoming him, for he believed that all were equal in the eyes of God. Thomas was also a fisherman, and after mass they had often talked of their favorite spots. Thomas's face was clean, his clothes neatly straight. He wasn't in uniform but in thick wool trousers and shirt, as if off duty. Alphonsus turned him again, and now saw the crust of hardened blood on the back of his head. As he removed his oils and stole from his fishing kit, Alphonsus scanned the trees, ready to become prone should he hear footsteps.

Thomas was middle aged, a bachelor who, Alphonsus sensed, was as private a person as he. Thomas lived in the RIC barracks, but in his conversations with Alphonsus never spoke of any of his mates. But of course one couldn't, in the same way that Alphonsus understood he would hear no mention of the Black and Tans and their tactics. Alphonsus, as he daubed the oils upon the cold face, assumed that Thomas had deplored all this, and Alphonsus didn't care to know different.

When he finished the last rites, Alphonsus sat for some time on a rock, looking at the body. How had Thomas come here? Had he been ambushed fishing? No rod or kit lay nearby, but those might have been spoils for the killer. He could go on speculating, but he couldn't avoid what he now planned to do. From his own bag Alphonsus extracted his trowel, the best he had been able to manage without being noticed. He walked in a circle around Thomas, looking for the softest and highest ground, and then knelt and began digging.

This act, he knew, transformed him. He had no business doing this. The dirt did not give way as easily as he'd imagined; he'd felt, coming out in the boat, that he could be back at the rectory by dusk. But the soil was choked with rocks. Hours into it, he stood back and looked at the pitiful rut he'd clawed out, and he laughed in despair.

"Tommy," he said to the body, "I damned well don't know what to do with you. This just isn't Christian, is it?" Tommy, on his side, stared out onto the lough.

Alphonsus peered up through the trees, not able to shed the sense that he was being watched. He had the feeling that the killer might come back, to see that the body was still there. The IRA wanted the body to be found, surely, so that a bloody raid by the Tans was inevitable. The killing of a fellow Irishman like Tommy would create doubt and ambivalence unless it was followed by the necessary retribution by the Brits. Was he being used in this? Did someone expect that Alphonsus himself was going to report the death? Or would the killer return, having thought things over, to put Tommy in a more conspicuous place?

His plan had been to bury Tommy, but Alphonsus now saw that he wasn't capable of finishing the job. The hole was barely two feet deep. Alphonsus recalled his grandfather's stories of the Famine, of skeletal men burying cloth-shrouded friends as packs of starving dogs gathered at the periphery, yelping with hunger and bloodlust, set to dig as soon as the living moved on.

"Forgive me, Tommy, but I can barely move now," Alphonsus said. "I thought my gardening had made me fit enough to undertake this."

A wind was picking up on the lough, making the water choppy and whitecapped. The row back would be dangerous if he didn't go soon. He felt a rising panic. He would have to drop Tommy into the deep waters — he saw this. He'd not be back until well after dark, but his midnight confession awaited. He'd have to be there or the killer would certainly have suspicions.

Down by the water he searched for a way to weight the body. Rocks were all around, but no means of attachment. His fishing kit could be loaded with them, but the top was loose and the ballast might fall out as the package sank. Alphonsus saw one way to do what he needed to do. Standing above the body, he removed his cassock, and then pulled off Thomas's pants and shirt.

Getting the cassock onto the body was easy. Thomas was a bigger man than he, but the cassock was loose. Alphonsus adjusted the braces of Thomas's pants and rolled up the pants and shirt cuffs so that he was clothed for the stealthy trip back to the rectory. In a pocket was a purse with Thomas's papers and a sizable bit of money. Alphonsus was surprised that this hadn't been taken.

The boat rode low on the water with two men in it, the dead one loaded down with stones, the live one weighted by the terror of being caught. Alphonsus had used his fishing line to bind the bottom of the cassock around Thomas's ankles to hold the rocks; the collar was snug at the neck. The last trace of sunlight was nearly gone. Alphonsus stroked hard against the winds, slicing out toward the rough middle of the lough.

He was a sinner now — he could see that. He would dump a dead man into the cold waters as if he were a load of garbage, would grant penance to a murderer. He would return to his rectory, slip past Mrs. Toole so that she wouldn't notice his inexplicable change of clothing, and spend the rest of his life trying to live with this. And all he wanted was for no one to be hurt. So be it. If this body somehow resurfaced or washed to shore, with a cracked skull and wrapped in a cassock, so be it. Or if the Tans correctly interpreted Tommy Shanahan's disappearance and overran Fenagh anyway, so be it. "So be it, Tom," Alphonsus said. "A week will pass and you won't turn up, and they'll know, they'll know."

He stopped rowing. The moon shone through a break in the clouds, giving definition to the far edges of the lough. To say a prayer at a moment like this seemed crude and sacrilegious, desperate and artificial. But he prayed now anyway, prayed for guidance.

Nothing came to him. He felt that matters were on an inevitable course and he could do nothing but send Tommy to the bottom and then go home. "Do as we must do," he said to the body.

He grabbed the shoulders of the cassock. He crouched in the boat, the balance becoming uncertain, and then he lurched and Tom hit the gunwale. The boat was listing. Water was pouring in. He had imagined a noiseless letting-go of the body, but now Alphonsus was in a fight, and in his panic he wasn't sure whether he was trying to shove the body away or pull it back on board. But neither was happening and now he was underwater, the coldness and dark shockingly sudden. He looked up and could see only a single blurred spot of weak light. He wanted to reach for it, that moon in the sky over on the other side of the surface. His hands were still clenched to the bunched fabric of his own cassock, now weighted with death, and he let go of it, and the solid block that was Thomas grazed his leg and ankle and then was gone.

Alphonsus had been hanging on to the side of the overturned boat for some minutes when he decided that he would not return to Fenagh. That he would survive was not a given; the water was cold enough and his arms were tired enough from the digging that he felt almost nothing, except for the dull pain of the thick muscles along his neck. But he clung on, the wind and waves rocking him in crests and swells, until he was desperate enough to push away from the boat and swim for shore.

His thought, as he crawled out of the water on his hands and knees, was of his hat, his black biretta, floating like an ornate ship far out of reach, its black pompon now a keel. He had seen it from the boat, puffed by the wind and etched by moonlight, unwilling to sink with the cassock. The boat, too, would be found, far off on the lough, known by those fishermen who knew him.

In the woods he undressed, squeezed water from his clothing. He considered trying to light a fire. Naked in the cold air, he plunged into the water again to clean himself, and then dressed in the wet woolen shirt and trousers. His black brogans squished loudly when he walked, but he was moving quickly. In no time he was well up the path and along the rutted highway toward Dublin. By dawn he would find a ride in a chicken lorry, and by that evening he would use Tommy Shanahan's wet money to get a room over a public house by the docks. Three days later, his clothes dry and black stubble making his face lose its delicacy of appearance, he would bribe a dock worker to get him into the steerage of the first ship leaving Ireland. The dock worker would ask, "Why are you going?" The answer would be this: that the stowaway was a royal constable from near Fenagh, that he was running away, and that he hoped no one would find out. And when these words were out, the dock worker's face would be twisted with revulsion and the story of his flight would be common knowledge in Fenagh in a few days' time.

*

My father, telling this story thirty-two years later in a wheelchair in the rest home where he would die, told me that this is how he came to be a man born in middle age, with a name picked from a city directory. He told me he felt the need to unburden himself, that my mother never knew, and that he was for that reason glad she had preceded him into death. He said this without a hint of expectation that I would say anything to console him, and I didn't. I couldn't. I was in my twenties then, leaning over the man who had hit me so hard and so frequently that I had gone to bed many nights wishing to be someone else, a different child. I should have said something. But I stared at him until a nurse came to us and said he needed to eat.

A few years ago I went to Ireland, for the simple reason that I am a devout Boston College football fan and that year they played a game in Dublin against West Point. I boarded an Aer Lingus 747 packed with alumni, and we sang drinking songs high over the Atlantic. Only on the day after the football game did I think to rent a car and take a drive. Asking in Dublin, I found no one who'd heard of Fenagh, but I set out toward Lough Ree, and on its eastern shore I got directions to the town. There I parked, and walked the length of its primary streets, and stood for a while in front of St. Enda's Church, without going in. At a small shop I talked to the keeper, a man older than I, and he told me he had a niece in Boston he sometimes went to visit. I told him I'd had a relative here, a Father Alphonsus.

"Of course," he said. "I've seen the plaque." He pointed me down the road toward a knoll overlooking the water. There, behind some overgrown brambles, I found an engraved plate, the size of an envelope maybe, mounted on a rock.

FATHER ALPHONSUS KELLY, RIP. DROWNED NOVEMBER 5, 1920. I stood on the knoll and looked at the harsh waters where this man had lost his life and become someone else. He was a man who became old and could not aspire to the better part of himself he believed he had squandered — who had come to find, I think, that in his exile he couldn't bring himself to try to be like Alphonsus, who indeed was a specter that floated over all our lives. Standing at the edge of the lough, I said a prayer for my father. I petitioned that he might be delivered from a purgatory of which I had been part.

Honored Guest

FROM HARPER'S MAGAZINE

SHE HAD BEEN HAVING a rough time of it and thought about suicide sometimes, but suicide was so corny and you had to be careful in this milieu that was eleventh grade because two of her classmates had committed suicide the year before and they had left twenty-four suicide notes between them and had become just a joke. They had left the notes everywhere, and they were full of misspellings and pretensions. Theirs had been a false show. Then this year a girl had taken an overdose of Tylenol, which of course did nothing at all, but word of it got out, and when she came back to school her locker had been broken into and was full of Tylenol, just jammed with it. Like, you moron. Under the circumstances, it was amazing that Helen thought of suicide at all. It was just not cool. You just made a fool of yourself. And the parents of these kids were mocked, too. They were considered to be suicide-enhancing, evil and weak, and they were ignored and barely tolerated. This was a small town. Helen didn't want to make it any harder on her mother than circumstances already had.

Her mother was dying and she wanted to die at home, which Helen could understand. She understood it perfectly, she'd say, but actually she understood it less well than she had. Or rather it had become clear that her mother's wish wasn't even what needed to be understood. Nothing needed to be understood.

There was a little brass bell on her mother's bedside table. It was the same little brass bell that had been placed at Helen's command when she was a little girl, sick upon occasion with some harmless little kid's sickness. She had just to reach out her hand and ring the bell and her mother would come or even her father. Her mother never used the bell now, she kept it there as sort of a joke, actually. Her mother was not utterly confined to bed. She moved around a bit at night and placed herself, or was placed by others, in other rooms during the day. Sometimes one of the women who had been hired to care for her during the day would even take her for a drive, out to see the icicles or to the bank window. Her mother's name was Lenore, and sometimes in the night her mother would call out this name, her own, Lenore! in a strong, urgent voice, and Helen in her own room would shudder and cry a little.

This had been going on for a while. In the summer, Lenore had been diagnosed and condemned, but she kept bouncing back, as the doctors put it, until recently. The daisies that bloomed in the fall down by the storm-split elm had come and gone, as had the little kids at Halloween. Thanksgiving had passed without comment, and it would be Christmas soon. Lenore was ignoring it. The boxes of balls and lights were in the cellar, buried deep. Helen had made the horrible mistake one night of asking her what she wanted for Christmas, and Lenore had said, "Are you stupid!" Then she said, "Oh, I don't mean to be so impatient. It's the medicine. My voice doesn't even sound right. Does my voice sound right? Get me something you'll want later. A piece of jewelry or something. Do you want the money for it?" She meant this sincerely.

At the beginning, they had talked eagerly like equals. This was more important than a wedding, this preparation. They even laughed like girls together remembering things. They remembered when Helen was a little girl before the divorce and they were all driving somewhere and Helen's father had been stopped for speeding and Lenore had wanted her picture taken with the state policeman and Helen had taken it. "Wasn't that mean!" Lenore said to Helen.

When Lenore died, Helen would go down to Florida and live with her father. "I've never had the slightest desire to visit Florida," Lenore would say. "You can have it."

At the beginning, death had given them the opportunity to be interesting. This was something special. There was only one crack at this. But then they lost sight of it somehow. It became a lesser thing, more terrible. Its meaning crumbled. They began waiting for it, terrible, terrible. Lenore had friends, but they called now, they didn't come over so much. "Don't come over," Lenore would tell them, "it wears me out." Little things started to go wrong with the house. Leaks, lights. The bulb in the kitchen would flutter when the water was turned on. Helen grew fat for some reason. The dog, their dog, began to change. He grew shy. "Do you think he's acting funny?" Lenore asked Helen.

She did not tell Helen that the dog had begun to growl at her. It was a secret growl, he never did it in front of anyone. He had taken to carrying around one of her slippers with him, he was almost never without it. He cherished her slipper.

"Do you remember when I put Grecian Formula on his muzzle because he turned gray so young?" Lenore said. "He was only about a year old and he began to turn gray? The things I used to do. The way I spent my time."

But now she did not know what to do with time at all. It seemed more expectant than ever. One couldn't satisfy it, one could never do enough for it.

She was so uneasy.

Lenore had a dream in which she wasn't dying at all. Someone else had died. People had explained this to her over and over again. And now they were getting tired of correcting her about this, impatient.

She had a dream of eating bread and dying. Two large loaves. Pounds of it, still warm from the oven. She ate it all, she was so hungry, starving! But then she died. It was the bread. It was too hot, was the explanation. There were people in her room, but she was not among them.

When she woke, she could feel the bread in her throat, scalding it. It was hot, gummy, almost liquid. She lay in bed on her side, her dark eyes open. It was four o'clock in the morning. She swung her legs to the floor. The dog growled at her. He slept in her room with her slipper, but he growled as she made her way past him. Sometimes self-pity would rise within her and she would stare at the dog, tears in her eyes, listening to him growl. The more she stared, the more sustained was the soft growl, as though the creature had no need to breathe.

She had a dream about a tattoo. This was a pleasant dream. She was walking away and she had the most beautiful tattoo. It covered her shoulders, her back, the back of her legs. It was unspeakably fine.

*

Helen had a dream that her mother wanted a tattoo. She wanted to be tattooed all over, a full custom body suit, but no one would do it. Helen woke protesting this, grunting and cold. She had kicked off her blankets. She pulled them up and curled tightly beneath them. There was a boy at school who had gotten a tattoo and now they wouldn't let him play basketball.

In the morning, Lenore said, "Would you get a tattoo with me? We could do this together. I don't think it's creepy," she added. "I think you'll be glad later. A pretty one, just small somewhere. What do you think?" The more she considered it, the more it seemed the perfect thing to do. What else could be done? She had given Helen her wedding ring, so what?

Her mother seemed happy. Her gaunt face seemed more familiar to Helen. "I'll get him to come over here, to the house. I'll arrange it," her mother said. Helen couldn't defend herself against this notion. She still felt sleepy, she was always sleepy. There was something wrong with her mother's idea, but not much.

But Lenore couldn't arrange it. When Helen returned from school, her mother said, "It can't be done. I'm so upset and I've lost interest, but I'll give you the short version. I called . . . I must have made twenty calls. At last I got someone to speak to me. His name was Smoking Joe and he was one hundred miles away, but he sounded as though he'd do it. And I asked him if there was any place he didn't tattoo, and he said, 'Faces, dicks, and hands.'"

"Mom!" Helen said. Her face reddened.

"And I asked him if there was any*one* he wouldn't tattoo, and he said, 'Drunks and the dying.' So that was that."

"But you didn't have to tell him. You won't have to tell him," Helen said.

"That's true," Lenore said dispiritedly. But then she looked angrily at Helen. "Are you crazy! Sometimes I think you're crazy!"

"Mom!" Helen said, crying. "I want you to do what you want."

"This was my idea, mine!" Lenore said. The dog gave a high nervous bark. "Oh dear," Lenore said. "I'm speaking too loudly." She looked at him as though to say how clever it was for both of them to realize this.

That night Lenore could not sleep. There were no dreams, nothing. High clouds swept slowly past the window. She got up and went into the living room, to the desk there. She looked with distaste at the desk, at all the objects in this room. There wasn't one thing here she'd want to take with her to the grave, not one. The dog had shuffled out of the bedroom with her and now lay at her feet, a slipper in his mouth, a red one with a little bow. She wanted to make note of a few things, clarify some things. She took out a piece of paper. The furnace turned on, and she heard something moving behind the walls. "Enjoy it while you can," she said to it. She sat at the desk, her back very straight, waiting for something. After a while, she looked at the dog. "Give me that," she said. "Give me that slipper." He growled but did not leave her side. She took a pen and wrote on the paper, *When I go, the dog goes. Promise me this.* She left it out for Helen.

Then she thought, That dog is the dumbest one I've ever had. I don't want him with me. She was amazed she could still think like this. She tore up the piece of paper. "Lenore!" she cried and wrung her hands. She wanted herself. Her mind ran stumbling, panting, through dark twisted woods.

When Helen got up, she would ask her to make some toast. Toast would taste good. Helen would press the GOOD MORNING letters on the bread. It was a gadget, like a cookie cutter. When the bread was toasted, the words were pressed down into it and you dribbled honey into them.

In the morning, Helen did this carefully, the way she always had. They sat together at the kitchen table and ate the toast. Sleet struck the windows. Helen looked at her toast dreamily, the golden letters against the almost black. They both liked the toast almost black.

Lenore felt peaceful. She even felt a little better. But it was a cruelty to feel a little better. A cruelty to Helen.

"Turn on the radio," Lenore said, "and find out if they're going to cancel school." If Helen stayed home today, she would talk to her. Important things would be said. Things that would still matter years from now.

Callers on a talk show were speaking about wolves. "There should be wolf control," someone said, "not wolf worship."

"Oh, I hate these people," Helen said.

"Are you a wolf worshiper?" her mother asked. "Watch out."

"I believe they have the right to live, too," Helen said fervently. Then she was sorry. Everything she said was wrong. She moved the dial on the radio. School would not be canceled. They never canceled it.

"There's a stain on that blouse," her mother said. "Why do your clothes always look so dingy? You should buy some new clothes."

"I don't want any new clothes," Helen said.

"You can't wear mine, that's not the way to think. I've got to get rid of them. Maybe that's what I'll do today. I'll go through them with Jean. It's Jean who comes today, isn't it?"

"I don't want your clothes!"

"No, why not? Not even the sweaters?"

Helen's mouth trembled.

"Oh, what are we going to do!" Lenore said. She clawed at her cheeks. The dog barked.

"Mom, Mom," Helen said.

"We've got to talk, I want to talk," Lenore said. What would happen to Helen, her little girl . . .

Helen saw the stain her mother had noticed on the blouse. Where had it come from? It had just appeared. She would change if she had time.

"When I die, I'm going to forget you," Lenore began. This was so obvious, this wasn't what she meant. "The dead just forget you. The important things, all the loving things, everything we . . ." She closed her eyes, then opened them with effort. "I want to put on some lipstick today," she said. "If I don't, when you come home, tell me."

Helen left for school just in time to catch the bus. Some of her classmates stood by the curb, hooded, hunched. It was bitter out.

"Hi," they said.

"All right."

In the house, Lenore looked at the dog. There were only so many dogs in a person's life, and this was the last one in hers. She'd like to kick him. But he had changed when she'd gotten sick, he hadn't been like this before. He was bewildered, he didn't like it — death — either. She felt sorry for him. She went back into her bedroom, and he followed her with the slipper.

At nine, the first in a number of nurse's aides and companions arrived. By three, it was growing dark again. Helen returned before four.

"The dog needs a walk," her mother said.

"It's so icy out, Mom, he'll cut the pads of his feet."

"He needs to go out!" her mother screamed. She wore a little lipstick and sat in a chair, wringing her hands.

Helen found the leash and coaxed the dog to the door. He looked out uneasily into the wet cold blackness. They moved out into it a few yards to a bush he had killed long before, and he dribbled a few drops of urine onto it. They walked a little farther, across the dully shining yard toward the street. It was still, windless. The air made a hissing sound. "Come on," Helen said. "Don't you want to do something?" The dog walked stoically along. Helen's eyes began to water with the cold. Her mother had said, "I want Verdi played at the service, Scriabin, no hymns." Helen had sent away for some recordings. How else could it be accomplished, the Verdi, the Scriabin . . . Once she had called her father and said, "What should we do for Mom?"

"Where have you been!" her mother said when they got back. "My God, I thought you'd been hit by a truck."

They ate supper, macaroni and cheese, something one of the women had prepared. Lenore ate it without speaking. She looked at the empty plate.

"Do you want some more, Mom?" Helen asked.

She shook her head. "One of those girls that comes says she'll take the dog."

Helen swallowed. "I think it would be good," she said.

"That's it, then. She'll take him tomorrow."

"Is she just going to see how it works out or what?"

"No, she wants him. She lives in an iffy neighborhood, and the dog, you know, can be impressive when he wants. I think better now than later. He's only five, five next month." She knew the dog's birthday. She laughed at this.

The next day when Helen came home from school, the dog was gone. His bowls were gone from the corner near the sink.

"At least I have my slipper back," Lenore said. She had it in her hand, the red slipper.

Helen was doing her homework. She was a funny kid, Lenore thought, there she was doing her homework.

"It's almost over for me," Lenore said. "I'm at the end of my life."

Helen looked up. "Mom," she said.

"I can't believe it."

"I'm a nihilist," Helen said. "That's what I'm going to be."

"You can't think you're going to be a nihilist," her mother said. "Are you laughing at me! I'm still your mother." She shook her fist.

"Mom, Mom," Helen said, "I'm not laughing." She began to cry.

"Don't cry," Lenore said dully.

Helen looked down at her textbook. She had underlined everything on one page. Everything! Stupid . . . She'd be stupid in Florida too, she thought. She could think about Florida only by being here with her mother. Otherwise, Florida didn't really exist.

Lenore said, "God is nothing. Okay? That's Meister Eckhart. But whatever is not God is nothing and ought to be accounted as nothing. Okay? That's someone else."

Helen didn't speak.

"I wasn't born yesterday," her mother said. "That's why I know these things. I wasn't even born last night." She laughed. It was snowing again. It had been snowing freshly for hours. First sleet, then colder, then this snow.

"Helen," her mother said. "Would you get me a snowball? Go out and make me one and bring it back."

Helen got up and went outside as though hypnotized. Sometimes she behaved like this, as though she were only an unwilling but efficient instrument. She could have thoughts and not think them. She was protected, and at the same time she was helping her mother to do her job, the job being this peculiar business.

The snow was damp and lovely. Huge flakes softly struck her face and felt like living things. She went past the bush the dog had liked, pushed her hands deeply in the snow, and made a snowball for her mother, perfect as an orange.

Lenore studied this. "This is good snow, isn't it?" she said. "Perfect snow." She packed it tighter and threw it across the room at Helen. It hit her squarely in the chest.

"Oh!" Lenore exclaimed.

"That hurt, Mom," Helen said.

"Oh, you," Lenore said. "Get me another."

"No!" Helen said. The thing had felt like a rock. Her breasts hurt. Her mother was grinning avidly at her.

"Get two, come on," her mother said. "We'll have a snowball fight in the house. Why not!"

"No!" Helen said. "This is . . . you're just pretending . . ."

Lenore looked at her. She pulled her bathrobe around herself. "I'm going to go to bed," she said.

"Do you want me to make some tea?" Helen said. "Let me make some tea."

"Tea, tea," Lenore mimicked. "What will you drink in Florida? You'll drink iced tea."

That night, Lenore dreamed she was on a boat with others. A white boat, clear lovely water. They were moving quickly, but there was a banging sound, arrhythmic, incessant, sad, it was sad. It's a banger, they said, the fish too big for the box, that's what we call them. Let it go, Lenore begged. Too late now, they said, too late now for it.

"Lenore!" she cried. She went into Helen's room. Helen slept with the light on, her radio playing softly, books scattered on her bed.

"Sleep with me," her mother said.

"I can't, please," Helen said. She shrank back.

"My God, you won't lie down with me!" her mother said. She had things from Helen's childhood still — little nightgowns, coloring books, valentines.

"All right, all right," Helen said. Her eyes were wild, she looked blinded.

"No, all right, forget it," Lenore said. She shook her head from side to side, panting. Helen's room was almost bare. There were no pictures, no pretty things, not even a mirror. Plastic was stapled to the window frames to keep out the cold. When had this happened? Lenore thought. Tomorrow, she thought. She shouldn't try to say anything at night. Words at night were feral things. She limped back to her room. Her feet were swollen, discolored; water oozed from them. She would hide them. But where would she hide them? She sat up in bed, the pillows heaped behind her back, and watched them. They became remote, indecipherable.

It became morning again. "Mother . . . Earth," said someone on the radio. "An egg?" Helen asked. "Do you want an egg this morning?"

"You should get your hair cut today," Lenore said. "Go to the beauty parlor."

"Oh, Mom, it's all right."

"Get it trimmed or something. It needs something."

"But nobody will be here with you," Helen said. "You'll be home by yourself."

"Go after school. I can take care of myself for an hour. Something wouldn't happen in an hour like that, do you think?" Lenore felt sly saying this. Then she said, "I want you to look pretty, feel good about yourself."

"I really hate those places," Helen said.

"Can't you do anything for me!" Lenore said.

Helen got off the bus at a shopping mall on the way back from school. "I don't have a reservation," she told the woman at the desk.

"You mean an appointment," the woman said. "You don't have an appointment."

She was taken immediately to a chair in front of a long mirror. The women in the chairs beside her were all looking in the mirror while their hairdresser stared into it too, and cut their hair. Everyone was chatting and relaxed, but Helen didn't know how to do this, even this, this simple thing.

Sometimes Helen dreamed that she was her own daughter. She was free, self-absorbed, unfamiliar. Helen took up very little of her thoughts.

She looked at the woman beside her, who had long wet hair and was smoking a cigarette. Above her shoe was a black parole anklet.

"These things don't work at all," the woman said. "I could take the damn thing off, but I think it's kind of stylish. Often I do take the damn thing off, and it's in one place and I'm in another. *Quite* another."

"What did you do?" Helen asked.

"I didn't do anything," the woman bawled. Then she laughed. She dropped her cigarette in the cup of coffee she was holding.

The washing, the cutting, the drying, all this took a long time. Her hairdresser was an Asian woman named Mickey. "How old do you think I am?" Mickey asked.

"Twenty," Helen said. She did not look at her, or herself, in the mirror. She kept her eyes slightly unfocused, the way a dog would.

"I am thirty-five," Mickey said, delighted. "I am one-sixteenth Ainu. Do you know anything about the Ainu?"

Helen knew it wasn't necessary to reply to this. Someone several chairs away said with disbelief, "She's naming the baby *what?*"

"The Ainu are an aboriginal people of north Japan. Up until a little while ago they used to kill a bear in a sacred ritual each year. The anthropologists were wild about this ritual and were disappointed when they quit, but here goes, I will share it with you. At the end of each winter, they'd catch a bear cub and give it to a woman to nurse. Wow, something! After it was weaned, it was given wonderful food and petted and played with. It was caged, but in all respects it was treated as an honored guest. But the day always came when the leader of the village would come and tell the bear sorrowfully that it must die, though they loved it dearly. This was a long oration, this part. Then everyone dragged the bear from its cage with ropes, tied it to a stake, shot it with blunt arrows that merely tortured it, then scissored its neck between two poles where it slowly strangled, after which they skinned it, decapitated it, and offered the severed head some of its own flesh. What do you think? Do you think they knew what they were doing?"

"Was there something more to it than that?" Helen said. "Did something come after that?" She really was a serious girl. Her head burned from the hair dryer that Mickey was wielding dramatically.

"These are my people!" Mickey said, ignoring her. "You've come a long way, baby! Maine or bust!" She sounded bitter. She turned off the dryer, removed Helen's smock, and with a little brush whisked Helen's shoulders. "Ask for Mickey another time," Mickey said. "That's me. Happy holidays."

Helen paid and walked out into the cold. The cold felt delicious on her head. "An honored guest," she said aloud. To live was like being an honored guest. The thought was outside her, large and calm. Then you were no longer an honored guest. The thought turned away from her and faded.

Her mother was watching television with the sound off when Helen got home. "That's a nice haircut," her mother said. "Now don't touch it, don't pull at it like that, for God's sake. It's pretty, you're pretty."

It was a ghastly haircut really. Helen's large ears seemed to float, no longer quite attached to her head. Lenore gazed quietly at the haircut.

"Mom," Helen said, "do you know there's a patron saint of television?"

Lenore thought this was hysterical.

"It's true," Helen said. "St. Clare."

Lenore wondered how long it would take for Helen's hair to grow back.

Later they were eating ice cream. They were both in their night-gowns. Helen was reading a Russian novel. She loved Russian novels. Everyone was so emotional, so tormented. They clutched their heads, they fainted, they swooned, they galloped around. The snow. The hoarfrost. What was hoarfrost, anyway? Russian snow had made Maine snow puny to Helen, meaningless.

"This ice cream tastes bad," her mother said. "It tastes like bleach or something." Some foul odor crept up her throat. Helen continued to read. What were they doing eating ice cream in the middle of winter, anyway? Lenore wondered. It was laziness. Something was creeping quietly all through her. She'd like to jump out of her skin, she would.

"You know," she said, "I believe that if Jesus walked into this house this minute, you wouldn't even raise your eyes."

Helen bit her lip and reluctantly put down the book. "Oh, Mom," she said.

"And maybe you'd be right. I bet he'd lack charisma. I'd bet my last dollar on it. The only reason he was charismatic before was that those people lived in a prerational time."

"Jesus isn't going to walk in here, Mom, come on," Helen said.

"Well, something is, something big. You'd better be ready for it." She was angry. "You've got the harder road," she said finally. "You've got to behave in a way you won't be afraid to remember. But you know what my road is? My road is the *new* road."

Like everyone, Lenore had a dread of being alone in the world, forgotten by God, overlooked. There were billions upon billions of people, after all. It wasn't out of the question.

"The new road?" Helen asked.

"Oh, there's nothing new about it," Lenore said, annoyed. She stroked her own face with her hands. She shouldn't be doing this to Helen, her little Helen. But Helen was so docile. She wasn't fighting this! You had to fight.

"Go back to what you were doing," Lenore said. "You were reading, you were concentrating. I wish I could concentrate. My mind just goes from one thing to another. Do you know what I was thinking of, did I ever tell you this? When I was still well, before I went to the doctor? I was in a department store. I was looking at a coat, and I must have stepped in front of this woman who was looking at coats, too . . . I had no idea . . . and she just started to stare at me. I was very aware of it, but I ignored it for a long time. I even moved away, but she followed me, still staring. Until I finally looked at her. She still stared, but now she was looking through me, *through* me, and she began talking to someone who was with her . . . she resumed some conversation with whoever was with her . . . all the while she was staring at me to show how insignificant I was, how utterly insignificant." Lenore leaned forward in her chair slightly toward Helen but then drew back, dizzy. "And I felt cursed. I felt as though she'd cursed me."

"What a creep," Helen said.

"I wonder where she picked that up," Lenore said. "I'd like to see her again. I'd like to murder her."

"I would, too," Helen said. "I really would."

"No, murder's too good for that one," Lenore said. "Murder's for the elect. I think of murder . . . sometimes I think . . . I wish someone would murder me. Out of the blue, without warning, for no reason. I wouldn't believe it was happening. It would be like not dying at all."

Helen sat in her nightgown. She felt cold. People had written books about death. No one knew what they were talking about, of course.

"Oh, I'm tired of talk," Lenore said. "I don't want to talk anymore. I'm tired of thinking about it. Why do we have to think about it all the time! One of those philosophers said that Death is the Big Thinker. It thinks the instant that was your life, right down to the bottom of it."

"Which one?" Helen asked.

"Which one what?"

"Which philosopher?"

"I can't recall," Lenore said. Sometimes Helen amused her, she really amused her.

Lenore didn't dream that night. She lay in bed panting. She wasn't ready, but there was nothing left to be done. The day before, the girl had washed and dried the bed sheets, and before she put them on again she had ironed them. Ironed them! They were just divine, still divine. It was the girl who loved to iron, she'd iron anything. Whatsername. Lenore got up and moved through the rooms of the house uncertainly. She could hardly keep her balance. Then she went down into the cellar. Her heart was pounding, it felt wet and small in her chest. She looked at the oil gauge on the furnace. It was a little over one quarter full. She wasn't going to order any more, she'd see what happened. She barely had the strength to get back upstairs. She turned on the little lamp that was on the breakfast table and sat in her chair there, waiting for Helen. She saw dog hairs on the floor, gathering together, drifting across the floor.

Helen felt sick, but she would drag herself to school. Her throat was sore. She heated up honey in a pan and sipped it with a spoon.

"I'm going to just stay put today," Lenore said.

"That's good, Mom, just take it easy. You've been doing too much." Helen's forehead shone with sweat. She buttoned up her sweater with trembling fingers.

"Do you have a cold?" her mother said. "Where did you get a cold? Stay home. The nurse who's coming this afternoon, she can take a look at you, write a prescription. Look at you, you're sweating. You've probably got a fever."

"I have a test today, Mom," Helen said.

"A test," Lenore marveled. She laughed. "Take them now, but don't take them later. They won't do you any good later."

Helen wiped at her face with a dishtowel.

"My God, a dishtowel!" Lenore said. "What's wrong with you? My God, what's to become of you?"

Startled, Helen dropped the towel. She expected to see her face on it almost. That was what had alarmed her mother so, Helen had wiped off her own face. Anyone knew better than to do that. She felt faint. She was thinking of the test, taking the test in a few hours. She took a fresh dishtowel from a drawer and put it on the rack.

Everyone at school knew Helen's mother was dying at home. Some of them thought it was cool. Others thought if she wasn't getting out clean, though, what was the point.

"What if I die today?" Lenore said suddenly. "I want you to be with me. My God, I don't want to be alone!"

"All this week there are tests," Helen said.

"Why don't I wait, then," Lenore said.

Tears ran down Helen's cheeks. She stood there stubbornly, looking at her mother.

"You were always able to turn them on and off," Lenore said, "just like a faucet. Crocodile tears." But with a moan she clutched her. Then she pulled away. "We have to wash these things," she said. "We can't just leave them in the sink." She seized the smudged glass she'd used to swallow her pills from and rinsed it in running water. She held it up to the window, and it slipped from her fingers and smashed against the sill. It was dirty and whole, she thought, and now it is clean and broken. This seemed to her profound.

"Don't touch it!" she screamed. "Leave it for Barbara — is that her name, Barbara?" Strangers, they were all strangers. "She never knows what to do when she comes."

"I have to go, Mom," Helen said.

"You do, of course you do," her mother said. She patted Helen's cheeks clumsily. "You're so hot, you're sick."

"I love you," Helen said.

"I love you, too," Lenore said. Then she watched her, walking down the street, toward the corner. It was growing lighter behind her. The mornings kept coming. She didn't like it.

On the bus, the driver said to Helen, "I lost my mother when I was your age. You've just got to hang in there."

Helen walked to the rear of the bus and sat down. She shut her eyes. A girl behind her snapped her gum and said,

"'Hang in there.' What an idiot."

The bus pounded down the snow-packed streets.

The girl with the gum had been the one who told Helen how ashes came back. Her uncle had died, and his ashes had come in a red shellacked box. It looked cheap, but it had cost fifty-five dollars and there was an envelope taped to the box with his name typed on it beneath a glassine window, as though he were being addressed to himself. This girl considered herself to be somewhat of an authority on the way these things were handled, for she had also lost a couple of godparents and knew how things were done as far south as Boston.

ANDREA BARRETT

The Behavior of the Hawkweeds

FROM THE MISSOURI REVIEW

FOR THIRTY YEARS, until he retired, my husband stood each fall in front of his sophomore genetics class and passed out copies of Gregor Mendel's famous paper on the hybridization of edible peas. This paper was a model of clarity, Richard told his students. It represented everything that science should be.

Richard paced in front of the chalkboard, speaking easily and without notes. Like the minor evolutionist Robert Chambers, he had been born hexadactylic; he was sensitive about his left hand, which was somewhat scarred from the childhood operation that had removed his extra finger. And so, although Richard gestured freely, he used only his right hand and kept his left in his pocket. From the back of the room, where I sat when I came each fall to hear him lecture, I could watch the students listen to him.

After he passed out the paper, Richard told the students his first, conventional version of Gregor Mendel's life. Mendel, he said, grew up in a tiny village in the northwestern corner of Moravia, which was then a part of the Hapsburg Empire and later became part of Czechoslovakia. When he was twenty-one, poor and desperate for further education, he entered the Augustinian monastery in the capital city of Brunn, which is now called Brno. He studied science and later taught at a local high school. In 1856, at the age of thirty-four, he began his experiments in the hybridization of the edible pea. For his laboratory he used a little strip of garden adjoining the monastery wall.

Over the next eight years Mendel performed hundreds of experiments on thousands of plants, tracing the ways in which characteristics were passed through generations. Tall and short plants, with white or violet flowers; peas that were wrinkled or smooth; pods that were arched or constricted around the seeds. He kept meticulous records of his hybridizations in order to write the paper the students now held in their hands. On a clear, cold evening in 1865, he read the first part of this paper to his fellow members of the Brunn Society for the Study of Natural Science. About forty men were present, a few professional scientists and many serious amateurs. Mendel read to them for an hour, describing his experiments and demonstrating the invariable ratios with which traits appeared in his hybrids. A month later, at the Society's next meeting, he presented the theory he'd formulated to account for his results.

Right there, my husband said, right in that small, crowded room, the science of genetics was born. Mendel knew nothing of genes or chromosomes or DNA, but he'd discovered the principles that made the search for those things possible.

"Was there applause?" Richard always asked at this point. "Was there a great outcry of approval or even a mutter of disagreement?" A rhetorical question; the students knew better than to answer.

"There was not. The minutes of that meeting show that no questions were asked and no discussion took place. Not one person in that room understood the significance of what Mendel had presented. A year later, when the paper was published, no one noticed it."

The students looked down at their papers and Richard finished his story quickly, describing how Mendel went back to his monastery and busied himself with other things. For a while he continued to teach and do other experiments; he raised grapes and fruit trees and all kinds of flowers, and he kept bees. Eventually he was elected abbot of his monastery, and from that time until his death he was occupied with his administrative duties. Only in 1900 was his lost paper rediscovered and his work appreciated by a new generation of scientists.

When Richard reached this point, he would look toward the back of the room and catch my eye and smile. He knew that I knew what was in store for the students at the end of the semester. After they'd read the paper and survived the labs where fruit flies bred in tubes and displayed the principles of Mendelian inheritance, Richard would tell them the other Mendel story. The one I told him, in which Mendel is led astray by a condescending fellow scientist and the behavior of the hawkweeds. The one in which science is not just appreciated, but bent by loneliness and longing.

I had a reason for showing up in that classroom each fall, and it was not just that I was so dutiful, so wifely. Richard was not the one who introduced Mendel into my life.

When I was a girl, during the early years of the Depression, my grandfather, Anton Vaculik, worked at a nursery in Niskayuna, not far from where Richard and I still live in Schenectady. This was not the only job my grandfather had ever had, but it was the one he liked the best. He had left Moravia in 1891 and traveled to the city of Bremen with his pregnant wife. From there he'd taken a boat to New York and then another to Albany. He'd meant to journey on to one of the large Czech settlements in Minnesota or Wisconsin, but when my mother was born six weeks early he settled his family here instead. A few other Czech families lived in the area, and one of those settlers hired my grandfather to work in a small factory that made mother-of-pearl buttons for women's blouses.

Later, after he learned more English, he found the nursery job that he liked so much. He worked there for thirty years; he was so skilled at propagating plants and grafting trees that his employers kept him on part time long past the age when he should have retired. Everyone at the nursery called him Tony, which sounded appropriately American. I called him Tati, a corruption of *tatínek*, which is Czech for "dad" and was what my mother called him. I was named Antonia after him.

We were never hungry when I was young, we were better off than many, but our daily life was a web of small economies. My mother took in sewing, making over jackets and mending pants; when she ironed she saved the flat pieces for last, to be pressed while the iron was cooling and the electricity was off. My father's wages had been cut at the GE plant and my older brothers tried to help by scrounging for odd jobs. I was the only idle member of the family, and so on weekends and during the summer my mother sometimes let me go with Tati. I loved it when Tati put me to work.

At the nursery there were fields full of fruit trees, peach and apple and pear, and long, low glass houses full of seedlings. I followed Tati around and helped him as he transplanted plants or worked with his sharp, curved knife and his grafting wax. I sat next to him on a tall wooden stool, holding his forceps or the jar of methylated spirits as he emasculated flowers. While we worked he talked, which is how I learned about his early days in America.

The only time Tati frowned and went silent was when his new boss appeared. Sheldon Hardy, the old chief horticulturalist, had been our friend; he was Tati's age and had worked side by side with Tati for years, cutting scions and whip-grafting fruit trees. But in 1931, the year I was ten, Mr. Hardy had a heart attack and went to live with his daughter in Ithaca. Otto Leiniger descended on us shortly after that, spoiling part of our pleasure every day.

Leiniger must have been in his late fifties. He lost no time telling Tati that he had a master's degree from a university out west, and it was clear from his white lab coat and the books in his office that he thought of himself as a scholar. In his office he sat at a big oak desk, making out lists of tasks for Tati with a fancy pen left over from better days; once he had been the director of an arboretum. He tacked the lists to the propagating benches, where they curled like shavings of wood from the damp, and when we were deep in work he'd drift into the glass house and hover over us. He didn't complain about my presence, but he treated Tati like a common laborer. One day he caught me alone in a greenhouse filled with small begonias we'd grown from cuttings.

Tati had fitted a misting rose to a pot small enough for me to handle, and I was watering the tiny plants. It was very warm beneath the glass roof. I was wearing shorts and an old white shirt of Tati's, with nothing beneath it but my damp skin; I was only ten. There were benches against the two side walls and another, narrower, propagating bench running down the center of the house. On one side of this narrow bench I stood on an overturned crate to increase my reach, bending to mist the plants on the far side. When I looked up Leiniger was standing across from me. His face was round and heavy, with dark pouches beneath his eyes.

"You're a good little helper," he said. "You help your grandpapa out." Tati was in the greenhouse next door, examining a new crop of fuchsias.

"I like it here," I told Leiniger. The plants beneath my hands were Rex begonias, grown not for their flowers but for their showy, ruffled leaves. I had helped Tati pin the mother leaves to the moist sand and then transplant the babies that rooted from the ribs.

Leiniger pointed at the row of begonias closest to him, farthest from me. "These seem a little dry," he said. "Over here."

I didn't want to walk around the bench and stand by his side. "You can reach," he said. "Just lean over a little farther."

I stood up on my toes and bent across the bench, stretching the watering pot to reach those farthest plants. Leiniger flushed. "That's right," he said thickly. "Lean toward me."

Tati's old white shirt gaped at the neck and fell away from my body when I bent over. I stretched out my arm and misted the begonias. When I straightened I saw that Leiniger's face was red and that he was pressed against the wooden bench.

"Here," he said, and he made a shaky gesture at another group of plants to the right of him. "These here, these are also very dry."

I was afraid of him, and yet I also wanted to do my job and feared that any sloppiness on my part might get Tati in trouble. I leaned over once again, the watering pot in my hand. This time Leiniger reached for my forearm with his thick fingers. "Not those," he said, steering my hand closer to the edge of the bench, which he was still pressed against. "These."

Just as the pot brushed the front of his lab coat, Tati walked in. I can imagine, now, what that scene must have looked like to him. Me bent over that narrow bench, my toes barely touching the crate and the white shirt hanging down like a sheet to the young begonias below; Leiniger red-faced, sweating, grinding into the wooden bench. And his hand, that guilty hand, forcing me toward him. I dropped the pot when I heard Tati shout my name.

Who can say what Leiniger had in mind? To Tati it must have looked as though Leiniger was dragging me across the begonias to him. But Leiniger was just a lonely old man and it seems possible to me, now, that he wanted only the view down my shirt and that one small contact with the skin of my inner arm. Had Tati not entered the greenhouse just then, nothing more might have happened.

But Tati saw the worst in what was there. He saw that fat hand on my arm and those eyes fixed on my childish chest. He had a small pruning knife in his hand. When he called my name and I dropped the pot, Leiniger clamped down on my arm. As I was tearing myself away, Tati flew over and jabbed his knife into the back of Leiniger's hand.

"Nemecky!" he shouted. *"Prase!"*

Leiniger screamed and stumbled backward. Behind him was the concrete block on which I stood to water the hanging plants, and that block caught Leiniger below the knees. He went down slowly, heavily, one hand clutching the wound on the other and a look of disbelief on his face. Tati was already reaching out to catch him when Leiniger cracked his head against a heating pipe.

But of course this is not what I told Richard. When we met, just after the war, I was working at the GE plant that had once employed my father and Richard was finishing his thesis. After my father died I had dropped out of junior college; Richard had interrupted his Ph.D. program to join the Navy, where he'd worked for three years doing research on tropical fungi. We both had a sense of urgency and a need to make up for lost time. During our brief courtship, I told Richard only the things that I thought would make him love me.

On our second date, over coffee and Italian pastries, I told Richard that my grandfather had taught me a little about plant breeding when I was young, and that I was fascinated by genetics. "Tati lived with us for a while, when I was a girl," I said. "He used to take me for walks through the empty fields of Niskayuna and tell me about Gregor Mendel. I still know a pistil from a stamen."

"Mendel's my hero," Richard said. "He's always been my ideal of what a scientist should be. It's not so often I meet a woman familiar with his work."

"I know a lot about him," I said. "What Tati told me — you'd be surprised." I didn't say that Tati and I had talked about Mendel because we couldn't stand to talk about what we'd both lost.

Tati slept in my room during the months before the trial; he was released on bail on the condition that he leave his small house in Rensselaer and stay with us. I slept on the couch in the living room and Leiniger lay unconscious in the Schenectady hospital. We were quiet, Tati and I. No one seemed to want to talk to us. My brothers stayed away from the house as much as possible and my father worked long hours. My mother was around, but she was so upset by what had happened that she could hardly speak to either Tati or myself. The most she could manage to do was to take me aside, a few days after Tati's arrival, and say, "What happened to Leiniger wasn't your fault. It's an old-country thing, what's between those men."

She made me sit with her on the porch, where she was turning mushrooms she'd gathered in the woods and laid out to dry on screens. Red, yellow, violet, buff. Some pieces were drier than others. While she spoke she moved from screen to screen, turning the delicate fragments.

"What country?" I said. "What are you talking about?"

"Tati is Czech," my mother said. "Like me. Mr. Leiniger's family is German, from a part of Moravia where only Germans live. Tati and Mr. Leiniger don't like each other because of things that happened in the Czech lands a long time ago."

"Am I Czech, then?" I said. "This happened because I am Czech?"

"You're American," my mother said. "American first. But Tati hates Germans. He and Leiniger would have found some way to quarrel even if you hadn't been there." She told me a little about the history of Moravia, enough to help me understand how long the Czechs and Germans had been quarreling. And she told me how thrilled Tati had been during the First World War, when the Czech and Slovak immigrants in America had banded together to contribute funds to help in the formation of an independent Czechoslovak state. When she was a girl, she said, Tati and her mother had argued over the donations Tati made and the meetings he attended.

But none of this seemed important to me. In the greenhouse, a policeman had asked Tati what had happened, and Tati had said, "I stuck his hand with my knife. But the rest was an accident — he tripped over that block and fell."

"Why?" the policeman had said. "Why did you do that?"

"My granddaughter," Tati had said. "He was . . . feeling her."

The policeman had tipped my chin up with his hand and looked hard at me. "Is that right?" he'd asked. And I had nodded dumbly, feeling both very guilty and very important. Now my mother was telling me that I was of no consequence.

"Am *I* supposed to hate Germans?" I asked.

A few years later, when Tati was dead and I was in high school and Hitler had dismembered Czechoslovakia, my mother would become loudly anti-German. But now all she said was, "No. Mr. Leiniger shouldn't have bothered you, but he's only one man. It's not right to hate everyone with a German last name."

"Is that what Tati does?"

"Sometimes."

I told my mother what Tati had shouted at Leiniger, repeating

the foreign sounds as best as I could. My mother blushed. "*Nemecky*
means 'German,'" she said reluctantly. "*Prase* means 'pig.' You must
never tell anyone you heard your grandfather say such things."

I did not discuss this conversation with Tati. All during that fall,
but especially after Leiniger died, I'd come home from school to
find Tati waiting for me on the porch, his knobby walking stick in
his hands and his cap on his head. He wanted to walk, he was
desperate to walk. My mother wouldn't let him leave the house
alone but she seldom found the time to go out with him; my brothers could not be bothered. And so Tati waited for me each afternoon like a restless dog.

While we walked in the fields and woods behind our house, we
did not talk about what had happened in the greenhouse. Instead,
Tati named the ferns and mosses and flowers we passed. He showed
me the hawkweeds — Canada hawkweed, spotted hawkweed, poor-
Robin's hawkweed. Orange hawkweed, also called devil's paint-
brush, creeping into abandoned fields. The plants had long stems,
rosettes of leaves at the base, small flowerheads that resembled
dandelions. Once Tati opened my eyes to them I realized they were
everywhere.

"*Hieracium,*" Tati said. "That is their real name. It comes from the
Greek word for hawk. The juice from the stem is supposed to make
your vision very sharp." They were weeds, he said: extremely hardy.
They grew wherever the soil was too poor to support other plants.
They were related to asters and daisies and dahlias — all plants
I'd seen growing at the nursery — but also to thistles and bur-
docks. I should remember them, he said. They were important.
With his own eyes he had watched the hawkweeds ruin Gregor
Mendel's life.

Even now this seems impossible: how could I have known someone of an age to have known Mendel? And yet it was true: Tati had
grown up on the outskirts of Brno, the city where Mendel spent
most of his life. In 1866, when they first met, there was cholera in
Brno and Prussian soldiers were passing through after the brief and
nasty war. Tati was ten then, and those things didn't interest him.
He had scaled the white walls of the Augustinian monastery of St.
Thomas one afternoon, for a lark. As he'd straddled the wall he'd
seen a plump, short-legged man with glasses looking up at him.

"He looked like my mother's uncle," Tati said. "A little bit."

Mendel had held out a hand and helped Tati jump down from

the wall. Around him were fruit trees and wild vines; in the distance he saw a clocktower and a long, low building. Where Tati had landed, just where his feet touched ground, there were peas. Not the thousands of plants that would have been there at the height of Mendel's investigations, but still hundreds of plants clinging to sticks and stretched strings.

The place was magical, Tati said. Mendel showed him the tame fox he tied up during the day but allowed to run free at night, the hedgehogs and the hamsters and the mice he kept, the beehives and the cages full of birds. The two of them, the boy and the middle-aged man, made friends. Mendel taught Tati most of his horticultural secrets and later he was responsible for getting him a scholarship to the school where he taught. But Tati said that the first year of their friendship, before the hawkweed experiments, was the best. He and Mendel, side by side, had opened pea flowers and transferred pollen with a camel-hair brush.

On the last day of 1866, Mendel wrote his first letter to Carl Nägeli of Munich, a powerful and well-known botanist known to be interested in hybridization. He sent a copy of his pea paper along with the letter, hoping Nägeli might help it find the recognition it deserved. But he also, in his letter, mentioned that he had started a few experiments with hawkweeds, which he hoped would confirm his results with peas.

Nägeli was an expert on the hawkweeds, and Tati believed that Mendel had only mentioned them to pique Nägeli's interest in his work. Nägeli didn't reply for several months, and when he finally wrote back he said almost nothing about the peas. But he was working on the hawkweeds himself, and he proposed that Mendel turn his experimental skills to them. Mendel, desperate for recognition, ceased to write about his peas and concentrated on the hawkweeds instead.

"Oh, that Nägeli!" Tati said. "Month after month, year after year, I watched Mendel writing his long, patient letters and getting no answer or slow answers or answers off the point. Whenever Nägeli wrote to Mendel, it was always about the hawkweeds. Later, when I learned why Mendel's experiments with them hadn't worked, I wanted to cry."

The experiments that had given such tidy results with peas gave nothing but chaos with hawkweeds, which were very difficult to hybridize. Experiment after experiment failed; years of work were wasted. The inexplicable behavior of the hawkweeds destroyed Mendel's belief that the laws of heredity he'd worked out with peas would be universally valid. By 1873, Mendel had given up completely. The hawkweeds, and Nägeli behind them, had convinced him that his work was useless.

It was bad luck, Tati said. Bad luck in choosing Nägeli to help him, and letting Nägeli steer him toward the hawkweeds. Mendel's experimental technique was fine, and his laws of heredity were perfectly true. He could not have known — no one knew for years — that his hawkweeds didn't hybridize in rational ways because they frequently formed seeds without fertilization. "Parthenogenesis," Tati told me — a huge, knobby word that I could hardly get my mouth around. Still, it sounds to me like a disease. "The plants grown from seeds formed this way are exact copies of the mother plant, just like the begonias we make from leaf cuttings."

Mendel gave up on science and spent his last years, after he was elected abbot, struggling with the government over taxes levied on his monastery. He quarreled with his fellow monks; he grew bitter and isolated. Some of the monks believed he had gone insane. In his quarters he smoked heavy cigars and gazed at the ceiling, which he'd had painted with scenes of saints and fruit trees, beehives and scientific equipment. When Tati came to visit him, his conversation wandered.

Mendel died in January 1884, on the night of Epiphany, confused about the value of his scientific work. That same year, long after their correspondence had ceased, Nägeli published an enormous book summarizing all his years of work. Although many of his opinions and observations seemed to echo Mendel's work with peas, Nägeli made no mention of Mendel or his paper.

That was the story I told Richard. Torn from its context, stripped of the reasons why it was told, it became a story about the beginnings of Richard's discipline. I knew that Richard would have paid money to hear it, but I gave it to him as a gift.

"And your grandfather saw all that?" he said. This was later on in our courtship; we were sitting on a riverbank, drinking Manhattans that Richard had mixed and enjoying the cold spiced beef and marinated vegetables and lemon tart I had brought in a basket. Richard liked my cooking quite a bit. He liked me too, but appar-

ently not enough; I was longing for him to propose but he still
hadn't said a word. "Your grandfather saw the letters," he said. "He
watched Mendel assembling data for Nägeli. That's remarkable.
That's extraordinary. I can't believe the things you know."

There was more, I hinted. What else did I have to offer him? Now
it seems to me that I had almost everything: youth and health and
an affectionate temperament; the desire to make a family. But then I
was more impressed than I should have been by Richard's education.

"More?" he said.

"There are some papers," I said. "That Tati left behind."

Of course I was not allowed in the courtroom, I was much too
young. After Leiniger died, the date of the trial was moved forward.
I never saw Tati sitting next to the lawyer my father had hired for
him; I never saw a judge or a jury and never learned whether my
testimony might have helped Tati. I never even learned whether, in
that long-ago time, the court would have accepted the testimony
of a child, because Tati died on the evening before the first day of
the trial.

He had a stroke, my mother said. In the night she heard a loud,
garbled cry and when she ran into the room that had once been
mine she found Tati tipped over in bed, with his head hanging
down and his face dark and swollen. Afterwards, after the funeral,
when I came home from school I no longer went on walks through
the woods and fields. I did my homework at the kitchen table and
then I helped my mother around the house. On weekends I no
longer went to the nursery.

Because there had been no trial, no one in town learned of my
role in Leiniger's death. There had been a quarrel between two old
men, people thought, and then an accident. No one blamed me
or my family. I was able to go through school without people pointing or whispering. I put Tati out of my mind, and with him the
nursery and Leiniger, Mendel and Nägeli and the behavior of the
hawkweeds. When the war came I refused to listen to my mother's
rantings and ravings. After my father died she went to live with one
of my married brothers, and I went off on my own. I loved working
in the factory; I felt very independent.

Not until the war was over and I met Richard did I dredge up the
hawkweed story. Richard's family had been in America for genera-

tions and seemed to have no history; that was one of the things that drew me to him. But after our picnic on the riverbank I knew for sure that part of what drew him to me was the way I was linked so closely to other times and places. I gave Richard the yellowed sheets of paper that Tati had left in an envelope for me.

This is a draft of one of Mendel's letters to Nägeli, Tati had written, on a note attached to the manuscript. *He showed it to me once, when he was feeling sad. Later he gave it to me. I want you to have it.*

Richard's voice trembled when he read that note out loud. He turned the pages of Mendel's letter slowly, here and there reading a line to me. The letter was an early one, or perhaps even the first. It was all about peas.

Richard said, "I can't believe I'm holding this in my hand."

"I could give it to you," I said. In my mind this seemed perfectly reasonable. Mendel had given the letter to Tati, the sole friend of his last days; then Tati had passed it to me, when he was no longer around to protect me himself. Now it seemed right that I should give it to the man I wanted to marry.

"To me?" Richard said. "You would give it to me?"

"Someone who appreciates it should have it."

Richard cherished Tati's letter like a jewel. We married, we moved to Schenectady, Richard got a good job at the college, and we had our two daughters. During each of my pregnancies Richard worried that our children might inherit his hexadactyly, but Annie and Joan were both born with regulation fingers and toes. I stayed home with them, first in the apartment in Union Street and then later, after Richard's promotion, in the handsome old house on campus that the college rented to us. Richard wrote papers and served on committees; I gave monthly dinners for the departmental faculty, weekly coffee hours for favored students, picnics for alumni on homecoming weekends. I managed that sort of thing rather well: it was a job, if an unpaid one, and it was expected of me.

Eventually our daughters grew up and moved away. And then, when I was nearly fifty, after Richard had been tenured and won his awards and grown almost unbearably self-satisfied, there came a time when the world went gray for me for the better part of a year.

I still can't explain what happened to me then. My doctor said it was hormones, the beginning of my change of life. My daughters, newly involved with the women's movement, said my years as a housewife had stifled me and that I needed a career of my own. Annie, our oldest, hemmed and hawed and finally asked me if her father and I were still sharing a bed; I said we were but didn't have the heart to tell her that all we did was share it. Richard said I needed more exercise and prescribed daily walks in the college gardens, which were full of exotic specimen trees from every corner of the earth.

He was self-absorbed, but not impossible; he hated to see me suffer. And I suppose he also wanted back the wife who for years had managed his household so well. But I could no longer manage anything. All I knew was that I felt old, and that everything had lost its savor. I lay in the window seat in our bedroom with an afghan over my legs, watching the students mass and swirl and separate in the quad in front of the library.

This was 1970, when the students seemed to change overnight from pleasant boys into uncouth and hairy men. Every week brought a new protest. Chants and marches and demonstrations; bedsheets hanging like banners from the dormitory windows. The boys who used to come to our house for tea dressed in blue blazers and neatly pressed pants now wore vests with dangling fringes and jeans with holes in them. And when I went to Richard's genetics class that fall, to listen to his first Mendel lecture, I saw that the students gazed out the window while he spoke or tipped back in their chairs with their feet on the desks: openly bored, insubordinate. A girl encased in sheets of straight blond hair — there were girls in class, the college had started admitting them — interrupted Richard midsentence and said, "But what's the *relevance* of this? Science confined to the hands of the technocracy produces nothing but destruction."

Richard didn't answer her, but he hurried through the rest of his lecture and left the room without looking at me. That year, he didn't give his other Mendel lecture. The students had refused to do most of the labs; there was no reason, they said, why harmless fruit flies should be condemned to death just to prove a theory that everyone already acknowledged as true. Richard said they didn't deserve to hear about the hawkweeds. They were so dirty, so destructive, that he feared for the safety of Mendel's precious letter.

I was relieved, although I didn't say that; I had no urge to leave my perch on the window seat and no desire to hear Richard repeat that story again. It seemed to me then that he told it badly. He muddled the dates, compressed the years, identified himself too closely with Mendel and painted Nägeli as too black a villain. By then I knew that he liked to think of himself as another Mendel, unappreciated and misunderstood. To me he looked more like another Nägeli. I had seen him be less than generous to younger scientists struggling to establish themselves. I had watched him pick, as each year's favored student, not the brightest or most original but the most agreeable and flattering.

That year all the students seemed to mutate, and so there was no favorite student, no obsequious well-dressed boy to join us for Sunday dinner or cocktails after the Wednesday seminars. As I lay in my window seat, idly addressing envelopes and stuffing them with reprints of Richard's papers, I hardly noticed that the house was emptier than usual. But at night, when I couldn't sleep, I rose from Richard's side and went down to the couch in the living room, where I lay midway between dream and panic. I heard Tati's voice then, telling me about Mendel. I heard Mendel, frantic over those hawkweeds, trying out draft after draft of his letters on the ears of an attentive little boy who sat in a garden next to a fox. *Highly esteemed sir, your honor. I beg you to allow me to submit for your kind consideration the results of these experiments.* How humble Mendel had been in his address, and yet how sure of his science. How kind he had been to Tati.

Some nights I grew very confused. Mendel and Nägeli, Mendel and Tati; Tati and Leiniger, Tati and me. Pairs of men who hated each other and pairs of friends passing papers. A boy I saw pruning shrubs in the college garden turned into a childish Tati, leaping over a white wall. During a nap I dreamed of Leiniger's wife. I had seen her only once; she had come to Tati's funeral. She stood in the back of the church in a brown dress flecked with small white leaves, and when my family left after the service she turned her face from us.

That June, after graduation, Sebastian Dunitz came to us from his lab in Frankfurt. He and Richard had been corresponding and they shared common research interests; Richard had arranged for Sebastian to visit the college for a year, working with Richard for the summer on a joint research project and then, during the fall and spring semesters, as a teaching assistant in the departmental laboratories. He stayed with us, in Annie's old bedroom, but he was little trouble. He did his own laundry and cooked his own meals except when we asked him to join us.

Richard took to Sebastian right away. He was young, bright, very well educated; although speciation and evolutionary relationships interested him more than the classical Mendelian genetics Richard taught, his manner toward Richard was clearly deferential. Within a month of his arrival, Richard was telling me how, with a bit of luck, a permanent position might open up for his new protégé. Within a month of his arrival, I was up and about, dressed in bright colors, busy cleaning the house from basement to attic and working in the garden. It was nice to have some company around.

Richard invited Sebastian to a picnic dinner with us on the evening of the Fourth of July. This was something we'd done every year when the girls were growing up; we'd let the custom lapse but Richard thought Sebastian might enjoy it. I fried chicken in the morning, before the worst heat of the day; I dressed tomatoes with vinegar and olive oil and chopped fresh basil and I made potato salad and a chocolate cake. When dusk fell, Richard and I gathered a blanket and the picnic basket and our foreign guest and walked to the top of a rounded hill not far from the college grounds. In the distance, we could hear the band that preceded the fireworks.

"This is wonderful," Sebastian said. "Wonderful food, a wonderful night. You have both been very kind to me."

Richard had set a candle in a hurricane lamp in the center of our blanket, and in the dim light Sebastian's hair gleamed like a helmet. We all drank a lot of the sweet white wine that Sebastian had brought as his offering. Richard lay back on his elbows and cleared his throat, surprising me when he spoke.

"Did you know," he said to Sebastian, "that I have an actual draft of a letter that Gregor Mendel wrote to the botanist Nägeli? My dear Antonia gave it to me."

Sebastian looked from me to Richard and back. "Where did you get such a thing?" he asked. "How . . . ?"

Richard began to talk, but I couldn't bear to listen to him tell that story badly one more time. "My grandfather gave it to me," I said, interrupting Richard. "He knew Mendel when he was a little boy." And without giving Richard a chance to say another word, without even looking at the hurt and puzzlement I knew must be on his face, I told Sebastian all about the behavior of the hawkweeds. I told the

story slowly, fully, without skipping any parts. In the gathering darkness I moved my hands and did my best to make Sebastian see the
wall and the clocktower and the gardens and the hives, the specta-
cles on Mendel's face and Tati's bare feet. And when I was done,
when my words hung in the air and Sebastian murmured apprecia-
tively, I did something I'd never done before, because Richard had
never thought to ask the question Sebastian asked.

"How did your grandfather come to tell you that?" he said. "It is
perhaps an unusual story to tell a little girl."

"It gave us something to talk about," I said. "We spent a lot of
time together, the fall that I was ten. He had killed a man — accidentally, but still the man was dead. He lived with us while we were
waiting for the trial."

Overhead, the first fireworks opened into blossoms of red and
gold and green. "Antonia," Richard said, but he caught himself. In
front of Sebastian he would not admit that this was something his
wife of twenty-five years had never told him before. In the light of
the white cascading fountain above us I could see him staring at
me, but all he said was, "An amazing story, isn't it? I used to tell it to
my genetics students every year, but this fall everything was so
deranged — I left it out, I knew they wouldn't appreciate it."

"Things are different," Sebastian said. "The world is changing."
He did not ask me how it was that my grandfather had killed a man.

The pace and intensity of the fireworks increased, until all of
them seemed to be exploding at once; then there was one final
crash and then silence and darkness. I had been rude, I knew. I had
deprived Richard of one of his great pleasures simply for the sake of
hearing that story told well once.

We gathered up our blanket and basket and walked home quietly. The house was dark and empty. In the living room I turned on
a single light and then went to the kitchen to make coffee; when I
came in with the tray the men were talking quietly about their work.
"I believe what we have here is a *Rassenkreis*," Sebastian said, and he
turned to include me in the conversation. In his short time with us,
he had always paid me the compliment of assuming I understood
his and Richard's work. "A German word," he said. "It means 'race-
circle' — it is what we call it when a species spread over a large area
is broken into a chain of subspecies, each of which differs slightly
from its neighbors. The neighboring subspecies can interbreed,

172 The Behavior of the Hawkweeds

but the subspecies at the two ends of the chain may be so different that they cannot. In the population that Richard and I are examining. . . ."

"I am very tired," Richard said abruptly. "If you'll excuse me, I think I'll go up to bed."

"No coffee?" I said.

He looked at a spot just beyond my shoulder, as he always did when he was upset. "No," he said. "Are you coming?"

"Soon," I said.

And then, in that dim room, Sebastian came and sat in the chair right next to mine. "Is Richard well?" he said. "Is something wrong?"

"He's fine. Only tired. He's been working hard."

"That was a lovely story you told. When I was a boy, at university, our teachers did not talk about Nägeli, except to dismiss him as a Lamarckian. They would skip from Mendel's paper on the peas to its rediscovery, later. Nägeli's student, Correns, and Hugo de Vries — do you know about the evening primroses and de Vries?"

I shook my head. We sat at the dark end of the living room, near the stairs and away from the windows. Still, occasionally, came the sound of a renegade firecracker.

"No? You will like this."

But before he could tell me his anecdote I leaned toward him and rested my hand on his forearm. His skin was as smooth as a flower. "Don't tell me any more science," I said. "Tell me about yourself."

There was a pause. Then Sebastian pulled his arm away abruptly and stood up. "Please," he said. "You're an attractive woman, still. And I am flattered. But it's quite impossible, anything between us." His accent, usually almost imperceptible, thickened with those words.

I was grateful for the darkness that hid my flush. "You misunderstood," I said. "I didn't mean . . ."

"Don't be embarrassed," he said. "I've seen the way you watch me when you think I am not looking. I appreciate it."

A word came back to me, a word I thought I'd forgotten. "*Prase,*" I muttered.

"What?" he said. Then I heard a noise on the stairs behind me, and a hand fell on my shoulder. I reached up and felt the knob where Richard's extra finger had once been.

"Antonia," Richard said. His voice was very gentle. "It's so late —

won't you come up to bed?" He did not say a word to Sebastian; upstairs, in our quiet room, he neither accused me of anything nor pressed me to explain the mysterious comment I'd made about my grandfather. I don't know what he said later to Sebastian, or how he arranged things with the Dean. But two days later Sebastian moved into an empty dormitory room, and before the end of the summer he was gone.

Nemecky, prase; secret words. I have forgotten almost all the rest of Tati's language, and both he and Leiniger have been dead for sixty years. Sebastian Dunitz is back in Frankfurt, where he has grown very famous. The students study molecules now, spinning models across their computer screens and splicing the genes of one creature into those of another. The science of genetics is utterly changed and Richard has been forgotten by everyone. Sometimes I wonder where we have misplaced our lives.

Of course Richard no longer teaches. The college retired him when he turned sixty-five, despite his protests. Now they trot him out for dedications and graduations and departmental celebrations, along with the other emeritus professors who haunt the library and the halls. Without his class, he has no audience for his treasured stories. Instead he corners people at the dim, sad ends of parties when he's had too much to drink. Young instructors, too worried about their jobs to risk being impolite, turn their ears to Richard like flowers. He keeps them in place with a knobby hand on a sleeve or knee as he talks.

When I finally told him what had happened to Tati, I didn't really tell him anything. Two old men had quarreled, I said. An immigrant and an immigrant's son, arguing over some plants. But Tati and Leiniger, Richard decided, were Mendel and Nägeli all over again; surely Tati identified with Mendel and cast Leiniger as another Nägeli? Although he still doesn't know of my role in the accident, somehow the equation he's made between these pairs of men allows him to tell his tale with more sympathy, more balance. As he talks he looks across the room and smiles at me. I nod and smile back at him, thinking of Annie, whose first son was born with six toes on each foot.

Sebastian sent me a letter the summer after he left us, in which he finished the story I'd interrupted on that Fourth of July. The young Dutch botanist Hugo de Vries, he wrote, spent his summers searching the countryside for new species. One day, near Hilversum, he came to an abandoned potato field glowing strangely in the sun. The great evening primrose had been cultivated in a small bed in a nearby park; the plants had run wild and escaped into the field, where they formed a jungle as high as a man. From 1886 through 1888, de Vries made thousands of hybridization experiments with them, tracing the persistence of mutations. During his search for a way to explain his results, he uncovered Mendel's paper and found that Mendel had anticipated all his theories. Peas and primroses, primroses and peas, passing their traits serenely through generations.

I still have this letter, as Richard still has Mendel's. I wonder, sometimes, what Tati would have thought of all this. Not the story about Hugo de Vries, which he probably knew, but the way it came to me in a blue airmail envelope, from a scientist who meant to be kind. I think of Tati when I imagine Sebastian composing his answer to me.

Because it was an answer, of sorts; in the months after he left I mailed him several letters. They were, on the surface, about Mendel and Tati, all I recalled of their friendship. But I'm sure Sebastian read them for what they were. In 1906, Sebastian wrote, after Mendel's work was finally recognized, a small museum was opened in the Augustinian monastery. Sebastian visited it, when he passed through Brno on a family holiday.

"I could find no trace of your Tati," he wrote. "But the wall is still here, and you can see where the garden was. It's a lovely place. Perhaps you should visit someday."

ANDREW COZINE

Hand Jive

FROM THE IOWA REVIEW

I WALK NORTH on Campbell Avenue away from Jefferson Park
Elementary School and Mrs. Hansen's third-grade class. I am walking the half mile to Grandma's house. Heat waves shimmer up off
the four lanes of asphalt to my left. Off on my right, toward the
park, the steady, buzzing hum of cicadas electrifies the afternoon. It
is a hundred degrees out, give or take, unusual but not too unusual
for the middle of May in Tucson, Arizona. I am taking care not to
step on the cracks in the sidewalk. When I step on a crack, I do the
thing: I count out loud from one to five, over and over, until it is
safe to stop. *One, two, three, four, five . . . one, two, three, four, five.* The
hum of the cicadas is drowned out by the engine noise from a wave
of cars traveling southbound; the cars pass, and the hum picks up
again right where it left off. The white heat of the sun burns into my
skin. I walk past the Catalina movie theater and into the shopping
center parking lot just as a group of older kids comes out of the
Walgreens. I don't know these kids, I've only seen them around on
the playground. They are laughing and shouting, making me nervous. I'm afraid they'll try to make me cry. The heat and the buzzing
and the shouts of these kids makes it hard to concentrate. I know
I'll slip up. I slip up. *One, two, three, four, five . . .*

I wait at the stoplight at Grant Road, hoping the other kids won't
come my way. I don't want to wait with them. I don't know what
they'll do. If they did try anything, my dad would do something
about it. He would call their parents or call the school or go and
have a talk with somebody. He would protect me. But what if something happened to Dad? I see my father spread out on the ground,

red-faced, an oily, bloody wound spreading out across his chest. Eyes glazed, mouth wide open. Dead. That's a bad thing to think you're a bad boy what if something really happened because you thought a thing like that? I do the thing, the other thing, to stop it from coming true: *I remember my E.S.P. I remember my E.S.P. I remember my E.S.P. I remember my E.S.P. I remember my E.S.P.*

The kids go off a different way. I am all alone at the curb, watching and waiting, still not sure after dozens of crossings when I'm allowed to go. The cars hiss and swish as they pass. Radios blare from open windows. I wait for five minutes, ten minutes. Sweat trickles down my cheeks and my clothes are sticky and wet against my skin. I am thinking, When I get across the street I will get a Baskin Robbins. When I get across the street I will go to The Book Stop and buy a book by the man who wrote *James and the Giant Peach.* When I get across the street I will go to Lown's Costumes and get some snap pops or a plastic dog barf, but I can't spend my whole allowance. I stare at the cracks in the sidewalk in front of me. The white glare begins to blur and the world gets foggy at the edges. *When I get, but I can't, I can't, what did I forget, what what did I oh no oh no what did I forget what did I forget I'm bad I'm bad what now what now oh no oh no oh no.* The pavement bucks up under my feet; I am swaying side to side. My heart is pushing up against my throat *heart attack heart attack like Grandpa* and my throat gets tight like my heart is trapped there blocking the air *I can't breathe I can't breathe help help I can't . . . help. . . .* The cars are close, too close, there's a horn honking and my feet are tripping forward *what did I do what did I do?* I know I did something, something very very bad. I know I'll pay for it, they'll say, What's wrong with you, William? My body is stopping short, lurching back the other way. I make a list: one, you didn't leave your sister at school, Grandma picked her up early; two, you weren't supposed to ride the bus home; three, you didn't forget a note for a field trip; four, you didn't have Spanish class after school; five. . . . It helps.

When I can see and breathe and move again, I shut my eyes and pray and run.

I am not crazy because of the words I say, and I am not stupid because I don't know how to cross the street. Brad Hubert and I are the smartest boys in the third grade. He does math a little better and I am the better reader. They separated us, put Brad in Miss Horner's third-grade class, even though we are friends. I am glad. I don't like competition; it makes me too nervous. I suspect they think we are the smartest boys in the whole school, that we could do sixth-grade work if they let us. Brad would want to move up to the sixth grade, I bet; I would not. I like to be where I'm supposed to be, where it's easy to be the best. The other kids come to me for help, even in math; one day I told them all to leave me alone, I was falling behind, and Mrs. Hansen called me up to her desk and told me to help them. She told me I had to, because I was smartest.

On the first day of third grade, I had to get up and go to the bathroom three times. I just get nervous a lot. Mrs. Hansen looked down at me the third time and said, "What's wrong with you, William? Do you have a problem?"

I still go to the bathroom a lot, but not three times. Not counting recess. Mrs. Hansen never asks what's wrong with me anymore. I think she thinks I'm okay.

I'm okay.

I walk down our driveway in the late afternoon to get the mail for Mom. She didn't work at the hospital today, so we didn't go to Grandma's house. The sun has fallen behind the big hill across the street, so the driveway and the house and the desert behind the house are painted in cool blue, quiet shadow. It is more peaceful here in the foothills, miles away from school and town. The only sounds are the cooings and twitterings of doves, Gambol quail, cactus wrens. And the voice, of course. The voice is a pain in the butt. It is me, but it's not me. I never do what it tells me to do, it's only trying to get me in trouble, but the voice is smarter and older than me, and sometimes it tricks me. It speaks with authority, so I listen.

Throw the mail away.

"No."

Throw some of the mail away. Throw away that, and that.

"No. Shut up."

If you won't throw out the mail, you have to ride your bike off the end of the driveway.

"Shut up. Lalalalalalalalalala shut up shut up shut up I'm not listening lalalalala."

I pass gas. Just a little. It slips out accidentally. Just in case God is watching, I do my other thing: *Excuse me, excuse me, excuse me, excuse me, excuse me.* Five times, ten times, twenty-five times. Always in multiples of five. I don't want any trouble.

Good, the voice says. *Now: the mail or the bike.*

The bike, I decide.

You have to ride as fast as you can. You have to start back up the road there to build up speed.

Okay, I decide. I take the mail in and ride my bike out to the designated starting line. It is a Schwinn Spirit of Seventy-Six, red, white, and blue. I take three deep breaths and start pedaling. Faster, faster. Forty yards, thirty yards, twenty, ten, don't stop, don't stop, don't think, don't think . . . go!

The end of our driveway, the part the voice refers to, is a concrete structure built up over a dry riverbed that runs parallel to the road. It is a five- or six-foot drop from the top of the concrete to the sand and rocks below. There are palo verde and mesquite tree limbs scattered over the surface of the riverbed, heavy and covered with thorns, but the rocks, some as big as pumpkins, are the real danger. I try to aim as I fly off the end of the concrete and feel the bike falling away below me, but the momentum I've built up is more powerful than I've figured on and I sail past the spot where I'd hoped to land. I close my eyes and let my body go limp, and I'm already crying from fear as I hit the rocks and dirt on my side and roll, roll. Sand scrapes at my face and forces its way into my mouth. My head hits a rock and I hear popping noises in my neck; pins of light swim up out of darkness and swirl in dizzy patterns. Sharp sticks like pencils jab into my arms and legs and, in the second before I stop moving, I sense a deeper shadow over me, something moving at me, heavy and powerful, at great speed. The bike. I throw my arms up over my head just as it hits me, a blow that knocks the wind out of me all over again. The handlebars jab into my ribs and I still, seventeen years later, carry the scar where a spinning pedal dug into my forearm. Thirty seconds of panic follow as I struggle to regain my breath; then, purple-faced, I limp back to the house with a sprained ankle and cuts and bruises everywhere.

I hope you're happy, I think. The voice is silent.

That night, Mom and Dad and I are sitting in the family room, listening to classical music, and I start to cry. What's wrong with me, they want to know. I tell them that the classical music makes me feel strange. I try to explain it but I can't find the right words, and I just get more and more confused. There's no way to tell them that I feel sad and hollow and empty inside because I know the music should make me feel happy, but I don't feel anything at all. People say it's beautiful like they say a sunset is beautiful, but to me it's just music, it's just a sunset. The sunset and the music are just there, they're not anything. Like me. I can't explain it. I feel numb.

Mom and Dad look at me curiously. That's a funny thing for an eight-year-old to be thinking, they say. And they're thinking more than that. They're wondering what's wrong with their son, what they did to deserve this, what they will do with me now. I'm ruined. I'm a bad egg. I'm a freak.

I go to bed and lie in the dark, staring at the top bunk. The voice comes and I tell it, beg it, will it to go away.

It stays.

In fourth and fifth grade things are worse. The voice is louder now and harder to control. Everything has to be repeated in five multiples of five, at the very least, to keep bad things from happening. Sometimes I have to excuse myself one hundred and twenty-five times for a single belch or fart. I try to convince the voice to let me just think out the repetitions in my head, but usually it makes me recite them out loud. Even then, I mumble in my smallest whisper. I try to convince myself that nobody notices. But I am cheating. The voice knows I am cheating; Grandpa Kiel, my mother's father, has another heart attack. *I'm sorry. I'm sorry.* At the hospital, the doctor comes into the little white room and tells us Grandpa is dead, and everyone is crying but me. I try to think about Grandpa. Grandpa used to tell me stories. He used to play his old jazz records for me: Bix Beiderbecke, Charlie Parker, the Dukes of Dixieland. I know this is sad, I see the word, "sad," hovering in the air before me, but all I feel is numb. Numb, empty, a little bit guilty, but not too guilty because I know it's only partly my fault. I did all my repetitions, every time, just like the voice told me. I only cheated a little. *Only partly only partly only partly only partly only partly.*

Ryan Brooks is my best friend now, and my sister Nancy and I go to his house after school instead of Grandma's. Mom pays Ryan's mom to watch us. I like it at Ryan's house because it's more comfortable than school. At school my old friends, Joey and Mike and John, don't hang out with me anymore; they like to play football and I don't. My girlfriend, Celia Parks, breaks up with me because she wants me to be a Christian, and I tell her I was raised a Presbyterian and I'm staying a Presbyterian, and that's that. The breakup makes me sad but I can't break with God. God would make me pay. My teacher, Mr. Peltier, looks at me funny because I'm losing my smartness; I'm not living up to the things I'm sure Mrs. Hansen and Mrs. Ek told him about me. All of it makes me nervous. Everything makes me nervous. But afternoons at Ryan's go by in the same pleasant way, day in and day out. We watch TV, we play superheroes, we walk to the schoolyard and play softball. We visit a girl down the street, Sarah, who has a retarded brother. The retard sits in front of the television and says, Fuck you fuck you fuck you shut up shut up shut up. *Family Feud* is his favorite show. *Treat him like you would anybody else,* Sarah's mom tells us. Sometimes the retard goes swimming with us, and I try to stay away from him so his freak germs don't swim through the water and soak into my skin. It's like when I had to stay at the weird family's house when Mom and Dad went out of town and they told me to take a shower. I pretended to take a shower but I really just turned on the water and sat on the toilet. I stay away from freaky people's water; I've got troubles of my own.

One day Ryan's little brother, Petey, decides he's in love with a little girl named Robin. We sing "Rockin' Robin" because it's fun to watch him turn red and go into fits. I can do it more than Ryan because Petey hits Ryan but he doesn't hit me. One time, though, I take it too far. We are out in the front yard, Ryan, Petey, Sarah, my sister Nancy, and I. I am singing the song and laughing and Petey tells me to stop, he begs, he pleads, but it's too much fun, too, too funny, and even when I try to stop I can't. *You'd better quit it,* he warns me, like he's got something up his sleeve. Some secret weapon. I keep on. *You better watch out.* I laugh. Petey chases me around but he doesn't hit me. He starts imitating me, this little second-grader, he hangs his head and shuffles around and starts to mumble: *Excuse me excuse me excuse me excuse me excuse me. . . .* I feel my face go red and start to burn. I feel shaky all over and dizzy, lightheaded. Ryan's mom comes out of the house at a fast trot. *Peter,* she yells. *Stop it. Stop that right now.* She grabs her son and shakes him. *I never, never want to hear you do that again.*

Ryan's mom drags Petey inside the house. But it's too late. We stand on the lawn in a little circle, heads down, silent. I can't pretend anymore that nobody knows, that everybody thinks I'm normal. *Treat him like you would anybody else.* I am just like the retard. I am a freak and I think it's a secret. They let me go to school, they let me read my books, go to friends' houses, ride my bike. But the whole time, they are watching me. They are letting me think I am just like anybody else.

But I am not the same. Not the same at all.

Everything changed in the summer before sixth grade. We moved to a new house a couple of miles away, and this meant a new school district and a new school, new teachers, new friends. I had a new routine: I could bike to my new school, and after school I could walk to friends' houses or invite them over to mine. The distance between school and home was no longer prohibitive. At around the same time, the voice went away. It just vanished, so mysteriously and unobtrusively that I didn't notice its absence for nearly a year. And, in much the same way, I stopped needing my verbal repetitions, my chants, my prayers, whatever they were. I was free. There was suddenly much more time in a day to get things accomplished: I formed a secret club with my friends; I competed in speech competitions and spelling bees; I started listening to the Beatles and the Rolling Stones a lot; and I watched *M*A*S*H* every afternoon, curling up calm and serene before the television with no unpleasant voices or compulsions to distract me.

But my problems weren't over, not by a long shot. Something had to replace the voice and the behaviors, and it turned out to be something worse and more freakish by far.

In sixth grade I rediscovered the hand jive.

The hand jive actually originated when I was around five years old, in an amusing and fairly harmless way. I was a big Mister Rogers fan; I wanted to be just like him and to have my own television program when I grew up. When I had to go to the bathroom, number two, I played out this fantasy: I would sit on the toilet and, watching myself in the bathroom mirror on the opposite wall, I'd play talk-show host. My *nom de guerre* was The Superdoozie Man, after the code word my parents had developed for bowel movements:

"Hello, welcome to The Superdoozie Man. I'm The Superdoozie Man, William Samuels. I hope everyone out there is having a great day. You should feel very special because you are a very special person. A lot of you kids send letters to me and call me up and you want to know, Are superdoozies bad? Should I feel bad for having superdoozies? No, superdoozies are totally natural. They are also called stools, or BMs. You should never call them poops, because you might get spanked. The Superdoozie Man never says bad words. Sometimes bad words just come out by accident, though, and you can't help it. Yesterday I called my uncle a bad word, but I didn't mean to. I said, 'Uncle David, you gucking, lucking, chucking, bucking . . .' and then I said a bad word by accident. 'F-U-C-K-ing,' in case you didn't know. But don't ever say that word. After Uncle David left, Dad spanked me. But your parents don't spank you because they hate you. They spank you because they love you. They love you very much because you are a very special person." Et cetera.

I believed I could see all of my viewers through the TV camera, just like the lady on *Romper Room* said she could. I believed I was the Voice of Authority. I believed I would be a great role model. I believed that parents would admire me and that I would make God and my family proud. The more I became immersed in my role, the more excited I became. I began to duck my head down and let my eyes fall out of focus, imagining my adult self on a television screen. One day, I felt an urge to hold my breath and constrict my vocal folds, i.e., to push the air trapped inside me up against my throat and hold it there, feel it burning my lungs. It is the thing people do when they lift something heavy, when they push out a bowel movement, when a woman has a baby. At the same time, I began to bend my arms at the elbows and flap them wildly, very very quickly, and then pull them in tight against my chest until the knuckles of my hands were pressing against my mouth. Flap out, pull in, flap out, pull in, alternating every five or ten seconds and keeping that air pressing tight against my throat. Occasionally, I would let loose with a sound effect or a tiny, excited squeak.

Before long, I was making up stories, movies, TV shows, cartoons, whenever I went to the bathroom. And the arm-flapping and constriction of my vocal folds helped me to simulate the same kind of excitement I imagined the viewer of my special programs might experience. For as long as I kept it up, I was lost in a totally private, totally satisfying world. I squeaked out theme songs, mood music, as I watched the images and narratives play out in my head, all the while pumping my arms furiously and sending blood racing to my brain. I was escaping into outer space, and it was as if all that body motion was required to launch my imagination and hold it suspended in those dark, isolated dream worlds.

I was fascinated. I was terrified.

The hand jive was born.

Back to third grade. Some of this may seem unrelated, but in my mind it all fits perfectly together:

Gina Betts, the neighbor girl who baby-sits us sometimes, is leading me out to our clubhouse in the desert. There's a growing feeling of excitement, but I don't know why. Gina is in the eighth grade at a private Catholic school, Saints Peter and Paul, and she is in love with a boy named Phil. All of her problems would be solved if she could just talk to Phil but, no, this is impossible. I only know the facts; I do not attempt to understand them.

"Gina, look, there's a tarantula."

"Come on."

"You told me to show you if I found a tarantula."

"Just come on. Hurry up."

Gina leads me under the branches of a palo verde and we skid on our butts down Slide Rock to the riverbed and the fort. I am getting really excited; anything better than a huge, hairy spider has got to be pretty good. As it turns out, Gina just has to go to the bathroom; she moves off into the weeds and drops her jeans and panties. Tinkles. "Don't you want to look?" she asks me finally.

I look. I look closer. I touch. Not as good as a tarantula, maybe, but hey, it's something new.

"Now you," she tells me. I eagerly strip down and let her look, look closer, touch.

"It's a lot smaller than my dad's," she says.

"It gets bigger," I tell her. "And it's going to grow."

"It's supposed to have hair."

I look down. "I don't know," I say, skeptically.

Gina leads me back over to the shade of the palo verde and we sit together. She shows me how to kiss like a movie star, with our mouths open. Her mouth is exciting and strange, especially the tongue. I like it. When she gets bored, we pull apart and head back home. "We have a secret now," Gina tells me as we walk through the deep sand of the riverbed. "Don't ever tell anybody our secret. If you don't, we can keep on doing it."

"Okay," I tell her.

A few weeks later, Gina and I have all kinds of new secrets. We are going steady, for one, and she has given me a little silver going-to-gether ring. I am not supposed to tell anyone what it means. We go on a date together to see *Return of the Pink Panther.* Nobody knows it's a real date but us. Her mom drives; the movie is good. I like the way Peter Sellers kung-fu fights with his Oriental cook. Gina has told me how people make babies, she has told me about "rubbers"; we have make-out sessions in my closet when she baby-sits. She gives me all her older brother's *Mad* magazines and makes me promise never to tell anyone anything. I like having secrets with her; I am tired of my own secrets. I know we are doing something wrong, something that is not normal, but, God knows, I'm used to that. It's good to have a little company.

The hand jive is driving me crazy. It has spread to my bedroom, where I hand jive while I draw superhero comic books. I am Colossal Kid, Joey Carroll is Super Star, Joey's friend Jerry is Black Lightning. Brad Hubert is Boy, a stupid name, and his Boy character is too powerful, has too many superpowers. But everyone got to make up their own name and powers, so what can I do? It is hard, though, coming up with supervillains who can give us a run for our money while Boy's around. I draw pages and pages of stories, adventures we will act out on the playground tomorrow, and when Dad walks in I am deep into the hand jive, squealing and flapping my arms.

"Son," he says. "Time for dinner. What are you doing?"

"Nothing," I say. "Drawing comics."

My voice sounds funny. Dad sees the embarrassment, the shame, in my face, and he leaves it alone. This happens every time Dad or Mom catches me at the hand jive; there is uncomfortable silence and then both parties act as if nothing was happening at all. This time, he turns without a word and marches back to the kitchen. Soon they will learn to knock before entering; they don't want to catch me any more than I want to be caught.

Weeks pass, and one day Gina and I are out playing in the driveway. "I see you from my bathroom window," Gina says. "I see you when you stand in front of your garage."

"I don't know what you're talking about," I tell her, but already I'm getting nervous.

"You stand there and flap your arms around. You make funny noises."

It is getting hard to breathe. My heart moves up and pushes against my throat. "No, I don't," I say.

"I watch you," Gina says. "I think it's funny."

I deny it again, but she's got me dead-to-rights. Mom had suggested that I spend more time outdoors, so I have moved the hand jive to the front yard. I only do it a couple of hours a week, maybe, and I had thought no one could see me. The houses on top of the hill looked so far away, fifty yards at least, and Gina's bathroom window, the only window in her house facing ours, is fogged over with a special kind of glass. I had thought I was safe.

"I'm going to tell your mom," Gina says.

"No, no," I tell her. "No, don't, Gina, please." Gina is angry because I lost her brother's *Mad* magazines, and now he's back from the Army and he wants them. Gina only smiles and walks up the driveway and into our house. I turn and run through the backyard and out into the desert. I run through the first line of trees and saguaros and out into the riverbed, the "wash," as we call it, and I keep running the half mile through it to the big hill and up it and onto the dirt road that leads deep into the foothills at the edge of the mountains. The sky is dark and grumbling. A slight rain begins to fall and I keep running. I run one mile, another half mile. I will run forever. I am not wearing shoes, I almost never do, and as I head up the steepest incline in the dirt road I step on a nail and it drives up into my foot. I shriek and fall into the weeds at the road's edge and lie there, sobbing, soaking wet. Every few minutes, I reach down and try to work the nail loose, but it won't come. I try to imagine growing up in my house, with them knowing about me, about my problem, my condition, and I can't. I know I will never go back.

An hour passes and the rain falls harder. I stop crying because it starts to hurt. Through the sheets of rain, I see Mom walking up the dirt road a hundred yards off. She is calling for me, and when she sees me she runs up the incline to where I am. Nancy, my little sister, told her when I ran off, and she has come to get me. I show her the nail and she pulls it loose. I am crying again.

"What's wrong, William? What is it?"

What's wrong, what's wrong. Everything's wrong. I can't feel a sunset, I can't feel music. I hear a voice in my head, and it pesters me and tells me to do bad things. I have to excuse myself fifty times when I belch or pass gas. I have to remember my E.S.P., over and over, all the time. I play hand jive with myself. I'm tired. I'm tired.

"You know, Mom. You know what's wrong with me."

"Tell me, honey."

Gina didn't really tell her at all. She was just scaring me.

"I said 'goddamnit' to Nancy," I tell Mom. It's true, too; I did say this, but it was several days before. "Gina said she was gonna tell on me."

Mom smiles. "It's okay, honey. It's okay. Just don't do it again."

I was going to tell Mom about Gina and me, about how we are engaged now and how we've been going steady for a month. But Gina has protected my secret and now I will protect her secret. Our secret. Because the hand jive is a lot like sexual feeling to me, and it will stay that way as I grow up. It is forbidden, exciting, disturbing, wrong. I know I'm strange for wanting to do it, but I can't stop wanting, I can't stop doing it. I am sick and awful, but I am the only one who knows just how sick and awful I am.

The skies are cracking, bellowing, and sheet lightning breaks across the clouds to the west of us. I stand and lean against Mom's shoulder, and she walks me home.

Around this time, my parents go to a Marriage Encounter to examine their marriage and discover ways to strengthen their family unit. It is a two- or three-day retreat, the one where I stay with the weird people and only pretend to use the shower, and when they return some changes are made. One of the changes involves Mom and Dad taking each of us kids out, individually, on family nights. Mom and Dad alternate with each child; Dad takes me out one week, and two weeks later I go out for a night with Mom. We do fun things together each time. I don't remember any of the things I do with Mom, though. Dad and I go miniature golfing one night, but we can't go to the go-cart place because Dad hears it is prohibitively expensive. One weekend Dad and I go camping together: it rains on our hike, we get lost, I get a bee sting on my hand that provokes an allergic reaction, and it rains so much during the night that we have to ditch our tent and sleep in the back of the car. I laugh a lot. I love my dad; he is always very funny when these things

happen, and I have a great time. It is one of the best weekends of
my life.

A few weeks or months later, Dad is driving me home from
someplace. I am still in the third grade. We are on Speedway Boulevard, in the middle lane, and I watch the Magic Carpet miniature
golf course go by on our right. Dad is telling me about sexual love,
because it is *time*, and he is telling me about heterosexuals and
homosexuals. He tells me that people get diseases from sexual love,
that they grow lumps on their sexual organs and that, eventually,
their brains can melt from these diseases. These are things that
Gina didn't know. Suddenly afraid, I tell him that my friend Joey
and I have touched each other's organs and rubbed them against
each other. I tell him we were pretending to be a man and woman,
that I don't think I sexual-love Joey. My father gives me a curious,
worried look, and then he tells me it is probably okay, that I probably don't have any diseases, but that I should never do that kind of
thing again. I ask him to examine my penis for irregularities anyway
(I have suspected for some time that the shape, size, and color of my
penis are extremely abnormal — Gina let me know it was too small
and bald — and now my worst fears are practically confirmed.) I
also ask him not to tell Mom about everything, and he says he
won't, and I ride home next to him thinking about how much of my
brain may have already melted and oozed down into the rest of my
body. At home, Dad spends a lot of time wandering around the
kitchen, talking to Mom, doing other things before getting around
to the examination, and I sit in front of the television watching a
show about Digby the Giant Dog and not even seeing it. Everything
is a foggy, anxious blur. *Come on, Dad, come on,* I think. I listen to my
brain sizzling away; I listen to it drip, drip, drip. Finally he takes me
to my bedroom and examines me and tells me I am just fine, and
then he reminds me not to do that sort of thing ever again, and that
if I want to I should come talk to him. I am relieved. But then he
gives me that look again, that curious, worried look, and I almost
wish I hadn't said anything and taken my chances.

What was he thinking when he gave me that look? I know what he
thought, what he still thinks, what he thinks all the time. He thinks
I am growing up to be a very strange boy, a boy he doesn't know and
doesn't really want to. A boy who plays naked with other boys. A boy
who sits around in his room drawing comics, flapping his arms and

making strange noises deep in his throat as he plans out the action and creates sound effects. That stuff, especially. A boy who doesn't like sports, who only plays soccer because he's told to, a boy who likes to go out in the desert by himself and do God Knows What. A boy who says *excuse me* fifty times in a row, for nothing. A very strange boy, indeed.

I stay in my room after he leaves and shut and lock the door. I close the blinds and sit down with my comics, and I hand jive my funny feelings away.

In sixth grade, I've forgotten all about the hand jive. Everything is better, everything is fine. I play with Jay Hardtke and Adam Zele. Mr. Thompson is angry because I don't take things seriously enough. My report card shows almost straight Cs. I have to go in for parent-teacher-student conferences. I'm having too much fun. I have so much potential, and I'm frittering it away. When am I going to grow up and take some responsibility? I'm always late to class in the mornings. It's as if I don't even care.

I love the word "frittering." It just sounds like a lot of fun. It sounds just like what I'm doing. And I don't hear the voice. I don't have to excuse myself or remember my E.S.P. five or twenty-five or a hundred and twenty-five times. I ride my bike on the moto-cross trail some bigger kids have made in the desert near my house. I go swimming at Skyline Country Club and watch the pretty, tanned older ladies in their tiny swimsuits. I tell jokes and make everybody laugh. And I don't care. I don't care. I don't care.

Near the end of the second quarter before Christmas break, I start thinking about Ronnie Newman. Ronnie is the biggest loser in the school. He is skinny, loaded with acne, ugly and stupid, and he's failed sixth grade five times. *Five* times. He is the sort of kid you know is headed for prison or worse. Not a tough, delinquent kid, just a weirdo. A Ted Bundy in the making. A Jeffrey Dahmer, Jr. The last kid you'd want to end up being like. Mr. Thompson calls me into the classroom during break one day and has me sit up close to him at his desk. William, he tells me, I like you a lot. I *like* you. But you're blowing it. And you know what I mean. I know how smart you are, you can't pretend with me. I've talked to you and talked to you, and I've given you more chances than anybody else. And I'll give you one last chance. But if you don't get your act together, I'm going to put you in the remedial learning classroom after Christmas break, and they'll hold you back this year. I mean it. You'll be in there with Ronnie Newman. You'll be held back with Ronnie Newman. Do you want to be like Ronnie Newman?

The Cs on my last report card, it turns out, have become Ds and, some of them, Fs. Mr. Thompson really is going to ship me out. I pedal home as fast as I can, crack all of my books, some of them for the first time, and I start to study. My chest constricts and my breathing quickens. My heart is back up there, beating against my throat. I study five and six hours a night to catch up on a semester's worth of social studies, reading, English, geography, math. I ace every test, every one, from that day forward. I contribute to classroom discussions, I volunteer for the toughest reading list in the sixth grade. I take make-up exams and ace those, too, and Mr. Thompson smiles and squeezes my shoulders and makes me want to go at it even harder.

At semester's end, I've earned myself five As and two Bs, and one of those Bs is a B-plus. Mr. Thompson makes a speech to the class with tears in his eyes. Dad and Mom take me out for dinner. Not knowing what else to do, unable to stop, I start diving into my assignments for the next semester. I study on Christmas Eve.

And, just like that, the hand jive is back.

I begin high school at Amphi High in the fall of 1981, and the hand jive is still with me. It is actually getting worse. I walk home from the bus stop with Ray Farley, a funny, popular kid, but he is too cool to hang out with the likes of me. We laugh and joke while we walk, but then he walks up his driveway and disappears. When Ray transfers out of Amphi, Geyr Greve transfers in, and I walk home with Geyr instead but the situation is the same. We throw rocks at each other as we walk, and that's fun, but then he walks on up his driveway and leaves me to my afternoon. I go to the kitchen and get a snack, and then I go to my bedroom and lock the door. Then I go into my bathroom and lock that door, too. And I hand jive. Hours pass. Outside the bathroom window, there is an old, rotting saguaro cactus skeleton. The skeleton's gray, weathered ribs rise up to a black, knobby point, and I imagine sometimes that Dad and Mom have allowed scientists to install a hidden camera in the knob so they can observe me. I always wonder why they haven't confronted me about all the time I spend in the bathroom, and this scenario provides some explanation, at least. I imagine turning on the television one day and seeing a PBS documentary all about me and my abnormalities. I know this is a paranoid, ridiculous notion, but I close the blinds on the window just in case. I crouch in the near darkness, shut out the world, and do my thing.

Amphitheater High School is a massive public school, population twenty-two hundred. I feel lost there; I am quiet, shy, unsure of myself most of the time. I feel I am five or ten different people crammed into a single body. My sharpest high school memories, in fact, read like the memories of a cross section of Amphi's population, like the recollections of a whole student body. I am highly active in drama class and more or less asleep everywhere else. I win the Best Actor award for my role in *You Can't Take It with You,* but I'm called into the assistant principal's office and threatened with suspension for cutting classes. I test into the "genius club" at Amphi, but I never attend a single meeting. I am sarcastic, cynical, sometimes mean. I submit to an underground humor magazine. I work out at the gym every day and make fun of Lippy Ford, the wrestler who lights cats on fire for fun on Saturday nights. Once, during squat reps, Lippy pulls the pin out of my Nautilus machine for a joke and the metal, unpadded footbar at the end of the leg extension bars swings back at me to carve permanent grooves in my shins. Another time he throws me up against my locker and sticks a loaded gun in my chest, cocks it, rubs the trigger with a greasy finger, laughs, and walks away. I keep making fun of him. I know I'm fairly good-looking, and I am willing to screw anything that moves. The really popular and pretty girls, though, look at me with a kind of wistful pity. I don't realize it's my seventies, "retro" look: dirty blue jeans, cheap button-down oxfords, and a "disco hair-do," parted straight down the middle. So I resign myself to dating wrestling cheerleaders instead of football cheerleaders, voluptuous freaks instead of pretty nice girls. Louise Chandler is both wrestling cheerleader and voluptuous freak; she smokes, listens to punk bands, and sneaks out her window at night to hang out in gay bars. One night, while I'm nibbling on her boobs in a backroom at a party, she begs me to rape her; I try my best, but I break down when she screams and cries and really struggles. She dumps me, disgusted. I am chosen to dance the senior jitterbug with our homecoming queen, the prettiest girl in school, and we take first prize. I throw a party at my boss's real estate office late one night and end up spread-eagled against the wall outside, ten police officers surrounding me with loaded assault rifles and barking dogs. I join the choir. I learn the trick of dating girls from other schools, nice, pretty girls who think I'm cute and sweet and don't have to worry about what their friends will think. Because their friends will never see me. This trick also makes two-timing easy and worry-free, for me and probably for them as well. I join the advanced Madrigal choir. I smoke grass. Disgusted with cheesy yearbook photos, I pose in the back of a convertible with a gorgeous brunette who feeds me grapes and strokes my hair. In our yearbook I am voted Best Actor in the Senior Class and, in the category of Class Clown, or so goes the rumor, I take second to Paul Potts. The ultra-popular Rawls girls drive me to school in their cherry red Mustang, but I am so intimidated by their glamour that I never, in nine months of twenty-minute rides, ever utter a word. Everyone looks at me the same way I look at myself: I'm a lot of bodies and a nobody, a funny, impressive kid who's almost-but-not-quite worth getting to know.

I avoid my parents. I keep that door locked. I read underground comic books and jerk off. The hand jive is my very best friend. No matter how hot and uncomfortable it gets at school, on the worst "nobody" days, I know it'll be okay.

I can come home and hand jive, hand jive, hand jive, all night long.

The last hand jive I remember hits me in the spring semester of my freshman year at college. I am sharing a room with Phil Green, an ultraconservative strait-laced kid from Fort Collins, Colorado. I have just bought the new R.E.M. album, *Fables of the Reconstruction,* and as I listen I get more and more excited. R.E.M. is the greatest, man; I love those murky mixes, that anxious, hard-driving beat and Michael Stipe's tentative growls and murmurs. I kneel down on the hard tile floor beside my bed and my arms start in with their tight, fast flapping. I grow red in the face, and I envision myself up on the stage singing unintelligibly just like Stipe. I have Stipe's voice, I am in Stipe's body. I am ultracool. I just know I'm wearing black, and all the women love it. I am jiving, I am jiving, all, of course, to the most thunderous applause.

Phil Green opens the door and walks in and stares. Our eyes

meet. I am kneeling there beside the bed, my arms frozen in mid-flap. He mumbles an apology, I say, "Oh, Jesus, Phil, you scared the hell out of me." And then there's nothing more to say. Phil grabs something off the desk, whatever he came in for, and leaves. And I realize, as I kneel alone in the dark, quiet room, that I can never, never do this thing again. I can't stand letting other people see it, and I can't stand to see it in myself.

When I was a little boy Dad told me that, when he was growing up, he liked to make strange, high-pitched squeaks when he was excited, too. That was the closest he ever came to discussing the hand jive with me. I wonder whether it is genetic; I wonder how my own kids will turn out. Mostly, though, I think about Dad. Sometimes, when he gets really excited about something, he shakes his arms a couple or three times and lets out a little yelp and gets red in the face. I wonder if he had the one hard moment, at some point, that I had, when he realized the world just wouldn't accept a hand-jiving man. I always thought his frenetic little bursts of excitement were sort of silly and stupid, but that was before I stopped my hand jive. I see them now for what they are, or what they are to me, anyway: a surrogate, a substitute. I find myself firing off these crazy yips and yelps more and more often these days. I get these strange little bursts of energy, and I've just got to let them loose. Smoking also helps a little.

I think, too, about all the time I lost to hand jiving while I was growing up. By my estimate, I spent a good year of my life, all told, doing the hand jive. It got me nothing. I imagined whole movies in my head, but I never got a good idea for a story or a play or a film script out of any of them. During junior high and high school, I mostly only envisioned short scenes of extravagant action and violence, the Hollywood formula: big guns, exploding cars, hot babes, and careless expletives. It did foster in me, though, a very active imagination, a very large and very real dream world, and I feel sometimes when I'm writing as though I'm tapping into that world, that feeling, again.

It feels good, but I can't explain why. That was sort of the point; hand jiving took me to a world beyond judgment, beyond reproach, beyond criticism. It was the ultimate passive, illusory escape. I don't know where the hand jive came from, where it went, or what it was, really, other than a nearly total waste of time and an embarrassment. And I've tried to discover why I needed such an absolute, self-annihilating escape, but I believe now I may never come close to the truth.

But it made me different, it made me special, it made me freakish. Like Prince Randian, the quadriplegic who rolled and lit his own cigarettes, or like Martin Laurillo the Neck-Twistin' Man or Legless Alvina Gibbs, I was different from everyone else in the world. Like any of those old Coney Island or Barnum and Bailey freaks who continue to fascinate me today, I carried with me everywhere a lonely, secret pride. I knew the whole truth about myself and believed I would horrify and repulse anyone who glimpsed that truth. The faces of those old human misfits, in the aging photographs I collect and in the 1932 MGM film *Freaks,* stare at me with that knowledge that I hid for so long from the rest of the world. Or I wish and pretend they knew, because they were kindred spirits who might have welcomed me into their fold. *We accept you, we accept you. One of us, one of us.* I live in Brooklyn now, and it's an easy ride on the F train to Coney Island. It's as far away from New York City as you can get on the B, D, F, and N subway trains, the end of those lines, and I go there some afternoons and listen to the barker at the freak show. Sometimes I pay to see the freaks: Painproof Man, Elastic Lady, the Human Blockhead. They are different from me, these people who have imposed freakishness upon themselves, but they are the only kinds of freaks allowed by law to hop on a stage. I like their easygoing pride and arrogance. I like the way they share their freakishness with the world as if it's a miraculous, beautiful secret, and assert at the same time their normalcy, their humanity, through the very fact that they're standing there before us, flesh and blood. Living, breathing people, like all of us but slightly different. Slightly special.

So here I go, mounting the stage for the first time, if only in print. I can hear that barker now, and he annoys me:

So here he is, folks, the Hand-jiving Man. An exhibitionist by nature, he can no longer hide his strange, twisted secret from the world. It is yours to see, ladies and gentlemen, live onstage and absolutely uncensored. He has spent years of his life on other worlds, and now you can see what his body does in his absence. A freakish, uncontrollable explosion of energy, folks, for your eyes only. He wants your sympathy, he wants your understanding, he wants to witness your wonder and pleasure, and if he can make a few bucks by

exploiting his condition that is just fine by him. The man with no shame.
Come on in, folks. Step right this way.

The barker annoys me because everything he says is true. I could
never hop on a real stage, though, willing or no. It would not be
much of a show. I cannot physically simulate the hand jive. Friends
who have read parts of this piece have asked me to try, and I do, but
I feel odd, self-conscious, and my arms will not react properly. My
heart and mind must lead; my body follows. And I do not want to
make an authentic leap into that world again. It is a mindless void,
a stupid habit, but for me it obviously has its attractions. I have
made my break from it, and I don't want to be seduced again.

For twenty years, it has been my proud, beautiful, odd, horrific
secret. And sometimes, when I'm feeling awfully normal, awfully
lonely, or awfully anxious, I have to admit that I almost miss it.

STEPHEN DOBYNS

So I Guess You Know What I Told Him

FROM PLOUGHSHARES

FLOYD BEEFUS was picking a tick off one of the springers when the gas man slipped on a cracked dinner plate on the cellar stairs and went bump, bump, bump, right to the bottom. "Yow!" went the gas man. The springer jumped but Floyd kept gripping him tight between his knees until he had cracked the tick between his forefinger and thumb, then he limped slowly to the cellar door.

The gas man lay in a heap at the bottom. He was a well-fed-looking fellow in a green shirt, green pants, and a little green cap. He was moaning and rubbing his leg.

"You hurt yourself?" called Floyd Beefus.

The gas man stared up the stairs at him with a confused look, as if his eyes had gone loose in his head. He was about forty, maybe twenty years younger than Floyd himself. "I think I broke my leg. I need an ambulance. You got a phone?"

"Nope," said Floyd. "No phone." He limped back to the springer and let him into the pen in the backyard before he peed on the rug. The springer had picked up the tick when they had been out hunting pheasants that morning. Floyd had thought the frost would have killed the ticks. It was early September and Floyd had a small farm outside of Montville, about twenty miles from Belfast. As he put the springer into his pen, he glanced around at the maples just beginning to turn color under the bright blue sky. Soon it would be hunting season and Floyd might get himself a nice buck. Frieda would appreciate that if she was still with them. After a moment, he went back inside to check on the gas man.

"You want an aspirin or maybe a Coca-Cola?" he called. He understood that the gas man posed a problem but he wasn't yet sure how to deal with it.

"Jesus, I'm in pain. You got to call a doctor." The gas man had stretched himself out a little with his head on the bottom step. He had a thick, red face. Floyd Beefus thought the man looked excitable and it made Floyd suck his teeth.

"I already told you I don't have no phone." Floyd had had a phone but he lost track of the bill and the phone had been temporarily disconnected. Frieda used to take care of all that. Floyd Beefus lowered himself onto the top step and gazed down at the gas man. He guessed he'd have to step over him if he went into the basement to fetch any of his tools.

"Then use a neighbor's phone. This is an emergency!"

"The nearest neighbor's two miles," said Floyd. "That'd be Harriet Malcomb in the mobile unit. Course I just call it a trailer. I'd be surprised if she had a phone. She don't even have a car. If you'd done this a week ago, then you would have caught some summer people, but the last of them left on Tuesday: Mike Prescott, a lawyer from Boston. Sometimes he has parties. I'd hate to tell what goes on."

"You can use my car."

"I can't drive no more on account of the Dewey."

"Dewey?"

"DWI."

The gas man was staring at him in a way that Floyd Beefus thought bordered on the uncivil. "You sure you don't want that aspirin?" added Floyd. "Or maybe a pillow?"

"I can't just lie here," said the gas man, letting the whine grow in his voice. "I could be bleeding internally!"

Floyd scratched the back of his neck. He saw cobwebs on the stairs that would never have been allowed to settle before his wife got sick. "I don't like to leave Frieda. She's up in bed." He started to say more, then didn't.

"Jesus," said the gas man, "don't you see this is a crisis situation? I'm a supervisor. I can't just lie here in your cellar. I could die here."

"Oh, you won't die," said Floyd. He considered the gas man's excitability. "If you're a supervisor, how come you're reading my meter?"

"We're understaffed. You got to get a doctor!"

Floyd pulled his pocket watch out of the pocket of his dungarees and opened the lid. It was shortly past ten-thirty.

"The visiting nurse should be here in a while. She usually shows up a little after lunchtime. Billy, that's my son, he took the Ford down to Rockland this morning. He said he'd be back by late afternoon. Had to go to the pharmacy down there. I don't see why they don't sell the damn stuff in Belfast. You'd think bedsores'd be the same in both places."

"After lunchtime?" said the gas man.

"Around one, one-thirty. Loretta likes to stop for the blue plate special out at the Ten-Four Diner. And if they have blueberry pie, she generally takes a slice. She's a fat old thing. She'll fix you right up."

"That could be three hours," said the gas man.

"Just about. You want to think again about that aspirin?"

"It upsets my stomach. You have any Tylenol?"

"Nope," said Floyd. "Course Frieda's got some morphine. I could give you a shot if you like. I've become practiced at it."

The gas man had big blue eyes and Floyd found himself thinking: Googly eyes.

"Morphine?"

"The visiting nurse brings it. A month ago Frieda only needed two shots a day. Now she needs four. Loretta, that's the nurse, she said she's seen patients taking six and even eight shots before their time's up. You sure you don't want a little shot? Loretta will be giving us some more."

The gas man shut his eyes. "I don't take morphine. Perhaps you could get me a glass of water. And I'll have some aspirin after all. God, it'd be just my luck to start puking."

The aspirin was above the bathroom sink. Before getting it, Floyd looked in on Frieda. She was sleeping. Her gray hair was spread out on the pillow around her face. Floyd thought of the tumor in her stomach. It didn't sleep; it just got bigger. The bedroom was full of medicines and an oxygen tank. It had a sweet hospital smell. Floyd himself had been sleeping in the spare room for six weeks and he still couldn't get used to it. He got the aspirin, then went downstairs for the water. One of the springers was barking but he was just being conversational.

Floyd had to wash out a glass. Since Frieda had been sick, he and Billy had been doing the cooking and cleaning up but it didn't come easy. A pot on the stove was still crusted with spaghetti sauce from two nights earlier.

Floyd descended the cellar stairs, watching out for the stuff that was on the steps: newspapers and empty Ball jars. He sat down above the gas man and handed him the water and bottle of aspirin. "You married?" he asked.

The gas man pried the top off the bottle of aspirin. "I got a wife," he said.

"Kids?"

"Two."

"I been married forty years," said Floyd. "We done it right after Frieda finished high school. I didn't graduate myself. Didn't need it back then."

The gas man didn't say anything. He took two aspirin, then took two more. There was sweat on his forehead. Floyd thought his face looked unhealthy but maybe it was the pain. The gas man drank some water, then shut his eyes.

"You like your wife?" asked Floyd.

The gas man opened his eyes. "Sure, I mean, she's my wife."

"How'd you feel if you didn't have her anymore?"

"What do you mean?"

"Well, if she died or went away."

"She wouldn't do that. Go away, I mean." The gas man's voice had an impatient edge.

"But what if she died?"

"I guess I'd be surprised."

"Is that all? Just surprised?"

"Well, she's thirty-eight. There's nothing wrong with her." The man took off his green cap and pushed a hand through his hair. It was dark brown with some gray at the temples.

"A car could hit her," said Floyd. "She could be struck down when crossing the street. It happens all the time."

"She pays attention. She looks both ways."

"It could still happen."

The gas man thought a moment, then got angry. "Can't you see I don't want to talk! I hurt and you won't even get help!"

Floyd pursed his lips. He sat above the gas man and looked down on his bald spot. "I already explained about that." He thought how the gas man's bald spot would get bigger and bigger till it ate up his whole head. "You live around here?" he asked.

"I live in Augusta."

"They got a lot of dangerous streets in Augusta," said Floyd. "I seen them."

The gas man sighed.

"Wouldn't you mind if your wife was hit by a car?"

"Mind, of course I'd mind! Jesus, what are you saying?"

"I'm just trying to get the picture," said Floyd.

"We got two kids, like I say. They're both still in school. Who'd take care of them?"

"My two oldest are grown up," said Floyd. "A daughter in Boston and my older boy in Portland. But they'd be here in a minute if Frieda got took worse. You sleep with your wife?"

"Of course I sleep with my wife. What are you getting at?" The gas man turned his head but it was hard to see Floyd seated behind him. Floyd had his arms folded across his knees and was resting his chin on his wrist.

"Me and Frieda, we can't sleep together no more. At first without her there I could hardly sleep at all. The bed seemed hollow, like it was no more than an empty shoe. She'd move around a lot in the night and she'd cry. She's scared but she won't say anything. I would've stayed right there in the old double bed but the visiting nurse said it would be better if I moved. At first I sat up in a chair with her but I couldn't do that for too many nights. Sleeping in the spare room feels like I done something wrong."

The gas man didn't speak for a moment. Then he said, "Can you get me a pillow for my head?"

Floyd got a pillow upstairs from Billy's room. His knee hurt from walking around the fields that morning and he moved slowly. Frieda was still asleep. He stood a moment in the doorway and watched her breathe. After she exhaled there was a pause that seemed to stretch on and on. Then she would breathe again and Floyd would relax a little. Her skin was the color of old egg cartons. He took the pillow back down to the gas man, who was rubbing his leg below the knee.

"I can feel the bone pressing against the skin," said the gas man. "It's sure to be bleeding inside. I could lose my whole leg." He had pulled up the green pant leg and showed Floyd the red bump in his skin where the bone was pressing.

Floyd put the pillow behind the gas man's head. "I broke my leg falling off the tractor once. I lay in the field for two hours and no harm was done except for the pain. It's not like cancer. The body can take a lot."

"It hurts," said the gas man.

"That's just your body telling you there's something wrong. You want me to haul you upstairs and put you on the couch?"

The gas man considered that. When he thought, he moved his tongue around in his mouth. "I think I better stay right here until the rescue squad shows up."

Floyd wasn't sure he could get the gas man up the stairs in any case. "You pray?" he asked.

"I'm not much for church," said the gas man.

"Me neither, but there's a Bible around somewheres if you need it. Frieda likes to look at it. Right up to last March she'd never been took sick. Never complained, always kept us going with her jokes. You ever been unfaithful to your wife?"

The gas man's head jerked on his pillow.

"Jesus, what kind of question is that?"

"I just wanted to know."

"My affairs are none of your business, absolutely none of your business."

Floyd settled himself more comfortably on the step. He was sorry that the gas man was so unforthcoming. "You know Belfast?"

"I been there."

"You know how it used to have those two chicken-processing plants? Penobscot Poultry and the other one. I forget its name. A guy named Mendelsohn run it. Every summer Belfast used to have a poultry festival with rides and activities in the city park. It used to be something special and high school bands would come from all over. And the Shriners, too."

The gas man didn't speak. He began rubbing his leg again. There was a bend in it that Floyd didn't think looked right.

"There was a woman who worked upstairs at Penobscot. She had a job putting the little piece of paper between the chicken parts and Styrofoam. Her name was Betsy. My, she liked to make trouble. She was never buttoned clear to the neck. About twelve years ago me and Frieda went to that poultry fair. The kids were young enough to still like it. I was drinking beer. That's always a mistake with me. After dark I got Betsy back on a tree stump. I was just unbuttoning myself when Frieda found me. Jesus, I already had Betsy's shorts off under her dancing skirt."

"Why are you telling me this?" The gas man stretched his neck to get a glimpse of Floyd.

"I was just thinking about it, that's all," said Floyd.

"Don't you see I don't care what you've done?"

"Then what do you want to talk about?" asked Floyd.

"I don't want to talk at all."

Floyd sat for a moment. The gas man had a fat gold wedding ring, then another ring with a blue stone on his right pinkie finger. He had shiny teeth and Floyd thought it was the kind of mouth that was used to eating a lot, the kind of mouth that enjoyed itself.

"How's your leg?" asked Floyd.

"It hurts."

"That aspirin help any?"

"It makes my stomach queasy."

"You sure you don't want a Coke?"

"I just want to get out of here. You got to take my car."

"The Dewey'd get me for sure," said Floyd, "and then there's Frieda. If she woke up, you couldn't do anything."

Floyd leaned back with his elbows on a step. The cellar was filled with evidence of forty years in this house: broken chairs, old bikes, tools, canning equipment, a dog bed for Bouncer, who had been dead fifteen years. The cellar had a musty smell. He wondered what he would do with this stuff when Frieda died. The thought of her death was like a pain in his body.

"You ever think," said Floyd, "that a bad thing happens to you because of some bad thing you've done?"

"What do you mean?" asked the gas man suspiciously.

"Well, that time I fell off the tractor and broke my leg was right after I'd been with Betsy at the poultry festival. Even when I fell I had the sense that something was giving me a shove. If I'd had two more seconds I'd've stuck it into her . . ."

"I don't want to hear about this," said the gas man.

"What I was wondering is maybe you've been doing something you shouldn't. You always play straight with your wife?"

"This is none of your business."

"You never felt temptation?"

"I only wanted to read your meter," said the gas man. "That's all, just your meter."

"You're a better man than I am. I felt temptation. I felt it every time I went into town. It wasn't that I don't love my wife. I was just exercising myself, so to speak. I'd go into Barbara's Lunch and just breathe heavily. Going into houses like you do, you must of felt temptation a whole lot."

"I don't want to talk about it. I'm a supervisor."

"But younger, when you were a plain gas man. Didn't some woman look at you and smile?"

"Why are you saying this?" asked the gas man. He spoke so forcefully that little drops of spit exploded from his lips. He tried to turn but couldn't quite see Floyd sitting behind him.

"You know," said Floyd, "after Frieda caught me behind the beer tent with Betsy McCollough, she'd look at me with such . . . disappointment. I don't mean right at the time. Then she was just angry. But later, at dinner or just walking across the room, she'd look up at me and I could see the wounding in her face. She still loved me and I loved her, too. It was eleven, almost twelve years later the cancer took hold of her, but I find myself thinking that my time with Betsy had opened the cancer to her. It made a little door for the cancer to enter."

The gas man had his face in his hands. He didn't say anything. The tips of his ears were all red.

"We were married right in Montville," said Floyd. "All our families were there, most of them dead now. We planned to be so happy. Even now, lying in bed, Frieda will look at me with that look of disappointment. Maybe that's too strong a word. She doesn't regret her marriage or regret having met me. It's like she thought I was a certain size and then she found out I was a little smaller. And I can never say she's wrong. I can't make myself bigger. When she was first sick, I used to make her dinners and bring her stuff and she appreciated it but it never made me as big a person as she used to think I was. And soon, you know, she'll be gone, and then I won't be able to explain anything or fix anything. All our time will be over."

The gas man didn't say anything.

"What d'you think about that?" asked Floyd.

"I just want a doctor," said the gas man.

"If you're so good," said Floyd, "then why won't you talk to me about it?"

"About what?"

"About what I done."

"Because I don't care," said the gas man. "Don't you understand it? I don't care."

"Fine gas man you are," said Floyd. He sat without speaking. He rubbed his knee and the gas man rubbed his leg.

"I don't mean to hurt your feelings," said the gas man.

"That's okay," said Floyd, "I'm not worth much."

"It's not what you're worth," said the gas man. "My leg's broken. I hurt. I'm preoccupied."

"You think I'm not preoccupied?" said Floyd. "My wife's dying upstairs and I can't do anything about it. I look in her face and I see the memories there. I see how I hurt her and how I said the wrong things and how I got angry and how I wasn't the man she hoped I'd be. I see that in her face and I see she's going to die with that. You think I'm not preoccupied?"

The gas man put his cap back on his head and pulled down the brim. "I don't know what to say. I come into this place. All I want is to read your meter. Why the hell can't you keep that stuff off the stairs? You think it's nice to be a gas man going into strange basements all the time? All I want is to get in and get out. Then I go home, eat dinner, watch some TV, and go to bed. Is that too much to ask? Instead, I slip on a dinner plate and you say I must've deserved it. I must've been cheating on my wife. All I want is to get my leg fixed. I'm sorry your wife's dying. I can't do anything about it. I'm just a gas man."

Floyd leaned back and sighed. He heard one of the springers howling. Frieda had a buzzer that sounded off in the kitchen if she needed anything. Apart from the springer, the house was silent except for the gas man's heavy breathing. Floyd felt dissatisfied somehow, like finishing a big meal and still being hungry. He looked at his watch. It was almost eleven-thirty.

"Old Loretta should be reaching the Ten-Four Diner in another hour," he said. "My, she loves to eat. I've known her even to have two pieces of pie with ice cream. If they got blueberry and if they got rhubarb, then I bet she'll have both."

"What's the latest she's gotten here?"

"Three o'clock."

The gas man groaned. "I hurt, I hurt a lot."

"There's still that morphine," said Floyd.

"No morphine," said the gas man.

"Anything else you want? Maybe a tuna fish sandwich?"

"You got any whiskey?"

"There might be some White Horse somewheres."

"Maybe a shot of that, maybe a double."

Floyd made his way back upstairs. He was sorry the gas man didn't want a tuna fish sandwich. He wanted to feed him, to have the gas man think well of him. Looking in on Frieda, he saw she had turned her head but that was all. She said the morphine gave her bright-colored dreams. She dreamt about being a kid or going to school or having children again. Rich, vigorous dreams and Floyd Beefus envied her for them. When he went to bed he was just grinding and grinding all night long like a tractor motor.

He poured the gas man half a glass of whiskey, then poured himself some as well. Floyd made his way back down the cellar stairs. He handed the gas man the bigger glass.

"Here you go," he said.

The gas man gripped it with both hands and took a drink, then he coughed. He had fingers like little sausages.

"You like being a supervisor?" asked Floyd.

"Sure."

"What do you like about it?"

"It commands respect."

"You ever fired anybody?"

"Well, sometimes you have to let somebody go."

"You feel bad about that?"

"I feel my duty is to the company and to the trust they put in me." The gas man took another drink.

Floyd couldn't imagine being a gas man or what it would be like going into people's houses. He had been a farmer all his life.

"You ever stole anything from them?"

The gas man cranked his head around. The whiskey had brought a little color to his nose. "Of course not!"

"Not even a ballpoint pen or a couple of paper clips?"

"They trust me."

"How long you worked for the company?"

"Almost twenty-three years."

"That's a big chunk of time. You must've done a lot of stuff for them."

"I've had a wide variety of experience." The gas man talked about the sort of things he had done: office work, fieldwork, repairing broken equipment. He finished his whiskey and Floyd gave him

another. The gas man took two more aspirins. It was just after twelve
o'clock.

"You won't change your mind about that sandwich?"

"I don't like tuna fish," said the gas man. "Maybe some toast with
a little butter. Not too brown."

Floyd went back up to the kitchen. The bread had a little mold
but he cut it off. He checked the toaster to make sure no mice had
gotten electrocuted. Sometimes they crept inside and got caught
like lobsters in a trap. Floyd wiped a plate off on his pant leg, then
he buttered the toast using a clean knife. Through the kitchen
window he saw four cows moseying in a line across the field. He and
Billy had milked all thirty before sunup. Floyd took the toast back
down to the gas man.

"How many houses can you go into in a single day as a gas man?"
asked Floyd.

"Maybe sixty out in the country, double that in the city." He had his
mouth full of toast and he wiped his lips with the back of his hand.

"And nothing strange ever happens?"

"In and out, that's all I want. Sometimes a dog gives you some
trouble. I'm like a shadow in people's lives."

"And you've never felt temptation?"

The gas man drank some whiskey. "Absolutely never."

"No women give you the eye?"

"Their lives don't concern me. It's their meters I'm after." The
gas man put the empty plate on the step. He was still chewing
slowly, getting a few last crumbs, running his tongue along the gap
between his teeth and his lower lip. "It's my duty not to get involved."

"But people must talk to you. A woman must give you a friendly
look."

"Oh, it's there all right," said the gas man. "I could be bad if I
wanted."

"You seen things."

"I seen a lot."

"It must be a burden sometimes."

"My duty's to the gas company, like I say. That's why they made
me supervisor, because I make the right decisions, or try to. They
appreciate my loyalty."

"What kind of things have you seen?" asked Floyd.

The gas man drank some more whiskey, then rested the glass on his thigh. "There was a woman in Augusta, a divorcée, who had it in mind to make trouble. I seen that."

"Good-looking?"

"A little thick, but good-looking. This was ten years ago."

"What'd she do?"

The gas man took off his cap again and wiped his brow. He set his cap carefully on the step beside him. "Well, the first time I went by her house she offered me a cup of coffee. I know that doesn't sound like much but it was just the beginning. She asked if I wanted a cup of coffee and if I wanted to sit down and rest a little. She was wearing a bathrobe, a cream-colored bathrobe. She had thick brown hair past her shoulders and it was nicely brushed."

"You take the coffee?"

"I always make a point of never taking anything."

"Then what happened?"

"A month later, I went by her house again. She was waiting for me. She followed me down to the basement when I went to read her meter. I turned around and she was standing right in front of me, still in her bathrobe, like she'd been wearing it for the entire month. I said howdy and she asked if I'd like to rest a little and I said I had to keep moving. Then she asked if I liked to dance and I said I didn't, that I hadn't danced since high school. So I walked around her and left."

"You think she wanted to dance right then?" asked Floyd. He liked dancing but he hadn't had much occasion in his life. When he was younger, there had been barn dances during the summer and sometimes he still recalled the smell of perfume and hay.

"I don't know if she wanted to dance," said the gas man. "I didn't think about it. I was in a hurry."

"She must have been lonely."

"A gas man doesn't socialize. It's like being a priest but you deal with meters instead. One time a man asked me for five dollars so he could feed his family. I didn't even answer him. I don't even like it when people ask me the time of day or what the weather is like outside. In and out, that's my motto."

"So what happened with the woman?" asked Floyd.

"So the third month I check her meter she doesn't follow me down to the basement. She was still wearing her robe and I thought she'd been drinking a little. She greeted me heartily, like I was an old friend. People have done that before trying to get around me. I just nodded. I go down in the basement and check her meter. When I start back up the basement stairs, she's standing at the top. She's taken off her bathrobe and she's wearing only this pink underwear, pink panties. Her titties are completely bare and she's pushing them up at me. Big, pink titties. She was blocking the door so I couldn't get through. 'Take me,' she says, like she thinks she's a cab or something."

"What did you do?" asked Floyd.

"I asked her to get out of my way, that I was in a hurry. She still didn't move. So I yelled at her. I told her I was a busy man and I didn't have time to waste. She took her hands away from her titties pretty quick, I can tell you. I said her behavior was awful and she should be ashamed."

"Then what happened?"

"She stepped aside and I left."

"And the next month?"

"The next month she was gone and the house was shut up. I didn't think much of it but a month later I asked one of her neighbors if she'd moved. I don't know why I asked but I kept thinking of her. Maybe it was because the woman seemed crazy. Anyway, the neighbor told me the woman was dead. One morning she just hadn't woken up. The neighbor said it was pills. She just took all the pills she could find. It was the neighbor who told me that the woman was a divorcée. She said the husband had gotten the kids and married someone else. I don't know when she died, just sometime during the month."

Floyd finished his whiskey. One of the springers was barking again. Floyd thought that no woman in his entire life had ever looked at him and said, "Take me," not even his wife. "You could have kept her alive," he said.

"What d'you mean?"

"You could have talked to her. She might still be around."

"She wanted sex. She was crazy."

"But you could have talked to her. She probably only wanted a little conversation."

"That's not my job. To me, she was only a person with a gas meter. In and out, like I say."

"What if you'd found her bleeding on the floor?"

"I would have called the cops."

"But the stuff she told you, it was like she was bleeding." Floyd regretted he had given the gas man any of his White Horse.

"It's not my job to deal with bleeding."

"You should've danced with her," said Floyd. "I would've danced with her. I would've danced till my feet fell off."

"We already know about you," said the gas man. "You and that woman behind the beer tent."

"You as good as killed her," said Floyd. He felt angry but knew that only a piece of his anger was connected to the gas man. The rest seemed a blanket over everything else. He didn't like the whole setup: people coming into and going out of this life and none of it being by choice.

Floyd heard Frieda's buzzer and he got to his feet. He felt dizzy from the whiskey. He made his way upstairs holding on to the banister. The gas man kept saying something but Floyd didn't pay any mind.

Frieda's eyes were only half open. "I would like some more water." Her voice was very soft.

Floyd got the water from the kitchen and put in a couple of cubes of ice. When he handed it to Frieda, he said, "There's a real jerk in the basement."

"Tell him to go away."

"I can't. He's broken his leg."

Frieda nodded solemnly. The morphine and her approaching death made her more accepting of the world's peculiarities.

"Then give him something to eat."

"I already did."

"Then just bear with it," she said.

When Floyd looked back down the basement stairs, he saw the gas man was holding his head in his hands. "More aspirin?" He found it hard to be polite.

"Leave me alone."

"Any food? Maybe a blanket?" It was approaching one o'clock. Loretta could be arriving in as little as half an hour.

"I don't want anything from you," said the gas man.

Floyd was about to turn away and fix himself some lunch, then he changed his mind. "That's why you fell," he said. "Because of that

woman who wanted to dance. That's the punishment you got, bust-
ing your dancing leg. Ten years ago, you said. That punishment's
been coming after you for a long time, just creeping along waiting
for its chance."

"Shut up!" said the gas man. "Shut up, shut up!"

Floyd told Billy about the gas man that night at dinner. Billy was a
thin, heavily freckled youngster in his late teens who wore old
dungarees and a gray University of Maine sweatshirt. His mother's
illness was like an awful noise in his ears.

"So the rescue squad is carrying this fellow out of the house," said
Floyd. "His hands were over his face but you could tell he was
crying. I was standing there holding the dog. The guy sees me.
'Damn you,' he says, 'Goddamn you to hell!'"

"After you'd been taking care of him and fed him?" asked Billy.
They were eating beans and franks.

"Some people have no sense of how to behave," said Floyd. "Some
people would act bad even in front of St. Peter. 'Damn you,' he
kept saying. Well, I wasn't going to take that in front of the rescue
squad. A man can be provoked only so far."

"I can't believe you kept your trap shut," said Billy.

"I don't like being messed with." Floyd paused with his fork
halfway to his mouth. "I guess you know what I told him."

"I bet you gave him the very devil."

"That's just the least of it," said Floyd.

JENNIFER C CORNELL

Undertow

FROM THE NEW ENGLAND REVIEW

IT WAS CLOSE to September and the date of the wedding when
my father started bringing us to Castlerock. After breakfast we'd
board the first train from Central Station that went south to Lam-
beg and Lisburn before turning north and arriving eventually beside the sea. We'd spend the rest of the day there on the rocks
above the beach, hurling stones into the oncoming waves and fishing without bait until it was time to catch the last train from Derry
home. The train leaned hard into the left shoulder just before the
platform came into sight, and as we moved towards the exits to be
ready when it stopped, I would watch the lights from the street
lamps on the far side of the Lagan wink on the spiral whenever a
fish rose up for air.

What's that flashing? I'd asked my father the first time I'd seen it.

Fairy lights, he answered.

Bullshit, Ricky said, under his breath. He was five years my senior,
thirteen and no longer a baby; rebellion came easily to him, like a
dog. We were fifty yards from the platform and the sign above him
told him No, but still he'd thrown his weight against the window,
pulled it down, and thrust his head out into the wind. He would not
take my father's hand as we stepped down from the train.

My mother was sitting at the kitchen table with John-O Noonan
when we got home. John-O's fingers were yellow from nailtip to
knuckle and his whole hand twitched with desire; there was no
smoking allowed in my mother's house.

It's happened again, she told my father.

Has it indeed? What's it of this time?

I'm flat out of paint, she said, so you'll have to go get some. I won't have that damn thing on the side of my house.

After our tea we went out to look at it. This time they'd painted flags and emblems, and every letter of the words that went with them was outlined in black and at least two feet high. The last time they'd done a map of the country with a pair of armed soldiers on either side, and before that there'd been a bright yellow shield on a powder blue background, and a list of the names of the most recent dead. Each time my mother had covered it over by climbing a stepladder and chucking buckets of paint at the house.

When do they do it, that's what I'd like to know, John-O said. He lived in the house which terraced ours, where he spent his days minding his sister's children and keeping his eye on the Help Wanted columns, in case something came up that my father could do. He shook his head with slow admiration. How the hell do they do it when youse're here all the time?

I wish to God I could catch them at it, my mother said. I don't care who they are. That's the last bit of painting they'd ever do.

It's a real shame, my father said.

Don't start with me, Joe, my mother told him. I've no time for hoods. I'll get that paint myself if I have to.

First thing tomorrow, he answered. The shops'll be closed now, anyway.

The next day my father and I lay on till eleven. My mother was working at the kitchen table when I went downstairs to make us tea. She'd been working steadily since early that morning but the sound of machinery hadn't disturbed us, because each sequin and pearl was sewn on by hand. By this time the shell of the dress was nearly finished — the bodice and skirt, the two mutton sleeves, the veil, the headdress, and the wide, four-foot train. She had still to complete the undergarments, and she'd promised to hem the girl's linens, embroider their edges, and inscribe the corners with the first letter of her name.

Your brother's gone out, my mother told me, so it's up to you to look after your father. Don't let him come home without that paint. I stood just behind her while the kettle boiled, skewering beads on her upright needle as soon as she'd fastened the previous one. Oh here, listen, she said, and reached under the fabric in search of her purse. The table was lost under cover of satin, a full bolt of chiffon lay unwrapped on the floor, and thick books of patterns sat on each chair, their insides fat with slips of paper, receipts, and newsprint torn into strips to mark a page. A spool of white thread, luv, she said, giving me money, say you want the kind for all types of fabric, and get me at least two hundred yards. I'd ask your daddy but you know he won't do it.

Because I don't think it's right, my father said from the threshold. Taking advantage of a foolish woman when you know rightly there won't be a wedding on the twenty-first. You can't have a wedding without a groom.

More's the pity, my mother said, and unnecessarily switched on her machine.

Well I won't be part of it, my father continued. I will not add to that girl's disappointment.

For God's sake, Joe, my mother said, it's none of my business what they want the clothes for. That girl placed an order same as anyone else.

A wedding gown's different, my father told her. Especially this.

I didn't ask to hear her life's story, Joe, my mother told him, and what she does with her money is her own affair. If she wants to waste it on fortunetellers that's got nothing to do with me.

I think we are obligated to protect the innocent, my father said quietly.

Fair enough, my mother answered, but only if they're mine. That girl pays good money, in advance and on time. I've got this family to worry about, Joe.

We spoke no more about it, though my father refused to come in the shop with me when I went in to purchase thread. We bought two tins of paint, a tray, and a roller, and were in the sitting room stirring the tins when Ricky came home with a sackful of chestnuts.

How come they're called conkers? I asked my father.

Why d'you think? Ricky said. He took one whose green armored shell had not broken and slapped it, palm open, against his head.

It began with a farmer, my father answered, who owned a good bit of land not far from Mullan Head. He was a man who didn't like to spend money, and it's not like he didn't have it to spend. Every night he sat in the dark so he wouldn't have to run the electric, and all the beasts on his farm had bad teeth and were spindly because he was too cheap to give them a decent feed. Now there was a tree on that land and the farmer didn't like it. Its shade kept him cold, he said, and it made his house dark. He blamed the tree for his own mean nature and one day he decided, I'll cut the thing down. But the tree saw him coming with his rolled-up sleeves and his heavy boots and the toothy new saw in his hand. It got so frightened it shook and heaved, and a whole shower of chestnuts fell on the farmer, sticking and pricking him with their rubbery spines. He was so bruised and battered he spent six weeks in hospital, and as soon as he got out he picked up and left. Then a husband and wife with two little children, a boy and a wee girl about your age, came to live in the house. They put a swing on the tree and built a conservatory and the house is so full of light now that they built a train past it, and if you're a good wee girly this evening and eat all your peas I'll show you it tomorrow on the way to Castlerock.

Joe, my mother said from the other room. How old is your daughter?

So why don't all trees throw conkers all the time?

Cuz it's all bollocks, that's why, Ricky said. They fall cuz the stems rot, that's why it's easy to knock 'em down.

You know what your problem is, Ricky? my mother called to him.

Humankind has grown impatient, my father answered. The cold facts of science take less time to tell.

The side of our house stayed white for six days. On the morning of the seventh my mother noticed the additional shadow when she stepped outside to bring in the milk.

Joe, she called from the bottom of the stairs, come here till you see this.

From the room next to mine I heard my parents' bed creak as my father rolled onto his back and sighed.

Ah, Belle, he said, it's not even seven.

They've left a ladder, my mother said, and I'll tell you right now they're not getting it back.

Not very good, is it? John-O said an hour or so later. Still in his dressing gown and pajamas, he'd seen our door lying open when he'd let the cat out and had jumped the low fence that ran between us, calling our names as he hurried into the house. My mother, lugging a tarpaulin and paint thinner, had nearly run over him as she backed out the door.

Different artist, my father answered. This wee fella's got no sense of color.

It's God awful, John-O said. I'm with you, missus — get rid of it. That bloody thing's hard on the eyes.

It's going today, my mother said firmly. I've a girl coming by for a fitting tomorrow, and this will not be the first thing she sees.

What time tomorrow? my father said suddenly.

For a moment my mother looked like she'd bitten her tongue. I know what you're thinking, Joe, she said, and it's not going to happen.

Go on, Belle. What time's she coming?

I should have known you'd pull something like this, my mother said bitterly. Why can't you stay out of it? It's got nothing to do with you.

Right! John-O said. See youse all later.

I just want to talk to her, Belle, that's all.

What for? What good'll it do? She's not getting a refund, you know, even if you do manage to make her change her mind.

C'mon now, folks, John-O said, don't do this outside.

It's not just about money, my father answered. It's her state of mind. What's going to happen to her two weeks from Friday? I'm not convinced she's going to survive.

All right, Joe, my mother said. I give up. Stay in if you want to tomorrow; just stay the hell out of my way today.

There now, John-O said cheerfully, that's better. Youse two had me worried there for a while.

We'd missed the first train to Derry but we did catch the second. Ricky stayed behind to help my mother; intending to keep the ladder as evidence, she'd said no when he'd asked for it and offered to let him paint the wall instead. When we arrived in Castlerock we headed at once for our regular café, where we each ordered a fish and chip dinner and my father explained why fish had it so bad — because they bore grudges, resenting all those who'd stood on four feet at the birth of Jesus, and the Dove for finding the olive branch, and all the rest of the animal kingdom for having a place set aside for them on the Ark. It didn't matter that God had conferred on them wisdom, that He'd warned them about the Flood in advance. And so they are regularly captured and eaten, they fall ill easily and are tormented by cats, and though they gasp with the effort of trying to buy freedom with secrets the Almighty had shared, they can never produce the human words necessary, never can make themselves understood. And that, said my father, is apt punishment for arrogance — that they die ignominiously, out of their element, impressive only because of their size.

Then our dinners were ready and he went up to fetch them. He came back with two plates and a plastic lemon, which he set down on the table next to the salt. If Ricky'd been with us he'd have been embarrassed, and my father would have explained yet again how he met my mother. She'd been the new girl at the local chippy where he went occasionally for a takeaway, and he'd asked her for a wedge of lemon, which naturally enough the shop didn't have. The dinner rush was at its most frantic when my mother put on her coat and took her umbrella and went down to a grocer two blocks away to buy my father a bagful of lemons with her own money, because there was something about his face she fancied though now she couldn't remember what. At this establishment, my father said as if I'd protested, my custom is valued. Did she really empty them out on top of you? I asked him. Right in my lap, he said. There must have been two or three dozen at least.

And then what happened?

Then? Then your mother was sacked and I was ejected. We never went near the place again.

After our dinner we walked to the beach. A buttress of rocks spilled into the sea, their surfaces pitted with shallow depressions, warm water puddles of algae and snails and keyhole limpets whose airtight seals resisted all efforts to pry their shells loose. A man hurled a stick and his dog sailed after and caught it each time in its open jaws, the wide arc of its body in motion continuing on into the water with the same compact force of those who ran barefoot from one rock to another to fling themselves off the final one, their knees to their chests and their arms wrapped around them, their hair and clothes still heavy with water from the previous jump. There's our friend, said my father, and I turned to see a horse approaching, its rider bouncing like a ball on a string as the horse's hooves pummeled the surf, leaving prints that the tide made more cavernous, brown sugar sand tumbling in on all sides. They'd been there every day since we first started coming. The man lived by himself in a one-room caravan staked to flat ground just beyond Castlerock, and he kept his horse on a small slab of pasture which belonged to no one and which he'd cleared himself. He's a nutter, Ricky had said when my father told us. Everyone says so. You must learn the difference between fraud and fiction, Ricky, my father said. It's true, Ricky'd said sullenly. There's even a petition to get him put out. The darkness of Mankind is truly untellable, my father said later, more to himself than to either of us. It shouldn't surprise me but it always does.

The man rode bareback and the horse wore no bridle, yet they pulled up beside us with the flourish expected when reins are drawn tight, hot breath expelled from the horse's nostrils, sand splashing over us with each sweep of its tail.

You're late today, the man said.

I know it, my father said. What about ye?

The man shrugged. Yerself?

We're all right, aren't we, luv? said my father. Do you still want a ride?

C'mon up, luv, the man said, and I reached for his hand. Up close the horse smelled like brass and worn leather; I filled my fists with its oily mane, my father put his hand on my ankle and I felt the knees of the man behind me press against the horse's ribs. We walked past the mouth of the tunnel, that long stretch of darkness from which trains hurtle out, startling their passengers with the sudden proximity of sand and seawater, of gulls suspended above black shards of rock. Then we turned and came back at a canter, my father too on the animal's strong back, past boys Ricky's age who were playing football, past new groups of people sitting on jackets drinking beer and soft drinks from oversized tins, up the very steps which led to the street. Look after yourself now, my father said. You worry too much, the other man told him, and urged the horse through the small crowd of children that had gathered around him and headed back the way we'd just come.

In Coleraine while we waited to transfer I stood at the edge of the platform to watch the incoming train, signaled by sirens and the lowering of booms, a mad dash of assorted pedestrians and small dogs on leads hurrying from one side of the road to the other before the train, with the same graceful movements of things buoyed by water, came round the corner and eased into the station.

Stand back now, my father said. Let them get off. But my eyes were not on the entrance but on the red diamond in the center of the train's yellow face. We'd chosen a car that was practically empty, so once we were settled with our tickets ready, our crisps on the table, our feet outstretched towards the seat across from us and our coats and umbrellas on the rack above our heads, I asked my father to tell me the story he'd promised the last time.

Oh yes, he said, I'd nearly forgotten. When the iron horse was first brought to Ireland, the other animals found it a bad-mannered beast. It was loud and filthy and single-minded, it stopped on no whim or for any diversion, just proceeded directly from A to B. To be so oblivious to the world around you was a dangerous condition, the other beasts said, for what if one of them happened to stop in its path? But once they realized that the train only ran on the tracks set down for it, and only at more or less predictable times, they began to enjoy its daily passage. They even grew rather possessive, and boasted about it when they'd had too much to drink. Our train can beat any bird flying, the beasts would say loudly, whenever birds were around to hear — which naturally the birds took as a challenge, and eventually they sent someone over to accept. But the two parties couldn't agree on the details of the contest, until finally the bird representative said How about this: you set the distance, and we'll set the course. The beasts were confident their man could travel over any terrain, so they said Okay, but we're not crossing water — and then congratulated themselves for being so clever. About the same time as all this was happening a new model of train was introduced. This one was even faster, the beasts read in the advertisements they found in the newspapers that passengers tossed from the windows, along with their cigarette butts and their empty tins. When the birds found this out, they tried to call the race off, but the beasts wouldn't let them. Instead they arranged for one round of pontoon, the winner to decide which train would be run. At the end of three rounds the beasts had a five, a two, and the Queen of Spades, while the birds had a hand adding up to fifteen. Each side asked for one more card. Twenty! the birds said when they got theirs, and if they'd been playing poker they'd have been hard to beat, for what they had in front of them was a straight flush of Hearts. The beasts sucked their teeth and said they were sorry but they didn't mean it, for their hidden card was the Three of Diamonds, and with the Ace they'd been given they'd just made twenty-one.

Listen! my father said as our train passed another, and I heard in the jolt and clatter of the tracks the sound of a deck of iron cards being shuffled. What about the race? I asked. Did the train beat the birds? Well, no, my father said. Sure the beasts had forgotten that a train can't run if there aren't any tracks. The birds chose a course that never crossed water, but it also didn't pass through A or B. As soon as they discovered the situation all the earth-moving beasts got stuck in right away, but no one could lift the rails from the stack in the depot, let alone move them to the ground they'd prepared. It was very frustrating, my father conceded, his arm growing heavy around my shoulders and his own gaze wandering to the scenery outside. I watched the outgoing tracks sprinting beside us, and imagined a pair of simultaneous tunnels, blind, flowered snouts and efficient fingers churning the soil up from below.

We reached our gate just as John-O was leaving, and it was clear from my mother's expression that she'd been trying to ease him out for some time. When John-O saw us his face brightened. My mother's brows drew together like curtains; she exhaled audibly and went back inside.

Talk sense to this woman, John-O pleaded, walking backwards in front of my father. She won't listen to me.

The dress was loosely assembled now. My father stooped to gather a fallen crinoline and struggled to drape it over the back of a chair, the garment appearing to defy gravity until my mother took it off him and dropped it back onto the floor.

I want to go to the council, get a sign put up.

A sign to say what?

Keep Off, that's what, my mother said irritably. I'm tired of wasting my time and money. It should be the council's problem, not mine.

Don't let her do it, John-O said to my father. She'll only annoy them. You're lucky they've let you paint the thing over. How many times has it been now? Three?

Four. If the council won't listen I'll go to the police.

You don't know who they are, John-O said. They could put you out first.

Is that right? Well just let them try.

It's not worth it, John-O said earnestly, even if it is just kids. Kids can be wee bastards, too, you know.

Where's Ricky? my father said after John-O went home.

Upstairs with Jason. Can't you hear that damn racket?

Go tell him to lower it, luv, my father said, and I had to twice before Ricky would. When I came down the second time my father, whose hands were cool even in summer, had placed his palms on the back of her neck, right where the spine makes its small mountain ridge, and was kneading her shoulders in generous handfuls, his own cheek resting on the top of her head.

I'm still going to do it, Joe, she said.

Ricky's friend left a short while later, and my father herded me upstairs to bed. I'm not tired, I told him, I slept on the train. Go on, luv, he said, lie down, close your eyes. Don't you worry. Everything's going to be okay. Here — tell me three things you saw today and I'll make you a story.

A tub in a field, I said. And a tree island. And a whole fence full of plastic bags.

Right, he said, here goes the first one. There once was a king whose greatest wish was for peace and quiet. Though his country had not been to war for many years, and though the land was fertile and the climate kind, still his people fought and bickered amongst themselves, and the king, as the arbiter of all disputes, found himself again and again called away from love or meditation to pass judgment on a trivial disagreement, or soothe the ego of some individual who felt insulted or slighted by somebody else. The king consulted with the greatest minds in study and politics, but no one could offer any good advice. Finally the king commissioned a wizard who said he'd cast a spell that'd do the trick — he'd send a fog so thick it'd cover the land like heavy cream, and when it cleared, all those thinking evil thoughts about another would be revealed for what they were. The king agreed, and for nine days afterwards a fog was on them, thicker on the ninth day than it had been on the first. When it cleared the sun was so brilliant that most folks just marveled — until they heard the embarrassed cries of the evil thinkers, caught stark naked in their bathtubs out in their fields for all the world to see. For the wizard had set an additional spell, so that all the vicious and petty people would be taking a bath at just the same time. The tubs that exposed them have been there ever since, collecting rain for the livestock to drink. The land itself has changed hands so often, hardly a soul remembers why they're there now. Are you asleep yet?

Not yet, I said, but I already was.

*

Not so long ago the Hardest Working Couple in the World were living with their children in Island Magee. Though the mother and father had earned the title by working continuously for more than ten months, even so they barely had enough for the bills and the shopping, and though Christmas was coming they hadn't been able to buy any gifts. On Christmas Eve on the road home from work the woman met an old man with such heavy wrinkles he had to use a forked branch to keep his brows up. What can I do to please my children? the woman asked him, because she was desperate for someone to talk to. We've labored long and hard but we're no richer for it. We don't even have stockings to hang over the hearth. Take one empty sack for each in your family and tie them to the fence that keeps your cows in, the old man said, and tomorrow your children will thank you for it. The woman did what he'd told her, and the next morning every sack was full of chocolate and oranges, picture books and pens and mechanical toys. A month or so later it was one child's birthday, and again his parents had no money to spare. On the off chance of a second miracle the woman tied another sack to the fence — and sure enough the next morning it was so heavy it pulled the fence after it on its way to the ground. Why should we work, the woman wondered as she watched her son enjoying his presents, when all we want can be had for the asking? But the spirit that filled the bags was no eedjit; it knew what their game was when later that night the woman and her husband covered their fence with empty sacks. The next morning all the sacks looked full from a distance, but up close it was clear they held only wind. The worst of it is the mother and father never learned their lesson: they kept leaving sacks on the fence for generations, and wasted so much time waiting for nothing they lost their title of Hardest Working Couple to a rival team from Markethill. And that's why there's plastic bags on the fences, because people are greedy past the point of good sense.

My mother put down her scissors and looked at me. He told you this.

I nodded.

What do you think of your father's stories?

I think he should sell them, John-O said. A letter requesting my father's attendance at an interview that afternoon had arrived the same morning, and John-O, who had spotted the post in the Job

Finder listings, was waiting in our kitchen to see him off. He'd make a fortune, John-O continued. Youse could get out of Belfast, buy a big house with at least fifteen bedrooms, a huge garden and a two-car garage — you could buy a good car with that kind of money. That's what I'd do if I was him.

Well, said my mother, he left a part out of this one. Farmers put bags on their fences to frighten their cows, luv. It's to keep them away from the wire so they don't try to get into other people's fields.

You could even go somewhere exotic, John-O said. I hear the weather's brilliant in Florida. An annual rainfall of less than three inches and sunshine ten months out of every year.

All right? said my father on his way past the kitchen. He'd come down the stairs at a run, his hand already reaching for the outside door.

Where's your tie? my mother demanded.

He patted his pocket. It's too warm, Belle. I'll put it on when I get there.

No, said my mother. Come over here. Stop fussing, Joe, she continued preemptively, it won't take a minute. Standing behind him she tugged at his waistband, and the cuffs of his trousers snapped to attention. How's that? Too tight?

I could borrow a belt, my father suggested.

It's done now, my mother said, and ran her razor down the short seam at the back of the garment and plucked the torn stitches out with a pin. Hand me that thread, luv, she said, and I snapped off a strand and moistened its end, and she pushed it through the eye of the needle she held with the same hand that gripped the thin fabric of my father's summer suit. There, she said after a minute, tugging his sleeves and smoothing his shoulders, her fingers running over his lapels till he caught her wrists and drew her to him, placing a kiss on each open palm. Go on, get out of here, she said, you'll be late, but she stood at our gate with me and John-O and even waved back to him as he waited for the bus.

All right, everybody, she said as the bus pulled away, show's over, back to work. But my mother's client was late for her fitting, and when John-O sent his niece over with cream buns later my mother agreed she had made enough progress to stop and have one with a quick cup of tea. It was some time after that when the girl rang our bell.

C'mon in, my mother shouted from the kitchen where she'd

taken a break from replacing a zipper to clean the grit out of Ricky's wounds. He'd been fighting again, though he wouldn't admit it. He'd told my mother he'd slipped on the ladder she'd told him expressly to stay away from, knowing the clout she was likely to give him would have been worse if he'd told her the truth. That's it there, my mother said before the girl could apologize, go ahead and try it on.

The girl took a step towards the dress and looked around her, at the no longer sterile roll of cotton and the bottle of alcohol on the kitchen counter, at Ricky's arm in my mother's firm grasp, at the teetering piles of new jeans and chinos purchased on sale from shops in the town, every one of them too long in the legs to be worn immediately and belonging to boys from our estate.

Where d'you want me?

Right here, my mother said. Ricky, go do something. He gave me a look as she released him, corked the bottle, and tossed the used swabs, but he needn't have bothered. I remembered the last time he'd gotten in trouble. He'd been one of a crowd of children who'd demolished a car that had been in an accident and was moved temporarily to the side of the road. The front left-hand corner had been shorn off on impact but apart from that there'd been little damage, and those who'd come running when they heard the collision were saying it was too bad the driver was uninsured when a boy took a stick and smashed the taillights. Within half an hour all the windows were broken, the roof had caved in, and someone had started an ineffectual fire in the foam rubber stuffing they'd pulled out of the backseat. That afternoon Ricky and I went out with my father, who'd been in town when it happened, and found the owner of the car sitting on the curb. Whose fault was it? my father asked him. It was his, the man said, but what does it matter? He's already got witnesses to say it was me. Later that night I'd informed on my brother, but my father said only, Yes, I know, and told me a story about Belfast Courthouse. A long time ago its four walls were formed out of living flora, a garden attended by Justice herself. But the crimes of Mankind had been so dazzling they had left Justice blind, and with no one to tend it the building itself had turned into stone, the gray marble leaves and flowers blackened by soot and ringing the pillars outside the Court the only reminder of what Justice once was. So is Ricky not going to get beaten, then? I'd asked. No, he said, that's not the point. People don't often get what's coming to them, one way or the other. The important thing is to keep trying to make sure they do.

The dress opened and closed by button only. At least three dozen ran from the small of the back towards the high collar, each one fastened through a tight elastic loop. My mother lay a board across two tins of paint and tested it briefly; then the girl stepped into it, the heavy folds of her skirts gathered high in both hands.

Are you redecorating? she asked.

All the time, my mother said. Lift up now; that's right.

I need to buy wallpaper myself, the girl said, holding her arms away from her sides. I was trying to get the house ready for Friday, but it's taking forever. I still have another two bedrooms to go, and I've done nothing else but that house all week.

How many bedrooms, altogether?

Five — well, four and a half, really. There's a wee room at the top that'd suit a child. It used to be part of the other back bedroom, but I put up a partition. We can always take it down again if we need the space. She dropped her arms on my mother's instruction and smiled. I retiled the bathroom, too, and lay new lino in the kitchen. I bought seeds to replant the garden, and a trellis for the side of the house, but I won't have the chance till after we've moved in.

If you don't mind me asking, my mother said, where are you getting the money for all this?

I won the pools, the girl said simply. I played the numbers Fortuna gave me and I won about two thousand pounds. My mother was on her knees adjusting the hem so the lace trim of the underskirt would show more clearly; she glanced up at the girl but did not pause. She's been right about other things, too, the girl continued. She knew my sister miscarried the first time, and told her she was pregnant again before she knew herself. She can tell things about you just by holding your hand.

I don't think I'd like that, my mother said. Turn this way, please.

I know, the girl said, I thought I wouldn't, either. But it's okay, it's nothing like I expected. She's awful good. My girlfriend saved for two years to put a deposit on a trip to Corfu, and the first thing Fortuna says to her is You're going to travel. And she told my mum she was going to get better and it was six months before she took sick again.

I don't know, my mother said. Here, try the veil on. The pools thing's impressive, but the rest of it sounds pretty familiar.

You should go, the girl said generously. She knew wee things about me I never told anyone. I was ill myself last year and she knew about it. She even knew what was in my head at the time.

Upstairs Ricky kicked a football through the door of his room onto the landing and down the stairs into the hall. I saw the ball bounce on its way past the kitchen and then heard the sound of it striking wood. Go easy! my mother warned him when he came in, but he only grinned.

Da's back, he said.

My father seemed surprised when he saw us together, the girl on her platform, my mother on her knees, myself on a chair in charge of the pin cushion, and Ricky with the football under his arm, spoiling his supper with the last cream bun.

This is my husband, my mother said through her teeth. The girl nodded quickly, flushed and self-conscious, but at that height even her awkwardness was elevated to grace. She wore the veil as it's worn after vows, the thin film of gauze spilling over her shoulders like freshly brushed hair. My father stood beneath her, gazing up.

You look very beautiful, he said.

It's lovely, isn't it? the girl said eagerly.

It's all right, my mother said, but I knew she was pleased. I'd helped her select the low, smooth bodice, and approved the change to sleeves which began off the shoulder and tapered to a point just past the wrist. I'd been there when she'd added a bustle, and replaced a full skirt which just brushed the ground with one more narrow, with a heavy train. Think elegant, my mother had said as we looked through the patterns. What we don't want is to make the thing vulgar. Feminine, yes, but not delicate, necessarily. Handsome? I'd offered. That's it, she'd said. Whatever else happens, at least she'll look strong.

We won't be much longer, my mother told him. Why don't you go next door for a while? I'll send Ricky over when the supper's ready.

No need, my father said heartily, almost before John-O came into the room. John-O, this is the wee girl that's getting married.

Oh, aye? John-O said. Congratulations. What's your fiancé do, by the way?

Not now, my mother said sharply. We're not finished here.

Fortuna says he'll be a baker. She says he'll come home with flour in his pockets, and he'll leave white footprints on the carpet when he takes off his shoes. She says I'll never smell another woman on him, only bread from the oven and marzipan.

My father's mouth opened, but when no words were coming John-O stopped waiting and turned back to the girl.

Is he from round here, your boyfriend?

Oh no, she said, he's from the country. That's why I got a house near Bellevue. Fortuna said he'd like it, being close to Cave Hill.

An outdoorsy type, is he?

He'll like having a garden, the girl said. He can make anything grow. I was just going to get roses, put a few bushes at the front of the house, but Fortuna said I should invest in a fruit tree or something, since she didn't see us moving house for a while. Course, I'm useless with flowers, and I can't cook. That's why Fortuna thinks we'll make a good match.

Right, my mother said, that's us finished. Could youse all get out while she changes, please?

After they'd gone she brought out the linens, four sets of sheets and eight pillowcases so heavy that when she set them down on the kitchen table loose scraps of thread and less durable fabrics jumped up in protest, and the hair around all three of our faces was moved by the puff of air she'd displaced. Your shift and things aren't finished yet, she told the girl, but I'll have them all ready for Wednesday. You can come and collect them any time after noon.

Can't I have them delivered? It's just I still have so much to do.

If you want, my mother said. It's a bit risky. Personally I like to have a good look at a thing before I pay the bill. But it's up to you. If you want them sent over I need the balance off you now.

That's okay, the girl said, I brought money with me. The bills she counted onto the table were still crisp and in sequence like the sheaves that spill from unmarked envelopes or are stacked and banded in open briefcases and pushed across deserted warehouse floors, and I thought of a trick that John-O had taught me, a way to fold bank notes to make the face printed on them smile or frown. That only works with the real ones, my father had added. All the forged ones do is grin.

It really is lovely, the girl said as she pulled on her coat.

I think it suits you, my mother said, following her out. You'll look well on the day. Are you getting your hair done?

Aye, I am, I'm putting it up. I brought in that picture you gave me, the one you drew the first time I came here. The girl in the salon said she could do something that'd set off the dress. I hope it's okay — I nearly rang you up to get your opinion, but you'd have to have seen it, really, to know. Here, why don't you come? she suggested suddenly. I've booked a wee room for the reception after — there's one right beside where they do the service.

Sorry, my mother said, but I'm up to my eyes in work at the minute. Thanks all the same.

It'd only be for an hour. There's another couple booked in for one o'clock. Please come. And think about going to see Fortuna. It's only five pounds for a palm reading, ten if you want the crystal ball.

My father sighed as he closed the door after her. So what d'you think? John-O asked him. Is she crazy?

No more than most.

Will there not be a wedding, then?

You never know, luv, he said. She might find someone yet. It's easier now, certainly, than it used to be. A long time ago there were rules about who you could marry. If a man fell in love with a widow, for example, he couldn't marry her unless he was a widower himself.

That's true enough, John-O said before my mother could protest. I heard about that on *Celebrity Squares*.

One boy in particular, my father continued, fell in love with a girl who was already married. Many years went by and the young man grew old, but he stayed a bachelor, for he knew he'd be no good as a husband without her as his wife. He spent his time writing bad poetry and romantic letters which of course he never sent, for the woman herself was happily married, and whatever his feelings he'd never do anything that might cause her pain. He wished no harm on her husband, either. In fact, he was almost resigned to a life as Love's martyr when word reached him that his beloved had been widowed at last. After a period of respectful courtship he crossed his fingers and made his proposal; naturally he was over the moon when she said Yes. To get round the rules he married a tree the following morning, chopped it down to be widowed around three o'clock, and that very evening joined his sweetheart in holy matrimony.

Married a tree, my mother repeated.

You see? Ricky said. If that girl's not crazy, what d'you call him?

It's all true, John-O protested. I remember the program.

If there is a wedding, I asked my mother, are you going to go?

I am not, she said. She glanced at my father. And neither are you.

Maybe we ought to, he said. She shouldn't be alone.

She's got family. Her sister'll be there. She'll be all right.

Aye, she will, Ricky said. If she can't find a man she can marry a tree.

What's going to happen? I asked my father when he came in later to kiss me good night. I don't know, luv, he said. Maybe she'll be lucky. Lots of people are.

I rolled towards the weight of him on the edge of my bed and for a long time his fingers brushed the hair from my brow and temple, smoothing and shaping it over my ear. We did not speak. I kept my eyes closed when he finished and he stood up without asking if I were asleep. I opened them only when his back was turned, and saw my mother in the doorway, watching him come.

Well? she asked. How'd it go?

He took her hand from her pocket and turned it over.

You'll have a long life, he said, and two lovely children. But you'll live in a house that brings only trouble, and you'll marry a man who'll be good for nothing and make your life seem longer still.

Did it not go well, then?

Not very.

Why, what happened?

He tilted her palm for a further reading but she put her other hand on his shoulder and he stopped and frowned and looked at her arm.

Tell me, she said.

What's there to tell? I'm thirty-eight years old; I've not worked in six years. How good could it go?

But you got an interview.

Yes, he said. There is that.

There'll be other jobs, she said, and though I could not see her face with the hall light behind her I imagined the way it had summoned its power the first morning she'd discovered they'd painted our wall.

We went to Portrush on the day of the wedding. My father asked John-O to come along with us, but he'd promised to take his nephew and niece to the zoo. There was a polar bear there that they wanted to see, which took two steps backwards for every twelve it walked front, and an elephant seal that spent most of its time under the water and only pretended to enjoy human company. Why does he do that? I'd asked my father. We'd been lucky; we were far from the Plexiglas when we saw the beast spew, the small group who'd gathered to laugh or admire stumbling backwards in confusion, holding their soaked shirts and blouses away from their skin. He's proud, my father explained, and he values his privacy. This is his way of pointing back.

It was strange not to transfer when we got to Coleraine. On good days the cast-iron bridge that vaulted the tracks was warm to the touch as I held on to the rail, the pigeons so bold on the ledge just beneath us that they barely noticed when we passed, their heads subsiding between their shoulders, the dreary stains and splotches of their city colors made as beautiful in the sunlight as the faint iridescence around their necks. But this time we stayed seated and watched other passengers collect their belongings and empty out of the small wooden doors which let the breeze in. A few people came on but walked through to Smoking, then the doors were snapped shut along the length of the carriage, I heard someone whistle, and the train pulled away.

The forecast had been hopeful and we'd brought food for a picnic. In a concrete shelter which faced the sea my mother announced the contents of the sandwiches she'd made and distributed them to us with a packet of crisps and carton of orange, and for a while there was only the sound of crunch and swallow, and the spluttering sighs of liquid reversing through straws.

A gull stalked the wall that bordered the walkway, harassing a dog in the shade underneath. We threw scraps and the gull descended, riding the air with wings outstretched as if it were lowered by invisible strings, and soon more arrived, each one as possessive of the air space in front of us as if it had the right of being there first. In the interest of fairness I threw a crust to the dog. It raised its chin to watch the bread land but apart from that it didn't move. No, my father agreed when I showed him, they aren't very intelligent. The Sixth Day of Creation was a busy one for God; the dogs had to wait for several hours while He was fashioning the other beasts, and by that time all the best attributes had been given out. Loyalty and patience and an affectionate nature seemed more attractive to them than intelligence at the time. Not such a poor choice, my mother said. No, my father responded. I don't think they regret it.

Here, Da, Ricky said, wait'll you see. He called the dog by some generic name and the animal rose from its haunches and came over, smiling and nodding and wagging its tail.

Sit, Ricky said, and the dog sat down indifferently like a man whose thoughts are somewhere else. Give us your paw, he said, and the animal did so with bored amusement, as if it were humoring a tiresome friend. Hand me a hammer, Ricky said with the same inflection, and the dog withdrew its right arm and lifted its left. See? Ricky said. You can tell'm anything. It's all got to do with your tone of voice. What do you want me to make him do?

Have him roll over, my mother said.

Fly round, Ricky said, addressing the dog, go on, fly round. The dog stretched lazily, its rump raised and waving till its chest touched the ground. That's it; now — throw bowlers! Ricky commanded, but the dog looked at him skeptically, its eyebrows raised. Throw bowlers, he said again, like an invitation, and the dog lay its ear on the tarmac and rolled onto its back. For some time preoccupied with its own hips and shoulders, it finally rose and shook itself violently, spattering us with flecks of saliva, fragments of glass, sand and lawn clippings and other footpath garbage. When it had finished it calmly accepted the crisps Ricky fed it and offered its ears to my father's caress.

When we headed for Waterworld the dog followed briefly, but soon was distracted by the sight of something at the far end of the beach. Let him go, son, my mother said when Ricky called after him. She squeezed my hand and gave me a wink, then slipped her arm through his as if she found walking difficult and she needed his help. They don't allow dogs where we're going, anyway.

The complex featured a selection of swimming pools and three water slides, twisting tunnels of bright colored plastic which plunged thirty feet into the water, jiggling like innards each time they were used, and a hidden machine which produced six-foot waves. The smell of chlorine was sharp close to the pools, and even the foyer was warm and damp. In the changing rooms at the back of the building wet swimsuits and towels slapped to the ground beside the benches and outside the stalls with the finality of things attracted by magnets, and steam rose from the threshold of water through which all new arrivals were required to pass. For a while I just stood by the railing and watched others pop from the slides with all the surprise of people whose chairs have been pulled out from under them. A siren erupted every half hour and those on the lip of the pool with their feet in the water twisted round on their palms and slipped over the side. Then the machine was switched on and the contents of the pool sloshed over its edges, slapping the steps at the opposite end where the concrete floor hurried up at an anxious angle and the water was so shallow it was still almost white. Because Ricky dared me I climbed the scaffolding which led to the slides. Some-one behind me gave me a push and I was carried down on a thin sheet of water, my hips riding furiously up the sides of the tube. All I could see was the white mouth of the exit swinging far in front, at the center of a world which was otherwise yellow, backlit and uni-form and almost translucent, and I thought of small, pallid insects and what they might see traversing the contours of delicate blos-soms, enveloped between a confluence of grooves.

When we got home my mother of course was the first to spot it, and she saw it as soon as we stepped from the bus. At the bottom of the mural men and women with various weapons stood with bowed heads against the ruins of battle while others fired a volley into the folds of a banner strung up with barbed wire and printed all over with shields and crests. Above all this a golden youth towered, his gaze flung backwards over his shoulder, his right arm raised and beckoning to the dark silhouettes of the marchers who followed him — Opportunity! Culture! their placards promised, Houses! Jobs! Education for All!

KATE BRAVERMAN

Pagan Night

FROM ZYZZYVA

SOMETIMES THEY called him Forest or Sky. Sometimes they called him River or Wind. Once, during a week of storms when she could not leave the van at all, not for seven consecutive days, they called him Gray. The baby with the floating name and how she carries him and he keeps crying, has one rash after another, coughs, seems to shudder and choke. It is a baby of spasms, of a twisted face turning colors. You wouldn't want to put his picture on the baby-food jar. You wouldn't want to carry his picture in your wallet, even if you had his photograph and she doesn't.

Of course, Dalton never wanted this baby. Neither did she. The baby was just something that happened and there didn't seem to be the time to make it not happen. They were on tour, two months of one-nighters between San Diego and Seattle and when it was over the band broke up. When it was over, they got drunk and sold the keyboards and video cameras for heroin. Then they were in San Francisco and she still had the apartment. Later, they had Dalton's van.

Then they had to leave San Francisco. Something about the equipment, the amplifiers Dalton insisted were his, that they had accrued to him by a process of decision and sacrifice. Then they had to wind through California with her belly already showing and all they had left were their black leather jackets and the silver-and-turquoise jewelry they had somehow acquired in Gallup or Flagstaff. Dalton kept talking about the drummer's kit, which he claimed was actually his, and they sold it in Reno and lived on the fortieth floor of an old hotel with a view of the mountains. They had room service for three weeks and by then she had stopped throwing up. After that there was more of Nevada and the van broke again on the other side of the state. There was the slow entry into Idaho, after mountains and desert and Utah and the snow had melted and then the baby they had almost forgotten about was born.

Dalton can't stand the baby crying. That's why she leaves the van, walks three miles into town along the river. When she has a dollar-fifty, she buys an espresso in the café where the waitress has heard of her band.

Sunny stays away from the van as long as she can. Sometimes someone will offer her a ride to the park or the zoo or the shopping mall and she takes it. She's let her hair grow out, the purple and magenta streaks are nearly gone, seem an accident that could have happened to anyone, a mislabeled bottle, perhaps. Dalton says it's better to blend in. He's cut his hair, too, and wears a San Diego Padres baseball cap. He says it makes him feel closer to God.

Willow. Cottonwood. Creek. Eagle. She could call the baby Willow. But Dalton refuses to give it a name. He resists the gender, refers to the baby as it, not he. Just it, the creature that makes the noise. But it doesn't cost any money. She still feeds it from her body and the rashes come and go. It's because she doesn't have enough diapers. Sunny puts suntan lotion on the baby's sores, massage oil, whatever is left in her suitcase from the other life. Once she covered the baby's rash with layers of fluorescent orange lipstick, the last of her stage makeup.

Sunny has begun to realize that if she can't keep the baby quiet, Dalton will leave her. It won't always be summer here. There will come a season when she can't just walk all day, or sit in the mall or the lobby of the granite city hall, pretending to read a newspaper. She won't be able to spend the entire winter in the basement of the museum where they have built a replica of the town as it was in the beginning, with its penny-candy store and nickel barber shop and baths for a quarter. She won't be able to spend five or six months attempting to transport herself through time telepathically. She could work in the saloon, find an Indian to watch the baby. Later she could marry the sheriff.

Today, walking by the river, it occurred to Sunny that this landscape was different from any other she had known. It wasn't the punched-awake, intoxicated glow of the tropics, seductive and inflamed. It didn't tease you and make you want to die for it. That's what she thought of Hawaii. And it wasn't the rancid gleam like spoiled lemons that coated everything in a sort of bad childhood waxy veneer flashback. That's what she thought of Los Angeles where they had lived for two years. In Los Angeles, afternoon smelled of ash and some enormous August you could not placate or forget. Los Angeles air reminded her of what happened to children in foster homes at dusk when they took their clothes off, things that were done in stucco added-on garages with ropes and pieces of metal and the freeway rushing in the background like a cheap sound track. It was in sync, but it had no meaning.

This Idaho was an entirely separate area of the spectrum. There was something unstable about it, as if it had risen from a core of some vast, failed caution. It was the end of restlessness. It was what happened when you stopped looking over your shoulder. It was what happened when you dared to catch your breath, when you thought you were safe.

Sunny feels there is some mean streak to this still raw, still frontier, place. This land knows it gets cold, winter stays too long, crops rot, you starve. This land knows about wind, how after storms the clouds continue to assemble every afternoon over the plain, gather and recombine and rain again and this can go on for weeks. Her shoes are always damp. Her feet are encased in white blisters. Always, the thunderheads are congregating and mating and their spawn is a cold rain.

Somedays the clouds are in remission, ringing the plain but staying low. On such afternoons, the three of them go down to the Snake River. They follow a dirt road to another dirt road and they've been instructed where to turn, near the hit-by-lightning willow. They park on a rise above the channel. Dalton leaves his guitar in the van and padlocks it, walks ahead of her and the baby with the fishing pole over his shoulder. They walk beneath black branches, find the path of smooth rocks down to the bank leading to a railroad bridge. It's a trestle over the Snake made from railroad ties with gaps between them and the tracks running down the center. This is how they cross the Snake, reach the other bank where the fishing is supposed to be good. There are tiny grassy islands Dalton can roll up his black jeans and wade out to. Dalton traded somebody in town for a fly-fishing rod. He probably traded drugs for the rod, though she realizes she hasn't seen her black leather jacket for more than a week.

On Sundays yellow with orioles and tiger monarchs and a sun that turns the grasses soft, Dalton takes them fishing on the far bank of the river. One late afternoon he caught four trout. Sunny could see their rainbows when the sun struck their skin. They looked sewed with red sequins. They were supposed to be sixteen inches. That was the rule for the South Fork of the Snake. Their trout were smaller, seven and eight inches, but they kept them anyway, cooked them on a stick over a fire they made near the van. Dalton said the eyes were the best part and he gave her one and it was white as a pried-open moon and she ate it.

Now she is walking into a yellow that makes her feel both restless and invigorated. A yellow of simultaneity and symbols and some arcane celebration she can vaguely sense. When she ate the trout eyes, they were like crisp white stones. She thought of rituals, primitive people, the fundamental meaning of blood. If one mastered these elements, it might be possible to see better in the dark. She shakes her head as if to clear it, but nothing changes. Her entire life is a network of intuitions, the beginning of words, like neon and dome, pine, topaz, shadow, but then the baby starts crying.

Sunny knows it's all a matter of practice, even silence and erasure and absence. What it isn't is also a matter of practice. In the same way you can take piano or voice and train yourself to recognize and exploit your range, you can also teach yourself not to speak, not to remember. That's why when Dalton asks what's she thinking, she says, "Nothing." It's a kind of discipline. What she's really thinking about is what will happen when summer is over. What will happen if she can't make the baby stop crying?

Sometimes when she is frightened, it calms her to think about Marilyn Monroe. Sunny knows all about Marilyn's childhood, the foster homes, the uncles who fondled her breasts, kissed her seven-year-old nipples, and they got hard. Then Marilyn knew she was a bad girl. She would always be a bad girl. It was like being at a carnival, a private carnival, just for her. There were balloons and streamers, party hats and birthday cakes with chocolate frosting and her name written in a neon pink. And no one could tell her no. She had liked to think about Marilyn Monroe when they were driving in the van between gigs. The band was in its final incarnation then. Sunny was already pregnant and it was called Pagan Night.

When Dalton asks her what she's thinking and she says, "Nothing," she is really imagining winter and how she is certain there won't be enough to eat. Dalton says he'll shoot a cow. There are cows grazing outside of town, off half the dirt roads and along the banks of the river. Or he'll shoot a deer, an elk, he'll trap rabbits. He's been talking to people in town, at the Rio Bar. He's traded something for the fly-fishing rig, but he still has both guns and the rifle. He'll never trade the weapons, not even for heroin, even if they could find any here.

Today, on this cool morning, Sunny has walked from the river to the zoo. Admission is one dollar, but the woman in the booth knows her and has started to simply wave her in.

Sunny passes through a gate near a willow and she would like to name the baby Willow. It would be an omen and it would survive winter. Then she is entering the zoo, holding her baby without a name. She sits with her baby near the swan pond until someone gives her a quarter, a sandwich, a freshly purchased bag of popcorn. They simply hand it to her.

She has memorized each animal, bird, and fish in this miniature zoo. The birds stand by mossy waterfalls of the sort she imagines adorn the swimming pools of movie stars. She sits nursing her baby that she is pretending is named Willow. If anyone asks, and she knows no one will, she is prepared to say, His name is Willow.

Later, she stands in a patch of sun by an exhibit featuring a glassed-in bluish pool that should contain a penguin or a seal, but is empty. It smells derelict, harsh and sour with something like the residue of trapped wind and the final thoughts of small mammals as they chew off their feet and bleed to death. You can walk down a flight of stairs and look through the glass, but nothing is swimming. She knows. She has climbed down twice.

Sunny likes to look at what isn't there, in the caged water whipped by sun. This is actually the grotto that is most full, with its battered streams of light like hieroglyphics, a language in flux, lost in shifting ripples.

She pauses in front of the golden eagle. It will not look at her, even when she whistles. The information stenciled to the cage says the golden eagle can live thirty years, longer than many movie stars, longer than Hendrix and Janis and Jim Morrison and James Dean. This particular bird will probably outlive her.

Sunny is thinking about how hungry she is, when someone offers her half a peanut butter and jelly sandwich. Actually, the woman has her child do this, reach out a baby arm to her as if she is now some declawed beast you could let your kid near.

Her own baby is wrapped in a shawl, the same shawl she had once laid across the sofa in the living room of her apartment in San Francisco. She had gone there to study modern dancing, tap, and ballet. Her father had wanted her to go to nursing school. If she went to nursing school, her father could believe she had finally forgotten. He could conclude that she was well and whole, and he could sleep without pills. His ulcer would disappear. He could take communion again.

Sunny took singing lessons and began to meet men with rock 'n' roll bands. Nursing school became white and distant. It became a sort of moon you could put between your teeth and swallow. She stopped envisioning herself in a starched cotton uniform with a stethoscope around her neck. What she wanted now was to smoke grass and hash and opium and stare out the window at Alcatraz. What she wanted to do was sniff powder drawn in lines across a wide square of mirror she kept on the side of the sofa, like a sort of magic screen where you could watch your face change forever.

Now, at the zoo, she stands on the wood slats surrounding the fish pond filled with keepers, twenty- and twenty-five- and thirty-inch rainbow trout. This is what keepers look like. On yellow Sundays, she and Dalton and the baby walk across the railroad trestle over the Snake River. But Dalton will never catch a fish this big.

She was afraid the first time they crossed the bridge. Dalton had to grab her hand. He hadn't touched her body since the baby was born. He had to pull her along. The bridge was higher than she had thought. The river was rushing underneath like a sequence of waves, but faster and sharper, without breath or cycles, and she was holding the baby. That day she was secretly calling the baby Sunday. And she was cradling Sunday with one arm and Dalton was holding her other hand, pulling her through the yellow. He was also holding the fishing rod he'd somehow procured at the Rio Bar, traded somebody something for, she is beginning to think it was her black leather jacket with the studs on the cuffs, the special studs sewed on by a woman who claimed she was a gypsy in Portland.

Dalton must think she won't need her leather jacket in winter. He isn't considering what she'll need in winter. Maybe they won't still be in Idaho. Maybe they won't still be together. And the bridge was wider than she had at first imagined. It was like a pier with its set of two railroad tracks down the center, one thinner, the other fatter, one unused set covered with rust. The bridge was made from railroad ties and there were gaps between them where a foot could get caught, something small could fall through. Dalton said, "Make a pattern. Step every other one. Don't look down." That's what she did, stepped every other one, didn't look down, but still she could hear the river in a kind of anguish beneath her and she was shaking.

"It's an abandoned bridge, isn't it?" she asked Dalton.

The first few times he said yes, but when they had crossed the fourth time, he said no. She stopped, found herself staring into sun. "What do you mean?" she demanded.

"Look at the rails. The larger set are clean. Trains do this." He pointed at the tracks. "Or they'd be covered with rust."

"What if the train came now? As we were crossing?" she finally asked.

"There are beams every twenty feet." Dalton pointed to a kind of metal girder. "We'd hang on the side until it passed."

She tries to imagine herself standing on the girder, holding the baby which in her mind is named Sunday in one of her arms. She cannot conceive of this. Instead she remembers, suddenly, a story Dalton once told her years ago, before they had gone on the road, when they first recited their secret information to each other, their collection of shame, where they were truly from, what had happened, what was irrevocable.

Dalton told her about a night in high school when he had been drinking beer with his friends. Perhaps it was spring. They had been drinking since dawn and now it was after midnight. It was Ohio. That's where Dalton was from. His friends had wandered down to the train station. His best friend had tried to hop a train. Johnny Mohawk. That's what they called him, Mohawk, because he said he was part Indian. Johnny Mohawk tried to hop a train and fell. It ran over him, amputating both legs, his right arm, and half of his left.

"He was so drunk, that's what saved him," Dalton explained. It must have been later. They were riding in a tour bus. They had an album out and the company had given them a roadie, a driver, and a bus. Outside was neon and wind and houses you didn't want to live in. "He was so drunk, he didn't feel it," Dalton was saying. "If he'd been more awake, the shock would have killed him."

Dalton glanced out the window, at some in-between stretch of California where there were waist-high grasses and wild flowers and a sense of too much sun, even in the darkness. She asked him what happened. She tried to imagine Johnny Mohawk, but she could not. Her mind refused to accommodate the brutal lack of symmetry, would produce only words like tunnel and agony, suffocate and scream. Even if she had gone to nursing school, even if she went right now, enrolled in the morning, she could do nothing about Johnny Mohawk. It would always be too late.

"It was the best thing ever happened to him," Dalton said. "He was on his way to becoming a professional drunk. Like his father, like his uncles and inbred cousins. After the accident, he got a scholarship to State. They gave him a tutor and a special car. Now he's an engineer for an oil company."

Sunny thinks about Johnny Mohawk as she stands in the zoo, in front of a grotto with grassy sides and a sleeping male and female lion. Their cage seems too small to contain them if they wanted to do anything other than sleep in the damp green grass. She wonders what would happen if she fell in, over the low metal bar.

Near her, a pregnant woman with three blond daughters, each with a different colored ribbon in their long yellow hair, tells her two-year-old, "Don't you climb up on that bar now. You fall in, there'd be no way to get you out. That hungry old lion would eat you right up."

Sunny feels the baby in her arms, how heavy it is, how it could so easily slide from her, through the bar, into the grassy grotto. She could never retrieve it. No one would expect her to.

Then she is walking past the one zebra. When Dalton asks her if she wants to talk about anything, she shakes her head, no. She is considering how filled each no is, glittering and yellow. Each no is a miniature carnival, with curled smiles and balloons on strings and a profusion of names for babies. And in this no are syllables like willow and cottonwood and shadow and Johnny Mohawk. And in this no is the railroad trestle above one hundred thousand rainbow trout.

Sunny's favorite exhibit is the snow leopard. It is strange that a zoo in a tiny town should have such an animal. They are so rare.

She reads what the snow leopard eats, mammals and birds. Its social life is solitary. How long does it live? Twenty-five years. Not quite long enough to see its first record go platinum. And it isn't really asleep on the green slope behind its grid of bars as much as it is simply turned away. Perhaps it is thinking about the past, and on its lip is something that isn't quite a smile. Or perhaps he is simply listening to birds.

There are always birds when they cross the railroad trestle on Sunday, the Snake below them, the bald eagles and blue herons and swallows and robins, orioles and magpies, in the air near their shoulders. And there is no schedule for the train. She's called Union Pacific five times, waited for the man in charge to come back from vacation, to come back from the flu, to be at his desk, and there is no way to predict when the train runs over this particular trestle. It's a local. It gets put together at the last moment, no one knows when.

When they cross the bridge on Sunday, she is obsessively listening for trains. And there are so many birds, fat robins, unbelievably red, and orioles, the yellow of chalk from fourth grade when she got an A and her teacher let her write the entire spelling list for the week on the blackboard. And ducks and Canadian geese and loons, all of them stringing their syllables across the afternoon, hanging them near her face like a kind of party streamer. The baby is named Sunday or Sometimes and she feels how heavy it is, how it could just drop from her arms.

It's become obvious that these fishing Sundays are not about catching trout. It's a practice for something else entirely, for leaving, for erasure, silence, and absence. She understands now. It's the end of July. She won't be able to feed the baby from her body indefinitely or walk through town all day, looking for trash cans where she can deposit the diapers she has used over and over again.

Now it is time to rehearse. They are involved in a new show with an agenda they don't mention. It's a rehearsal for abandoning the baby. She practices leaving it on the bank, walking fifty steps away, smoking a cigarette. Then she rushes back to retrieve it, to press it against her. If she simply took a slightly longer path from the bank, permitted herself to smoke a joint, a third or fourth cigarette, she might not remember exactly where she placed the baby, not with all the foliage, the vines and brush, bushes and trees, the whole bank an ache of greenery. Something could have interceded, a sudden aberration in the river current or perhaps a hawk. She wouldn't be blamed.

In the children's petting zoo, a gray rabbit mounts a white one. Another white rabbit eats from a bowl. They eat and mate, eat and mate. In the winter, Dalton says he'll shoot a deer. He's made a deal with somebody at the Rio Bar, something about sharing and storing. There are always cattle, fish, rabbits, beavers, and otters that can be trapped.

During the day, Dalton says he's working on songs. He still has both guitars. He can only write music when the baby isn't crying or coughing. She wants to name the baby Music or Tears. Once she tells Dalton she wants to name the baby Bay. She remembers the apartment they had with the view of the bridge, the way at midnight the wind felt like a scalded blue. It was when everything seemed simultaneously anesthetized and hot. It was a moment she remembers as happy.

"It's not time to name it," Dalton said. He was strumming his twelve-string. He said many African tribes didn't name a baby until it had survived a year. Dalton looked at her and smiled. His lips reminded her of Marilyn Monroe.

That's when she realized each day would have to be distinct and etched. She licks the baby's face. She sits on a bench in the sun at the zoo by a pond with a mossy waterfall in the center. There are swans in this pond. She closes her eyes and smells the baby and decides to name him Swan. She kisses his cheek and whispers in his ear, "Your name is Swan. Your name is Moss. Your name is Bye-Bye."

"What are you thinking?" Dalton asks. It was during the storm two weeks ago. He was drinking tequila. Rain struck the van and she thought of rocks and bullets and time travel.

"Nothing," she replied.

Wind. Hidden networks. The agenda that sparks. You know how night feels without candles, without light bulbs, maps, schedules. This is what we do not speak of Bye-bye-bye, baby. Bye-bye-bye.

Everyday, Dalton says he's going to write songs while she is gone. He has a joint in his mouth, curled on his side in the back of the van on a ridge above the Snake River where they now live. He has a bottle of vodka tucked into his belt. The vodka is gone when she comes back. Sunny has to knock again and again on the side of the van, has to kick it with her foot, has to shout his name, until he wakes up.

Each day must be separate, an entity, like a species, a snow leopard, a zebra, or a rainbow trout. Each one with a distinct evolution and morphology, niches, complex accidents. Last Sunday, she smoked a joint and drank tequila. Then they crossed the river on the railroad ties. She has a pattern, left foot, skip one with the right, left foot, skip one with the right, don't look down.

She knows it will happen on a Sunday, perhaps next Sunday. Dalton will say, "Come over, look at this."

"I can't. I'm feeding the baby," she will answer.

"Put it down a second," he'll say. "You've got to see this."

She'll place the baby in the center of soft weeds. She'll follow the sound of his voice, find Dalton on the bank with a great trout, twenty inches, thirty inches long. It will be their keeper and she will bend down, help him pull it in. Her feet will get wet. She will use her hat for a net, her red hat that says Wyoming Centennial 1990. The seconds will elongate, the minutes will spread into an afternoon, with no one counting or keeping track. When they've pulled the trout in, when they've finished the tequila, it will be dark. They will begin searching for the baby, but there will be only shadow. No one could say they were at fault. No one could say anything. No one knows about them or the baby, and the van has got at least five thousand miles left in it. They could be in New York or Florida in two days.

Perhaps it will be a Sunday when they are crossing the bridge. She'll be holding the baby named Sometimes or Swan or Willow, and they'll have to leap onto the steel girders as the train rushes by. The baby will drop from her arms into the Snake and it will be taken on the current like Moses.

They will never mention the falling. They will not speak of it, not once. It will just be something caught in the edge of their smile, like a private carnival that went through town and maybe you saw it once and too briefly and then it was gone.

She knows Dalton believes they are purer, more muscle and bone, closer to an archetypal winter beyond artifice. That was part of why they called the band Pagan Night. They are animals, barbarians, heathens. They are savage and recognize this, its possibilities and what it costs. In China and India, girl children are often drowned at birth. There are fashions of surviving famines engraved on the nerves.

Maybe this Sunday they will be crossing the bridge when the train erupts from a spoil of foliage and shadow, willows and heron and orioles. Dalton will have left his guitar in the van, padlocked with his paperback myths of primitive people. Perhaps it will be a Sunday after Dalton returned from the Rio Bar with heroin. They will have cooked it up and had it that night, all night, and the next day, all day, until it was finished and there was nothing left, not even in the cotton in the spoon.

When she stands on the Sunday railroad trestle, she will think about ineluctable trajectories. There is a destiny to the direction and journey of all objects, stars and birds, babies and stones and rivers. Who can explain how or why that snow leopard came from Asia to reside in an obsolete grotto in a marginal farming town among barley and potato fields in southern Idaho? What shaped such a voyage, what miscalculations, what shift of wind or currents, what failure of which deity?

Sunny knows exactly what she will be thinking when it happens. There are always acres of sun and their fading. It is all a sequence of erasures and absences. Who is to say flesh into water or flesh into rock is not a form of perfection? What of Moses on the river with an ineluctable destiny to be plucked from reeds by a princess? Perhaps on some fishing Sunday when the baby is named Swallow or Tiger and falls from her arms, someone on a distant bank will look up and say they saw the sudden ascension of a god.

First, Body

FROM ANTAEUS

TWO NURSES with scissors could make a man naked in eleven seconds. Sid Elliott had been working Emergency eight months and it amazed him every time. Slicing through denim and leather, they peeled men open faster than Sid's father flayed rabbits.

Roxanne said it would take her longer than eleven seconds to make him naked. "But not that much longer." It was Sunday. They'd met in the park on Tuesday, and she hadn't left Sid's place since Friday night. She was skinny, very dark-skinned. She had fifteen teeth of her own and two bridges to fill the spaces. "Rotted out on smack and sugar. But I don't do that shit anymore." It was one of the first things she told him. He looked at her arms. She had scars, hard places where the skin was raised. He traced her veins with his fingertips, feeling for bruises. She was never pretty. She said this too. "So don't go thinking you missed out on something."

He took her home that night, to the loft in the warehouse overlooking the canal, one room with a high ceiling, a mattress on the floor beneath the window, a toilet behind a screen, one huge chair, one sink, a hot plate with two burners, and a miniature refrigerator for the beer he couldn't drink anymore.

"It's perfect," she said.

Now they'd known each other six days. She said, "What do you see in me?"

"Two arms, two ears. Someone who doesn't leave the room when I eat chicken."

"Nowhere to go," she said.

"You know what I mean."

He told her about the last boy on the table in Emergency. He'd fallen thirty feet. When he woke, numb from the waist, he said, *Are those my legs?* She lay down beside him, and he felt the stringy ligaments of her thighs, the rippled bone of her sternum; he touched her whole body the way he'd touched her veins that night in the park, by the water.

He sat at his mother's kitchen table. "What is it you do?" she said.
"I clean up."
"Like a janitor?"
Up to our booties in blood all night, Dr. Enos said.
"Something like that."
She didn't want to know, not exactly, not any more than she'd wanted to know what his father was going to do with the rabbits.
She nodded. "Well, it's respectable work."
She meant she could tell her friends Sid had a hospital job.
He waited.
"Your father would be proud."
He remembered a man slipping rabbits out of their fur coats. His father had been laid off a month before he thought of this.

Tonight his mother had made meatloaf, which was safe — as long as he remembered to take small bites and chew slowly. Even so, she couldn't help watching, and he kept covering his mouth with his napkin. Finally he couldn't chew at all and had to wash each bite down with milk. When she asked, *Are you happy there?* he wanted to tell her about the men with holes in their skulls, wanted to bring them, trembling, into this room. Some had been wounded three or four times. They had beards, broken teeth, scraped heads. The nurses made jokes about burning their clothes.

But the wounds weren't bullet holes. Before the scanners, every drunk who hit the pavement got his head drilled. "A precautionary measure," Dr. Enos explained. "In case of hemorrhage."
"Did the patient have a choice?"
"Unconscious men don't make choices."
Sid wanted to tell his mother that. *Unconscious men don't make choices.* He wanted her to understand the rules of Emergency: first, body, then brain — stop the blood, get the heart beating. No fine-tuning. Don't worry about a man's head till his guts are back in his belly.

Dr. Enos made bets with the nurses on Saturday nights. By stars and fair weather they guessed how many motorcyclists would run out of luck cruising from Seattle to Marysville without their helmets, how many times the choppers would land on the roof of the hospital, how many men would be stripped and pumped but not saved.

Enos collected the pot week after week. "If you've bet on five and only have three by midnight, do you wish for accidents?" Dr. Roseland asked. Roseland never played. She was beyond it, a grown woman. She had two children and was pregnant with the third.

"Do you?" Enos said.

"Do I what?"

Enos stared at Roseland's swollen belly. "Wish for accidents," he said.

Skulls crushed, hearts beating, the ones lifted from the roads arrived all night. Enos moved stiffly, like a man just out of the saddle. He had watery eyes — bloodshot, blue. Sid thought he was into the pharmaceuticals. But when he had a body on the table, Enos was absolutely focused.

Sid wanted to describe the ones who flew from their motorcycles and fell to earth, who offered themselves this way. *Like Jesus.* His mother wouldn't let him say that. *With such grace.* He wished he could make her see how beautiful it was, how ordinary, the men who didn't live, whose parts were packed in plastic picnic coolers and rushed back to the choppers on the roof, whose organs and eyes were delivered to Portland or Spokane. He was stunned by it, the miracle of hearts in ice, corneas in milk. These exchanges became the sacrament, transubstantiated in the bodies of startled men and weary children. Sometimes the innocent died and the faithless lived. Sometimes the blind began to see. Enos said, "We save bodies, not souls."

Sid tasted every part of Roxanne's body: sweet, fleshy lobe of the ear, sinewy neck, sour pit of the arm, scarred hollow of the elbow. He sucked each finger, licked her salty palm. He could have spent weeks kissing her, hours with his tongue inside her. Sometimes he forgot to breathe and came up gasping. She said, "Aren't you afraid of me?"

And he said, "You think you can kill me?"

"Yes," she said, "anybody can."

She had narrow hips, a flat chest. He weighed more than twice what she did. He was too big for himself, always — born too big, grown too fast. Too big to cry. Too big to spill his milk. At four he looked six; at six, ten. Clumsy, big-footed ten. Slow, stupid ten. *Like living with a bear,* his mother said, something broken every day, her precious blown-glass ballerina crumbling in his hand, though he held her so gently, lifting her to the window to let the light pass through her. He had thick wrists, enormous thumbs. Even his eyebrows were bushy. *My monster,* Roxanne said the second night, *who made you this way?*

"How would you kill me?" he said. He put one heavy leg over her skinny legs, pinning her to the bed.

"You know, with my body."

"Yes, but how?"

"You know what I'm saying."

"I want you to explain."

She didn't. He held his hand over her belly, not quite touching, the thinnest veil of air between them. "I can't think when you do that," she said.

"I haven't laid a finger on you."

"But you will," she said.

He'd been sober twenty-seven days when she found him. Now it was forty-two. Not by choice. He'd had a sudden intolerance for alcohol. Two shots and he was on the floor, puking his guts out. He suspected Enos had slipped him some Antabuse and had a vague memory: his coffee at the edge of the counter, Enos drifting past it. Did he linger? Did he know whose it was? But it kept happening. Sid tried whiskey instead of rum, vodka instead of whiskey. After the third experiment he talked to Roseland. "Count your blessings," she said. "Maybe you'll have a liver when you're sixty." She looked at him in her serious, sad way, felt his neck with her tiny hands, thumped his back and chest, shined her flashlight into his eyes. When he was sitting down, she was his height. He wanted to lay his broad hand on her bulging stomach.

No one was inclined to offer a cure. He started smoking pot instead, which was what he was doing that night in the park when Roxanne appeared. *Materialized,* he said afterward, *out of smoke and air.*

But she was no ghost. She laughed loudly. She even breathed loudly — through her mouth. They lay naked on the bed under the open window. The curtains fluttered and the air moved over them.

"Why do you like me?" she said.

"Because you snore."

"I don't."

"How would you know?"

"It's my body."

"It does what it wants when you're sleeping."

"You like women who snore?"

"I like to know where you are."

He thought of his sister's three daughters. They were slim and quick, moving through trees, through dusk, those tiny bodies — disappearing, reassembling — those children's bodies years ago. Yes, it was true. His sister was right. Better that he stayed away. Sometimes when he'd chased them in the woods, their bodies frightened him — the narrowness of them, the way they hid behind trees, the way they stepped in the river, turned clear and shapeless, flowed away. When they climbed out downstream, they were whole and hard but cold as water. They sneaked up behind him to grab his knees and pull him to the ground. They touched him with their icy hands, laughing like water over stones. He never knew where they might be, or what.

He always knew exactly where Roxanne was: behind the screen, squatting on the toilet; standing at the sink, splashing water under her arms. Right now she was shaving her legs, singing nonsense words, *Sha-na-na-na-na*, like the backup singer she said she was once. "The Benders — you probably heard of them." He nodded but he hadn't. He tried to picture her twenty-four years younger, slim but not scrawny. Roxanne with big hair and white sequins. Two other girls just like her, one in silver, one in black, all of them shimmering under the lights. "But it got too hard, dragging the kid around — so I gave it up." She'd been with Sid twenty-nine days and this was the first he'd heard of any kid. He asked her. "Oh yeah," she said, "of course." She gave him a look like, *What d'you think — I was a virgin?* "But I got smart after the first one." She was onto the second leg, humming again. "Pretty kid. Kids of her own now. I got pictures." He asked to see them, and she said, "Not *with* me."

"Where?" he said.

She whirled, waving the razor. "You the police?"

She'd been sober five days. That's when the singing started. "If you can do it, so can I," she'd said.

He reminded her he'd had no choice.

"Neither do I," she said, "if I want to stay."

He didn't agree. He wasn't even sure it was a good idea. She told him she'd started drinking at nine: stole her father's bottle and sat in the closet, passed out and no one found her for two days. Sid knew it was wrong, but he was almost proud of her for that, forty years of drinking — he didn't know anyone else who'd started so young. She had conviction, a vision of her life, like Roseland, who said she'd wanted to be a doctor since fifth grade.

Sid was out of Emergency. Not a demotion. A lateral transfer. That's what Mrs. Mendelson in Personnel said. Her eyes and half her face were shrunken behind her glasses.

"How can it be lateral if I'm in the basement?"

"I'm not speaking literally, Sid."

He knew he was being punished for trying to stop the girl from banging her head on the wall.

Inappropriate interference with a patient. There was a language for everything. Sterilized equipment contaminated.

Dropped — he'd dropped the tray to help the girl.

"I had to," he told Roxanne.

"Shush, it's okay — you did the right thing."

There was no reward for doing the right thing. When he got the girl to the floor, she bit his arm.

Unnecessary risk. "She won't submit to a test," Enos said after Sid's arm was washed and bandaged. Sid knew she wasn't going to submit to anything — why should she? She was upstairs in four-point restraint, doped but still raving; she was a strong girl with a shaved head, six pierced holes in one ear, a single chain looped through them all. Sid wanted Enos to define *unnecessary.*

Now he was out of harm's way. Down in Postmortem. The dead don't bite. *Unconscious men don't make choices.* Everyone pretended it was for his own sake.

Sid moved the woman from the gurney to the steel table. He was not supposed to think of her as a woman, he knew this. She was a body, female. He was not supposed to touch her thin blue hair or wrinkled eyelids — for his own sake. He was not supposed to look at her scars and imagine his mother's body — three deep puckers in one breast, a raised seam across the belly — was not supposed to see the ghost there, imprint of a son too big, taken this way, and later another scar, something else stolen while she slept. He was not to ask what they had hoped to find, opening her again.

Roxanne smoked more and more to keep from drinking. She didn't stash her cartons of cigarettes in the freezer anymore. No need. She did two packs a day, soon it would be three. Sid thought of her body, inside: her starved, black lungs shriveled in her chest, her old, swollen liver.

He knew exactly when she started again, their sixty-third day together, the thirty-ninth and final day of her sobriety.

He drew a line down her body, throat to belly, with his tongue. She didn't want to make love. She wanted to lie here, beneath the window, absolutely still. She was hot. He moved his hands along the wet, dark line he'd left on her ashy skin, as if to open her.

"Forget it," she said. The fan beat at the air, the blade of a chopper, hovering. He smelled of formaldehyde, but she didn't complain about that. It covered other smells: the garbage in the corner, her own body.

They hadn't made love for nineteen days. He had to go to his mother's tonight but was afraid to leave Roxanne naked on the bed, lighting each cigarette from the butt of the last one. He touched her hip, the sharp bone. He wanted her to know it didn't matter to him if they made love or not. If she drank or not. He didn't mind cigarette burns on the sheets, bills missing from his wallet. As long as she stayed.

The pictures of his three nieces in his mother's living room undid him. He didn't know them now, but he remembered their thin fingers, their scabbed knees, the way Lena kissed him one night — as a woman, not a child, as if she saw already how their lives would be — a solemn kiss, on the mouth, but not a lover's kiss. Twelve years old, and she must have heard her mother say, *Look Sid, maybe it would be better if you didn't come around — just for a while — know what I mean?* When he saw her again she was fifteen and fat, seven months pregnant. Christina said, *Say hello to your uncle Sid,* and the girl stared at him, unforgiving, as if he were to blame for this too.

These were the things that broke his heart: his nieces on the piano and the piano forever out of tune; dinner served promptly at six, despite the heat; the smell of leather in the closet, a pile of rabbit skin and soft fur; the crisp white sheets of his old bed and the image of his mother bending, pulling the corners tight, tucking them down safe, a clean bed for her brave boy who was coming home.

Those sheets made him remember everything, the night sweats, the yellow stain of him on his mother's clean sheets. He washed them but she knew, and nothing was the way they expected it to be, the tossing in the too-small bed, the rust-colored blotches in his underwear, tiny slivers of shrapnel working their way to the surface, wounding him again. *How is it a man gets shot in the ass?* It was a question they never asked, and he couldn't have told them without answering other questions about what had happened to the men who stepped inside the hut, who didn't have time to turn and hit the ground, who blew sky-high and fell down in pieces.

He touched his mother too often and in the wrong way. He leaned too close, tapping her arm to be sure she was listening. He tore chicken from the bone with his teeth, left his face greasy. Everything meant something it hadn't meant before.

She couldn't stand it, his big hands on her. He realized now how rarely she'd touched him. He remembered her cool palm on his forehead, pushing the hair off his face. Did he have a temperature? He couldn't remember. He felt an old slap across his mouth for a word he'd spit out once and forgotten. He remembered his mother licking her thumb and rubbing his cheek, wiping a dark smudge.

He thought of the body he couldn't touch — then or now — her velvety, loose skin over loose flesh, soft crepe folding into loose wrinkles.

His father was the one to tell him. They were outside after dinner, more than twenty years ago, but Sid could see them still, his father and himself standing at the edge of the yard by the empty hutches. Next door, Ollie Kern spoke softly to his roses in the dark. Sid could see it killed his father to do it. He cleared his throat three times before he said, "You need to find your own place to live, son." Sid nodded. He wanted to tell his father it was okay, he understood, he was ready. He wanted to say he forgave him — not just for this, but for everything, for not driving him across the border one day, to Vancouver, for not suggesting he stay there a few days, alone, for not saying, "It's okay, son, if you don't want to go."

Sid wanted to say no one should come between a husband and a wife, not even a child, but he only nodded, like a man, and his father patted his back, like a man. He said, "I guess I should turn on the sprinkler." And Sid said, "I'll do it, Dad."

They must have talked, after that, many times. But in Sid's mind, this was always the last time. He remembered forever crawling under the prickly juniper bushes to turn on the spigot as the last thing he did for his father. Remembered forever how they stood, silent in the dark, listening to water hitting leaves and grass.

He was in the living room now with his mother, after all these years, drinking instant coffee made from a little packet — it was all she had. It was still so hot. She said it. *It's still so hot.* It was almost dark, but they hadn't turned on the lights because of the heat, so it was easy for Sid to imagine the shadow of his father's shape in the chair, easy to believe that now might have been the time his father said at last, *Tell me, son, how it was, the truth, tell me.* It was like this. Think of the meanest boy you knew in sixth grade, the one who caught cats to cut off their tails. It's like that. But not all the time. Keep remembering your eleven-year-old self, your unbearable boy energy, how you sat in the classroom hour after hour, day after day, looking out the window at light, at rain. Remember the quivering leaves, how you felt them moving in your own body when you were a boy — it's like that, the waiting, the terrible boredom, the longing for something to happen, *anything,* so you hate the boy with the cat but you're thrilled too, and then you hate yourself, and then you hate the cat for its ridiculous howling and you're glad when it runs into the street crazy with pain — you're glad when the car hits it, smashes it flat. Then the bell rings, recess is over, and you're in the room again — you're taking your pencils out of your little wooden desk. The girl in front of you has long, shiny braids you know you'll never touch, not now, not after what you've seen, and then you imagine the braids in your hands, limp as cats' tails, and Mrs. Richards is saying the words *stifle, release, mourn,* and you're supposed to spell them, print them on the blank page, pass the paper forward, and later you're supposed to think the red marks — her sharp corrections, her grade — matter.

He could be more specific. If his father wanted to know. At night, you dig a hole in red clay and sleep in the ground. Then there's rain. Sheets and rivers and days of rain. The country turns to mud and smells of shit. A tiny cut on your toe festers and swells, opens wider and wider, oozes and stinks, an ulcer, a hole. You think about your foot all the time, more than you think about your mother, your father, minute after minute, the pain there, you care about your foot more than your life — you could lose it, your right big toe, leave it here, in this mud, your foot, your leg, and you wonder: How many pieces of yourself can you leave behind and still be called yourself? Mother, father, sister — heart, hand, leg. One mosquito's trapped under your net. You've used repellent — you're sticky with it, poisoned by it — but she finds the places you've missed: behind your ear, between your fingers. There's a sweet place up your sleeve, under your arm. And you think, *This is the wound that will kill me.* She's threading a parasite into your veins. These are the enemies: mud, rain, rot, mosquito. She's graceful. She's not malicious. She has no brain, no intentions. She wants to live, that's all. If she finds you, she'll have you. She buzzes at your head, but when she slips inside there's no sound.

It's still so hot. He wants to bang the keys of the out-of-tune piano. He wants a racket here, in his mother's house. He longs for all the dark noise of Roxanne, his plates with their tiny roses smashing to the floor two nights ago, his blue glasses flying out of the drainer. She wanted a drink, and he said she could have one, and she told him to go fuck himself, and then the dishes exploded. He thinks of her walking through the broken glass, barefoot, but not cutting her feet, brilliant Roxanne. *Roxanne Roxanne.* He has to say her name here, now, bring her into this room where the silent television flickers like a small fire in the corner. He wants to walk her up the stairs to that boy's room, wants her to run her fingers through the silky fur of rabbit pelts in the closet, wants to explain how fast his father was with the knife but too old, too slow, to collect tolls for the ferry. He wants to show her the tight corners of the white sheets, wants her to touch him, here, in this room, to bring him back together, who he was then, who he is now.

So he is saying it, her name. He is telling his mother, *I've been seeing someone,* and his mother is saying, *That's nice, Sid — you should bring her to dinner,* and he understands she means sometime, in some future she can't yet imagine, but he says, *Next week?*

She sips at her too-hot coffee, burns her pursed lips, says, *Fine, that would be fine.*

Roxanne will never agree to it. He knows this. He sees the glow of her cigarette moving in the dark, hand to mouth. He knows he won't ask because he can't bear the bark of her laughter. He doesn't turn on the light, doesn't speak. He sees what's happening, what will happen — this room in winter, the gray light leaking across the floor, the windows closed, the rain streaming down the glass.

He lies down beside her. She snubs out her cigarette, doesn't light another, says nothing but moves closer, so the hair of her arm brushes the hair of his.

He knows she hasn't eaten tonight, hasn't moved all day, living on cigarettes and air, a glass of orange juice he brought her hours ago. Roxanne. But she must have stood at the windows once while he was gone, he sees that now: the blinds are down; the darkness is complete, final, the heat close. There's only sound: a ship's horn on the canal; a man in the distance who wails and stops, wails and stops, turning himself into a siren. She rolls toward him, touches his lips with her tongue, presses her frail, naked body against him. He feels the bones of her back with his fingers, each disc of the spine. He knows he can't say anything — now or forever — such tender kisses, but he's afraid she'll stop, that she'll break him here, on this bed, so he holds back, in case she says she's tired or hungry, too hot, though he's shaking already, weeks of wanting her pulled into this moment. He touches her as if for the first time, each finger forming a question: *Here and here, and this way, can I?* He's trembling against his own skin, inside. If she says *no*, he'll shatter, break through himself, explode. She's unbuttoning his shirt, unzipping his pants, peeling him open. She's tugging his trousers down toward his feet but not off — they shackle him. And he knows if they make love this way, without talking, it will be the last time. He wants to grab her wrists and speak, but he can't — the silence is everything, hope and the lack of it. He wants the dark to come inside him, to be him, and there are no words even now, no sounds of pleasure, no soft murmurs, no names, no gods, only their skin — hot, blurred — their damp skin and the place where his becomes hers no longer clear, only her hair in his mouth, her eyes, her nose, her mouth in his mouth, her nipple, her fingers, her tongue in his mouth, brittle Roxanne going soft now, skinny Roxanne huge in the heat of them, swollen around him, her body big enough for all of him and he's down in her, all the way down in the dark and she has no edges, no outline, no place where her dark becomes the other dark, the thinning, separate air, and he doesn't know his own arms, his own legs, and still he keeps moving into her, deeper and deeper, feeling too late what she is, what she's become, softer and softer under him, the ground, the black mud, the swamp swallowing him — he's there, in that place, trying to pull himself out of it, but his boots are full of mud — he's thigh-deep falling facedown in the swamp, and then he feels fingernails digging into his back, a bony hand clutching his balls. He tries to grab her wrist but she's let go — she's slipped away from him, and he knows he never had a chance — this swamp takes everyone. He's gasping, mouth full of mud, and then there's a word, a name, a plea: *Stop, Sid, please,* and then there's a body beneath him, and then there's his body: heavy, slick with sweat, and then there's a man sitting on the edge of a mattress, his head in his hands, and then there's the air, surprising and cool, the fan beating and beating.

He opens the shades and rolls a joint, sits in the big chair, smoking. She's fallen asleep — to escape him, he thinks, and he doesn't blame her. If his father moved out of these shadows, Sid would say, Look at her. It was like this, exactly like this. After the rain, after the toe heals, after you don't die of malaria. The sniper's bullet whizzes past your ear, and you're almost relieved. You think, This is an enemy you'll know. Bouncing Bettys and Toe Poppers jump out of the ground all day. Two wounded, two dead. The choppers come and take them all. You expect it to happen and it does, just after dark: one shot, and then all of you are shooting — you tear the trees apart. In the morning, you find them, two dead boys and a girl in the river. Her blood flowers around her in the muddy water. Her hands float. Her long black hair streams out around her head and moves like the river. She's the one who strung the wire, the one who made the booby trap with your grenade and a tin can. She tried to trip you up, yesterday and the day before. She's the sniper who chose you above all others. Her shot buzzed so close you thought she had you. She looks at the M-16 slung over your shoulder. She looks at your hands. She murmurs in her language which you will never understand. Then she speaks in your language. She says, Your bullet's in my liver. She tells you, Your bullet ripped my bowel.

She says, Look for yourself if you don't believe me. You try to pull her from the water. You slip in the mud. The water here knows her. The mud filling your boots is her mud. Slight as she is, she could throw you down and hold you under.

How would you kill me?

You know, with my body.

But you get her to the bank. You pull her from the river. Then the medic's there and he tells you she's dead, a waste of time, *unnecessary risk*, and you tell him she wasn't dead when you got there, she wasn't, and you look at her lying on the bank, and she's not your enemy now — she's not anyone's enemy — she's just a dead girl in the grass, and you leave her there, by the river.

Sid thinks of the doctors at the hospital, their skills, how they use them, their endless exchanges — merciful, futile, extravagant — hearts and lungs, kidneys and marrow. What would they have given her; what would they have taken?

If his mother had looked out the window soon enough, if Sid had been there to carry him to the car, his father could have been saved by a valve; but the man was alone, absolutely, and the blood fluttering in his heart couldn't flow in the right direction. So he lay there in his own backyard, the hose in his hand, the water running and running in the half dark.

Sid no longer knows when Roxanne will be lying on his bed and when she won't. She's got her own life, she tells him, and suddenly she does: friends who call at midnight, business she won't describe. One night she doesn't come home at all, but the next morning she's there, downstairs, hunched in the entryway, one eye swollen shut. *Mugged*, she says. *Son of a bitch.* And he knows what's happened. Even her cigarettes stolen. She forages for butts, checking the ashtray, the garbage. There aren't many. She's smoked them down to the filters almost every time, but she finds enough to get by while he runs to the store for a carton, for juice and bread, a jar of raspberry jam. He wants her to eat, but she won't. She doesn't give a shit about that. She doesn't give a shit about him. One line leads to the next. He nods, he knows this. She says she loves whiskey more than she loves him — the park, the tracks, the ground more than a mattress on the floor. She says the bottle's always there and sometimes he's not and who the fuck does he think he is, Jesus?

And he says no, he never saved anyone. And then she's crying, beating his chest with her fists, falling limp against him, sobbing so hard he thinks her skinny body will break and he holds her until she stops and he carries her to the bed. He brings her orange juice, the jar of jam, ice in a rag for her swollen eye. She eats jam by the spoonful but no bread. He combs her tangled hair. He lays her down and she wants to make love but they don't, he can't, and he doesn't go to work that day but he does the next and then she's gone.

Days become weeks become winter, the one he imagined, the rain on the window. She's here but not here. She's left the smell of her hair on the pillow, her underpants in a ball beneath the bed, the butts of her cigarettes in the ashtray. He sees her everywhere. She's the boy in the hooded sweatshirt huddled on the stoop, whispering, *I got what you need,* trying to sell crack or his own thin body. She's the bloated woman asleep on a bench in the park, the newspaper over her face coming apart in the rain. She's the bearded man at Pike's Market who pulls fishbones from the trash to eat the raw flesh. She's the dark man cuffed and shoved into the cruiser. She turns to stare out the back window, blaming him. She's the girl on Broadway with blond hair shaved to stubble. She's fifteen. She wears fishnets under ripped jeans, black boots, a leather jacket with studded spikes along the shoulders. She smacks gum, smokes, says *Fuck you* when he looks too long. He wants to stop, wants to warn her of the risks, wants to say, *Just go home.* But she can't, he knows; at least it's strangers on the street, not someone you know. *And anyway, what about you?* she'd say. She'd drop her cigarette, grind it out. She'd whisper, *I saw Roxanne — she's not doing too good, she's sick — so don't be giving me any shit about risk.*

She's the scarred man on the table with his twice-cleaved chest and gouged belly. When they open him, they'll find things missing. She's the woman without a name, another body from the river. He knows her. She rises, floating in the dirty water.

Dr. Juste says, "Shove her up there on the slab any way you can."

This one's fat. That's the first thing Sid notices. Later there will be other things: the downy hair on her cheeks, the long black hairs sprouting from her blotched legs, the unbelievable white expanse of her breasts. And she's dead, of course, like the others.

But she's not exactly like them, not dead so long, not so cold or stiff. He'd thought he could no longer be surprised, but she surprises him, Gloria Luby, the fattest dead person he has ever seen.

She weighs 326 pounds. That gives her 83 on Sid and the gravity of death.

Dr. Juste turns at the door. He's lean and hard, not too tall, bald; he has a white beard, the impatience of a thin man. He says, "You'll have to roll this one." He says, "She won't mind."

Now they're alone, Gloria and Sid. She was a person a few hours ago, until the intern blasted her eyes with light and the pupils stayed frozen. Sid can't grasp it, the transformation. If she was a person in the room upstairs, she's a person still. He imagines her, upstairs, alive in her bed, a mountain of a woman in white, her frizz of red hair matted and wild, no one to comb it. Blind, unblinking as a queen, she sat while the interns clustered around her and the head resident told them about her body and its defeats, the ravages of alcohol and the side effects of untreated diabetes: her engorged cirrhotic liver, the extreme edema of her abdomen, fluid accumulating from her liver disease, which accounted for her pain — Were they listening to her moan? — which put pressure on her lungs till she could barely breathe — Did they see her writhing under the sheets? It was the gastrointestinal bleeding that couldn't be stopped, even after the fluid was drained from the belly.

She pissed people off, getting fatter every day, filling with fluids and gases, seventeen days in all. If she'd lived two more, they would have taken her legs, which Dr. Juste says would have been a waste because it wouldn't have saved her but might have prolonged this. Sid wanted to ask what he meant, exactly, when he said *this*.

She's valuable, now, at last: she's given herself up, her body in exchange for care. In an hour, Dr. Juste will begin his demonstration and Gloria Luby will be exposed, her massive mistakes revealed.

Sid thinks they owe her something, a lift instead of a shove, some trace of respect. He won't prod. He isn't going to call another orderly for help, isn't going to subject Gloria Luby to one more joke. *How many men does it take to change a light bulb for a fat lady?*

Later, he may think it isn't so important. Later, he may realize no one was watching, not even Gloria Luby. But just now this is his only duty: clear, specific. It presented itself.

None, she has to turn herself on. He knew what Juste would say when the interns gathered: *Shall we cut or blast?*

A first-timer might be sick behind his mask when they opened her abdomen and the pools of toxins began to drain into the grooves of the metal table, when the whole room filled with the smell of Gloria Luby's failures. But everyone would keep laughing, making cracks about women big enough for a man to live inside. He knew how scared they'd be, really, looking at her, the vastness of her opened body, because she *was* big enough for a man to crawl inside, like a cow, like a cave. Hollowed out, she could hide him forever. Some of them might think of this later, might dream themselves into the soft swamp of her body, might feel themselves waking in the warm, sweet, rotten smell of it, in the dark, in the slick, glistening fat with the loose bowels tangled around them. They might hear the jokes and wish to speak. Why didn't anyone notice: there's a man inside this woman, and he's alive? But he can't speak — she can't speak — the face is peeled back, the skull empty, and now the cap of bone is being plastered back in place, and now the skin is being stitched shut. The autopsy is over — she's closed, she's done — and he's still in there, with her, in another country, with the smell of shit and blood that's never going to go away, and he's not himself at all — he's her, he's Gloria Luby — bloated, full of gas, fat and white and dead forever.

It could happen to anyone. Anytime. Sid thinks, The body you hate might be your own; your worst fear might close around you, might be stitched tight by quick, clever hands. You might find yourself on this table. You might find yourself sprawled on a road or submerged in a swamp; you might find yourself in a bed upstairs, your red hair blazing, your useless legs swelling. Shadows come and go and speak, describing the deterioration of your retinas, the inefficiency of your kidneys, the necessity of amputation due to decreasing circulation in the lower extremities. *Extremities.* Your legs. They mean your legs. You might find yourself facedown in your own sweet backyard, the hose still in your hand.

He doesn't think about God or ask himself what he believes — he knows: he believes in her, in Gloria Luby, in the 326-pound fact of her body. He is the last person alive who will touch her with tenderness.

The others will have rubber gloves, and masks, and knives.

So he is going to lift her, gently, her whole body, not her shoulders, then her torso, then her terrible bruised thighs. She's not in pieces — not yet — she's a woman, and he is going to lift her as a woman. He is going to move her from the gurney to the table with the strength of his love.

He knows how to use his whole body, to lift from the thighs, to use the power of the back without depending on it. He crouches. It's a short lift, but he's made it harder for himself, standing between the gurney and the table. If he pressed them together, they'd almost touch — a man alone could roll her.

He squats. He works his arms under her, surprised by the coolness of her flesh, surprised, already, by her unbelievable weight.

For half a second, his faith is unwavering, and he is turning with her in his arms; they're almost there, and then something shifts — her immense left breast slaps against his chest, and something else follows — her right arm slips from his grasp, and he knows, close as they are, they'll never make it, an inch, a centimeter, a whole lifetime — lost. He feels the right knee give and twist, his own knee; he feels something deep inside tear, muscles wrenching, his knee springing out from under him, from under them. And still he holds her, trying to take the weight on the left leg, but there's no way. They hit the gurney going down, send it spinning across the room. The pain in his knee is an explosion, a booby trap, a wire across a path and hot metal ripping cartilage from bone, blasting his kneecap out his pant leg.

When they hit the floor, his leg twists behind him, and he's howling. All 326 pounds of Gloria Luby pin him to the cold concrete.

She amazes him. She's rolled in his arms so his face is pressed into her soft belly. The knee is wrecked. He knows that already, doesn't need to wait for a doctor to tell him. *Destroyed.* He keeps wailing, though there's no point, no one in that room but the woman on top of him, insisting she will not hear, not ever. There's no one in the hallway, no one in the basement. There are three closed doors between Sidney Elliott and all the living.

He has to crawl out from under her, has to prod and shove at her thick flesh, has to claw at her belly to get a breath. Inch by inch he moves, dragging himself, his shattered leg, across the smooth floor. He leaves her there, just as she is, facedown, the lumpy mound of her rump rising in the air.

*

Dr. Enos is trying not to smile while Sid explains, again, how it happened. Everyone smiles, thinking of it, Sid Elliott on the floor underneath Gloria Luby. They're sorry about his leg, truly. It's not going to be okay. There'll be a wheelchair, and then a walker. In the end, he'll get by with a cane. If he's lucky. It's a shame, Dr. Roseland tells him, to lose a leg that way, and Sid wonders if she thinks there are good ways to lose a leg. He remembers the boy on the table. He remembers all the boys. *Are those my legs?*

He's drifting in and out. He hears Roxanne laughing in the hallway. Then he sees her at the window, her mouth tight and grim as she sucks smoke.

She wants to know if it's worth it, the risk, the exchange: Gloria Luby's dignity for his leg. The *idea* of her dignity. She laughs, but it's bitter. She tells him he's a failure; she tells him how they found Gloria Luby. It took six orderlies to get her on the slab. They grunted, mocking her, cursing him.

He sleeps and wakes. Roxanne's gone. Even her smoke is gone. He asks the nurse, a thin, dark-skinned man, *Where is she?* And the nurse says, *Where's who, baby? Nobody been here but you and me.*

His father stands in the corner, shaking his head. He can't believe Sid's come back from the jungle, nothing worse than shrapnel in his ass, only to get it from a three-hundred-pound dead woman in a hospital in Seattle. Three-twenty-six, Sid says. *What?* Three hundred and twenty-six pounds. His father looks as if he wants to weep, and Sid's sorry, not for himself — he'd do it again. He's sorry for his father, who's disappointed, and not just in him. He's been standing in the closet in Sid's old room all these years, sobbing in the musty dark, pressing his face into the soft rabbit fur. He's been in the other room, in the summer heat, listening to Sid plead with Roxanne, *Just let me lick you.* He's been in the kitchen, watching Sid's mother fry pork chops, chop onions, mash potatoes. He's tried to tell her something and failed. He's stood there, silent in the doorway, while she and Sid sat at the table chewing and chewing. Now, at last, when he speaks to his son, he has nothing to tell him, no wisdom to impart, only a phrase to mutter to himself, *What a waste, what a waste,* and Sid knows that when he says it he's not thinking of the leg. He wants to forgive his father for something, but the old man's turned down his hearing aid. He looks befuddled. He says, *What is it, Sid?*

The nurse shows him the button to press when the pain comes back. *Straight into your IV, babe. No need to suffer. Just give yourself a little pop. Some people think they got to be strong, lie there sweating till I remind them. Not me, honey — you give me one of those, I'd be fine all the time.* He grins. He has a wide mouth, bright teeth; he says, *You need me tonight honey, you just buzz.*

Gloria Luby lies down beside him. She tells him, *I was exactly what they expected me to be. My brain was light, my liver heavy; the walls of my heart were thick. But there were other things they never found.* She rolls toward him, presses herself against him. Her soft body has warmth but no weight. She envelops him. She says, *I'll tell you now, if you want to know.*

The blond girl with the spikes on her jacket leans in the doorway. Outside, the rain. Behind her, the yellow light of the hall. She's wearing her black combat boots, those ripped fishnets, a sheer black dress, a black slip. She says, *Roxanne's dead. So don't give me any of that shit about risk.* He turns to the wall. He doesn't have to listen to this. *All right then,* she says, *maybe she's not dead. But I saw her — she don't look too good.*

She comes into the room, slumps in the chair by the bed. She says, *I heard all about you and that fat lady.*

She's waiting. She thinks he'll have something to say. She lights a cigarette, says, *Wanna drag?* And he does, so they smoke, passing the cigarette back and forth. She says, *Roxanne thinks you're an idiot, but who knows.* She grinds the cigarette out on the floor, then stuffs the filter back in the pack, between the plastic and the paper. She says, *Don't tell anybody I was here.*

The nurse brings Sid a wet cloth, washes his face, says, *You been talking yourself silly, babe.*

You know what I did?

The nurse touches Sid's arm, strokes him elbow to wrist. *You're famous here, Mr. Elliott — everybody knows what you did.*

*

Roxanne sits on the windowsill. She says, *Looks like you found yourself another sweetheart.*

Sid's forehead beads with sweat. The pain centers in his teeth, not his knee; it throbs through his head. He's forgotten the button on his IV, forgotten the buzzer that calls the nurse. Roxanne drifts toward the bed like smoke. She says, *Does it hurt, Sid?* He doesn't know if she's trying to be mean or trying to be kind. She says, *This is only the beginning.* But she presses the button, releases the Demerol into the tube. She stoops as if to kiss him, but doesn't kiss. She whispers, *I'm gone now.*

Sidney Elliott stands in a white room at the end of a long hallway. He's alone with a woman. He looks at her. He thinks, Nobody loved you enough or in the right way.

In some part of his mind, he knows exactly what will happen if he lifts her, if he takes her home, but it's years too late to stop.

He tries to be tender.

He prays to be strong.

DON DeLILLO

The Angel Esmeralda

FROM ESQUIRE

THE OLD NUN rose at dawn, feeling pain in every joint. She'd been rising at dawn since her days as a postulant, kneeling on hardwood floors to pray. First she raised the shade. That's the world out there, little green apples and infectious disease. Banded light fell across the room, steeping the tissued grain of the wood in an antique ocher glow so deeply pleasing in pattern and coloration that she had to look away or become girlishly engrossed. She knelt in the folds of the white nightgown, fabric endlessly laundered, beaten with swirled soap, left gristled and stiff. And the body beneath, the spindly thing she carried through the world, chalk pale mostly, and speckled hands with high veins, and cropped hair that was fine and flaxy gray, and her bluesteel eyes — many a boy and girl of old saw those peepers in their dreams.

She made the sign of the cross, murmuring the congruous words. *Amen,* an olden word, back to Greek and Hebrew, *verily* — touching her midsection to complete the body-shaped cross. The briefest of everyday prayers yet carrying three years' indulgence, seven if you dip your hand in holy water before you mark the body.

Prayer is a practical strategy, the gaining of temporal advantage in the capital markets of Sin and Remission.

She said a morning offering and got to her feet. At the sink she scrubbed her hands repeatedly with coarse brown soap. How can the hands be clean if the soap is not? This question was insistent in her life. But if you clean the soap with bleach, what do you clean the bleach bottle with? If you use scouring powder on the bleach bottle, how do you clean the box of Ajax? Germs have personalities. Different objects harbor threats of various insidious types. And the questions turn inward forever.

An hour later she was in her veil and habit, sitting in the passenger seat of a black van that was headed south out of the school district and down past the monster concrete expressway into the lost streets, a squander of burned-out buildings and unclaimed souls. Grace Fahey was at the wheel, a young nun in secular dress. All the nuns at the convent wore plain blouses and skirts except for Sister Edgar, who had permission from the motherhouse to fit herself out in the old things with the arcane names, the wimple, cincture, and guimpe. She knew there were stories about her past, how she used to twirl the big-beaded rosary and crack students across the mouth with the iron crucifix. Things were simpler then. Clothing was layered, life was not. But Edgar stopped hitting kids years ago, even before she grew too old to teach. She knew the sisters whispered deliciously about her strictness, feeling shame and awe together. Such an open show of power in a bird-bodied soap-smelling female. Edgar stopped hitting children when the neighborhood changed and the faces of her students became darker. All the righteous fury went out of her soul. How could she strike a child who was not like her?

"The old jalop needs a tune-up," Gracie said. "Hear that noise?"

"Ask Ismael to take a look."

"Ku-ku-ku-ku."

"He's the expert."

"I can do it myself. I just need the right tools."

"I don't hear anything," Edgar said.

"Ku-ku-ku-ku? You don't hear that?"

"Maybe I'm going deaf."

"I'll go deaf before you do, Sister."

"Look, another angel on the wall."

The two women looked across a landscape of vacant lots filled with years of stratified deposits — the age-of-house garbage, the age-of-construction debris, and vandalized car bodies. Many ages layered in waste. This area was called the Bird in jocular police parlance, short for bird sanctuary, a term that referred in this case to a tuck of land sitting adrift from the social order. Weeds and trees grew amid the dumped objects. There were dog packs, sightings of hawks and owls. City workers came periodically to excavate the site, the hoods of their sweatshirts fitted snug over their hard hats, and they stood warily by the great earth machines, the pumpkin-mudded backhoes and dozers, like infantrymen huddled near advancing tanks. But soon they left, they always left with holes half dug, pieces of equipment discarded, Styrofoam cups, pepperoni pizzas. The nuns looked across all this. There were networks of vermin, craters chocked with plumbing fixtures and Sheetrock. There were hillocks of slashed tires laced with thriving vine. Gunfire sang at sunset off the low walls of demolished buildings. The nuns sat in the van and looked. At the far end was a lone standing structure, a derelict tenement with an exposed wall where another building had once abutted. This wall was where Ismael Muñoz and his crew of graffiti writers spray-painted a memorial angel every time a child died in the neighborhood. Angels in blue and pink covered roughly half the high slab. The child's name and age were printed in cartoon bubbles under each angel, sometimes with cause of death or personal comments by the family, and as the van drew closer Edgar could see entries for TB, AIDS, beatings, drive-by shootings, blood disorders, measles, general neglect and abandonment at birth — left in Dumpster, forgot in car, left in Glad bag Xmas Eve.

"I wish they'd stop already with the angels," Gracie said. "It's in totally bad taste. A fourteenth-century church, that's where you go for angels. This wall publicizes all the things we're working to change. Ismael should look for positive things to emphasize. The townhouses, the community gardens that people plant. The townhouses are nice, they're clean. Walk around the corner you see ordinary people going to work, going to school. Stores and churches."

"Titanic Power Baptist Church."

"It's a church, it's a church, what's the difference? The area's full of churches. Decent working people. Ismael wants to do a wall, these are the people he should celebrate. Be positive."

Edgar laughed inside her skull. It was the drama of the angels that made her feel she belonged here. It was the terrible death these angels represented. It was the danger the writers faced to produce their graffiti. There were no fire escapes or windows on the memorial wall and the writers had to rappel from the roof with belayed ropes or sway on makeshift scaffolds when they did an angel in the lower ranks. Ismael spoke of a companion wall for dead graffitists, flashing his wasted smile.

"And he does pink for girls and blue for boys. That really sets my teeth on edge."

"There are other colors," Edgar said.

"Sure, the streamers that the angels hold aloft. Big ribbons in the sky. Makes me want to be sick in the street."

They stopped at the friary to pick up food they would distribute to the needy. The friary was an old brick building wedged between boarded tenements. Three monks in gray cloaks and rope belts worked in an anteroom, getting the day's shipment ready. Grace, Edgar and Brother Mike carried the plastic bags out to the van. Mike was an ex-fireman with a Brillo beard and wispy ponytail. He looked like two different guys front and back. When the nuns first appeared he'd offered to serve as guide, a protecting presence, but Edgar had firmly declined. She believed her habit and veil were safety enough. Beyond these South Bronx streets people may look at her and think she exists outside history and chronology. But inside the strew of rubble she was a natural sight, she and the robed monks. What figures could be so timely, costumed for rats and plague?

Edgar liked seeing the monks in the street. They visited the homebound, ran a shelter for the homeless; they collected food for the hungry. And they were men in a place where few men remained. Teenage boys in clusters, armed drug dealers — these were the men of the immediate streets. She didn't know where the others had gone, the fathers, living with second or third families, hidden in rooming houses or sleeping under highways in refrigerator boxes, buried in the potter's field on Hart's Island.

"I'm counting plant species," Brother Mike said. "I've got a book I take out to the lots."

Gracie said, "You stay on the fringes, right?"

"They know me in the lots."

"Who knows you? The dogs know you? There are rabid dogs, Mike."

"I'm a Franciscan, okay? Birds light on my index finger."

"Stay on the fringes," Gracie told him.

"There's a girl I keep seeing, maybe twelve years old, runs away when I try to talk to her. I get the feeling she's living in the ruins. Ask around."

"Will do," Gracie said.

When the van was loaded they drove back to the Bird to do their business with Ismael and to pick up a few of his crew who would help them distribute the food. What was their business with Ismael?

They gave him lists that detailed the locations of abandoned cars in the north Bronx, particularly along the Bronx River, which was a major dump site for stolen joy-ridden semistripped gas-siphoned pariah-dog vehicles. Ismael sent his crew to collect the car bodies and whatever parts might remain unrelinquished. They used a small flatbed truck with an undependable winch and a motif of souls-in-hell graffiti on the cab, deck, and mud flaps. The car hulks came here to the lots for inspection and price-setting by Ismael and were then delivered to a scrap-metal operation in remotest Brooklyn. Sometimes there were forty or fifty cannibalized car bodies dumped in the lots, museum-quality — bashed and rusted, hoodless, doorless, windows deep-streaked like starry nights in the mountains.

When the van approached the building, Edgar felt along her midsection for the latex gloves she kept tucked in her belt.

Ismael had teams of car-spotters who ranged across the boroughs, concentrating on the bleak streets under bridges and viaducts. Charred cars, upside-down cars, cars with dead bodies wrapped in shower curtains all available for salvage inside the city limits. The money he paid the nuns for their locational work went to the friary for groceries.

Gracie parked the van, the only operating vehicle in human sight. She attached the vinyl-coated steel collar to the steering wheel, fitting the rod into the lock housing. At the same time Edgar force-fitted the latex gloves onto her hands, feeling the secret reassurance of synthetic things, adhesive rubberized plastic, a shield against organic menace, the spurt of blood or pus and the viral entities hidden within, submicroscopic parasites in their protein coats.

Squatters occupied a number of floors. Edgar didn't need to see them to know who they were. They were a civilization of indigents subsisting without heat, lights or water. They were nuclear families with toys and pets, junkies who roamed at night in dead men's Reeboks. She knew who they were through assimilation, through the ingestion of messages that riddled the streets. They were foragers and gatherers, can-redeemers, the people who yawed through subway cars with paper cups. And doxies sunning on the roof in clement weather and men with warrants outstanding for reckless endangerment and depraved indifference and other offenses requiring the rounded Victorian locutions that modern courts have adopted to match the woodwork. And shouters of the Spirit, she knew this for a fact — a band of charismatics who leapt and wept on the top floor, uttering words and nonwords, treating knife wounds with prayer.

Ismael had his headquarters on three and the nuns hustled up the stairs. Grace had a tendency to look back unnecessarily at the senior nun, who ached in her movable parts but kept pace well enough, her habit whispering through the stairwell.

"Needles on the landing," Gracie warned.

Watch the needles, sidestep the needles, such deft instruments of self-disregard. Gracie couldn't understand why an addict would not be sure to use clean needles. This failure made her pop her cheeks in anger. But Edgar thought about the lure of damnation, the little love bite of that dragonfly dagger. If you know you're worth nothing, only a gamble with death can gratify your vanity.

Ismael stood barefoot on dusty floorboards in a pair of old chinos rolled to his calves and a bright shirt worn outside his pants and he resembled some carefree Cuban ankle-wading in happy surf.

"Sisters, what do you have for me?"

Edgar thought he was quite young despite the seasoned air, maybe early thirties — scattered beard, a sweet smile complicated by rotting teeth. Members of his crew stood around smoking, uncertain of the image they wanted to convey. He sent two of them down to watch the van and the food. Edgar knew that Gracie did not trust these kids. Graffiti writers, car scavengers, probably petty thieves, maybe worse. All street, no home or school. Edgar's basic complaint was their English. They spoke an unfinished English, soft and muffled, insufficiently suffixed, and she wanted to drum some hard *g*'s into the ends of their gerunds.

Gracie handed over a list of cars they'd spotted in the last few days. Details of time and place, type of vehicle, condition of same.

He said, "You do nice work. My other people do like this, we run the world by now."

What was Edgar supposed to do, correct their grammar and pronunciation, kids suffering from malnutrition, unparented some of them, some visibly pregnant — there were at least four girls in the crew. In fact she was inclined to do just that. She wanted to get them in a room with a blackboard and to buzz their minds with Spelling and Punctuation, transitive verbs, *i* before *e* except after *c*. She wanted to drill them in the lessons of the old Baltimore Catechism. True or false, yes or no, fill in the blanks. She'd talked to Ismael about this and he'd made an effort to look interested, nodding heavily and muttering insincere assurances that he would think about the matter.

"I can pay you next time," Ismael said. "I got some things I'm doing that I need the capital."

"What things?" Gracie said.

"I'm making plans I get some heat and electric in here, plus pirate cable for the Knicks."

Edgar stood at the far end of the room, by a window facing front, and she saw someone moving among the poplars and ailanthus trees in the most overgrown part of the rubbled lots. A girl in a too-big jersey and striped pants grubbing in the underbrush, maybe for something to eat or wear. Edgar watched her, a lanky kid who had a sort of feral intelligence, a sureness of gesture and step — she looked helpless but alert, she looked unwashed but completely clean somehow, earth-clean and hungry and quick. There was something about her that mesmerized the nun, a charmed quality, a grace that guided and sustained.

Edgar said something and just then the girl slipped through a maze of wrecked cars and by the time Gracie reached the window she was barely a flick of the eye, lost in the low ruins of an old firehouse.

"Who is this girl," Gracie said, "who's out there in the lots, hiding from people?"

Ismael looked at his crew and one of them piped up, an undersized boy in spray-painted jeans, dark-skinned and shirtless.

"Esmeralda. Nobody know where her mother's at."

Gracie said, "Can you find the girl and then tell Brother Mike?"

"This girl she being swift."

A little murmur of assent.

"She be a running fool this girl."

Titters, brief.

"Why did her mother go away?"

"She be a addict. They un, you know, predictable."

If you let me teach you not to end a sentence with a preposition, Edgar thought, I will save your life.

Ismael said, "Maybe the mother returns. She feels the worm of remorse. You have to think positive."

"I do," Gracie said. "All the time."

"But the truth of the matter there's kids that are better off without their mothers or fathers. Because their mothers or fathers are dangering their safety."

Gracie said, "If anyone sees Esmeralda, take her to Brother Mike or hold her, I mean really hold her until I can get here and talk to her. She's too young to be on her own or even living with the crew. Brother said she's twelve."

"Twelve is not so young," Ismael said. "One of my best writers, he does wildstyle, he's exactly twelve more or less. Juano. I send him down in a rope for the complicated letters."

"When do we get our money?" Gracie said.

"Next time for sure. I make practically, you know, nothing on this scrap. My margin it's very minimum. I'm looking to expand outside Brooklyn. Sell my cars to one of these up-and-coming countries that's making the bomb."

"Making the what? I don't think they're looking for junked cars," Gracie said. "I think they're looking for weapons-grade uranium."

"The Japanese built their navy with the Sixth Avenue el. You know this story? One day it's scrap, next day it's a plane taking off a deck. Hey, don't be surprise my scrap ends up in North, you know, Korea."

Edgar caught the smirk on Gracie's face. Edgar did not smirk. This was not a subject she could ever take lightly. Edgar was a cold-war nun who'd once lined the walls of her room with aluminum foil as a shield against nuclear fallout from communist bombs. Not that she didn't think a war might be thrilling. She daydreamed many a domed flash in the film of her skin, tried to conjure the burst even now, with the USSR crumbled alphabetically, the massive letters toppled like Cyrillic statuary.

They went down to the van, the nuns and three kids, and with the two kids already on the street they set out to distribute the food, starting with the hardest cases in the projects.

They rode the elevators and walked down the long passageways. Behind each door a set of unimaginable lives, with histories and memories, pet fish swimming in dusty bowls. Edgar led the way, the five kids in single file behind her, each with two bags of food, and Gracie at the rear, carrying food, calling out apartment numbers of people on the list.

They spoke to an elderly woman who lived alone, a diabetic with an amputated leg.

They saw a man with epilepsy.

They spoke to two blind women who lived together and shared a seeing-eye dog.

They saw a woman in a wheelchair who wore a FUCK NEW YORK T-shirt. Gracie said she would probably trade the food they gave her for heroin, the dirtiest street scag available. The crew looked on, frowning. Gracie set her jaw, she narrowed her pale eyes and handed over the food anyway. They argued about this, not just the nuns but the crew as well. It was Sister Grace against everybody. Even the wheelchair woman didn't think she should get the food.

They saw a man with cancer who tried to kiss the latexed hands of Sister Edgar.

They saw five small children bunched on a bed being minded by a ten-year-old.

They went down the passageways. The kids returned to the van for more food and they went single file down the passageways in the bleached light.

They talked to a pregnant woman watching a soap opera in Spanish. Edgar told her if a child dies after being baptized, she goes straight to heaven. The woman was impressed. If a child is in danger and there is no priest, Edgar said, the woman herself can administer baptism. How? Pour ordinary water on the forehead of the child, saying, "I baptize thee in the name of the Father and of the Son and of the Holy Ghost." The woman repeated the words in Spanish and English and everyone felt better.

They went down the passageways past a hundred closed doors and Edgar thought of all the infants in limbo, unbaptized, babies in the seminether, hell-bordered, and the nonbabies of abortion, a cosmic cloud of slushed fetuses floating in the rings of Saturn, or babies born without immune systems, bubble children raised by computer, or babies born addicted — she saw them all the time, bulb-headed newborns with crack habits, they resembled something out of peasant folklore.

They heard garbage crashing down the incinerator chutes and they walked one behind the other, three boys and two girls forming one body with the nuns, a single swaybacked figure with many moving parts. They rode the elevators down and finished their deliveries in a group of tenements where boards replaced broken glass in the lobby doors.

Gracie dropped the crew at the Bird just as a bus pulled up.

What's this, do you believe it? A tour bus in carnival colors with a sign in the slot above the windshield reading SOUTH BRONX SURREAL. Gracie's breathing grew intense. About thirty Europeans with slung cameras stepped shyly onto the sidewalk in front of the boarded shops and closed factories and they gazed across the street at the derelict tenement in the middle distance.

Gracie went half berserk, sticking her head out the van and calling, "It's not surreal. It's real, it's real. You're making it surreal by coming here. Your bus is surreal. You're surreal."

A monk rode by on a rickety bike. The tourists watched him pedal up the street. They listened to Gracie shout at them. They saw a man come along with battery-run pinwheels he was selling, brightly colored vanes pinned to a stick, and he held a dozen or so in his hands with others jutting from his pockets and clutched under his arms, plastic vanes spinning all around him — an elderly black fellow in a yellow skullcap. They saw this man. They saw the ailanthus jungle and the smash heap of mortified cars and they looked at the six-story slab of painted angels with streamers rippled above their cherub heads.

Gracie shouting, "This is real, it's real." Shouting, "Brussels is surreal. Milan is surreal. This is the only real. The Bronx is real."

A tourist bought a pinwheel and got back in the bus. Gracie pulled away muttering. In Europe the nuns wear bonnets like cantilevered beach houses. That's surreal, she said. A traffic jam developed not far from the Bird. The two women sat with drifting thoughts. Edgar watched children walk home from school, breathing air that rises from the oceans and comes windborne to this street at the edge of the continent. Woe betide the child with dirty fingernails. She used to drum the knuckles of her fifth-graders with a ruler if their hands were not bright as minted dimes.

A clamor rising all around them, weary beeping horns and police sirens and the great saurian roar of fire-engine Klaxons.

"Sister, sometimes I wonder why you put up with all this," Gracie said. "You've earned some peace and quiet. You could live upstate and do development work for the order. How I would love to sit in the rose garden with a mystery novel and old Pepper curled at my feet." Old Pepper was the cat in the motherhouse upstate. "You could take a picnic lunch to the pond."

Edgar had a mirthless inner grin that floated somewhere back near her palate. She did not yearn for life upstate. This was the truth of the world, right here, her soul's own home, herself — she saw herself, the fraidy child who must face the real terror of the streets to cure the linger of destruction inside her. Where else would she do her work but under the brave and crazy wall of Ismael Muñoz?

Then Gracie was out of the van. She was out of the seat belt, out of the van and running down the street. The door hung open. Edgar understood at once. She turned and saw the girl, Esmeralda, half a block ahead of Gracie, running for the Bird. Gracie moved among the cars in her clunky shoes and frump skirt. She followed the girl around a corner where the tour bus sat dead in traffic. The tourists watched the running figures. Edgar could see their heads turn in unison, pinwheels spinning at the windows.

All sounds gathered in the dimming sky.

She thought she understood the tourists. You travel somewhere not for museums and sunsets but for ruins, bombed-out terrain, for the moss-grown memory of torture and war. Emergency vehicles were massing about a block and a half away. She saw workers pry open subway gratings in billows of pale smoke and she said a fast prayer, an act of hope, three years' indulgence. Then heads and torsos began to emerge, indistinctly, people coming into the air with jaws skewed open in frantic gasps. A short circuit, a subway fire. Through the rearview mirror she spotted tourists getting off the bus and edging along the street, poised to take pictures. And the schoolkids going by, barely interested — they saw tapes of actual killings on TV. But what did she know, an old woman who ate fish on Friday and longed for the Latin mass? She was far less worthy than Sister Grace. Gracie was a soldier, a fighter for human worth. Edgar was basically a junior G-man, protecting a set of laws and prohibitions. She heard the yammer of police cars pulsing in stalled traffic and saw a hundred subway riders come out of the tunnels accompanied by workers in incandescent vests and she watched the tourists snapping pictures and thought of the trip she'd made to Rome many years ago, for study and spiritual renewal, and she'd swayed beneath the great domes and prowled the catacombs and church basements and this is what she thought as the riders came up to the street, how she'd stood in a subterranean chapel in a Capuchin church and could not take her eyes off the skeletons stacked there, wondering about the monks whose flesh had once decorated these metatarsals and femurs and skulls, many skulls heaped in alcoves and catty-corners, and she remembered thinking vindictively that these are the dead who will come out of the earth to lash and cudgel the living, to punish the sins of the living — death, yes, triumphant — but does she really want to believe that, still?

Gracie edged into the driver's seat, unhappy and flushed.

"Nearly caught her. We ran into the thickest part of the lots and then I was distracted, damn scared actually, because bats, I couldn't believe it, actual bats — like the only flying mammals on earth?" She made ironic wing motions with her fingers. "They came swirling up out of a crater filled with medical waste. Bandages smeared with body fluids."

"I don't want to hear it," Edgar said.

"I saw, like, enough used syringes to satisfy the death wish of entire cities. Dead white mice by the hundreds with stiff flat bodies. You could flip them like baseball cards."

Edgar stretched her fingers inside the milky gloves.

"And Esmeralda somewhere in those shrubs and junked cars. I'll bet anything she's living in a car," Gracie said. "What happened here? Subway fire, looks like."

"Yes."

"Any dead?"

"I don't think so."

"I wish I'd caught her."

"She'll be all right," Edgar said.

"She won't be all right."

"She can take care of herself. She knows the landscape. She's smart."

"Sooner or later," Gracie said.

"She's safe. She's smart. She'll be all right."

And that night, under the first tier of scratchy sleep, Edgar saw the subway riders once again, adult males, females of childbearing age, all rescued from the smoky tunnels, groping along catwalks and led up companion ladders to the street — fathers and mothers, the lost parents found and gathered, shirt-plucked and bodied up, guided to the surface by small faceless figures with Day-Glo wings.

And some weeks later Edgar and Grace made their way on foot across a patch of leaf rot to the banks of the Bronx River near the city limits where a rear-ended Honda sat discarded in underbrush, plates gone, tires gone, windows lifted cleanly, rats ascratch in the glove compartment, and after they noted the particulars of abandonment and got back in the van, Edgar had an awful feeling, one of those forebodings from years long past when she sensed dire things about a pupil or a parent or another nun and felt stirrings of information in the dusty corridors of the convent or the school's supply room that smelled of pencil wood and composition books or the church that abutted the school, some dark knowledge in the smoke that floated from the altar boy's swinging censer, because things used to come to her in the creak of old floorboards and the odor of clothes, other people's damp camel coats, because she drew News and Rumors and Catastrophes into the spotless cotton pores of her habit and veil.

Not that she claimed the power to live without doubt.

She doubted and she cleaned. That night she leaned over the washbasin in her room and cleaned every bristle of the scrub brush with steel wool drenched in disinfectant. But this meant she had to immerse the bottle of disinfectant in something stronger than disinfectant. And she hadn't done this. She hadn't done it because the regression was infinite. And the regression was infinite because it is called infinite regression. You see how doubt becomes a disease that spreads beyond the pushy extrusions of matter and into the elevated spaces where words play upon themselves.

And another morning a day later. She sat in the van and watched Sister Grace emerge from the convent, the rolling gait, the short legs and squarish body, Gracie's face averted as she edged around the front of the vehicle and opened the door on the driver's side.

She got in and gripped the wheel, looking straight ahead.

"I got a call from the friary."

Then she reached for the door and shut it. She gripped the wheel again.

"Somebody raped Esmeralda and threw her off a roof."

She started the engine.

"I'm sitting here thinking, Who do I kill?"

She looked at Edgar briefly, then put the van in gear.

"Because who do I kill is the only question I can ask myself without falling apart completely."

They drove south through local streets, the tenement brick smoked mellow in the morning light. Edgar felt the weather of Gracie's rage and pain — she'd approached the girl two or three times in recent weeks, had talked to her from a distance, thrown a bag of clothing into the pokeweed where Esmeralda stood. They rode all the way in silence with the older nun mind-reciting questions and answers from the Baltimore Catechism. The strength of these exercises, which were a form of perdurable prayer, lay in the voices that accompanied hers, children responding through the decades, sylla-ble-crisp, a panpipe chant that was the lucid music of her life. Question and answer. What deeper dialogue might right minds devise? She reached her hand across to Gracie's on the wheel and kept it there for a digital tick on the dashboard clock. Who made us? God made us. Those clear-eyed faces so believing. Who is God? God is the Supreme Being who made all things. She felt tired in her arms, her arms were heavy and dead and she got all the way to Lesson 12 when the projects appeared at the rim of the sky, upper windows white with sunplay against the broad dark face of beaten stone.

When Gracie finally spoke she said, "It's still there."

"What's still there?"

"Hear it, hear it?"

"Hear what?" Edgar said.

"Ku-ku-ku-ku."

Then she drove the van down past the projects toward the painted wall.

When they got there the angel was already sprayed in place. They gave her a pink sweatshirt and pink and aqua pants and a pair of white Air Jordans with the logo prominent — she was a running fool, so Ismael gave her running shoes. And the little kid named Juano still dangled from a rope, winched down from the roof by the old hand-powered hoist they used to grapple cars onto the deck of the truck. Ismael and others bent over the ledge, attempting to shout correct spellings down to him as he drifted to and from the wall, leaning in to spray the interlaced letters that marked the great gone era of wildstyle graffiti. The nuns stood outside the van, watching the kid finish the last scanted word and then saw him yanked skyward in the cutting wind.

ESMERALDA LOPEZ

12 YEAR

PETECTED IN HEVEN

They all met on the third floor and Gracie paced the hollow room. Ismael stood in a corner smoking a Phillies Blunt. The nun did not seem to know where to begin, how to address the nameless thing that someone had done to this child she'd so hoped to save. She paced, she clenched her fists. They heard the gassy moan of a city bus some blocks away.

"Ismael. You have to find out who this guy is that did this thing."

"You think I'm running here? El Lay Pee Dee?"

"You have contacts in the neighborhood that no one else has."

"What neighborhood? The neighborhood's over there. This here's the Bird. It's all I can do to get these kids so they spell a word on the freaking wall. When I was writing we did subway cars in the dark without a letter misspell."

"Who cares about spelling?" Gracie said.

Ismael exchanged a secret look with Sister Edgar, giving her a snaggle smile from out of his history of dental neglect. She felt weak and lost. Now that Terror has become local, how do we live? she thought. The great thrown shadow dismantled — no longer a launched object in the sky named for a Greek goddess on a bell krater in 500 B.C. What is Terror now? Some noise on the pavement very near, a thief with a paring knife or the stammer of casual rounds from a passing car. Someone who carries off your child. Ancient fears called back, they will steal my child, they will come into my house when I'm asleep and cut out my heart because they have a dialogue with Satan. She let Gracie carry her grief and fatigue for the rest of that day and the day after and the two or three weeks after that. Edgar thought she might fall into crisis, begin to see the world as a spurt of blank matter that chanced to make an emerald planet here and a dead star there, with random waste between. The serenity of immense design was missing from her sleep, form and proportion, the power that awes and thrills. When Gracie and the crew took food into the projects, Edgar waited in the van, she was the nun in the van, unable to face the people who needed reasons for Esmeralda.

Mother of Mercy pray for us. Three hundred days.

Then the stories began, word passing block to block, moving through churches and superettes, maybe garbled slightly, mistranslated here and there, but not deeply distorted — it was clear enough that people were talking about the same uncanny occurrence. And some of them went and looked and told others, stirring the hope that grows on surpassing things.

They gathered after dusk at a windy place between bridge approaches, seven or eight people drawn by the word of one or two, then thirty people drawn by the seven, then a tight silent crowd that grew bigger but no less respectful, two hundred people wedged onto a traffic island in the bottommost Bronx where the expressway arches down from the terminal market and the train yards stretch toward the narrows, all that industrial desolation that breaks your heart with its fretful Depression beauty — the ramps that shoot tall weeds and the old railroad bridge spanning the Harlem River, an openwork tower at either end, maybe swaying slightly in persistent wind.

Wedged, they came and parked their cars if they had cars, six or seven to a car, parking tilted on a high shoulder or in the factory side streets, and they wedged themselves onto the concrete island between the expressway and the pocked boulevard, feeling the wind come chilling in and gazing above the wash of madcap traffic to a billboard floating in the gloom — an advertising sign scaffolded high above the riverbank and meant to attract the doped-over glances of commuters on the trains that ran incessantly down from the northern suburbs into the thick of Manhattan money and glut.

Edgar sat across from Gracie in the refectory. She ate her food without tasting it because she'd decided years ago that taste was not the point. The point was to clean the plate.

Gracie said, "No, please, you can't."

"Just to see."

"No, no, no, no."

"I want to see for myself."

"This is tabloid. This is the worst kind of tabloid superstition. It's horrible. A complete, what is it? A complete abdication, you know? Be sensible. Don't abdicate your good sense."

"It could be her they're seeing."

"You know what this is? It's the nightly news. It's the local news at eleven with all the grotesque items neatly spaced to keep you watching the whole half hour."

"I think I have to go," Edgar said.

"This is something for poor people to confront and judge and understand if they can and we have to see it in that framework. The poor need visions, okay?"

"I believe you are patronizing the people you love," Edgar said softly.

"That's not fair."

"You say the poor. But who else would saints appear to? Do saints and angels appear to bank presidents? Eat your carrots."

"It's the nightly news. It's gross exploitation of a child's horrible murder."

"But who is exploiting? No one's exploiting," Edgar said. "People go there to weep, to believe."

"It's how the news becomes so powerful it doesn't need TV or newspapers. It exists in people's perceptions. It becomes real or fake-real so people think they're seeing reality when they're seeing something they invent. It's the news without the media."

Edgar ate her bread.

"I'm older than the pope. I never thought I would live long enough to be older than a pope and I think I need to see this thing."

"Pictures lie," Gracie said.

"I think I need to see it."

"Don't pray to pictures, pray to saints."

"I think I need to go."

"But you can't. It's crazy. Don't go, Sister."

But Edgar went. She went with a shy quiet type named Janis Loudermilk, who wore a retainer for spacey teeth. They took the bus and subway and walked the last three blocks and Sister Jan carried a portable phone in case they needed aid.

A madder orange moon hung over the city.

People in the glare of passing cars, hundreds clustered on the island, their own cars parked cockeyed and biaswise, dangerously near the streaming traffic. The nuns dashed across the boulevard and squeezed onto the island and people made room for them, pressed bodies parted to let them stand at ease.

They followed the crowd's stoked gaze. They stood and looked. The billboard was unevenly lighted, dim in spots, several bulbs blown and unreplaced, but the central elements were clear, a vast cascade of orange juice pouring diagonally from top right into a goblet that was handheld at lower left — the perfectly formed hand of a female Caucasian of the middle suburbs. Distant willows and a vaguish lake view set the social locus. But it was the juice that commanded the eye, thick and pulpy with a ruddled flush that matched the madder moon. And the first detailed drops plashing at the bottom of the goblet with a scatter of spindrift, each fleck embellished like the figurations of a precisionist epic. What a lavishment of effort and technique, no refinement spared — the equivalent, Edgar thought, of medieval church architecture. And the six-ounce cans of Minute Maid arrayed across the bottom of the board, a hundred identical cans so familiar in design and color and typeface that they had personality, the convivial cuteness of little orange people.

Edgar didn't know how long they were supposed to wait or exactly what was supposed to happen. Produce trucks passed in the rumbling dusk. She let her eyes wander to the crowd. Working people, she thought. Working women, shopkeepers, maybe some drifters and squatters but not many, and then she noticed a group near the front, fitted snug to the prowed shape of the island — they were the charismatics from the top floor of the tenement in the Bird, dressed mainly in floppy white, tublike women, reedy men with dreadlocks. The crowd was patient, she was not, finding herself taut with misgiving, hearing Gracie in her head. Planes dropped out of the darkness toward La Guardia, splitting the air with throttled booms. She and Sister Jan traded a sad glance. They stood and looked. They stared stupidly at the juice. After twenty minutes there was a rustle, a sort of human wind, and people looked north, children pointed north, and Edgar strained to catch what they were seeing.

The train.

She felt the words before she saw the object. She felt the words although no one had spoken them. This is how a crowd brings things to single consciousness. Then she saw it, an ordinary commuter train, silver and blue, ungraffitied, moving smoothly toward the drawbridge. The headlights swept the billboard and she heard a sound from the crowd, a gasp that shot into sobs and moans and the cry of some unnameable painful elation. A blurted sort of whoop, the holler of unstoppered belief. Because when the train lights hit the dimmest part of the billboard, a face appeared above the misty lake and it belonged to the murdered girl. A dozen women clutched their heads, they whooped and sobbed, a spirit, a godsbreath passing through the crowd.

Esmeralda.

Esmeralda.

Edgar was in body shock. She'd seen it but so fleetingly, too fast to absorb — she wanted the girl to reappear. Women holding babies up to the sign, to the flowing juice, let it bathe them in baptismal balsam and oil. And Sister Jan talking into Edgar's face, into the jangle of voices and noise.

"Did it look like her?"

"Yes."

"Are you sure?"

"I think so," Edgar said.

"Did you ever see her up close?"

"Neighborhood people have. Everyone here. They knew her for years."

Gracie would say, What a horror, what a spectacle of bad taste. She knew what Gracie would say. Gracie would say, It's just the undersheet, a technical flaw that causes an image from the papered-over ad to show through when sufficient light shines on the current ad.

Edgar saw Gracie clutching her throat, clawing theatrically for air.

Was she right? Had the news shed its dependence on the agencies that reported it? Was the news inventing itself on the eyeballs of walking talking people?

But what if there was no papered-over ad? Why should there be an ad under the orange juice ad? Surely they removed earlier ads.

Sister Jan said, "What now?"

They waited. They waited only eight or nine minutes this time before another train approached. Edgar moved, she tried to edge and gently elbow forward, and people made room, they saw her — a nun in a veil and long habit and winter cape followed by a sheepish helpmeet in a rummage coat and headscarf, holding aloft a portable phone.

They saw her and embraced her and she let them. Her presence was a verifying force, a figure from a universal church with sacraments and secret bank connections — she elects to follow a course of poverty, chastity and obedience. They embraced her and then let her pass and she was among the charismatic band, the gospelers rocking in place, when the train lamps swung their beams onto the billboard. She saw Esmeralda's face take shape under the rainbow of bounteous juice and above the little suburban lake and it had being and disposition, there was someone living in the image, a

distinguishing spirit and character, the beauty of a reasoning creature — less than a second of life, less than half a second and the
spot was dark again.

She felt something break upon her. She embraced Sister Jan.
They shook hands, pumped hands with the great-bodied women
who rolled their eyes to heaven. The women did great two-handed
pump shakes, fabricated words jumping out of their mouths, trance
utterance, Edgar thought — they're singing of things outside the
known deliriums. She thumped a man's chest with her fists. Everything felt near at hand, breaking upon her, sadness and loss and
glory and an old mother's bleak pity and a force at some deep level
of lament that made her feel inseparable from the shakers and
mourners, the awestruck who stood in tidal traffic — she was nameless for a moment, lost to the details of personal history, a disem-
bodied fact in liquid form, pouring into the crowd.

Sister Jan said, "I don't know."

"Of course you know. You know. You saw her."

"I don't know. It was a shadow."

"Esmeralda on the lake."

"I don't know what I saw."

"You know. Of course you know. You saw her."

They waited for two more trains. Landing lights appeared in the
sky and the planes kept dropping toward the runway across the
water, another flight every half minute, the backwashed roars over-
lapping so everything was seamless noise and the air had a stink of
smoky fuel. They waited for one more train.

How do things end, finally, things such as this — peter out to some
forgotten core of weary faithful huddled in the rain?

The next night a thousand people filled the area. They parked
their cars on the boulevard and tried to butt and pry their way onto
the traffic island but most of them had to stand in the slow lane of
the expressway, skittish and watchful. A woman was struck by a
motorcycle, sent swirling into the asphalt. A boy was dragged a
hundred yards, it is always a hundred yards, by a car that kept on
going. Vendors moved along the lines of stalled traffic, selling flowers, soft drinks and live kittens. They sold laminated images of
Esmeralda printed on prayer cards. They sold pinwheels that never
stopped spinning.

The night after that the mother showed up, Esmeralda's lost mother, and she collapsed with flung arms when the girl's face appeared on the billboard. They took her away in an ambulance that was followed by a number of TV trucks. Two men fought with tire irons, blocking traffic on a ramp. Helicopter cameras filmed the scene and the police trailed orange caution tape through the area — the very orange of the living juice.

The next night the sign was blank. What a hole it made in space. People came and did not know what to say or think, where to look or what to believe. The sign was a white sheet with two microscopic words, SPACE AVAILABLE, followed by a phone number in tasteful type.

When the first train came, at dusk, the lights showed nothing.

And what do you remember, finally, when everyone has gone home and the streets are empty of devotion and hope, swept by river wind? Is the memory thin and bitter and does it shame you with its fundamental untruth — all nuance and wishful silhouette? Or does the power of transcendence linger, the sense of an event that violates natural forces, something holy that throbs on the hot horizon, the vision you crave because you need a sign to stand against your doubt?

Edgar held the image in her heart, the grained face on the lighted board, her virgin twin who was also her daughter. She recalled the smell of jet fuel. This became the incense of her experience, the burnt cedar and gum, a retaining medium that kept the moment whole, all the moments, the stunned raptures and swells of fellow feeling.

She felt the pain in her joints, the old body raw with routine pain, pain at the points of articulation, prods of sharp sensation in the links between bones.

She rose and prayed.

Pour forth we beseech thee, O Lord, thy grace into our hearts.

Ten years if recited at dawn, noon and eventide, or as soon thereafter as possible.

EDWARD FALCO

The Artist

FROM THE ATLANTIC MONTHLY

JIM HAD the rearview mirror tilted so that he could see into the backseat, where Alice, his two-year-old daughter, appeared and disappeared and reappeared out of the darkness as the car passed under streetlight after streetlight. He had been driving for more than an hour, trying to get her to sleep, and her eyes were still open. He located the dimmer control for the dashboard lights and increased the brightness just slightly, so that he could read the time.

"Daddy," Alice said dreamily, "is it the fairy place?"

"Not yet," Jim answered. It was almost nine. He dimmed the lights. "If you close your eyes, we'll get there faster."

Alice closed her eyes, which surprised him. She was usually harder to fool than that.

A moment later she was sleeping. Each time the light swept over her, she seemed to sink deeper into the car seat, her shoulder-length brown hair blending with the seat's brown padded leather. Jim straightened out the mirror and turned the car around. When he drove Alice to sleep, he rarely traveled more than a few minutes' distance from his house, so that he wouldn't have to waste time driving back once she was out. He was efficient. At forty-six, he was father to three children, all under ten; husband to a doctor; owner of an advertising firm; and, finally, an artist, a video artist, creating pieces that were thought of by some as "experimental" films. He didn't think of them as films, and he didn't think of them as experiments — but he sometimes used the term himself.

A set of spotlights came on automatically as he pulled into his driveway. He parked the car, lifted Alice from her seat, and carried

her up a sloping walk surrounded by flower boxes thick with blos-
soming azaleas. The polished mahogany door at the front of the
house was open to let in the early-summer evening breezes. Jim
opened the screen door and stepped into a house so quiet it surprised him. Jake, his four-month-old, would be asleep by now, but
Melissa, the nine-year-old, should have been up and around. And
he didn't hear his wife, Laura, on the phone or running the dish-
washer or doing something somewhere, as he would have expected.
The house was just plain quiet which almost never happened. He
carried Alice up a short flight of stairs into the living room and
noticed Melissa's sneakers and socks on the rug next to the baby
grand. If he hadn't been afraid of waking Alice, he would have
called out for Laura or Melissa. Instead he continued on silently
toward the back of the house. He found his wife and daughter in
the kitchen, sitting at the table with a man who looked to be in his
fifties. He had hair down to the middle of his back, pulled into a
braid. He wore multiple earrings and a gold nose ring. Where the
top two buttons of his shirt were open, Jim could see the bright
colors of a tattoo. From the way the three of them sat staring up at
him, with grins on their faces, Jim guessed that he was supposed to
recognize the stranger. At first he didn't. Then, little by little, he saw
the boyish face of Tony Diehl compose itself within the weathered
face of the stranger. "Tony?"

Tony touched his chest with his fingertips. "Who else, man?" He
stood and opened his arms, offering Jim an embrace.

Laura said, "He came just a few minutes after you took off with
Alice." Before dinner she had gone jogging while Jim watched the
kids, and she was still wearing her skintight spandex outfit. She
looked good. She was five years younger than Jim — and she looked
younger than that.

Melissa said, "He's been telling us stories about you, Dad, when
you were young."

Laura got up to take Alice from Jim. "Your father's still a young
man."

"Oh please," Melissa said. "Forty-six is hardly young."

Jim handed Alice to Laura. He asked Tony, "How'd you find me?"

Tony grabbed Jim's hand, shook it once, and then pulled him
close and wrapped his arms around him. He stepped back and
looked him over. "Christ, man," he said. "Twenty? Twenty-five years?"

Jim looked at Melissa and made a little motion with his head that told her she should go to bed.

"I want to stay up," Melissa said. "I want to hear about all the trouble you used to get into."

Jim said, "What have you been telling her?"

Tony answered, "None of the juicy stuff. Don't worry."

"Pleeease," Melissa said.

Laura, who had been standing quietly in the doorway with Alice, told Melissa to go get her nightgown on. "I'll get them off to bed," she said. "Why don't you guys make yourselves drinks downstairs, and I'll join you when I'm done?"

Tony said, "Sounds good to me."

"I'm going to take Tony out to a bar." Jim put his arm around Laura and kissed her on the forehead. Then he directed Tony toward the living room. On the steps down to the front door he said, speaking loudly and without looking back at Laura, "We have a lot to catch up on." When he looked up, he saw Laura still standing by the kitchen with Alice on her shoulder, her mouth open a little. He called, "I'll be back late. Don't wait up."

Tony waved to her. "Hey. It was nice."

Jim reached around Tony and opened the screen door, his body leaning into Tony's, nudging him out.

"Hey, man," Tony said as Jim pulled the mahogany door closed tight behind him, "are you hustling me out of your house?"

Jim had on his standard summer outfit: loafers without socks, lightweight khaki pants, and a solid-color T-shirt. He said, "It's getting cool," and went to the back of his car, where a linen jacket was hanging from a hook above the side window. He put on the jacket and took out Alice's car seat while Tony watched.

"What?" Tony said. He opened his hands, as if surprised. "Are you mad at me? I should have called, right?"

Jim put the car seat in the trunk and pointed to the passenger door, indicating that Tony should get in.

"Jesus Christ." Tony got in the car. When Jim got in and started the engine, Tony said again, "Jesus Christ. Some welcome."

"What is it, Tony?" Jim started for the expressway. "Am I not being friendly enough?"

"Hey," Tony said, "we did hang out a lot of years." He flipped the sun visor down and looked at himself in the mirror. "Have I changed that much?" He pointed at the gold ring in his nose. "It's the nose ring, right? The nose ring's got you freaked?"

"You're a funny guy, Tony."

"What's funny? You want to see something funny? Here, I'll show you my tattoo." He started to unbutton his shirt.

Jim grabbed his arm. "Stop it. Tell me why you're here."

Tony leaned back in his seat as if he were suddenly tired.

Jim turned and looked at him. The boyishness he remembered was gone entirely. Tony's skin had hardened and thickened: it looked as though it would feel ragged to the touch. His eyes seemed to have sunk into their sockets, and he had small fatty growths around each eyelid. He was forty-two, four years younger than Jim, and he looked like a man in his late fifties or early sixties, a man who had led a rough life. "So where am I taking you?"

"I thought we were going for a drink."

"You want a drink?"

"Sounds good to me."

"Fine. I know a bar. You want to tell me what's up?"

"I'm insulted," Tony said. He was lying back in his seat as if too exhausted to move. "After all the years we hung out, I can't stop in to say hello? A social visit?"

"What's the gun for?"

"The gun?" He reached around and touched the middle of his back. "I didn't think you'd see. I mean, I *know* your old lady didn't see nothing." He took a nine-millimeter Beretta out from under the back of his shirt. He placed it on the console between them. "Let me tell you what's happening, man. You'll understand."

Jim said, "Isn't this a social visit?"

"You haven't changed, bro." Tony sat up straight. "Actually, man, I can't believe you. Look at you! You look like Don Johnson, *Miami Vice*. Slick." He slapped Jim's stomach. "How come you don't have a gut, like me?" He held his belly with both hands. "And what kind of car is this, Jimmy?" He looked around the interior. "I never seen a car like this."

"It's a Rover."

"A what?"

"A Rover."

"What the hell's a Rover? Sounds like a dog."

Jim said, "Tell me what's going on."

"I've got a problem. Never mind the drink. You have to take me into the city." Tony stopped and seemed to think about how to continue. Then his thought process apparently shifted. "But, Jimmy, man," he said, "look at you. Stony Brook, Long Island. This is like where the rich people live, right? You're like rich now. You got a doctor wife. You got your own business. You live in a goddamn mansion. You look great, your wife's a piece of ass — I mean, what is this? You're unbelievable, man." Tony reached over and slapped him on the stomach again. "I'm proud of you, man. I'm still a small-time drug-dealing jerk-off, and look at you. I'm proud of you, Jimmy. I mean it."

Jim checked the side-view mirror as he picked up speed on the entrance ramp to the Long Island Expressway. He pulled the car over to the extreme left-hand lane and accelerated to seventy. "What kind of trouble are you in? What do you need?"

"Don't you want to know how I know all this stuff about you?"

"I haven't kept a low profile."

"That's the truth. *The Village Voice!* Not that I would have recognized you from the picture. Where's the curly hair down to your ass?"

"It was never down to my ass. Since when do you read *The Village Voice?*"

"I don't," Tony said. "Ellis showed me."

Jim seemed surprised. "I thought Ellis would have moved on a long time ago."

"Oh," Tony said. "Like, me, you're not surprised I'm still small-time — but Ellis . . . Man, you don't know Ellis. Don't even think you know Ellis. The guy you knew, those years . . . he's like completely gone, totally. He don't even exist anymore."

"What happened to him?"

"Drugs. Twisted stuff. He's a sick puppy, man. If he's alive another month, I'll be surprised."

"Why? What's he got?"

"Not like that," Tony said. He pointed to his temple. "He's sick this way. He's out of his mind. He's not even human anymore, Jimmy. You won't believe the stuff he's into. I tell you some of the things he's done, you'll puke right here, man. Right in the car."

Jim pulled into the slow lane, behind a tractor-trailer. He pointed to the gun on the console beside him. "Put that on the floor or something. I want to pass this truck." Tony put the gun on the floor in the back, and Jim pulled into the passing lane. They were both quiet for a long time then, driving in silence in the dark. When they left Nassau County and entered the city, streetlights suddenly appeared above the road.

"Remember those two guys?" Tony said, as if the lights had suddenly waked him.

Jim didn't answer. He knew what Tony was referring to without having to think about it. "We're in the city," he said. "You want to tell me where we're going? You want to tell me what the hell I'm doing here?" Tony had slumped down in his seat and put his knees up on the dash. Jim knew that Tony was staring up at him, checking his reaction.

Tony reached down into his pocket and came up with a fat manila envelope. He opened the top. "Ten thousand dollars," he said. "I need you to give this to Ellis for me."

Jim took the money and held it up in front of the steering wheel. The bills stuffed into the envelope were held tight with a thick rubber band. He dropped the envelope onto the console. "What's this?"

"It's Ellis's. Jimmy, my man, Ellis has got millions in his place. All in envelopes just like this. He's out of his mind."

"Millions?"

"You don't believe me." Tony put his right hand over his forehead, closed his eyes, and pointed to Jim with his left hand. He looked like a magician about to identify a card. "Look at the back of the envelope. What's the number?"

Jim looked at the back of the envelope. The number was written large with a black marker. "One hundred and sixty-two."

"You do the math."

"Ellis has got a hundred and sixty-two envelopes stashed in his place, each with ten thousand dollars?"

"More. And he counts them. Two, three times a day. Religious."

"Somebody would have killed him for it by now."

"Jimmy . . . Ellis is . . . Everybody's scared of him. Everybody."

"This is the same Ellis I used to play chess with? This is the Ellis who was our supplier?"

"No, man. I told you. That Ellis is long dead. This is some other guy." Tony reached over his head and turned on the interior light. He said, "Look at me, man," and he leaned close to Jimmy.

Jim squinted and reached to turn off the light.

Tony smacked his hand away. "I'm serious," he said. "Look at me."

Jim turned to look at him and then turned back to the road. "I looked at you," he said. "Will you turn off the light?"

"Just listen a minute." He put his hand on Jim's shoulder. "I need you to do me this favor, but you have to understand about Ellis. You can't tell just to look at him." He paused for a moment and then turned off the light. "We're almost there," he said. "I'll tell you a few things."

"Thank you."

"Ellis owns this building; he lives on the top floor — the whole floor. He's got a freezer set up in his living room. He'll show it to you. He shows it to everybody. When he opens it, you're going to see a cop in it." He pointed out of the car, to the right. "Take this exit," he said.

Jim pulled the car to the right, slowed down, and exited onto a cobblestone avenue strewn with garbage. "Where the hell are we?"

"South Bronx. Just stay on this a couple of miles."

Jim slowed down to twenty miles an hour, and even then the cobblestones tested the suspension. The streets on either side of him were empty. Whole blocks had been gutted by fire. "A cop," he said. "He's got a cop in a freezer."

"A dead cop."

"Is this a joke, Tony?"

"I wish."

"You want me to believe this crap? Ellis has got a dead cop in a freezer in his living room, a couple of million dollars scattered around in envelopes . . . It's a joke. What else? Anything else you want to tell me about him?"

"Could I make this up, Jimmy? Really? Ask yourself, if I were lying, would I tell you stuff this wild?" Tony clasped his hands behind his neck and tapped his foot. "I'm getting nervous just coming up here." He jerked around and retrieved the gun from the back floor. "I haven't told you the half of it." He leaned forward and put the Beretta into its holster behind his back. "He sleeps with little girls from the neighborhood. He pays their junkie mothers and they come over in the morning and bathe him — these three little girls. They carry water to his bath. I'm talking eight, nine years old. Same thing at night. It's like some sort of ceremony, some sort of ritual. They fill the tub and then . . ." Tony stopped and shook his head, disgust apparently overcoming him. "He wants me dead, Jimmy, and the guy's a stone-cold, pure-insane murderer. He's got this machete . . ." Again Tony stopped and shook his head. He pointed out the window. "Turn right here."

Jim turned right onto a wide, well-lit boulevard. The area seemed to improve some: the streets were paved, the buildings weren't bombed out, here and there people were sitting on stoops. Along-side him Jim could feel Tony's nervousness. "Let me ask you some-thing, Tony. If Ellis is so bad, why are you still hanging with him?"

"Let me ask you something first," Tony said. "How come it's different for you? You know what I mean? You tell me."

"What do you think? You think the gods picked me up and put me someplace else?"

"So tell me," Tony said. "All I know now is, one day no Jimmy. Twenty years later they're writing about you in the paper. You're a big deal."

Jim looked at his wrist, as if checking a watch. "How long have I got? Five minutes?"

"Give me the short version."

"The short version . . . At twenty-five I split to the West Coast, hung out, met this crowd of people who were into art. They got me into school; I busted my ass, got my degrees, met my wife in gradu-ate school, got married, had kids, moved back east . . ." He stopped and looked at Tony. "Then you showed up."

"You know what I think?" Tony said. "I think the gods picked you up and put you someplace else."

Jim was quiet for a moment. "Okay," he said. "I'm not arguing."

"Amen."

"And you?"

"I don't know," Tony said. "Me . . . I got married once. It lasted a couple of years. I hated working. I lifted all day, I loaded trucks. Never had any money." He grimaced at the memory. "I don't know," he said again. "We couldn't have any kids, she wanted kids . . . I screwed around a lot . . ." He stopped and seemed to drift off.

Jim said, "So now you're working for Ellis again, and . . . ? What happened?" He picked up the money in the envelope. "You ripped him off?"

"Right," Tony said mockingly. "I ripped off envelope number one hundred and sixty-two, hoping he wouldn't miss it. Pull over here."

He pointed to an empty parking space in front of an apartment building that looked seven or eight stories high. "We're here."

Jim parked the car. He turned off the engine and slipped the keys into his pocket. He turned to look at Tony, who was looking back at him intently. Tony picked up the envelope and handed it to Jim. "He gave it to me, Jimmy. He handed it to me, just like I'm handing it to you. Then he gets that look that scares me, and he goes, 'You stole my money, Tony. You know what I got to do, don't you?' I go, 'What money? This money?' I try to give him back the envelope. He turns around, goes into the other room, I hear him taking the machete down off the wall — and I split. This is last week. Now I hear from everybody on the street that I'm a dead man. Kill me, you get an envelope. Ten thousand dollars."

Jim leaned back against his door. "And you didn't do anything, Tony. Anything at all."

"What do you mean, am I innocent? Neither one of us is innocent, Jimmy. But I didn't snake Ellis — that's what we're talking about."

"You want me to go up there and see this maniac and tell him what? For old times' sake, he should stop being a lunatic?"

"Listen —"

"If this guy's so crazy, why do I want to deal with him?"

"Jimmy, listen to what I'm trying to tell you." Tony stopped and looked up at the car's ceiling, as if pausing to find the right words. "Ellis is about to be dead — soon. He's like a guy who's reached the end of some kind of twisted road. It's hard to explain this, but I know. I'm sure. He's trying to wrap things up. It's all gotten too warped, even for Ellis. The guy wants to die."

"This is just something you know. Intuitively."

"Yeah, intuitively. But other stuff, too. Like, in the past month he's been showing everybody his money. And he shows everybody the dead cop. Everybody. And he's been ripping people off, ripping them off big time. He hurts people every chance he gets." Tony hesitated for a moment and then shrugged. "And he's wasted a couple of guys. Not street scum. These were guys with connections. With his own hands, with that fucking machete. I mean, Jimmy, he knows what he's doing. Somebody's going to kill him. He won't live out the month."

Jim held the envelope in front of him. "So let's say you're right.

Why is he going to take this back from me? If what you say is the case, he wants you dead. Like wrapping up loose ends. Maybe he'll want me dead too."

"He doesn't want you dead. He wants you to make a movie about him."

"He wants what?"

"He wants you to make a movie about him. That's all he's talked about since he saw the article."

"He wants me to make a movie about him?"

"It fits, man. It's like the end of his life, like his memoirs. He's been writing it all down, like a script. When he gets it done, he plans on coming out to see you."

Jim turned away from Tony. At the entrance to the apartment building, in front of its thick glass doors, someone had left a McDonald's bag with a cup and a fries container next to it. Jim said, "Tony, I don't make movies."

Tony said, "You want my advice, don't tell Ellis that."

"And what am I supposed to tell him?"

"Listen, Jimmy. I wouldn't ask for this favor if I thought it would screw you. You're an old friend. We were tight once. All you have to do is go up there, tell him Tony told you he wants you to make this movie about him, tell him you'll make it if he'll take the money back and let it be known he's not looking for Tony's head anymore. That's all you got to do. He'll go for it. I know he'll go for it. He asks you why, tell him old times' sake. Tell him you been through some stuff with me — he knows that anyway."

"Except I don't make movies. What I do is nothing like a movie."

"It don't matter," Tony said. "You're not listening to me. Tell him you're going to get Steven Spielberg to direct the thing. Tell him Clint Eastwood's going to play him, and it'll open in a million theaters all over the world. Tell him anything. It doesn't matter. In a month he'll be dead." Tony touched Jim's knee. "This isn't going to cost you, Jimmy. You keep me alive, and it doesn't cost you anything."

"Except," Jim said, "what happens if in a month he's not dead?" He looked through the dark car to Tony. Their eyes met and locked. He said, "I'm sorry, Tony. I can't do this."

"Yeah, you can," Tony said without hesitating. "Remember those two guys in SoHo? Their friends got a long memory, Jimmy."

"You'd blackmail me?"

Tony took the Beretta out of its holster and laid it on the console between them. "Take this if it makes you feel safer. This is my life we're talking about. If you won't do it because it's decent, because you owe me at least something — then you force me to push you a little."

Jim looked out the window at the litter in front of the building. Then he got out of the car, holding the envelope. When he reached the glass doors, he found that they were locked. Beyond them was a small empty space and then another set of glass doors leading into a carpeted lobby, where a young man wearing a crisp white shirt, a thin yellow tie, and a lightweight navy blue jacket sat at a desk. He was watching a portable television. Jim knocked on the glass, and when the man didn't look up, he grabbed the handle and rattled the door. The man at the desk jumped, startled. When he focused on Jim, he looked him up and down a moment. Then he hit a button. Jim heard a click and pulled open one of the doors. When he reached the second set of doors, they were locked. The young man grinned and pointed to a telephone hanging on the wall. Jim picked up the phone. The man put a handset to his ear. Jim said, "Ellis Tyler. Top floor."

The man stared at him through the door as he spoke into the handset. "Who are you?"

"James Renkowski."

"'James Renkowski' don't tell me a thing, ace." The grin had disappeared. "What do you want?"

"I'm looking for Ellis. I'm an old friend."

"An old friend," he repeated. The grin reappeared — more a sneer than a grin. He put the handset down on the desk and pulled another phone in front of him by yanking at a gray wire. He pushed a few numbers and spoke to someone. Then he hung up and stared at Jim unblinkingly until an elevator door at the back of the lobby opened and another two young men stepped out. Like the kid at the desk, they were dressed neatly, wearing white shirts and narrow ties under summer jackets. When they reached the first set of doors, Jim heard a loud click and they pulled the doors open. They both nodded casually toward him in the way of a greeting. Jim nodded back.

The ride up was quick. His escorts stood one on either side of him. They were relaxed and quiet, and he didn't feel any pressure to speak. When they reached the top floor, the elevator opened onto a small carpeted area where two chairs bracketed a door that looked as though it was made of solid steel. One of the young men sat down heavily, as if tired, and the other opened the metal door for Jim.

Jim hesitated a moment and then stepped into a room that was dark and smelled of incense. His shoes partly disappeared into a plush black rug. The room contained a black leather couch and a teak coffee table. Jim was about to take a seat on the couch when Ellis wandered into the room. He entered casually, his eyes on the floor, hands in his pockets, absorbed in his thoughts. When he looked up, he appeared almost surprised to see Jim. "This is a shock," he said, his voice soft, nearly a whisper. "You're one person I thought I'd never see again." While he spoke, he kept his hands in his pockets. He was dressed immaculately. His clothes — a dark blue suit and silk shirt buttoned to the collar — were tailored to a body as thin and lanky as a marathon runner's. He was tall, six foot something, and — just as Jim remembered — he stooped slightly, habitually, from the shoulders down, in the manner of a tall man used to dealing constantly with shorter people. His long hair was slicked back on his head, and he wore glasses with thin lenses in sleek frames. He said, "You've caught me at an awkward time, Jimmy. I have a business meeting coming up."

It took Jim a moment to respond. When he spoke, he was surprised at the ease in his voice and manner. "Ellis," he said. "You look different."

"You think so?" Ellis spread his arms and looked down at himself. Then he seemed to remember. "That's right," he said. He pointed at Jim and his eyes brightened a little. "You knew me in my fat days." Then he put his hands back in his pockets. "A long time ago, Jimmy."

"You look good."

"I'd invite you in . . ."

"No," Jim said. "That's okay. I'm here because of Tony." He reached into his jacket pocket and took out the manila envelope.

When he saw the envelope, Ellis touched his hands to his temples. "I should have guessed," he said. Then he added, as if surprised at himself, "It didn't occur to me."

Jim said, "It wasn't a meeting I was prepared for either." He extended the money toward Ellis.

Ellis took the envelope and tossed it onto the coffee table. He said, "Come in for a minute."

Jim followed Ellis through a series of dark rooms into a large open area that appeared to serve as a combination living room, bedroom, dining room, and bath. One wall was a row of open windows with a view of the Manhattan skyline. A line of crepe curtains fluttered in a breeze. The other walls were solid and barren: no art, no ornamentation of any kind. In one part of the room a teak dining table was surrounded by straight-backed chairs. In another part was a queen-sized bed in a teak frame. Next to the bed was a freestanding marble bathtub with brass claw legs. Next to the bathtub were three brass buckets the size of small garbage cans. As Jim walked past the open windows, his knees went loose and watery from the height. He glanced down at the street and noticed, several blocks away, a newspaper kiosk next to a public telephone.

Ellis said, "I'm sorry I can't be more sociable, Jimmy." He took a seat on a couch and motioned Jim to sit across from him.

Jim took a seat, and Ellis made a gesture with his hands indicating that Jim should talk.

"He wants you to take the money back."

"What does he think — that because we all used to be friends . . . ?"

"Something like that," Jim said. "He asked me to cut a deal with you."

"A deal?"

"He thought you might be interested in having me do a movie. About you. About your life. He thought —"

"A movie?" Ellis said. "You don't make movies, Jimmy." He opened his hands as if to ask Jim what he was talking about. "I've read about you. I saw your show. What you do, it's a kind of poetry with visual images."

"That's true," Jim said. "But I thought —"

Ellis put his hand up. "Stop, Jimmy. Don't embarrass both of us. Tony's not worth it." He turned around on the couch and leaned toward the windows, drawing in a deep breath of air as if he needed the fresh air from the open windows to help him breathe. He filled his lungs and exhaled slowly. Then he turned back to Jim. "The fool tried to steal from me. He took an envelope with ten thousand dollars and replaced it with one with a few hundred. He thought I wouldn't notice. If I ever see him again, I'm going to kill him. If anybody who works for me ever sees him, they'll kill him." Ellis leaned forward. "There's nothing you can do for him."

Jim said, "Ellis . . ."

"Jimmy." Ellis's face tightened, and a hard note came into his voice. "Come here," he said. "Let me show you something." Ellis put his hands on his knees and lifted himself from the couch as if it were an effort, and Jim followed him into an adjacent room with an eight-foot-by-three-foot waist-high rectangular structure situated at its center like an altar or a cenotaph. The structure was covered with red drapery. At the back of the room was a worktable with a huge metal vise at one end. On the worktable a chainsaw rested next to a power drill and a set of pliers. A machete at least three feet long hung on the wall above the table. The blade was blood-stained, and there were lines of blood on the wall.

Jim said, "How long you been into woodworking, Ellis?"

Ellis looked at the worktable and then back to Jim. He didn't laugh. He pulled the red drapery off the structure, revealing it to be a freezer with a thick black cord that trailed off into the black carpet. He said, "This is something I learned from you," and lifted the heavy white door of the freezer. Inside was a young man in a blue New York City police uniform. He looked like he wasn't yet twenty years old. His skin was an ugly deep hue of purple. His eyes were open under bushy black eyebrows. Half of his body was encased in ice, as if he were floating in it, his chest and face and the tops of his legs protruding above the cloudy surface.

Jim said, "You didn't learn this from me, Ellis."

"When you were just coming up, you cracked a guy's head open with a blackjack. Big public place, some bar. Everybody knew who you were."

"You've got the wrong guy. Never happened."

"No, I don't, Jimmy." Ellis grasped the edge of the freezer with both hands and leaned over it, looking down at the frozen body. "I'll tell you something nobody else knows." Still leaning over the freezer, he looked back at Jim. "I didn't kill him. He's like a road kill. I found him. That's why the cops have no idea. There's nothing to connect me. I just saw him on the street, threw him in my trunk, took off. But I tell all the punks I have to deal with, all the small-time pushers — like you used to be — that I wasted him. They come in here, see a dead New York cop in a freezer, they'd put an ice pick through their mother's heart before they'd screw me."

Jim turned his back to the freezer. Through the room's open door he could see the living room windows and the lights of Manhattan.

Ellis said, "So now we don't have to talk any more about Tony."

Jim didn't respond, and then Ellis was quiet for a time. When he turned around, he saw that Ellis was still leaning over the freezer, staring down at the frozen body, but his eyes seemed vacant. Jim said, "I'd better go, then."

Ellis nodded. He reached into the freezer and rubbed away frost covering the metal badge pinned to the cop's uniform. "Shield 3266," he said, and he closed the lid. Then he put a hand on Jim's back and led him out of the apartment to the elevator, motioning the young men stationed outside the apartment to stay where they were. When the elevator doors opened, he put a hand on Jim's shoulder. "You got lucky," he said. "Don't let it get screwed up on you." Then he pushed him into the elevator and turned away before the doors closed. Jim watched him walk back to his apartment as the two young men stood on either side of the door, as stiff as palace guards.

Tony was waiting for him on the street, leaning back into the shadows of a small alley between apartment buildings. Jim had already walked past him when he stepped out of the darkness. "Jimmy," he said.

Jim laughed. He said, "You don't have to hide, Tony. It's straightened out."

"He went for it?"

"You're surprised?"

"No, I'm not surprised." He slapped Jim on the shoulder, a kind of congratulations or thanks. "I know Ellis, man. I know him like I know myself. What'd he say?"

"He's like a little kid. He's talking about who's going to play who, where we're going to shoot it, that kind of stuff."

"And me? What'd he say about me?" He took Jim by the arm and pulled him back into the shadows of the alley.

Jim reached out and held Tony by the shoulders. "Look," he said,

"I can't tell you he's happy with you. You have to go up and deal with him. You have to explain yourself to him."

"He's going to burn me, man. I know it."

"No," Jim said. "We have a deal. I make the movie, he doesn't hurt you."

"He doesn't *hurt* me, or he doesn't *kill* me?"

"He doesn't do anything to you."

"Are you sure, Jimmy? Because that guy can hurt people so bad they'd rather be dead."

Jim said, "No, Tony. This is a formality. This is for show. You got to go humble yourself up there. You know what it is. He'll make you grovel. He'll make sure the others see. You have to do it, Tony. It's for business."

Tony looked down at the ground as if thinking things over. When he looked up, he said, "You sure about this, Jimmy?"

"Absolutely, Tony." Jim took Tony's hand and held it between his two hands. "It's cool," he said. "He wants Tom Cruise to play you in the movie."

Tony shouted, "Tom Cruise!" Then he laughed.

"All right, listen, can I go home now?" Jim reached into his jacket pocket for his car keys. "My wife'll be asking me questions for the next six months."

Tony stepped back for a moment as if to look Jim over, and then embraced him tightly. "You saved my life, man. I got to thank you."

Jim whispered, "I just hope you're right, Tony. About Ellis not being around another month."

Tony stepped back. "Was I right about the movie?"

Jim smiled. Then he shook hands with Tony, and Tony hugged him one more time before walking away, out of the shadows and into the lights from the apartment building.

Jim watched from the driver's seat of his car as Tony waited for a short while on the street and then disappeared behind the glass doors. Within a minute or two he heard the muted sound of shouting voices, one of them clearly Tony's. Then silence. He drove to the newspaper kiosk he had seen from Ellis's apartment and parked in front of the pay phone. When he stepped out of his car, he heard a scream, distinctly, though he couldn't tell for certain where it came from. He looked up and found Ellis's windows. He kept his eyes on the windows as he picked up the phone and dialed 911. He could see Ellis's apartment. The crepe curtains had been sucked out by the breeze. They fluttered over the street. He gave the operator Ellis's name, the location of the apartment building, and the apartment number. He told her about the dead cop. The operator didn't sound interested. She wanted his name. He told her the dead cop's badge number and hung up.

He drove a block or two away and found another place to park where he could still see Ellis's windows. A second or two after he turned off the lights and ignition, two police cars sped past him. Then police cars and paddy wagons and unmarked cars were speeding down every street and through every intersection in sight, sirens screaming. Ellis came to a window and looked out. His hair was wild. He was no longer wearing his jacket, and his shirt was open to the waist, as if the buttons had all been ripped off. The three young men came, and one pulled him away while another closed the window. They disappeared, and a minute later the sound of gunshots crackled over the street. It lasted only a minute or two, but a thousand shots seemed to have been fired in that time. Then Ellis appeared again at the window, this time in the arms of a burly cop. Other uniforms seemed to be wrestling with the cop who had Ellis. A brawl was going on. The burly cop broke away from the others and the window shattered and half of Ellis's body hung out the window for a second — and then he was flying toward the ground, his arms extended in front of him as if he were diving. Jim got out of the car and walked to the entrance of the apartment building, where a crowd was gathering behind police lines. He waited until the ambulances came and men and women in blue coats began carrying away bodies in black zippered bags. After he counted five bodies, he left.

On the way back to Stony Brook he practiced not thinking. He tried to concentrate on his home and family, on his life with his wife and children, on projects that engaged him. When a disturbing thought or image came to mind — Ellis flying through the window, the shattered glass around him like the surface of water breaking, or Tony embracing him on the street, thanking him for saving his life — when such an image or thought came to mind, he would stop thinking and make himself go numb until it dissolved. Then he returned to thinking about his everyday life. For most of the ride home he was numb and empty of thought, and at one point he felt himself getting shaky with the fear that something terrible had happened, that his life would change, that he wouldn't be able to go on living the life he had built with Laura, for Melissa and Alice and Jake, and for himself. He shook his whole body, like a dog shaking water from its coat, and he told himself that he would do what he had to do, as always.

At home he found everyone asleep. In their bedroom Laura lay on her back, with the baby alongside her in a cradle. Alice had crawled into bed with her. She lay on her stomach with her head snug against her mother's breast and one leg flung on top of her mother's knee. Jim quietly removed a pair of pajamas from his dresser, went to the basement to shower, and returned to join Laura and Alice in bed. He checked the alarm clock on the headboard. It was only a little after midnight. In an hour or two Melissa would wake up and try to get into bed with everyone else. She was going through a stage of regular bad dreams, and most nights Jim would have to hold her and comfort her and persuade her to go back to her own bed. Usually she'd tell him that she was afraid of her bed — she was afraid that something was under it. He'd take her back to her room and show her that nothing was under the bed, and then he'd lie with her for a while and she'd huddle close to him, careful that no part of her body extended over the edge of the mattress. This night, he thought, he'd let her sleep with them.

Alongside him Alice moved slightly, and he laid the palm of his hand on her small shoulder, her soft skin warm and comforting. He tried to close his eyes, but they kept opening, as if with a will of their own. He imagined he was lying on a raft, a cedar raft of logs strapped together, and got to the point where he could feel the bed rocking, as if it were floating, and in his mind's eye he saw the stripped white logs of the raft as they drifted over a sea of murky water — but still he couldn't fall asleep. Hours later, when the quality of the darkness began to soften and the first few birds began to chirp and squawk, when he started working out in his mind the structure for one of his video pieces, when he began thinking about images and the way he might put them together, the image of Ellis flying from the window, the image of the young cop in the freezer, the bodyguards, Tony — when he began shaping and structuring the project in his mind, when he knew for sure that one day he would begin to work on it, then the tension in his muscles eased up some, and he closed his eyes, and when the sun came up, he was sleeping.

MAX GARLAND

Chiromancy

FROM THE NEW ENGLAND REVIEW

SHE HELD HIS HAND in hers and said he would live a long time. He had a lifeline that was practically ridiculous. *Look,* she said, and traced the downcurve with a fingernail. Truly, it ran all the way from the webbing of the thumb to the veins of the wrist and promised a vast pile of years. *I'd be surprised if you died at all,* she said, then moved her hand to the ignition, at which sign he slid from the car, felt the black snap of vertigo from the tequila, leaned down to say good night, and watched as she pulled from the curb and started the drive toward her husband and assorted sons.

I could die tonight, he thought. *I could die in a minute or two.* The only complication was the feeling that he hadn't suffered enough, and although he was no Buddhist, he recognized the dishonor in this. Under the streetlight he looked down at his own hand as if examining an object fallen from space. He could make out the bumps and squiggles, meanderings and pointless hieroglyphs, a modest chain of epidermal hills, a lone callus. I might as well be reading the entrails of a bird, he thought, or studying a map of the moon. Although his memory for the arcane was excellent, his newspaper columns laden with scraps of local history and hearsay, he couldn't for the life of him remember which mound of the palm was Venus, which Jupiter or Saturn. He couldn't recall where logic resided, or libertinage might dwell. The streetlamp threw a blue, moony light on the subject, and he thought for the first time about how naked the hand looked, how almost indecent, the opened palm of the hand.

*

How many men do you marry? she wondered as she drove, a little wobbly from the margaritas. Although it wasn't really a question, but more along the lines of saying, *Look at all the fireflies tonight.* Or, watching her middle son dress himself that morning — shoes on the proper feet, his shirt turned rightside out, thinking, *God, how quickly this happens.*

Whereas some women she knew, many in fact, felt oppressed by the presence of a single husband, the sheer mastodon weight of the man, she felt just the opposite. In these drawling Kentucky river towns, you need all the husbands you can gather, she thought. You need the one you really married, the historical husband; in her case an actual teacher of history at the junior college. The man waiting even as she drove — one boy put to bed, she checked the Toyota clock; yes, the two-year-old in bed by now, the middle son clomping morosely up the stairs, and the third, the nine-year-old, no doubt waiting up for her.

But you need smaller, briefer husbands. Husbands who sweep in like rainstorms and make the air more breathable. Sharers of harmless intimacies. Receivers of throwaway flirtations. Coffee break husbands, browsing through the gallery husbands.

And what about the sales representatives who visit the gallery once a month, crisp clockwork husbands who take you to lunch and behave as if their manners had been gleaned from old Gig Young movies?

Or the haunted Southern painter husband whose studio you visit two or three times a year? A white flurry of paint on the eyelashes. Instant coffee in the cup, oily toxins in the air. Maybe he has disheveled himself a little extra for your coming? Maybe his wife is really unfortunately away?

You don't sleep with the spare husbands, of course, though they sometimes fail to understand a point so fine. In all honesty, there is some inner debate on this. *Take tonight,* reading his hand by dashboard light, speedometer light. A small debate, she thought as she drove, her own hands prompt at 10:00 and 2:00 on the wheel like any good inebriate.

. . . and what does it mean to have a hand instead of a hoof, paw, wing, fin, tentacle? he immediately sat at his desk and wrote in his journal because what he wanted to do was drive the twenty-odd miles to her

farm and stand there like an imbecile, swatting the bat-sized mosquitoes and staring at the house lights. That would be proper suffering, wouldn't it? He ran a hand through his hair, dislodged a grain of margarita salt from a corner of his mustache, flicked it across the page. *And what is this contraption of 27 bones?* he wrote, remembering the number from the gallery brochure, because it was exactly the kind of sentence he could not include in the article he would write on tonight's opening, "The Art of the Hand," a traveling exhibit of images of the human hand she had booked into the gallery. It had been a little far-fetched for western Kentucky, but the regulars had turned out — the doctors' wives, the high school art teachers with their few troubled students in tow, someone from the Chamber of Commerce, decked-out members of the local art guild.

The show had included paintings by minor contemporaries: abstract and photo-realistic hands, a small collection of photographs, even a mixed-media collage incorporating medical x-rays — the spectral hands of infants, the burled, mineralized hands of the aged. And, of course, the huge medieval chiromancy chart, the elaborately framed piece with angels and constellatory beasts swirling around an enormous human palm, every inch mapped and labeled with the Latin names of planets and emotions. After the brief palm-reading episode in her car, he wished he had studied it closer.

Let's see, she had said, then reached for his hand, surprising him. Not that they hadn't touched before. There was a small, tame history of brushes and pecks, airy smooches of greeting and goodbye. Sometimes her husband was at her side; occasionally, another woman at his. Though not for a while now.

In a town where the ship of marital love sailed early and often, he found himself among the holdouts, the rather conspicuous landlubbers. Though it wasn't a tiny town by Kentucky standards — the junior college, the regional mall, an outlying clutch of chemical factories, bargeworks, a spreading apron of suburbs — the unmarried life still carried its unmistakable stigma. Like slow-witted children, single men and women were introduced, and reintroduced. The town's loose change needing to be gathered, converted to crisp currency and tucked into the vault.

Nevertheless, he had managed a bachelorhood, not so much by

design as by continually falling for firmly married women. His first married love had been his fourth-grade teacher, a woman with a Tidewater accent and a premature silver streak in her hair that had reminded him of the tail of a comet. It seemed to him now that there was never a time before this, that even in infancy, probably even in the womb itself, it had occurred to him to want only what was complete without him.

Therefore, he found himself drifting to her side during whatever social events the town could muster — occasional dinners, the local concert series, her own gallery's openings. Since the newspaper office was near the gallery they sometimes met for lunch. Lately, even meeting her on the street, he felt all the familiar apparatus start to churn — the quick tightening of the abdominals, the straightening of the spine, the annoying surge of perked-up chemistry. One minute he was buoyant, almost witty in her presence, and the next minute the awareness of his own foolishness came gliding down like a thunderhead.

All of which proved to him, as he had written in other journals, that hopeless love had no instructional value, taught absolutely nothing. It was a realm to which trial and error did not apply.

It seemed as if such mistakes were too *embedded* to learn from. Even thinking back on them, as he tended to do, merely deepened the wayward grooves.

Not that he hadn't attempted more conventional loves — single women, reasonable women. But at some point the distraction always arrived, and not only for him. He noticed the women themselves checking the depths of mirrors and store windows, looking around in restaurants and movie theaters as if someone were missing. Hadn't they also sensed it — the paucity, the incorrectness of *two*? That perhaps the triangle, after all, was the more perfect romantic shape. Take away one side and the others flail and drift, or else snap together too sharply, like scissors.

Take tonight, the newspaper husband. She stopped to roll down a window at the last light before the town fizzled into long rivery outskirts. He was probably the kindest, if maybe not the smartest of the little husbands. Of course, both qualities, she realized, may have been the symptoms of love. You see these things coming. See them over the months, the extra courtesies and attentions.

She had even seen it in the articles he wrote for the newspaper, gamely promoting whatever she brought to the gallery. Praising the local watercolorists, a misty, prolific lot whose patronage helped support the gallery, but whose paintings always looked as if they had suffered minor rain damage. Praising the regional wildlife painters, whose creatures posed on branches and stones, their faces as perturbed and two-dimensional as Byzantine martyrs. *A ruggedness appropriate to the outdoors,* he had written of their work. Which qualified as praise in her book.

Certainly she saw it coming over the table tonight. The restaurant where they had stopped for drinks after the opening had undergone a recent transformation from nautical motif to southwestern decor, a trend that had swept the country a decade ago and finally dawdled its way into the Bluegrass. To soften the blow, they were offered enormous half-priced margaritas, salt encrusted like old spells around their rims. The walls had taken on the sheenless peach of sunset. Where buoys and fish netting had hung, there were Navaho rugs, their sharp oracular patterns lit by strings of chili-pepper lights. In the newly installed window box was a miniature horizon of cacti, some drooping and wounded like figures from Dali, others dreamily phallic and untouchable.

It's not a good town for the lonely, he had said, in the middle of a gossipy rundown of the guests at the opening. Or maybe it was *good time.* Whichever, it was a subject they had touched on before. A boring and necessary part of living where they lived — this moaning about the limits, the insularity, as if somewhere existed a place where the lonely lived happily, possibly danced in the streets. *Why do people stay here?* he had asked, meaning, of course, *Why do we stay?* meaning they were in this together — the wrong place, the wrong life. She watched him lean toward her, fetchingly rumpled in his all-day white newspaperman's shirt, sleeves shot to the elbows as if he were about to wash his face in the margarita.

It was amazing how it all still worked — the scraggle of mustache, the showing of the naked forearms, letting the candlelight glaze them like honey buns. Even the inevitable migration of the goblets until his stood rim to rim with hers. Had she actually heard the small grinding sound of salt on salt?

Not that she was really worried about herself. You can deflect the husbands, she knew. Sometimes talking about her sons was enough. Occasionally, even bringing out the photographs. She could see, however, that along his particular evolutionary branch the defenses against blind love had not been well laid. And although she wasn't worried, it did occur to her that it might be a bad idea, drinking tequila so close to the birthplace of bourbon, that there might be some sort of curse involved.

And it was strange, she thought now, following the Toyota's beam along the pocked and cratered county highway, how you can see it coming, slow and blatant as a moon, and still not quite get out of the way. See it sagging in his shirt. See it tugging like a moth at the corners of his mouth. How the words of such a man become a gradual unfurling, a laying out, the man spreading the weather-beaten map of himself on the table as if you might actually choose to navigate in that bleak direction.

Carpal, metacarpal, phalanges, he wrote, exhausting all the bones he knew by name. *The vestigial nails,* he came up with, although he could have sworn there was some purpose in the raking of hers across his palm tonight, an event that had sent an old-fashioned romantic shiver, like a tiny arrow of Novocaine, into his teeth and gums. *Drummers and twiddlers,* he scribbled, watching his fingers. *Hapless fondlers and probers,* he wrote, because like countless others he had tumbled into small-town journalism from the ark of literary ambition. The obligatory, half-finished novel. Long Wolfian meditations stashed in folders and accordion files.

In this way he knew they were alike: he had seen some of her college paintings on his one trip to the farm for an open house soon after the gallery opened. There had been a certain Munch or Roualt quality about the paintings, a sober, almost charred cast to the subjects as if they had been unearthed from volcanic ruins. He was no expert, but it seemed obvious she had invested too much to graciously abandon. Even though she ran the gallery well, gave the town more occasion for art than the town knew it needed, he recognized in her what he felt in himself — the shirtsleeve efficiency, the cultural boosterism of the thwarted. Hadn't she admitted this?

But he presumed too much. Blabbing about his own loneliness, implying a kinship there as well. Why invent this drama? Why insist upon playing the ancient role of the town bachelor, tapping at the lives of married women for the sound of something hollow? In whose life would there not be something hollow?

He looked down at his fingers again, the ridges, whorls, arches, and vague deltas of the fingertips, the swirling patterns that could identify criminals and dead men, even long-buried men, he knew, although he no longer covered crime. Even a burned man, a coroner had once told him, if not burned to an absolute cinder, could be known by the ashy loop and flourish of a single fingertip.

She reached to roll down the opposite window of the Toyota, nearly spilling the car onto the gravelly roadside. There was a new rush of air, a heightened sound, almost a *racket* of crickets. Porchlights were scattered, and fireflies shone everywhere except in the sweep of headlights. *Look at all the fireflies,* she actually spoke the words. But to whom did she imagine speaking? The little newspaper husband? Her real husband, husband of record, who not only taught history, but existed as an almost sedimentary force in her life? Their marriage had begun so long ago now it seemed like a pact made by ambitious children. Their nights and years drifted down and hardened. Then more nights after that. Finally, you had this dry land appearing, a kind of mutually created continent. No fear of drowning, no shudder of waves. Only occasionally did the question nag. Another life? A small debate?

But whose fault was anybody's choice? Who was really to blame? The decision to return to his hometown after college had been mutual, hadn't it? The idea of the gallery had been hers. There was the unused studio space above it, east light every morning of the year. That had been part of the plan, hadn't it, to paint in the mornings? Doesn't everyone have a plan to paint in the mornings?

You marry a man, after all, who is the very soul of patience. A man who frowns and laments over the essays of the local junior college students, their ideas so faithfully cribbed from *Encyclopedia Americana* he knows the language by heart. And in summer, isn't he practically a house-husband, if such a thing is possible in these latitudes?

But still, does any woman fail to give up more than the man she marries? Fail to put more of herself aside? Isn't every husband's diaper changing, skillet wielding, even *fathering,* just a bit of a favor? Doesn't he, the man waiting even at this moment, possibly up to his elbows in dishwater, doesn't even he wear it like just the tiniest stain on his sleeve?

She was thinking like her friends now. The ones with husbands hunkered over their remote controls. Big boys sitting in front of their dinner plates waiting for the loaves and fishes, the manna to fall.

She couldn't pretend it was the same for her. Yet, she had wanted to touch the smitten man tonight, as if that were the solution to anything. If only there were more of the body, she thought. If only there were some neutral place, a kind of *home free*. Maybe a third shoulder, a small safe plane of the brow, some bland appendage you could touch without everything going damp and rhythmic.

He reached across the desk and unfolded the brochure from the opening, a small maplike pamphlet written by someone referred to as an "art anthropologist." "It is the hand that separates man from the other hominids," the brochure read, as if this were a good thing. Specifically, it was the thumb, the famous opposable thumb that did the separating, that made man such a stellar mechanic. Capable of flexion and rotation, it was the thumb that made painting itself possible, the writer went on to say. All art, in fact, even writing, sprang from the suppleness of the human thumb.

He picked up his pen and watched the dip and wiggle, sure enough the words spilling forth. So relentless, he thought. *Such a hoarder, such a perfect tool of desire,* he watched the hand confess across the page. It occurred to him that even the writing of this proved the point, this attempt to nail down the measliest scrap of time. Every little drifting moment some poor fool has to stitch across a page.

A paw would be better than this, he wrote. *A fin, a flipper.* He thought of the afternoon he had spent at the Brookfield Zoo in Chicago researching his annual summer travel piece for the paper. After watching the dolphin show — the hoop-jumping, tail-walking, the grinning and chattering of the animals — he had taken the stairs to the underwater observation windows. There were three of them, bottle-nosed dolphins — gliding, slowly ascending and dipping, grazing against one another in a kind of barreling dance, occasionally even brushing the thick observation glass. He remembered how, even in that small space, they had seemed unbelievably serene. He tried to describe it now, scribbling past the margins of the journal — how the dolphins would rise, momentarily weightless, then suddenly dive as if the notion of gravity had just occurred to them, as if physics were a matter of whimsical choice. Even trapped as they were, the dolphins moved through the water with something he wished he knew — almost a grace, not the easy athletic sense of the word, but the grace of old hymnbooks, the kind used in Appalachian funerals.

Remembering them now, he was sure their serenity had something to do with their lack of hands. With those blunt gray flippers, what could the dolphins ever be tempted to cling to? Not even their own children could they hold. Wouldn't that be a kind of happiness? Whatever the creatures reached for simply turned to water, propelling them forward and away.

The night air swept through the car, almost chilly. She thought of him walking to work that morning and wondered if he had left his car behind for tonight's possibility, the lift home, the stopping for drinks. Strangely, it made her think of her eldest son, a solid girl-hater at the moment. The mere mention of girlfriends sent him into a fit of such vehemence even his younger brothers seemed puzzled, though they tried to imitate him. Yet, she suddenly envisioned her son on a night like this years from now, sitting across from a woman, wanting something that no amount of common ground, no quantity of spilled pathos, could gain for him. How do you prepare any child for that?

She wished she really understood chiromancy. All she knew she had learned from the huge medieval chart in the exhibit, just enough to follow the main lines — heartline, headline, lifeline. Just enough to act on the impulse, to predict love and a long life for him in the car tonight. Maybe it was just as well she didn't know more. There had been that moment in front of his house, the distinct feeling that if she had held his hand any longer, if she so much as rested a finger in the soft middle, it would have closed on her. It would have closed exactly the way her own infant sons' hands had once grasped and held whatever foreign thing wandered across them.

He read back over what he had written in the journal. The words already seemed absurd to him, inflated boozy snippets. This is why they don't serve drinks at the office, he thought. *Hands? Dolphins?* What did dolphins have to do with this? And what did he know about them anyway? He had watched for fifteen minutes through a pane of thick, smudged glass. Who could be sure what any other creature felt? Maybe it was even worse for them. Maybe the dolphins' famous smile was no more than a blubbery mask. Maybe all that bright chatter, the chirping and coded clicks, were not the sounds of merriment at all. For all anyone knew, the dolphins could be crying something as human as *hold me,* as they sped through the oceans and zoos, inconsolable.

He slapped the journal shut. If he had a wise friend, he knew what such a friend would say to him now — In love? You're in love with the idea of it, some phony painting of love: the womanly farm, the domestic trappings, the ready-made passel of sons, the eternal tricycle overturned in the drive. Look at what you've written, the friend would say. You haven't even mentioned her name.

But he had no such friend, nor did he particularly want one. What *had* he wanted tonight? What had he expected? After the months of conversations, lunches, small confidences, did he really think she took his hand out of anything but consolation? Did he imagine she might continue reading his palm all the way up the wrist, run a finger along the inside of the elbow, maybe trace the blank shell of an ear?

He reopened the journal. *Blank shell of an ear,* he wrote, apropos of nothing, then flicked off the lamp and sat there, let himself think of her, his hands on the desk in front of him like depleted puppets, or the hands of someone posing for a portrait in the dark.

The fireflies were even thicker as she entered the bottomland near the farm. They seemed almost as constant as stars, the new ones sweeping into the sockets of the old, the flickering nearly canceled by the car's movement. A few had even dashed against the windshield, their green chemical wreckage fading in slow leaks and pulses across the glass.

There must be thousands of drives like this every night, she thought. *Fireflies, porchlights, headlights.* Drives like little divorces. The wind wrestled a tiny wrapper along the floor, almost swept a torn page from a coloring book out the window. She took a hand from the wheel and gathered her hair, held it in a fist at the base of her neck like a girl on a date in a movie. She felt odd; not drunk, or guilty, almost happy in fact, as if once again she had discovered the secret of marriage in this subtle polygamy. The strange sense that even at this late hour of entrenchment — joint mortgages, insurance policies, children nestled in bed — you *could* still ruin your life. There was that slim possibility, that remnant weight of decision. And was it too perverse, too roundabout, to think that what could still be ruined, could still be valued, or even saved?

Let's see your fortune, she had said to him in the car. And now it seemed she reached for his hand simply because something had to be reached for, and better the hand than the cheek, or the fleck of salt in his mustache, which she might at least have mentioned, or brushed away, or in another life, even tasted?

Thousands of porchlights, thousands of little divorces. Though some, of course, are harder than others, she thought, turning from the asphalt onto the long gravel drive. And what can anyone say about that moment of absolute wavering? Which for her, she realized now, had come, not over the margaritas, nor even reading his palm in the car, but just after she pulled from the curb, and halfway down the block looked up to suddenly see him — little reversed man in the rearview mirror, looking down into his own deciphered hand, the hand she knew he imagined moving over her, under her, the hand she had said would live so long.

JAMAICA KINCAID

Xuela

FROM THE NEW YORKER

MY MOTHER DIED at the moment I was born, and so for my whole life there was nothing standing between me and eternity; at my back was always a bleak, black wind. I could not have known at the beginning of my life that this would be so; I only came to know this in the middle of my life, just at the time when I was no longer young and realized that I had less of some of the things I used to have in abundance and more of some of the things I had scarcely had at all. And this realization of loss and gain made me look backward and forward: at my beginning was this woman whose face I had never seen, but at my end was nothing, no one; there was nothing between me and the black room of the world. I came to feel that for my whole life I had been standing on a precipice, that my loss had made me vulnerable, that it had made me hard and helpless; on knowing this, I became overwhelmed with sadness and shame and pity for myself.

When my mother died, leaving me a small child vulnerable to all the world, my father took me and placed me in the care of the same woman he paid to wash his clothes. It is possible that he emphasized to her the difference between the two bundles; one was his child, perhaps not the only child of his in the world but the only child he had had with the only woman he had married so far, the other was his soiled clothes. He would have handled one more gently than the other, he would have given more careful instructions for the care of one than for the other, he would have expected better care for one than the other — but which one I do not know, because he was a vain man, his appearance was very important to him. That I was a burden to him then, I know; that his soiled clothes were a burden to him then, I know; that he did not know how to take care of me by himself, that he did not know how to clean his own clothes himself then, I know.

He had lived in a very small house with my mother. He was poor, but it was not because he was good; he had simply not done enough bad things yet to get rich. The house was on a hill, and he had walked down the hill balancing in one hand his child, in the other his clothes, and he gave them, bundle and child, to this woman. She was not a relative of his or of my mother's; her name was Eunice Paul, and she had six children already, the last one still a baby. That was why she still had some milk to give me, but in my mouth it tasted sour, and I would not drink it. She lived in a house that was far from other houses, and from it there was a broad view of the sea and the mountains, and when I was irritable and unable to console myself she would prop me up on a pile of old clothes and place me under a tree, and at the sight of that sea and those mountains, so unpitying, I would exhaust myself in tears.

Ma Eunice was not unkind: she treated me just the way she treated her own children — but that is not to say that she was kind to her own children. In a place like this, brutality is the only real inheritance and cruelty is sometimes the only thing freely given. I did not like her, and I missed the face I had never seen; I looked over my shoulder to see if someone was coming, as if I were expecting someone to come, and Ma Eunice would ask me what I was looking for, at first as a joke, but when, after a time, I did not stop doing it, she thought that it meant I could see spirits. I could not see spirits at all, I was just looking for that face, that face I would never see, even if I lived forever.

I never grew to love this woman my father left me with, this woman who was not unkind to me but who could not be kind because she did not know how — and perhaps I could not love her because I, too, did not know how. She fed me food forced through a sieve when I would not drink her milk and did not yet have teeth; when I grew teeth, the first thing I did was to sink them into her hand as she fed me. A small sound escaped her mouth then, more from surprise than from pain, and she knew this for what it was — my first act of ingratitude — and it put her on her guard against me for the rest of the time we knew each other.

Until I was four I did not speak. This did not cause anyone to lose a minute of happiness; there was no one who would have worried about it in any case. I knew I could speak, but I did not want to. I saw my father every fortnight, when he came to get his clean clothes. I never thought of him as coming to visit me; I thought of him as coming to pick up his clean clothes. When he came, I was brought to him, and he would ask me how I was, but it was a formality; he would never touch me or look into my eyes. What was there to see in my eyes then? Eunice washed, ironed, and folded his clothes; they were wrapped up like a gift in two pieces of clean nankeen cloth and placed on a table, the only table in the house, waiting for him to come and pick them up. His visits were quite steady, and so when one time he did not appear as he usually did I noticed it. I said, "Where is my father?"

I said it in English — not patois French or English but plain English — and that should have been the surprise; not that I spoke but that I spoke English, a language I had never heard anyone speak. Ma Eunice and her children spoke the language of Dominica, which is French patois, and my father, when he spoke to me, spoke that language also. But no one noticed; they only marvelled at the fact that I had finally spoken. That the first words I said were in the language of a people I would never like or love is not now a mystery to me; almost everything in my life to which I am inextricably bound is a source of pain.

I was then four years old and saw the world as a series of sketches, soft strokes in charcoal; and so when my father would come and take his clothes away I saw only that he suddenly appeared on the small path that led from the main road to the door of the house in which I lived and then, after completing his mission, disappeared as he turned onto the road, where it met the path. I did not know what lay beyond the path; I did not know if after he passed from my sight he remained my father or dissolved into something altogether different and I would never see him again in the form of my father. I would have accepted it.

I did not talk and I would not talk.

One day, without meaning to, I broke a plate, the only bone-china plate that Eunice had ever owned, and the words "I am sorry" would not pass my lips. The sadness she expressed over this loss fascinated me; it was so intense, so overwhelming, so deep: she grabbed the thick pouch that was her stomach, she pulled at her hair, she pounded her bosom, large tears rolled out of her eyes and down her cheeks, and they came in such profusion that if they had become a new source of water, as in a myth or a fairy tale, my small self would not have been surprised. I had been warned repeatedly by her not to touch this plate, for she had seen me look at it with an obsessive curiosity. I would look at it and wonder about the picture painted on its surface, a picture of a wide-open field filled with grass and flowers in the most tender shades of yellow, pink, blue, and green; the sky had a sun in it that shone but did not burn bright; the clouds were thin and scattered about like a decoration, not thick and banked up, not harbingers of doom; it was nothing but a field full of grass and flowers on a sunny day, but it had an atmosphere of secret abundance, happiness, and tranquillity; underneath this picture, written in gold letters, was the word "Heaven." Of course it was not a picture of Heaven at all. It was a picture of the English countryside idealized, but I did not know that, I did not know that such a thing as the English countryside existed. And neither did Eunice; she thought that this picture was a picture of Heaven, offering as it did a promise of a life without worry or care or want.

When I broke the china plate on which this picture was painted, and caused Ma Eunice to cry so, I did not immediately feel sorry, I did not feel sorry shortly after; I only felt sorry long afterward, and by then it was too late to tell her so, she had died by then; perhaps she went to Heaven and it fulfilled what was promised on that plate. When I broke the plate, she cursed my dead mother, she cursed my father, she cursed me. The words she used were without meaning; I understood them, but they did not hurt me, for I did not love her. And she did not love me; she made me kneel down on her stone heap — which was situated in a spot that got direct sun all day long — with my hands raised high above my head and with a large stone in each hand. She meant to keep me in this position until I said the words "I am sorry," but I would not say them, I could not say them. It was beyond my own will; those words could not pass my lips then. I stayed like that until she exhausted herself cursing me and all whom I came from.

And should this punishment, redolent as it was in every way of

the relationship between captor and captive, master and slave, with
its motif of the big and the small, the powerful and the powerless,
the strong and the weak, and against a background of earth, sea,
and sky, and Eunice standing over me, metamorphosing into a
succession of things furious and not human with each syllable that
passed her lips; with her dress of a thin, badly woven cotton, the
bodice of a contrary color and pattern that clashed with the skirt;
her hair uncombed, unwashed for many months, wrapped in a
piece of old cloth that had been unwashed for longer than her hair;
the dress had once been new and clean, and dirt had made it old
but dirt had made it new again by giving it shadings it did not have
before, and dirt would finally cause it to disintegrate altogether, but
she was not a dirty woman, she washed her feet every night; the day
was clear, it was not the rainy time, some men were on the sea
casting nets for fish, but they would not catch too many because it
was a clear day; and three of her children were eating bread and
they rolled up the inside of the bread into small pebblelike shapes
and threw it at me as I knelt there and they laughed at me; and the
sky was without a cloud and there was not a breeze, a fly flew back
and forth across my face, sometimes landing on a corner of my
mouth; an overripe breadfruit fell off its tree, and that sound was
like a fist meeting the soft, fleshy part of a body . . . All this, all this I
can remember — should it have made a lasting impression on me?

But as I was kneeling there I saw three land turtles crawling in
and out of the small space under the house, and I fell in love with
them, I wanted to have them near me, I wanted to speak only to
them each day for the rest of my life. Long after my ordeal was over
— resolved in a way that did not please Ma Eunice, for I did not say
I was sorry — I took all three turtles and placed them in an en-
closed area where they could not come and go as they pleased and
where they were completely dependent on me for food. I would
bring to them the leaves of vegetables, and water in seashells. I
thought them beautiful, with their shells dark-gray with faint yellow
circles, their long necks, their unjudging eyes, the slow deliberate-
ness of their crawl. But they would withdraw into their shells when I
did not want them to, and when I called them they would not come
out; to teach them a lesson, I took some mud from the riverbed and
covered up the small hole from which each neck would emerge,
and I allowed it to dry; I covered over the place where they lived

with stones, and for days afterward I forgot about them. When they came into my mind again, I went to take a look at them in the place where I had left them. They were by then all dead.

It was my father's wish that I be sent to school. It was an unusual request; girls did not attend school. I shall never know what made him do such a thing. I can only imagine that he desired such a thing for me without giving it too much thought, because in the end what could an education do for someone like me? I can only say what I did not have; I can only measure it against what I did have and find misery in the difference. And yet, and yet — it was for that reason that I came to see for the first time what lay beyond the path that led away from my house.

I can so well remember the feel of the cloth of my skirt and blouse — coarse because it was new — a green skirt and beige blouse, a uniform, its colors and style mimicking the colors and style of a school somewhere else, somewhere far away; and I had on a pair of brown canvas shoes and brown cotton socks which my father had got for me, I did not know from where. And to mention that I did not know where these things came from, to say that I wondered about them is really to say that this was the first time I had worn such things as shoes and socks, and they caused my feet to ache and swell and the skin to blister and break, but I was made to wear them until my feet got used to it. That morning was a morning like any other, so ordinary it was profound: it was sunny in some places and not in others, and the two (sunny, cloudy) occupied different parts of the sky quite comfortably; the green of the trees, the red burst of the flowers from the flamboyant trees, the sickly yellow fruit of the cashew, the smell of lime, the smell of almonds, the coffee on my breath, Eunice's skirt blowing in my face, and the stirring up of the smells that came from between her legs, which I shall never forget, and whenever I smell myself I am reminded of her; the river was low, so I did not hear the sound of the water rushing over stones; the breeze was soft, so the leaves did not rustle in the trees.

And I had these sensations of seeing, smelling, and hearing during my journey down the path that began at Eunice's door and ended where it met the road; and when I reached the road and placed my newly shod foot on it, that was the first time I had done so; I was aware of this. It was a road of small stones and dirt tightly packed together, and each step I took was awkward; the ground shifted, my feet slipped backward. The road stretched out ahead of me and then it vanished in a bend; we kept walking toward this bend and then we came to the bend and the bend gave way to more of the same road and then another bend. We came to my school long before the end of the last bend: it was a small building with one door and four windows; it had a wooden floor; there was a lizard crawling along a beam in the roof; there were three long desks lined up one behind the other; there was a large wooden table and a chair facing the three long desks; on the wall behind the wooden table and chair was a map; at the top of the map were the words "The British Empire." Those were the first words I learned to read.

In that room there were always boys; I did not sit in a schoolroom with other girls until I was older. I was not afraid in that new situation: I did not know how to be that then and do not know how to be that now. I was not afraid then, because my mother had already died, and that is the only thing a child is really afraid of; when I was born my mother was dead, and I had already lived all those years with Eunice, a woman who was not my mother and who could not love me, and I had lived without my father, never knowing when I would see him again, so I was not afraid for myself in this situation. (And if it is not really true that I was not afraid then, it was not the only time that I did not admit to myself my own vulnerability.)

At the time, each thing as it took place stood out in my mind with a sharpness that I now take for granted; it did not then have a meaning, it did not have a context, I did not yet know the history of events, I did not know their antecedents. My teacher was a woman who had been trained by Methodist missionaries; she was of the African people, that I could see, and she found in this a source of humiliation and self-loathing, and she wore despair like an article of clothing, like a mantle, or a staff on which she leaned constantly, a birthright which she would pass on to us without effort. She did not love us; we did not love her; we did not love one another, not then, not ever. There were seven boys and myself. The boys, too, were all of the African people. My teacher and these boys looked at me and looked at me: I had thick eyebrows; my hair was coarse, thick, and wavy; my eyes were set far apart from each other and they had the shape of almonds; my lips were wide and narrow in an unexpected way. I was of the African people, but not exclusively.

My mother was a Carib woman, and when they looked at me this is what they saw; and it was my teacher who, at the end of the day, in bidding me good evening, called me Miss Boiled Fish — she thought me pale and weak.

I started to speak quite openly then — to myself frequently, to others only when it was absolutely necessary. We spoke English in school — proper English, not patois — and among ourselves we spoke French patois, a language that was not considered proper at all, a language that a person from France could not speak and could only with difficulty understand. I spoke to myself because I grew to like the sound of my own voice. It had a sweetness to me, it made my loneliness less, for I was lonely and wished to see people in whose faces I could see something of myself. Because who was I? My mother was dead; when I saw my father I could not tell what I meant to him.

I learned to read and write very quickly. My memory, my ability to retain information, to remember the tiniest detail, to recall who said what and when, was regarded as unusual, so unusual that my teacher, who was trained to think only of good and evil and whose judgment of such things was always mistaken, said I was evil, I was possessed — and to establish that there could be no doubt of this she pointed to the fact that my mother was a Carib woman.

My world, then — silent, soft, and vegetablelike in its vulnerability, subject to the powerful whims of others, diurnal, beginning with the pale opening of light on the horizon each morning and ending with a sudden onset of dark at the beginning of each night — was both a mystery to me and the source of much pleasure. I loved the face of a gray sky, porous, grainy, wet, following me to school for mornings on end, shooting down soft arrows of water on me; the face of that same sky when it was a hard, unsheltering blue, a backdrop for a cruel sun; the harsh heat that eventually became a part of me, like my blood; the massive trees, the stems of some of them the size of small trunks, that grew without restraint, as if beauty were only size, and which I could tell apart by closing my eyes and listening to the sound the leaves made when they rubbed together; and I loved that moment when the white flowers from the cedar tree started to fall to the ground with a silence that I could hear, their petals at first still fresh, a soft kiss of pink and white, then a day later crushed, wilted, and brown, a nuisance to the eye; and the river that had become a small lagoon when one day on its own it changed its course, on whose bank I would sit and watch families of birds, and frogs laying their eggs, and the sky turning from black to blue and blue to black, and rain falling on the sea beyond the lagoon but not on the mountain that was beyond the sea.

It was while sitting in this place that I first began to dream about my mother; I had fallen asleep on the stones that covered the ground around me, my small body sinking into this surface as if it were a bed of feathers. I saw my mother come down a ladder. She wore a long white gown, the hem of it falling just above her heels, and that was all of her that was exposed, just her heels; she came down and down, but no more of her was ever revealed. Only her heels, only the hem of the gown. At first I longed to see more, and then I became satisfied just to see her heels coming down toward me. When I awoke, I was not the same child I had been before I fell asleep. I longed to see my father and to be in his presence constantly.

On a day that began in no special way that I can remember, I was taught the principles involved in writing an ordinary letter. A letter has six parts: the address of the sender, the date, the address of the recipient, the salutation or greeting, the body of the letter, the closing of the letter. It was well known that a person in the position I was expected to occupy — the position of a woman, and a poor one — would have no need whatsoever to write a letter, but the sense of satisfaction it gave everyone connected with teaching me this, writing a letter, must have been immense. I was beaten and harsh words were said to me when I made a mistake. The exercise of copying the letters of someone whose complaints or perceptions or joys were of no interest to me did not make me angry then; it only made me want to write my own letters, letters in which I would express my own feelings about my own life, as it appeared to me at seven years old. I started to write to my father. "My Dear Papa," I wrote, in a lovely, decorative penmanship, a penmanship born of beatings and harsh words. I would say to him that I was mistreated by Eunice in word and deed and that I missed him and loved him very much. I wrote the same thing over and over again. It was without detail; it was without color. It was nothing but the plaintive cry of a small, wounded animal: "My Dear Papa, you are the only person I have left in the world, no one loves me, only you can, I am beaten with words, I am beaten with sticks, I am beaten with stones, I love you more than anything, only you can save me." These words were not meant for my father at all, but the person for whom they were meant — I could see only her heel. Night after night I saw her heel, only her heel coming down to meet me.

I wrote these letters without any intention of sending them to my father; I did not know how to do that, to send them. I folded them up in such a way that if they were torn along the folds they would make eight small squares. There was no mysterious significance to this; I did it to make them fit more neatly under a large stone just outside the gate to my school. Each day, as I left, I would place a letter I had written to my father under it. I had, of course, written these letters in secret, during the small amount of time allotted to us as recess, or during some time when I was supposed to be doing other work but had finished before I was noticed. Pretending to be deeply involved in what I was supposed to be doing, I would write my father a letter.

This small cry for help did not bring me instant relief. I recognized my own misery, but that it could be alleviated — that my life could change, that my circumstances could change — did not occur to me.

My letters did not remain a secret. A boy named Roman had seen me putting them in their secret storage place and, behind my back, he removed them. He had no empathy or pity; any instinct to protect the weak had been destroyed in him. He took my letters to our teacher. In my letters to my father I had said, "Everyone hates me, only you love me," but I had not truly meant these letters to be sent to my father, and they were not really addressed to my father; if I had been asked then if I really felt that everyone hated me, that only my father loved me, I would not have known how to answer. But my teacher's reaction to my letters, those small scribblings, was fascinating to me — a tonic. She believed the "everybody" I referred to was herself, and only herself. She said that my words were calumny, a lie, libellous, that she was ashamed of me, that she was not afraid of me. My teacher said all this to me in front of the other pupils at my school. They thought I was humiliated, and they felt joy to see me brought so low. I did not feel humiliated at all. Her teeth were crooked and yellow, and I wondered then how they had

got that way. Large half-moons of perspiration stained the under-
arms of her dress, and I wondered if when I became a woman I, too,
would perspire so profusely and how it would smell. Behind her
shoulder on the wall was a large female spider carrying its sac of
eggs, and I wanted to reach out and crush it with the bare palm of
my hand, because I wondered if it was the same kind of spider or a
relative of the spider that had sucked saliva from the corner of my
mouth the night before as I lay sleeping, leaving three small, painful bites. There was a drizzle of rain outside; I could hear the sound
of it on the galvanized roof.

She sent my letters to my father, apparently to show me that she
had a clear conscience. She said that I had mistaken her scoldings,
which were administered out of love for me, as an expression of
hatred and that this showed that I was guilty of the sin called pride.
And she said that she hoped I would learn to tell the difference
between the two, love and hate. And when she said this I did look in
her face to see if I could tell whether it was true that she loved me
and to see if her words, which so often seemed to be a series of
harsh blows, were really an expression of love. Her face to me then
did not appear loving, and perhaps I was mistaken — perhaps I was
too young to judge, too young to know.

I did not immediately recognize what had happened, what I had
done: however unconsciously, however without direction, I had,
through the use of some words, changed my situation, I had perhaps even saved my life. To speak of my own situation, to myself or
to others, is something I would always do thereafter. It is in that way
that I came to be so extremely conscious of myself, so interested in
my own needs, so interested in fulfilling them, aware of my griev-
ances, aware of my pleasures. From this unfocussed, childish expression of pain, my life was changed, and I took note of it.

My father came to fetch me wearing the uniform of a jailer. To him
this had no meaning, it was without significance. He was returning
to Roseau from the village of St. Joseph, where he had been carrying out his duties as a policeman. I was not told that he would arrive
on that day, I had not expected him. I returned from school and
saw him standing at the final bend in the road that led to the house
in which I lived. I was surprised to see him, but I would only admit
this to myself; I did not let anyone know.

The reason I had missed my father so — the reason he no longer came to the house in which I lived, bringing his dirty clothes and taking away clean ones — was that he had married again. I had been told about this, but it was a mystery to me what it might mean; it was not unlike when I had been told that the world was round and it was the first time I had heard such a thing. I thought, What could it mean, why should it be? My father had married again. He took my hand, he said something, he spoke in English, his mouth had begun to curl around the words he spoke, and it made him appear benign, attractive, even kind. I understood what he said: He had a home for me now, a good home; I would love his wife, my new mother; he loved me as much as he loved himself, perhaps even more, because I reminded him of someone he knew with certainty he had loved even more than he had loved himself. I would love my new home; I would love the sky above me and the earth below.

The word "love" was spoken with such frequency that it became a clue to my seven-year-old mind, a clue that the love being spoken of did not exist. My father's eyes grew small and then they grew big; he believed what he said, and that was a good thing, because I did not. But I would not have wanted to stop this progression, this going away from here; and though I did not believe him I did not have any reason not to, and I was not yet cynical, I did not yet think that behind everything I heard lay another story altogether.

I thanked Eunice for taking care of me. I did not mean it, I could not mean it, but I would mean it if I said it now. I did not say goodbye. All my belongings were in a muslin knapsack, and my father placed it in a bag that was strapped on the donkey he had been riding. He placed me on the donkey, and then he sat behind me. And this was how we looked as my back was turned on the small house in which I spent the first seven years of my life: a man and his small daughter on the back of a donkey at the end of an ordinary day, a day that had no meaning if you were less than a smudge on a page covered with print. I could hear my father's breath, it was not the breath of my life; the back of my head touched his chest from time to time; I could hear the sound of his heart beating through the shirt of his uniform, a uniform that made people afraid when they saw him coming toward them. His presence in my life then was a good thing, and it was too bad that he had not thought of changing his clothes. It was too bad that I noticed he had not done so; it was too bad that such a thing would matter to me.

This new experience of leaving the past behind — of going from one place to another and knowing that whatever had been would remain just as it had been — was something I immediately accepted, a gift. This simple movement, the turning of your back to leave something behind, is among the most difficult to make, but once it has been made you cannot imagine that it was at all hard to accomplish. I had not been able to do it all by myself, but I could see that I had set in motion the events that would make it possible. If I were ever to find myself sitting in that schoolroom again, or sitting in Eunice's yard again, sleeping in her bed, eating with her children, none of it would have the same power it had once had over me — the power to make me feel helpless and ashamed of my own helplessness.

I could not see the look on my father's face as we rode, I did not know what he was thinking, I did not know him well enough to guess. He set off down the road in the opposite direction from the schoolhouse. This stretch of road was new to me, and yet it had a familiarity that made me sad. Around each bend was the familiar dark green of the trees that grew with a ferociousness that no hand had yet attempted to restrain, green unrelenting and complete; nothing could be added to it and nothing could be taken away from it. Each precipice along the road was steep and dangerous, and a fall down one of them would result in death or a lasting injury. And each climb up was followed by a slope down, at the bottom of which clustered, along the road, a choke of flowering plants, each plant with a purpose not yet known to me. And each curve that ran left would soon give way to a curve that ran right.

The day then began to have the colors of an ending, the colors of a funeral, gray and mauve, and my sadness became manifest to me. I was a part of a procession of sadness, which was moving away from my old life, a life I had lived then for only seven years. I did not become overwhelmed, though. The dark of night came on with its usual suddenness. My father placed an arm around me then, as if to ward off something — a danger I could not see in the cool air, an evil spirit, a fall. His clasp was at first gentle; then it grew tighter; it had the strength of an iron band. I did not become overwhelmed.

We entered the village in the dark. There were no lights anywhere, no dog barked, we did not pass anyone. We entered the house in which my father lived, and there was a light coming from a beautiful glass lamp, something I had never seen before; the light was fuelled by a clear liquid that I could see through the base of the lamp, which was embossed with the heads of animals unfamiliar to me. The lamp was on a shelf, and the shelf was made of mahogany, its brackets curling in the shape of two tightly closed paws. The room was crowded, containing a chair on which two people could sit at once, two other chairs on which only one person could sit, and a small, low table draped with a piece of white linen. The walls of the house and the partition that separated this first room from the other rooms of the house were covered with a kind of paper, and the paper was decorated with small pink roses. I had never seen anything like this before, except once, while looking through a book at my school — but the picture I had seen then was a drawing, illustrating a story about the domestic life of a small mammal who lived in a field with his family. In their burrow, the walls had been covered with similar paper. I had understood that story about the small mammal to be a pretense, something to amuse a child, but this was my father's very real house, a house with a bright lamp in a room, and a room that seemed to exist only for an occasional purpose.

At that moment I realized that there were so many things I did not know, not including the very big thing I did not know — my mother. I did not know my father; I did not know where he was from or whom and what he liked; I did not know the land whose surface I had just crossed on an animal's back; I did not know who I was or why I was standing there in that room of occasional purpose with the lamp. A great sea of what I did not know opened up before me, and its treacherous currents pulsed over my head repeatedly until I was sure I was dead. I had only fainted. I opened my eyes soon after that to see the face of my father's wife not too far above mine. She had the face of evil. I had no other face to compare it with; I only knew that this was the face of evil as far as I could tell. She did not like me. I could see that. She did not love me. I could see that. I could not see the rest of her right away — only her face. She was of the African people and the French people. It was night-time and she was in her own house, so her hair was exposed; it was smooth and yet tightly curled, and she wore it parted in the middle and plaited in two braids that were pinned up in the back. Her lips were shaped like those of people from a cold climate: thin and ungenerous. Her eyes were black, and not with beauty but with deceit. Her nose was long and sharp, like an arrow; her cheekbones were also sharp.

She did not like me. She did not love me. I could see it in her face. My spirit rose to meet this obstacle. No love. I could live in a place like this. I knew this atmosphere all too well. Love would have defeated me. Love would always defeat me. In an atmosphere of no love I could live well; in this atmosphere of no love I could make a life for myself. She held a cup to my mouth; one of her hands brushed against my face, and it felt cold; she was feeding me a tea, something to revive me, but it tasted bitter, like a bad potion. My small tongue allowed no more than a drop of it to come into my mouth, but the bad and bitter taste of it warmed my young heart. I sat up. Our eyes did not meet and lock; I was too young to throw out such a challenge. I could then act only on instinct.

I was led down a short hallway to a room. It was to be my own room. My father lived in a house in which there were so many rooms that I could occupy my own. This small event immediately became central to my life: I adjusted to this evidence of privacy without question. My room was lit by a small lamp, the size of my fist, and I could see my bed: small, of wood, a white sheet on its copra-filled mattress, a square, flat pillow. I had a washstand, on which stood a basin and an urn that had water in it. I did not see a towel. (I did not then know how to wash myself properly in any case, and the lesson I eventually got came with many words of abuse.) There was not a picture on the wall. The walls were not covered with paper; the bare wood — pine — was not painted. It was the plainest of plain rooms, but it had in it more luxury than I had ever imagined; it offered me something I did not even know I needed; it offered me solitude.

All of my little being, physical and spiritual, could find peace here, in this little place where I could sit and take stock.

I sat down on the bed. My heart was breaking; I wanted to cry, I felt so alone. I felt in danger, I felt threatened; I felt as each minute passed that someone wished me dead. My father's wife came to say goodnight, and she turned out the lamp. She spoke to me then in French patois; in his presence she had spoken to me in English. She would do this to me through all the time we knew each other, but that first time, in the sanctuary of my room, at seven years old, I recognized this as an attempt on her part to make an illegitimate of me, to associate me with the made-up language of people regarded as not real — the shadow people, the forever humiliated, the forever low. Then she went to the part of the house where she and my father slept; it was far away; I could hear the sound of her footsteps fade; I could hear their voices as they spoke, the sounds swirling upward to the empty space beneath the ceiling; they had a conversation; I could not make out the words; the emotions seemed neutral, neither hot nor cold; there was some silence; there were short gasps and sighs; there was the sound of people sleeping, breath escaping through their mouths.

I lay down to sleep, to dream of my mother — for I knew I would do that, I knew I would make myself do that. She came down the ladder again and again, over and over, just her heels and the hem of her white dress visible; down, down, I watched her all night in my dream. I did not see her face. I was not disappointed. I would have loved to see her face, but I didn't long for it anymore. She sang a song, but it had no words; it was not a lullaby, it was not sentimental, not meant to calm me when my soul roiled at the harshness of life; it was only a song, but the sound of her voice was like treasure found in an abandoned chest, a treasure that inspires not astonishment but contentment and eternal pleasure.

All night I slept and in my sleep saw her feet come down the ladder, step after step, and I heard her voice singing that song, sometimes humming, sometimes through an open mouth. To this day she will appear in my dreams from time to time, but never again to sing or utter a sound of any kind — only as before, coming down a ladder, her heels visible and the white hem of her garment above them.

I came to my father's house in the blanket of voluptuous blackness that was the night; a morning naturally followed. I awoke to the same landscape that I had always known, each aspect of it beyond reproach, at once beautiful, ugly, humble, and proud; full of life, full of death, able to sustain the one, inevitably to claim the other.

My father's wife showed me how to wash myself. It was not done with kindness. My human form and odor were an opportunity to heap scorn on me. I responded in a fashion by now characteristic of me: whatever I was told to hate I loved. I loved the smell of the thin dirt behind my ears, the smell that comes from between my legs, the smell in the pits of my arms, the smell of my unwashed feet. Whatever about me caused offense, whatever was native to me, whatever I could not help and was not a moral failing — those things about me I loved with the fervor of the devoted. Her hands as they touched me were cold and caused me pain. In her was a despair rooted in a desire long thwarted; she had not yet been able to bear my father a child. She was afraid of me; she was afraid that because of me my father would think of my mother more often than he thought of her. On that first morning, she gave me some food, and it was old, moldy, as if she had saved it especially for me, in order to make me sick. I did not eat what she offered after that; I learned then how to prepare my own food and made this a trait by which others would know me: I was a girl who prepared her own food.

Parts of my life then, incidents in my life then, seem, when I remember them now, as if they were taking place in a very small, dark place, a place the size of a doll's house, and the doll's house is at the bottom of a cellar, and I am way up at the top of the stairs peering down into this little house trying to make out exactly what is happening down there. And sometimes when I look down at this scene certain things are not in the same place they were in the last time I looked; different things are in the shadows, different things are in the light.

Who was my father? Not just who was he to me, his child — but who was he? He was a policeman, but not an ordinary policeman; he inspired more than the expected amount of fear for someone in his position. He made appointments to see people, men, at his house, the place where he lived with his family — this entity of which I was now a sort of member — and he would make these people wait for hours or he wouldn't show up at all. They waited for him, sometimes sitting on a stone that was just inside the gate of the yard, sometimes pacing back and forth from inside the yard to outside the yard, causing the gate to creak, and this always made his wife cross, and she would complain to these people, speaking rudely to them, the rudeness way out of proportion to the annoyance of the creaky gate. They waited for him without complaint, sometimes falling asleep standing up, sometimes falling asleep as they sat on the ground. They waited, and when he did not show up they left and returned the next day, hoping to see him; sometimes they did,

sometimes they did not. He suffered no consequences for his behavior; he just treated people in this way. He did not care, or so I
thought at first — but of course he did care; it was well thought out,
this way he had of causing suffering; he was part of a whole way of
life on the island which perpetuated pain.

At the time I came to live with him, he had just mastered the
mask that he wore for the remainder of his life: the skin taut, the
eyes small and drawn back as though deep inside his head, so that it
wasn't possible to get a clue to him from them, the lips parted in a
smile. He seemed trustworthy. His clothes were always ironed, clean,
spotless. He did not like people to know him very well; he tried
never to eat food in the presence of strangers or in the presence of
people who were afraid of him.

Who was he? I ask myself this all the time, to this day. Who was
he? He was a tall man; his hair was red; his eyes were gray. He must
have loved me then, he had told me so. I never heard him say words
of love to anyone. He wanted me to continue going to school, but I
did not know why. It was a great sacrifice that I should go to school,
because, as his wife often pointed out, I would have been more
useful at home. He gave me books to read. He gave me a life of
John Wesley, and as I read it I wondered what the life of a man so
full of spiritual tumult and piety had to do with me. My father had
become a Methodist and attended church every Sunday; he taught
Sunday school. The more money he had, the more he went to
church. And the richer he became, the more fixed the mask of his
face grew, so that now I no longer remember what he really looked
like when I first knew him long ago, before I came to live with
him. And so my mother and father then were a mystery to me: one
through death, the other through the maze of living; one I had
never seen, the other I saw constantly.

The world I came to know was full of treachery, but I did not
remain afraid, I did not become cautious. I was not indifferent to
the danger my father's wife posed to me, and I was not indifferent
to the danger she thought my presence posed to her. So in my
father's house, which was her home, I tried to cloak myself in an
atmosphere of apology. I did not in fact feel sorry for anything
at all, and I had not done anything, either deliberately or by accident, that warranted my begging for forgiveness, but my gait was a
weapon — a way of deflecting her attention from me, of persuad-

ing her to think of me as someone who was pitiable, an ignorant child. I did not like her, I did not wish her dead, I only wanted her to leave me alone.

I would lie in my bed at night and turn my ear to the sounds that were inside and outside the house, identifying each noise, separating the real from the unreal: whether the screeches that crisscrossed the night, leaving the blackness to fall to the earth like so many ribbons, were the screeches of bats or of someone who had taken the shape of a bat; whether the sound of wings beating in that space so empty of light was a bird or someone who had taken the shape of a bird. The sound of the gate being opened was my father coming home long after the stillness of sleep had overtaken most of his household, his footsteps stealthy but sure, coming into the yard, up the steps, his hand opening the door to his house, closing the door behind him, turning the bar that made the door secure, walking to another part of the house; he never ate meals when he returned home late at night. The sound of the sea then, at night, could be heard clearly, sometimes as a soft swish, a lapping of waves against the shore of black stones, sometimes with the anger of water boiling in a cauldron resting unsteadily on a large fire. And sometimes, when the night was completely still and completely black, I could hear, outside, the long sigh of someone on the way to eternity; and this, of all things, would disturb the troubled peace of all that was real: the dogs asleep under houses, the chickens in the trees, the trees themselves moving about, not in a way that suggested an uprooting, just a moving about, as if they wished they could run away. And if I listened again I could hear the sound of those who crawled on their bellies, of those who carried poisonous lances, and those who carried a deadly poison in their saliva; I could hear the ones who were hunting, the ones who were hunted, the pitiful cry of the small ones who were about to be devoured, followed by the temporary satisfaction of the ones doing the devouring: all this I heard night after night. And it ended only after my hands had travelled up and down all over my own body in a loving caress, finally coming to the soft, moist spot between my legs, and a gasp of pleasure had escaped my lips which I would allow no one to hear.

Contributors' Notes

ANDREA BARRETT lives with her husband in Rochester, New York. She is the author of the novels *Lucid Stars, Secret Harmonies, The Middle Kingdom,* and *The Forms of Water.* Her stories have appeared in numerous magazines, including *Story, American Short Fiction, New England Review,* and *Mademoiselle,* as well as in the anthology *American Voices: Best Short Fiction by Contemporary Authors.* "The Behavior of the Hawkweeds" will appear in her collection of short fiction, *Ship Fever & Other Stories,* forthcoming from W. W. Norton.

▪ For the last several years, I've been writing about the lives of scientists. I once meant to be a zoologist myself, and although I was derailed after a very brief bout in graduate school, I retain a passion for natural history and the texture and language of naturalists' lives. Mendel's life, in all its obsessive wonder and sadness, has long had a particular grip on me; as a child, long before I had any real understanding of Mendel or his work, I once tried to repeat his pea experiment.

I started this story in 1992, simply as an exploration of Mendel's life and this cruel, crucial incident with the hawkweeds. But after working on it for some time, and learning a little about the historical tensions between Czechs and Germans in Mendel's corner of Moravia, I realized that I wanted to write something more than a purely biographical fiction. I thought there might be ways to weave some of those tensions into the story and to make Mendel's experience resonate with the life of a contemporary scientist. Everything else in the story — Antonia, her grandfather Tati, the incident in the greenhouse; Richard with his hexadactyly and frustrated ambitions; the impatient students and the visiting professor from Germany — was imagined from there. Union College, in Schenectady, New

York, was where I spent my undergraduate years; two decades later it (or my vague memories of it) became the setting for the story.

KATE BRAVERMAN is the author of four books of poetry, a trilogy of novels about Los Angeles, *Lithium for Medea* (1979), *Palm Latitudes* (1988), and *Wonders of the West* (1993), and the 1990 short story collection, *Squandering the Blue*. She lives in Los Angeles with her husband, Alan, and daughter, Gabrielle. She was included in *The Best American Short Stories* in 1991 and in the *O. Henry Prize Stories* in 1992.

- "Pagan Night" was written during the second of three consecutive summers I spent on the Snake River in Idaho. The town was lyrical and strange, a farming community with unusual effects. It was like a Mormon Nepal. We rented a house on thirty acres. I saw the same silos every day from the window where I wrote, the fields of potatoes and barley. My twin silos and I loved them, and the thunderstorms and constant yellow heat. There was a trestle we would cross to fish the Snake and it terrified me, the thought a train might come. It gave me nightmares.

I wrote "Pagan Night" by going out to stalk it. I call that method writing. I went out armed, with a tape recorder, to hunt, outwit, wound, and then capture the story. I roamed all day, starting with a walk by the river. I saw a couple, flagrantly punk in so conservative a milieu, and I began to inhabit her, the stranger with magenta hair. I went to the zoo. By then, I was carrying a fictional baby. By nightfall, I had the entire story on four tapes and I was delirious.

For three weeks, I would intermittently transcribe a tape, and then stop the machine as I found places where I wanted to riff. I love rewriting. It's an entirely improvisational event. It's like playing guitar with an album, adding sound, filling out the sound, harmonizing, developing rhythms.

The tape recorder frees you from the page. It liberates you from the "study." It frees you from the patriarchal assumptions of what literature is and how it is made. I was trying to divest myself of conventional narrative and its limitations. For me as a millennial writer, there is only time and space. Time as internal thought or the rush of consciousness, and space as landscape. I believe thought is plot and landscape is definition, shape. I should mention that my editor, Howard Junker, cut four pages from the beginning of the story, and that really sculpted it. It was like a facelift. He brought out the good cheekbones of the thing.

With the tape recorder, the writer *enters* the world as she writes. It is the end of passivity and walls. The more kinetic, the better. It's like juggling with fire. The artist as arsonist. I have tapes of stories where I'm jogging or bike riding, and I'm breathing so hard, I can't transcribe them, can't hear the words over my breath.

The great aspect of the tape recorder is that you speak faster than you write. If you're doing internal work, you're closer to the actual spin of the mind, whirl of words, the fantastic speed of association. You're on the flow. You know what the river knows. Print of blue heron. Scar of moon. You open your arms and drift to God.

JENNIFER C CORNELL'S collection of short stories, *Departures*, won the 1994 Drue Heinz Prize for Literature and was published by the University of Pittsburgh Press. She teaches creative writing at Oregon State University in Corvallis, where she is working on a second collection and completing a nonfiction book on representations of Northern Ireland in contemporary British television drama.

▪ "Undertow" began as a story about a child's first romantic fascination with a woman from the traveling community, complicated by a number of even weaker subplots whose nature — like that of the original theme — embarrasses me too much to talk about now. But luckily (for once) I tend to procrastinate, and I work so slowly when I produce at all that by the time I got around to seriously writing the thing, the corner near Belfast city center where the woman sold fruit had been scheduled for renovation, and she had moved on. I remember her as a woman of arresting beauty, and by her complexion, her self-assurance, and her style of dress, she stood out from all other women I had encountered until then. I did not like losing her — I have saved the sections I wrote describing her — and I suspect the image of her has influenced the character that the narrator's mother became in her absence.

With the story altered in this way, other (better) ideas had room to take over. As a student at Magee College, I took the train from Belfast to Derry (a two-and-a-half-hour trip each way) twice a week for almost three years. Standing at the station in Coleraine one afternoon, I imagined an explanation involving playing cards for the large purple diamond on the face of the train that was coming toward us — and more important, imagined a child who would ask questions about it, and the parent who would answer in a way I'd want to hear. I spent the ride home making up explanations for what I saw in the fields and towns the train passed through. Originally I was going to give the child nightmares, corruptions of the stories her father told (since part of what I wanted to talk about was the failure of imagination to transform one's experience), but I am learning to suppress my impulse toward pessimism for the good of my fiction, or at least to express it more subtly, less simplistically, to even admit some reason for hope.

This impulse was the basis for the final image: an impossible blend of two Belfast wall murals, one Loyalist, the other Republican. Such murals are infamous; to many they have defined Northern Ireland: no film set in Belfast seems free of them, and as a consequence they are often what visitors to the city most want to see. I'd always been struck by how different the murals from the two traditions were stylistically, thematically, even in terms of what they suggested about the world view and self-conception of the artists who created them. These differences depressed me; they seemed to confirm the breadth and depth of the divisions between us. Nevertheless, these two murals — both powerful visual images, full of an idealism I empathized with, even shared, but which seemed futile, ultimately doomed — had always moved me, even made me feel proud, both of them, though they arose out of aspirations that were in diametric opposition and were, at least on one level, celebrations of a tradition of violence which I abhorred, intellectually. I wanted "Undertow" to address that ambivalence — my identification with both traditions, my admiration for the power of the images they'd produced, and my angry confusion at the imposition of these images, designed to intimidate one's own, as well as one's enemies, even if the space on which they appear is "public" in the strictest sense. Out of all this came a family I'm fond of, and an opportunity to celebrate a city and a community — by which I mean all the people of Northern Ireland — to whom I owe an enormous debt.

ANDREW COZINE lives in Mountain View, California, with his wife, Stefani, and their two small dogs. He attended Colorado College and is currently enrolled in the Columbia University Writing Program and at work on a novel. This is his first published piece.

▪ The material in this story is mostly autobiographical. I wrote it for a course taught by Joyce Johnson at Columbia. Originally I'd meant to write a story about all the odd people around me when I was growing up, but once I'd started writing about my own odd ways I couldn't stop.

I grew up wishing most of my best friends would move away. I wasn't just a hand-jiving freak, I was a freak magnet. There was my best friend, Jodie, the smallish third-grader who appears in this story as Joey, the boy with whom I played house. Jodie had a shrunken look to him, and he was always acting tough to make up for it. A cliché, I know, but that was Jodie all over. He got us in lots of trouble. In third grade we'd sneak out his window at night, strip naked, and flash police cars. In fifth grade our favorite pastime was the rock fight, where we'd stand twenty feet apart and hurl large stones at each other. It was around this same time that my worst best friend, Patrick Gunn, hit puberty. He'd chase me around his bedroom with a hard-on, and he was always trying to grab me between the legs: in class, at the video arcade, wherever the fancy struck him. Patrick had a long, devilish face and very pale skin; he always frightened me a little, but never more so than the time he confessed to raping his family's orange tabby, Archibald. It didn't help that during his confession Patrick was rubbing his penis against my bare right thigh.

So these were my friends, the playground pariahs. We were all still playing out superhero adventures down by the baseball diamond when the normal kids had graduated to football. Should I go on to mention the other superheroes? Ronnie and Edgar and the rest of them? Ronnie's still in prison, as far as I know. Edgar shot himself in the head on graduation from medical school. Even Paul, my best friend in kindergarten, won't embarrass me anymore. He hung himself from a rafter in his father's study, clutching a photograph of his sister in her bra and panties.

But the whole time I was growing up, these fellows were my life outside of the hand jive. I wondered why they were the ones the other kids ganged up on during recess. My green-haired friend Edsel, especially, was always getting pummeled and laughed at, usually for eating his boogers. I wondered why it was always Edsel and Jodie and Patrick, never me. I was weird enough to deserve these other strange boys as friends. Why didn't the normal kids pick up on my weirdness and attack me, too?

In high school I ran into a girl from elementary school named Elizabeth Dobbins. I recognized her immediately, though she looked nothing like the chubby girl who threw up on her desk in Mrs. Elk's second-grade class. I said hello to Elizabeth but, though we'd shared a classroom for three years, she didn't remember me at all. "I'm the one who told all the kids you threw up in Mrs. Elk's class," I prompted her. "You hated me for that." Elizabeth laughed politely, still shaking her head, and cut the conversation short. Was this her long-awaited revenge? I don't think so. I think the episode comes closer to revealing what I was like as a child than anything in this story of mine. Whenever these friends of mine touched me, for example, skin on skin, I used to act out a series of pantomimes, taking care not to let them see me. I'd scoop up their strangeness in the palm of one hand, ball it up with both hands, and toss it away. This was something I had to do. I didn't want my friends' strangeness infecting me. The other kids could point and laugh at Edsel, Jodie, and Patrick, but not at me. I was so concerned about my own counting and chanting and hand-jiving, so anxious to blend in and not attract attention, that I became — to lots of the people I grew up around — the little boy who wasn't.

How did I come to write this piece? It was driven by guilt, partly, for feeling ashamed of those friends of mine. For defending some of them only sometimes, others of them not at all. We were the same, my friends and I; they were only more untethered. It sounds strange to say, after all this, that I had a happy childhood. Appearances to the contrary, I swear I did.

PETER HO DAVIES, who was born in England in 1966, has been living in the United States since 1992. He received a B.S. in physics from the University of Manchester, a B.A. in English from Cambridge University, and an M.A. in creative writing from Boston University. His work has appeared in Britain in *Critical Quarterly* and in the United States in *The Antioch Review, The Harvard Review,* and *The Greensboro Review.* In 1993, he was awarded a Transatlantic Review Prize from the Henfield Foundation, and he has since completed a fellowship at the Fine Arts Work Center in Provincetown.

▪ "The Ugliest House in the World" was supposed to be a simple story. I had the central events, the child's death and the trout-tickling scene, in mind right from the start. But perhaps because I had them so early, the story refused to stop there. The character of Kate began to get away from me, and then that of the narrator, and then that of Kate *and* the narrator. Thematic concerns — the idea of home, the reach of guilt — started to make themselves felt, and finally the image of the Ugliest House began to assert itself.

I still couldn't quite give up on the idea of a simple story, but I liked nearly all of these awkward elements, even if I couldn't put them all together. In the end, I laid out all my half-finished scenes on a coffee table . . . and put my head in my hands. I had at least three separate openings, all of which I liked, none of which were sufficient. So I used them all, one after another. As suddenly and simply as that, the story was already half written. From there it was only a short leap to the notion that I could use all my various title ideas as subheads, and somehow they made the rest of the story manageable. (It's tempting, in retrospect, to call this process inspiration, but the truth was something more like desperation.)

As to where the story originates, most of it derives from secondhand experience. The circumstances of the child's death, tragically, occurred much as related. The outlook and jargon of young doctors I absorbed from three ex-roommates. As for the Ugliest House, in reality it's known as "The Ugly House" (*Tŷ Hyll,* in Welsh), and any visitor to North Wales is likely to drive past it. I went inside for the first time not too long ago, and my one regret is that I was unable to include the detail that the amount of land that went with the house was determined by how far you could throw an ax from each corner.

EDWARD J. DELANEY was born in 1957 in Fall River, Massachusetts, where he lives with his children, Kieran and Caitlin. A graduate of Fairfield University and Boston University, he began his career as a journalist, writing for *The Denver Post* and other newspapers. His short stories have appeared in *The Atlantic Monthly, Greensboro Review, Carolina Quarterly,* and other magazines. He teaches at Roger Williams University in Bristol, Rhode Island.

▪ I began by writing a story with a contemporary setting in which a lapsed priest sits in an insurance company cafeteria telling a coworker about how a bogus confession and his compulsion to act on it led to his downfall. I liked it well enough, but found myself wanting to push it back to a setting in which the priest's downfall is more resounding, from greater heights to greater depths. It led me to Ireland in the 1920s, but I would not claim the authority or experience to make it seem firsthand. So I hedged by putting in the narrator, who both gave the story distance that comes with reminiscence and also linked it to the present.

I'm always interested in the stories in which we assume or change roles and why it happens. Of course, it's too mysterious to fully grasp, but I suppose the reason to write is to search for some understanding of how one person becomes another, or how we can live unintended lives, or how we can somehow struggle against the identities we've formed for ourselves. The moment in which one person becomes another is both renewal and tragedy, a death and a birth; in this story I wanted to try to grasp such an event in some small way.

The story took shape through the autumn of 1992. I knew the ending first and went back to form a path to it. I am not one of those people who is able to write a story not knowing how it will turn out. It was slow going, a little each day, and in a lot of research I felt able to create a setting around the story. C. Michael Curtis at *The Atlantic* asked me to change the first sentence of the story, to move along more quickly. Otherwise, it is as it formed.

DON DELILLO has published ten novels. His short stories have appeared in a number of national magazines and literary quarterlies. He has won the National Book Award and the PEN/Faulkner Award for Fiction.

▪ This story began with the idea of a face on a billboard. I knew at once that the face was an apparition of someone sainted or otherwise dead, and that crowds would gather to see the face, and that the face would drift in and out of the graphic art on the billboard, and the other thing I knew was that the face would be a woman's or a girl's. All this happened years before I wrote the story. The story is everything else. It's the ten thousand things I saw, heard, made up, and threw together to get me to the face on the billboard.

STEPHEN DOBYNS has published eight volumes of poetry and seventeen novels. His most recent book of poems is *Velocities: New and Selected Poems, 1966-1992* (Viking Penguin, 1994). His most recent novels are *The Wrestler's Cruel Study* (Norton, 1994) and *Saratoga Fleshpot* (Norton, 1995). His book of poems, *Common Carnage,* will be published by Viking Penguin in March 1996. His book of essays on poetry, *Best Words, Best Order,* will be published by St. Martins Press at the same time. He is completing a book of short stories, *Eating Naked and Other Stories.*

▪ I had the title of this story, "So I Guess You Know What I Told Him," long before I had the actual story. My friend Ray Carver was one of the main reasons I moved to Syracuse. Some months after he died, I was sitting with a few friends and we were talking about Ray, and the sorts of things he might be writing were he alive. This led to possible story titles, and my contribution was "So I Guess You Know What I Told Him."

About five years after that, I was in a motel room in Moscow, Idaho, with a bad cold. I was doing a week's teaching at the University of Idaho, but because of my cold I didn't feel like socializing. I had been writing short stories for a couple of months, going at them in a way, which for me was entirely different. That too owed a lot to Ray Carver. I had once asked him how he had written a particular story and he said the first sentence had come into his head and he had just followed it. The first sentence was something like: "He was vacuuming the living room floor when the telephone rang."

In any case, I was trying to do the same. After all, that was how I wrote poems, while novels went through a long process of note-taking and outlining. But when I tried to do that note-taking and outlining with short stories I was unable to produce anything but anecdotes.

So there I was in a motel in Moscow, Idaho, with my cold and my box of Kleenex and my computer, and I began putting down first sentences to see if any might lead someplace. One of the first was the sentence "Floyd Beefus was picking a tick off one of the springers when the gas man slipped on a cracked dinner place on the cellar stairs and went bump, bump, bump, right to the bottom."

What evolved was a story set in Waldo County, Maine, where I lived for a few years. In language and situation, the story was completely unlike Ray, but because I was thinking of him, I gave the story my "Ray Carver" title: "So I Guess You Know What I Told Him." It keeps Ray alive in my head. It would have amused him.

William Trevor, in his *Paris Review* interview, described the short story as the "art of the glimpse." My story takes two people who have fairly usual lives and to each it introduces a little shock that jars them from their daily routines. This lets them see themselves from a slightly different perspective and maybe they learn something about themselves that they did not know before or had hidden from themselves. They experience this glimpse and, ideally, the reader experiences it as well.

One writes to find out why one is writing and my first drafts produced a jumble of material which I revised over the next year. The story takes us to one point: when the gas man realizes that he has been lying to himself. When I began the story, I had no idea this would happen. The revision process exists to make it seem that no other outcome is possible.

One of the reasons I write is that I constantly learn from the process of writing. I am constantly a student, I find new questions to ask about the craft. This also makes it exciting and I can persuade myself that I am getting better. Those conversations with Ray Carver began a process of thinking which led me to some discoveries about writing (even if others had learned them long before). The title of my story and its method, in a rather private way, seek to honor those discoveries.

EDWARD FALCO is the author of a novel, *Winter in Florida* (Soho, 1990), a collection of short stories, *Plato at Scratch Daniel's & Other Stories* (University of Arkansas Press, 1990), a chapbook of prose poems, *Concert in the Park of Culture* (Tamarack Editions, 1984), and a collection of hypertext poems, *Sea Island,* brought out in early 1995 by Eastgate Systems. In 1996, the University of Notre Dame Press will publish *Acid,* his second collection of short stories, which includes "The Artist." *Acid* is the recipient of the Richard Sullivan Prize from the Creative Writing Program at the University of Notre Dame. Other stories in the collection have been published in *TriQuarterly, Ploughshares, The Southern Review, The Virginia Quarterly Review, The Southwest Review, Quarterly West, The New Virginia Review,* and elsewhere. Falco has also won the Emily Clark Balch Prize for Short Fiction from *The Virginia Quarterly Review* and the Mishima Prize for Innovative Fiction from *The Saint Andrews Review,* as well as a Dakin Fellowship from the Sewanee Writers' Conference and the Governor's Award for the Screenplay from the Virginia Festival of American Film. He lives in Blacksburg, Virginia, where he teaches writing and literature at Virginia Tech.

▪ I think of "The Artist" as being, on one level, about escaping the past, how such an escape always involves a kind of murder, a killing off of old selves — but I was also thinking about art and artists when writing the story, about the way the process of creating art can expiate the past, or at least provide a temporary escape from it; about the way artists can take a nightmarish reality and turn it into something fascinating, sometimes even into something beautiful: Wilfred Owen writing about World War I, or Tim O'Brien writing about Vietnam, or Dorothy Allison writing about brutality and poverty. In Jim Renkowski, I imagined an artist who would do anything, anything at all, to maintain the order he has achieved in his life. Jim sees his world as precarious, like that cedar raft he imagines in the story's final paragraph. He's willing to do whatever is necessary to stay afloat.

The point of origin for the story, however, is located in Ellis, the drug dealer who, by the time we meet him, has traveled so far down the road of a twisted and perverse life — a life in which order is as dead as that cop in the freezer — that he needs to end it. Ages ago, when I spent a good deal of time hanging out in bars and playing chess, I knew a guy who was a chess player and who, on occasion, sold marijuana. When I knew him, I liked him. Years later I heard horrific stories about him, rumors of a strange and violent life. The stories shocked me. I have no idea if they were true, but they stayed with me, and they led, eventually, to "The Artist." I began with the image of a child in a car seat, appearing and disappearing behind bands of light as she is being driven to sleep along the streets of a suburb. I always wanted to use that image, which comes out of my own life, out of years of driving around my sleep-resistant daughter until she finally conked out. The image led me to the character of Jim Renkowski, an artist who has put together a good life. Then, as usual, trouble entered the picture, this time in the character of Tony, an associate of Ellis's, the drug dealer Jim knew in his distant past, a fictional creation fleshed out of the rumors of the real character I knew so many years ago — and the story took off from there.

MAX GARLAND grew up in western Kentucky where he worked as a rural mail carrier for many years. His first book of poems, *The Postal Confessions,* won the 1994 Juniper Prize. Other awards include an NEA Fellowship for Poetry and a James Michener Fiction Fellowship. He lives and teaches in Madison, Wisconsin.

- "Chiromancy" began with a single image, the image of a woman reading a man's palm by the light of her car speedometer. I tried to write a poem about it, a kind of meditation on the human hand. Then the characters began to assert themselves, and I decided to look at the same moment from different points of view. Since I'm no Robert Browning, I couldn't wrestle the dual interior monologues into poetry. So "Chiromancy" became something else.

It's hard to say more without beginning to steal from the story, or lapse into a bad paraphrase. Besides, what one says about a story is often as fictional as the story itself, and much more embarrassing.

ELLEN GILCHRIST was born in the Mississippi delta and lived part of her life in the Midwest. She has published twelve books of fiction, two books of poetry, and a collection of essays. She is the recipient of the National Book Award for Fiction and many other awards. *The Stucco House* is included in her latest collection of stories, *The Age of Miracles,* published by Little, Brown.

- I was writing at white heat when I wrote this story. For several months I had been writing stories as fast and hard as I could think them up. It was late in the evening when the idea for this one came to me. I *never* write in the late afternoon or night; I don't even like that time of day. But the impulse to write this story was so strong that I turned on the lamps around my typewriter and wrote until a draft was finished. By the time I went to bed I knew that I had been given a real gift. I was able to accept it because I had been writing stories for weeks and had the skills of my craft at hand.

JAIMY GORDON's second novel, *She Drove Without Stopping,* appeared in 1990 from Algonquin Books. Gordon is also the author of *Shamp of the*

City-Solo, a novel (McPherson & Company), and *Circumspections from an Equestrian Statue,* a novella (Burning Deck). With Peter Blickle, she translates from the German, most recently *Lost Weddings,* a novel by Maria Beig (Persea Books, 1990). She has been a fellow of the Fine Arts Work Center, Provincetown, and the Bunting Institute, Radcliffe College. In 1991 she won an Academy-Institute Award for fiction from the American Academy and Institute of Arts and Letters. She teaches in the creative writing program at Western Michigan University.

▪ When I was in my twenties, I worked for some years at Charles Town and Shenandoah Downs, at that time adjacent half-mile thoroughbred racetracks in West Virginia. I wrote "A Night's Work" to see if I could still conjure up the rinky-dink atmosphere of that life, the peculiar alliances it bred, and the vanishing tricks it worked on money.

As for the structure of the story: sometimes I poke around in folktale motif indexes to see if there might be something worth stealing. I ruminate happily on motifs like *the dog's certificate* or *the witch secretly substitutes her own daughter for the bride* or *the ox as mayor.* Usually I don't get around to writing the story. In "A Night's Work," I finally put to use Stith Thompson's motif K2151 from *The Folktale,* 1941: *the corpse handed around.* Thompson gives this brief description: "A corpse is handed around from one dupe to another. Each is accused of the murder and the trickster is paid to keep silence."

And that is more or less the plot of "A Night's Work." In my version, the corpse has three stops on its travels, although I do my best to divert attention from the symmetry of the tale with naturalistic furnishings and Runyonesque dialogue. (But Runyon's hoods who talk always in present tense are truer to the racetrack life than one would suppose. In racetrack parlance, the verb *to win* has neither tense nor number. "He win" or "She win" is always correct.)

Finally, although "A Night's Work" is in no way autobiographical, the story is a sort of cartoon of an unorthodox marriage — my own. When Nurse Pigeon makes money by hauling around Kidstuff's corpse, she is genuinely trying to save his honor, though this happens to coincide with her self-interest. Likewise, when I exhort my dear one to be loyal, serviceable, and true, it is his soul I am trying to save, though in my rush to improve him I may overlook his own puny efforts to be a mensch. Just so, Nurse Pigeon misreads Kidstuff's.

"A Night's Work" is dedicated to my mentor John Hawkes because he has written about racehorses better than anyone. His horses, however, are a lot classier than the ones I used to know.

GISH JEN is the author of two novels, *Typical American* (1991) and *Mona,* which will be published in 1996. She has received grants from the National

Endowment for the Arts, the James Michener/Copernicus Society, the Bunting Institute, and the Massachusetts Artists' Foundation. She lives in Massachusetts with her husband and son.

▪ I have written only two novels, but in both cases I found that three quarters of the way through, a short story popped out of me, quite unbidden. The first story that came this way was the basis of my second book, *Mona.* Will "Birthmates" be the basis of a third? We'll see.

I wrote "Birthmates" so fast that I cannot remember writing it. I remember only the feeling that I had of many big bubbles rising to the surface; I remember laughing. I felt as though I was on holiday, even as I was remembering times of great personal difficulty, and I think now that much of the laughter had to do with a feeling of difficulty surmounted; it was the laughter of distance finally achieved, of glorious escape.

The personal difficulty had to do with infertility and the termination of a much wanted pregnancy owing to genetic problems. That abortion was one of the most painful experiences of my life, and it of course remains no laughing matter. But aspects of my experience had become something I could consider in an irreverent way, and I cannot express how good it felt to be able to joke about any of it — how whole I felt again, finally, and how much I credited the process of writing for that feeling. For you write out of something you know or feel, but you write yourself into something you never would have expected.

Before I went to graduate school, I thought writing was about transcendence. Then I went to graduate school, and I thought it was about point of view. And now I know again that writing is indeed about transcendence, except that transcendence is a matter of point of view. The truly personal material out of which "Birthmates" was written was almost too painful to consider. So it was that I had to write it without considering it. I concentrated mostly on the background material, on getting the welfare hotel and the world of minicomputers right — only to discover that, in the course of composition, I had somehow composed myself.

THOM JONES is a visiting instructor at the Iowa Writer's Workshop. His second story collection, *Cold Snap,* was published by Little, Brown in June.

▪ I witnessed the opening scene of my story years ago in Africa. What struck me at the time was that the doctors and pilot were not of the usual "do-good" sort that one sees at the missions. They were hard core, so to speak. But I had forgotten all of that, and simians did not especially reemerge into my consciousness until my daughter asked for a cat and we answered an ad for a "female, tabby, declawed." When I picked up the cat, she slashed at me with her rear claws. I thought it was just nerves. I figured she would calm down in our happy home, but when she didn't I called the previous owner back and he told me that he had a confession to make: our new cat had been placed in the pen with the celebrated gorilla Ivan, who was in residence in a South Tacoma shopping mall. Whenever "Bobbie" fell asleep, Ivan would grab her and bounce her against the walls like a Ping-Pong ball. To spare her life, this saintly gorilla keeper told the owner that Ivan had killed Bobbie and placed the ad. Apparently animal activists were crusading on behalf of Ivan, who was the only privately owned gorilla in America. Michael Jackson wanted to adopt him, and so forth. Bobbie was meant to become his friend, but Ivan had recently killed a bird. A cat had worked that way with some other Washington State gorilla. Or something. Spotting a photograph of Ivan in *People* magazine, I thought, with a certain resentment, Well, good for you, Ivan. But what about Bobbie, who has been permanently traumatized?

In the meantime I had been working as a janitor at a public high school, had a bad back, and with Ivan then on my mind, I used to kid a certain teacher that I wanted to import a baboon — an African animal as common and detested as the American crow, but also smart, useful, and an underexploited source of labor. I wanted a durable Highlands baboon to pick up the classroom debris that was too large for my vacuum — pencil stubs, used condoms, hypodermic syringes, broken crack pipes, spent bullet cartridges, et cetera. I would call this baboon Odette. She would help me save on aspirin, acupuncture, chiropractic, Alexander technique, and so forth. Thus, in my imagination, George Babbitt became a character for me. After I wrote the drunken monkey scene, the rest of the story followed as if by magic. I certainly never expected the Odette I knew and loved to become a Rosicrucian, have a sex-change operation, then steal both my money and my passport, hop on a plane, and go back to Africa to reemerge as "George." Neither did I anticipate that she would become an alcoholic, opium smoker, and so forth. Still further, I didn't expect that "she" would become popular and adored. Just after the story appeared in *The New Yorker,* perfect strangers began to stop me in public and say, "Thom Jones, sir, what happens to the monkey? Does the leopard get it or does it live?" I was surprised at this since I didn't think short story writers were necessarily recognized on the street.

Perhaps "George" is at an AA meeting somewhere in Kinshasa as we speak, or perhaps the leopard did get her. I can only speculate. I haven't gotten any postcards from her, and although she betrayed me in a sense, I ain't no janitor no more and I do wish to thank her for that. I guess that's what you call a love/hate relationship. In any case, my back feels like a daisy and I wish George Babbitt the best, wherever she may be.

JAMAICA KINCAID is the author of *Annie John, A Small Place,* and *Lucy.* Her first book, *At the Bottom of the River,* received the Morton Dauwen Zabel Award of the American Academy and Institute of Arts and Letters. A staff writer for *The New Yorker*, she was born in Antigua and lives in Vermont.

AVNER MANDELMAN was born in Israel in 1947, immigrated to Canada in 1973, and received his M.B.A. from Stanford Business School in 1976. He received an M.A. in English and creative writing from San Francisco State College in 1993 and is working on a novel while continuing a career as a trader and investor. He lives near Stanford University with his wife and two children.

▪ My stories have two aims: first, to make you unable to stop reading, and second, to leave you unable to stop thinking of what you have read.

The first part is usually the result of form: mostly technical and rhetorical devices. I will say little about them, because they often come out sounding like cooking recipes or a sex manual. The second part, though, is easy to explain: to make you remember my story, I must agitate you deeply. And to do that, I must first of all agitate myself.

How does a writer agitate himself?

The best way is to write against the grain — your own. Find out your most cherished belief, the essence of your soul, and prove it wrong — in a story.

In "Pity" I set out to undermine my own moral belief, which is imbued through and through with the dark Jewish God (a far more interesting character, by the way, than the pale Christian deity): He is *El N'kamott,* a God of vengeance, before He is *El Rahúm,* a God of pity. Indeed, the Talmud says that he who pities the guilty will end up having to harm the innocent. The very act of pitying a criminal, then, is not only foolish, according to Jewish morality, but actually sinful. I, too, believe this, most strongly. And so, to produce the highest possible agitation in myself, I set out to write a story proving this morality wrong.

First, I created a partly unpleasant narrator and set him upon catching the mass murderer of his family — and of mine. It took about two weeks to build him up inside me, brick by brick. Then, after some research (perusing period newspapers, Paris city maps, and so on), I plunked this built-up creature in the middle of the action, wound his spring, and let him run toward the ending, where I intended to show him that if Nazis can learn to pity strangers, so can he (and I) learn to pity Nazis.

But then, even as I was writing that last scene, forcing myself to feel the Nazi's surprised compassion — and the narrator's terror at his own sudden feeling for his enemy — something happened: the Nazi smiled — and my story went to hell.

For what was the meaning of this smile? Was it truly beatific, or was it mocking to the end? Did the Nazi really take pity on the girl, or was he about to go back just to throw his pursuer (and me) into moral confusion

— a final act of revenge, if you will, on us both? — And so, finally, which morality did I prove right? Which wrong?

I can't stop thinking about it.

DANIEL OROZCO, who was born and raised in San Francisco, now lives in Seattle. He has studied creative writing at San Francisco State University and the University of Washington, where he is in the Ph.D. English program. Prior to the publication of "Orientation," he had two stories published in the *Santa Clara Review.*

▪ After graduating from Stanford University in 1979, having no idea what I wanted to do with my life, I registered with a temporary employment agency. I was soon hired at the University of California Medical Center, where I ended up working in various clerical capacities, off and on, for about ten years. It was, for the most part, very tedious work with very nice people about whom I knew very little. Near the tail end of my clerical career there, while taking classes at San Francisco State, I became reacquainted with the work of Chekhov. It struck me then — as it does still — that no other writer has been so adept at portraying the vagaries of unrequited love with such humane and unremitting clarity. So I set out to write a contemporary Chekhovian love story about an office romance. I wrote several versions of this story, all bad, and all proving the futility, I think, of trying to "do Chekhov."

By 1991 I was a full-time student, working as a temp between semesters. That summer I was assigned to an office on the twelfth floor of the Kaiser Building in downtown Oakland. The floor plan was laid out so that a main hallway traversed the length of the building. One side of this hallway consisted of doors to private offices, while the other side opened out onto the main work area, which consisted entirely of modular office cubicles. If you craned your neck and stood on your toes from anywhere in the hallway, there would come into view an expanse of cubicles that receded toward a horizon of shatterproof floor-to-ceiling windows, through which could be seen the shatterproof floor-to-ceiling windows of other downtown office buildings.

About six months later, I had to turn in a story for a workshop. I wanted to tackle that office romance again (*sans* the neo-Chekhovian pretensions), and when I recalled that rat-maze image from the twelfth floor of the Kaiser Building, the voice of a narrator came to me. As I worked on the first few drafts, the voice embodied itself as an omniscient guide, orienting a new employee to the workings of the office, conducting an initiate through the topography of the cubicles and of the lives contained therein. The unrequited-love story I had originally intended to write is gone . . . sort of. With every revision I made — adding and deleting characters, shuffling scenes and episodes, playing with the rhythms of language — the story became less and less about any particular one of its characters, and more about *all* of them, a kind of collective love story, perhaps, assembled and told by an all-knowing narrator — part gossip, part god — whose litany of intimate knowledge reveals much more about the vagaries of love and loneliness than any of us might care to know.

STEVEN POLANSKY lives in Minnesota with his wife and two sons. He resigned his position at St. Olaf College, where he was professor of English and creative writing, and now writes fiction.

• When I hear myself talk about my own work, I don't know what to believe. As I was writing "Leg," I would say to my wife, "I don't know where this one comes from." By which, I suppose, I hoped to suggest I'd tapped into something deeper and darker than usual — that I had, in this instance, caught wind of some mysterious afflatus. Maybe what I really meant was that "Leg" was hard, and not much fun, to write.

I live in a small Minnesota town where people are uneasy with things figurative and insubstantial. After "Leg" appeared in *The New Yorker,* I felt I needed to write a letter — a kind of affidavit — to our local paper, attesting that I still had both legs and a reasonably good rapport with my oldest son.

I like to take advice; I don't like to get it. Someone told me once that a writer's business is to choose what is most unlikely and make that seem inevitable. I thought about this when I was writing "Leg."

I asked an editor, who didn't like "Leg," if perhaps he'd like it more if he knew I was Jewish. He said he wouldn't. I like it more, knowing that.

I owe thanks to Daniel Menaker, my editor at *The New Yorker,* and to Mary Kierstead, his colleague there, both of whom helped make this story presentable. They also told me that Steven, not Steve, was the name for a writer who took himself seriously, and they were right.

MELANIE RAE THON is the author of two novels, *Meteors in August* and *Iona Moon,* and a collection of stories, *Girls in the Grass.* Originally from Kalispell, Montana, she now teaches in the Graduate Writing Program at Syracuse University. Her most recent fiction has appeared in *Ploughshares, Antaeus, Paris Review, Bomb, Story,* and *Ontario Review,* and the anthologies *Circle of Women* and *Women on Hunting.*

• Every story begins with a mystery. I never met Sid Elliott. He was a man with a cane at a lecture, the history of autopsy. He told my friend Mary he'd destroyed his knee trying to lift a woman the size of Gloria Luby. I wanted to understand: *Who was this man, and why did he attempt the impossible?* I had these images of the shattered knee, the dead woman — that's all. The first draft came in a rush, a single morning of nonstop writing, Sid's story pouring out in his own voice. I discovered his passion for Roxanne, his fear of his nieces, his journey through Vietnam. I saw his clumsy, overgrown body. I began to imagine living in a body like that.

I spent months in my mind with Sid, and each day I glimpsed another piece — his father with a hose, a dark-haired girl in the river, a man pulling fishbones from the garbage — but I never found an "explanation" for what he'd done with Gloria. Sid couldn't answer my questions. Watching him day after day only led me to a deeper mystery, the grace of his compassion. He was the last person alive who would touch Gloria Luby with tenderness. Somehow he knew nobody ever loved her enough or in the right way.

JOY WILLIAMS has written two collections of stories, *Taking Care* and *Escapes*, as well as three novels. In 1993, she received the Strauss Living Award from the American Academy of Arts and Letters. She lives in Key West.

▪ This was an extremely difficult story for me to write and I could not get *out*, I could not get out of the story. Writing it did not break up the frozen sea within, this is no ax, the sea remains as heavy and unyielding as ever. Everything here seems to me to be cold and hopeless and unresolved. There is such a distance between the living and the dead, it cannot be traveled really. So I perpetrate a lie here. I pretend to traverse some of the distance the living share. All art is about nothingness: our apprehension of it, our fear of it, its approach. We're on the same trail, we hurry along, soon we'll meet. There are details along the way, of course. Even here there are tattoos and hairdressers and ice cream and dogs with slippers. But these are just details, which protect us as long as they can from nothingness, the dear things.

100 Other Distinguished Stories of 1994

SELECTED BY KATRINA KENISON

Editorial Addresses of American and Canadian Magazines Publishing Short Stories

When available, the annual subscription rate, the average number of stories published per year, and the name of the editor follow the address.

African American Review
Stalkes Hall 212
Indiana State University
Terre Haute, IN 47809
$20, 25, Joe Weixlmann

Agni Review
Creative Writing Department
Boston University
236 Bay State Road
Boston, MA 02115
$12, 13, Askold Melnyczuk

Alabama Literary Review
Smith 253
Troy State University
Troy, AL 36082
$10, 21, Theron E. Montgomery

Alaska Quarterly Review
Department of English
University of Alaska
3221 Providence Drive
Anchorage, AK 99508
$8, 28, Ronald Spatz

Alfred Hitchcock's Mystery Magazine
1540 Broadway
New York, NY 10036
$34.97, 130, Cathleen Jordan

Amelia
329 East Street
Bakersfield, CA 93304
$25, 12, Frederick A. Raborg, Jr.

American Letters and Commentary
Suite 56
850 Park Avenue
New York, NY 10021
$5, 4, Jeanne Beaumont, Anna Rabinowitz

American Literary Review
University of North Texas
P.o. Box 13615
Denton, TX 76203
$10, 14, Scott Cairns, Barbara Rodman

American Short Fiction
Parlin 108
Department of English
University of Texas at Austin

Austin, TX 78712-1164
$24, 32, Joseph Krupa

American Voice
332 West Broadway
Louisville, KY 40202
*$15, 20, Sallie Bingham, Frederick
  Smock*

American Way
P.O. Box 619640
DFW Airport
Texas 75261-9640
$72, 50, Jeff Posey

Analog Science Fiction/Science Fact
1540 Broadway
New York, NY 10036
$34.95, 70, Stanley Schmidt

Another Chicago Magazine
Left Field Press
3709 North Kenmore
Chicago, IL 60613
$8, 16, Sharon Solwitz

Antaeus (ceased publication)
100 West Broad Street
Hopewell, NJ 08525
$30, 12, Daniel Halpern

Antietam Review
82 West Washington Street
Hagerstown, MD 21740
$5, 8, Suzanne Kass

Antioch Review
P.O. Box 148
Yellow Springs, OH 45387
$25, 11, Robert S. Fogarty

Apalachee Quarterly
P.O. Box 20106
Tallahassee, FL 32316
$15, 4, Barbara Hamby

Appalachian Heritage
Besea College
Besea, KY 40404
$18, 6, Sidney Saylor Farr

Ascent
P.O. Box 967

Urbana, IL 61801
$9, 8, group editorship

Asimov's Science Fiction Magazine
Bantam Doubleday Dell
1540 Broadway
New York, NY 10036
$39.97, 27, Gardner Dozois

Atlantic Monthly
745 Boylston Street
Boston, MA 02116
$15.94, 12, C. Michael Curtis

Baffler
P.O. Box 378293
Chicago, IL 60637
$16, Thomas Frank, Keith White

Bellowing Ark
P.O. Box 45637
Seattle, WA 98145
$15, 7, Robert R. Ward

Beloit Fiction Journal
P.O. Box 11, Beloit College
Beloit, WI 53511
$9, 14, Clint McCown

Black Warrior Review
P.O. Box 2936
Tuscaloosa, AL 35487-2936
$11, 13, Mark S. Drew

Blood & Aphorisms
Suite 711
456 College Street
Toronto, Ontario
MGG 4A3 Canada
$18, 20, Hilary Clark

BOMB
New Art Publications
594 Broadway, 10th floor
New York, NY 10012
$18, 6, Betsy Sussler

Border Crossings
Y300-393 Portage Avenue
Winnipeg, Manitoba
R3B 3H6 Canada
$23, 12, Meeka Walsh

Boston Review
Building E53
Room 407
Cambridge, MA 02139
$15, 6, editorial board

Boulevard
P.O. Box 30386
Philadelphia, PA 19103
$12, 17, Richard Burgin

Briar Cliff Review
3303 Rebecca Street
P.O. Box 2100
Sioux City, IA 51104-2100
$4, 4, Tricia Currans-Sheehan

Bridge
14050 Vernon Street
Oak Park, MI 48237
$8, 10, Helen Zucker

BUZZ
11835 West Olympic Blvd.
Suite 450
Los Angeles, CA 90064
$14.95, 12, Renee Vogel

Callaloo
Johns Hopkins University Press
701 West 40th Street, Suite 275
Baltimore, MD 21211
$25, 6, Charles H. Rowell

Calyx
P.O. Box B
Corvallis, OR 97339
$18, 11, Margarita Donnelly

Canadian Fiction
Box 946, Station F
Toronto, Ontario
M4Y 2N9 Canada
$34.24, 23, Geoffrey Hancock

Capilano Review
Capilano College
2055 Purcell Way
North Vancouver,
British Columbia
V7J 3H5 Canada
$25, 12, Robert Sherrin

Carolina Quarterly
Greenlaw Hall 066A
University of North Carolina
Chapel Hill, NC 27514
$10, 13, Bettina Entzminger, Brenda Thissen

Catalyst
236 Forsyth Street
Suite 400
Atlanta, GA 30303
$10, Pearl Cleage

Chariton Review
Division of Language & Literature
Northeast Missouri State University
Kirksville, MO 63501
$9, 6, Jim Barnes

Chattahoochee Review
DeKalb Community College
2101 Womack Road
Dunwoody, GA 30338-4497
$15, 21, Lamar York

Chelsea
P.O. Box 773
Cooper Station
New York, NY 10276
$11, 6

Chicago Review
5801 South Kenwood
University of Chicago
Chicago, IL 60637
$15, 20, Andy Winston

Christopher Street
P.O. Box 1475
Church Street Station
New York, NY 10008
$27, 50, Tom Steele

Cimarron Review
205 Morrill Hall
Oklahoma State University
Stillwater, OK 74078-0135
$12, 15, Gordon Weaver

Colorado Review
Department of English
Colorado State University

Fort Collins, CO 80523
$15, 8, David Milofsky

Columbia
404 Dodge
Columbia University
New York, NY 10027
*$13, 14, Susan Perry, Caitlin
   O'Neil*

Commentary
165 East 56th Street
New York, NY 10022
$39, 5, Norman Podhoretz

Concho River Review
English Department
Angelo State University
San Angelo, TX 76909
$12, 7, Terence A. Dalrymple

Confrontation
English Department
C. W. Post College of Long Island
   University
Greenvale, NY 11548
$8, 25, Martin Tucker

Conjunctions
Bard College
Annandale-on-Hudson, NY 12504
$18, 6, Bradford Morrow

Crab Creek Review
4462 Whitman Avenue North
Seattle, WA 98103
$8, 3, Linda Clifton

Crazyhorse
Department of English
University of Arkansas
Little Rock, AR 72204
$10, 13, Judy Troy

Cream City Review
University of Wisconsin, Milwaukee
P.O. Box 413
Milwaukee, WI 53201
*$10, 30, Kathleen Lester, Patricia
   Montalbano, Andrew Ribera*

Crescent Review
P.O. Box 15069
Chevy Chase, MD 20825-5069
$21, 23, J. Timothy Holland

Critic
205 West Monroe Street, 6th floor
Chicago, IL 60606-5097
$20, 4, Julie Bridge

Crosscurrents
2200 Glastonbury Road
Westlake Village, CT 91361
$18, 10, Linda Brown Michelson

Cut Bank
Department of English
University of Montana
Missoula, MT 59812
$12, 20, David Belman

Daughters of Nyx
Rose's Fairy Tale Emporium
P.O. Box 1187
White Salmon, WA 98672
Kim Antieu

Denver Quarterly
University of Denver
Denver, CO 80208
$15, 5, Brian Kiteley

Descant
P.O. Box 314, Station P
Toronto, Ontario
M5S 2S8 Canada
$20, 20, Karen Mulhallen

Descant
Department of English
Texas Christian University
Box 32872
Fort Worth, TX 76129
*$12, 16, Stanley Trachtenberg, Betsy
   Colquitt, Harry Opperman*

Eagle's Flight
P.O. Box 832
Granite, OK 73547
$5, 10, Rekha Kulkarni

Elle
1633 Broadway
New York, NY 10019
$24, 2, John Howell

Epoch
251 Goldwin Smith Hall
Cornell University
Ithaca, NY 14853-3201
$11, 23, Michael Koch

Esquire
250 West 55th Street
New York, NY 10019
$17.94, 12, Rust Hills

event
c/o Douglas College
P.O. Box 2503
New Westminster, British Columbia
V3L 5B2 Canada
*$15, 18, Christine Dewar, Maurice
   Hodgson*

Fantasy & Science Fiction
143 Cream Hill Road
West Cornwall, CT 06796
$26, 75, Edward L. Ferman

Farmer's Market
P.O. Box 1272
Galesburg, IL 61402
$10, 18, Jean C. Lee

Fiction
Fiction, Inc.
Department of English
The City College of New York
New York, NY
$7, 15, Mark Mirsky

Fiction International
Department of English and
   Comparative Literature
San Diego State University
San Diego, CA 92182
$14, Harold Jaffe, Larry McCaffery

Fiddlehead
UNB Box 4400
University of New Brunswick

Fredericton, New Brunswick
E3B 5A3 Canada
$16, 20, Don McKay

Florida Review
Department of English
University of Central Florida
P.O. Box 25000
Orlando, FL 32816
$7, 14, Russell Kesler

Folio
Department of Literature
The American University
Washington, D.C. 20016
$10, 12, Elisabeth Poliner

Four Quarters
LaSalle University
20th and Olney Avenues
Philadelphia, PA 19141
$8, 10, John J. Keenan

Free Press
P.O. Box 581
Bronx, NY 10463
$25, 10, J. Rudolph Abate

Geist
1062 Homer Street #100
Vancouver, Canada
V6B 2W9
$20, 5, Stephen Osborne

Georgia Review
University of Georgia
Athens, GA 30602
$18, 10, Stanley W. Lindberg

Gettysburg Review
Gettysburg College
Gettysburg, PA 17325
$18, 22, Peter Stitt

Glimmer Train Stories
812 SW Washington Street
Suite 1205
Portland, OR 97205
*$29, 40, Susan Burmeister, Linda
   Davies*

Good Housekeeping
959 Eighth Avenue
New York, NY 10019
$17.97, 7, Arleen L. Quarfoot

GQ
350 Madison Avenue
New York, NY 10017
$19.97, 12, Thomas Mallon

Grain
Box 1154
Regina, Saskatchewan
S4P 3B4 Canada
$19.95, 21, J. Jill Robinson

Grand Street
131 Varick Street
New York, NY 10013
$40, 20, Jean Stein

Granta
2-3 Hanover Yard
Noel Road Islington
London, England N1 8BE
$32, 12, Bill Buford

Green Mountain Review
Box A 58
Johnson State College
Johnson, VT 05656
$12, 23, Tony Whedon

Greensboro Review
Department of English
University of North Carolina
Greensboro, NC 27412
$8, 16, Jim Clark

Gulf Coast
Department of English
University of Houston
4800 Calhoun Road
Houston, TX 77204-3012
$22, 10, Susan Davis, Amy Storrow

Gulf Stream
English Department
Florida International University
North Miami Campus

North Miami, FL 33181
$4, 6, Lynne Barrett, John Dufresne

Habersham Review
Piedmont College
Demorest, GA 30535-0010
$12, David L. Greene, Lisa Hodgens Lumkin

Hadassah
50 West 58th Street
New York, NY 10019
$4, 2, Zelda Shluker

Harper's Magazine
666 Broadway
New York, NY 10012
$18, 9, Lewis H. Lapham

Hawaii Review
University of Hawaii
Department of English
1733 Donaghho Road
Honolulu, HI 96822
$15, 40, Robert Sean MacBeth, Kalani Chapman

Hayden's Ferry Review
Matthews Center
Arizona State University
Tempe, AZ 85287-1502
$10, 10, Tim Schell, Amy Sage

High Plains Literary Review
180 Adams Street, Suite 250
Denver, CO 80206
$20, 7, Robert O. Greer, Jr.

Hudson Review
684 Park Avenue
New York, NY 10021
$24, 8, Paula Deitz, Frederick Morgan

Hyphen
3458 W. Devon Ave., No. 6
Lincolnwood, IL 60659
$12, 8, Matthew Adrian, Margaret Lewis

Image
3100 McCormick Ave.

Wichita, KS 67213
$30, 12, Gregory Wolfe

Indiana Review
316 North Jordan Avenue
Bloomington, IN 47405
$12, 13, rotating editorship

Innisfree
P.O. Box 277
Manhattan Beach, CA 90266
$20, 100, Rex Winn

Interim
Department of English
University of Nevada
4505 Maryland Parkway
Las Vegas, NV 89154
$8, A. Wilber Stevens

Iowa Review
Department of English
University of Iowa
308 EPB
Iowa City, IA 52242
$18, 20, David Hamilton

Iowa Woman
P.O. Box 680
Iowa City, IA 52244
$18, 15, Marianne Abel

Italian Americana
University of Rhode Island
College of Continuing Education
199 Promenade Street
Providence, RI 02908
$15, 6, Carol Bonomo Albright

Jewish Currents
22 East 17th Street, Suite 601
New York, NY 10003-3272
$20, 8, editorial board

Journal
Department of English
Ohio State University
164 West 17th Avenue
Columbus, OH 43210
$8, 5, Kathy Fagan, Michelle Herman

Kalliope
Florida Community College
3939 Roosevelt Blvd.
Jacksonville, FL 32205
$10.50, 12, Mary Sue Koeppel

Kansas Quarterly
Department of English
Denison Hall
Kansas State University
Manhattan, KS 66506
$20, 8, Ben Nyberg, John Rees, G. W. Clift

Karamu
English Department
Eastern Illinois University
Charleston, IL 61920
$6.50, 8, Peggy L. Brayfield

Kenyon Review
Kenyon College
Gambier, OH 43022
$22, 18, Marilyn Hacker

Kinesis
P.O. Box 4007
Whitefish, MT 59937-4007
$18, 6, David Hipschman

Kiosk
English Department
306 Clemens Hall
SUNY
Buffalo, NY 14260
9, Robert Rebein

Laurel Review
Department of English
Northwest Missouri State University
Maryville, MO 64468
$8, 20, Craig Goad, David Slater,
* William Trowbridge*

Left Bank
Blue Heron Publishing, Inc.
24450 N.W. Hansen Road
Hillsboro, OR 97124
$14, 6, Linny Stoval

Literal Latté
Suite 240

61 East 8th Street
New York, NY 10003
$25, 12, Jenine Gordon

Literary Review
Fairleigh Dickinson University
285 Madison Avenue
Madison, NJ 07940
$18, 10, Walter Cummins

Lost Creek Letters
Box 373A
Rushville, MO 64484
$15, 10, Pamela Montgomery

Louisiana Literature
Box 792
Southeastern Louisiana University
Hammond, LA 70402
$10, 8, David Hanson

McCall's
110 Fifth Avenue
New York, NY 10011
$15.94, 6, Laura Manske

Mademoiselle
350 Madison Avenue
New York, NY 10017
$28, 10, Ellen Welty

Madison Review
University of Wisconsin
Department of English
H. C. White Hall
600 North Park Street
Madison, WI 53706
$14, 8, Andrew Hipp, Richard Gilman

Malahat Review
University of Victoria
P.O. Box 1700
Victoria, British Columbia
V8W 2Y2 Canada
$15, 20, Derk Wynand

Manoa
English Department
University of Hawaii
Honolulu, HI 96822
$18, 12, Robert Shapard, Frank Stewart

Massachusetts Review
Memorial Hall
University of Massachusetts
Amherst, MA 01003
$15, 6, Mary Heath, Jules Chametzky, Paul Jenkins

Matrix
c.p. 100 Ste.-Anne-de-Bellevue
Quebec
H9X 3L4 Canada
$15, 8, Linda Leith, Kenneth Radu

Michigan Quarterly Review
3032 Rackham Building
University of Michigan
Ann Arbor, MI 48109
$18, 10, Laurence Goldstein

Mid-American Review
106 Hanna Hall
Department of English
Bowling Green State University
Bowling Green, OH 43403
$12, 11, Rebecca Meacham

Minnesota Review
Department of English
State University of New York
Stony Brook, NY 11794-5350
$12, 10, Jeffrey Williams

Mirabella
200 Madison Avenue
New York, NY 10016
$17.98, 6, Amy Gross

Mississippi Review
University of Southern Mississippi
Southern Station, P.O. Box 5144
Hattiesburg, MS 39406-5144
$15, 25, Frederick Barthelme

Missouri Review
1507 Hillcrest Hall
University of Missouri
Columbia, MO 65211
$15, 23, Speer Morgan

Ms.
230 Park Avenue

New York, NY 10169
$45, 7, *Marcia Ann Gillespie*

Nassau Review
English Department
Nassau Community College
One Education Drive
Garden City, NY 11530-6793
Paul A. Doyle

Nebraska Review
Writers' Workshop, ASH 212
University of Nebraska
Omaha, NE 68182-0324
$10, 10, *Art Homer, Richard Duggin*

New Delta Review
Creative Writing Program
English Department
Louisiana State University
Baton Rouge, LA 70803
$7, 9, *Stephen Schoen, Tony Whitt*

New England Review
Middlebury College
Middlebury, VT 05753
$18, 16, *T. R. Hummer*

New Letters
University of Missouri
4216 Rockhill Road
Kansas City, MO 64110
$17, 21, *James McKinley*

New Orleans Review
P.O. Box 195
Loyola University
New Orleans, LA 70118
$25, 4, *Ralph Adamo*

New Quarterly
English Language Proficiency
 Programme
University of Waterloo
Waterloo, Ontario
N2L 3G1 Canada
$14, 26, *Peter Hinchcliffe, Kim Jernigan,
 Mary Merikle, Linda Kenyon*

New Renaissance
9 Heath Road

Arlington, MA 02174
$11.50, 5, *Louise T. Reynolds*

New Yorker
25 West 43rd Street
New York, NY 10036
$32, 45, *Tina Brown*

Nimrod
Arts and Humanities Council
 of Tulsa
2210 South Main Street
Tulsa, OK 74114
$10, 10, *Francine Ringold*

North American Review
University of Northern Iowa
1222 West 27th Street
Cedar Falls, IA 50614
$18, 13, *Robley Wilson, Jr.*

North Dakota Quarterly
University of North Dakota
P.O. Box 8237
Grand Forks, ND 58202
$15, 13, *William Borden*

Northwest Review
369 PLC
University of Oregon
Eugene, OR 97403
$14, 10, *Hannah Wilson*

Oasis
P.O. Box 626
Largo, FL 34649-0626
$22, 14, *Neal Storrs*

Ohio Review
Ellis Hall
Ohio University
Athens, OH 45701-2979
$16, 10, *Wayne Dodd*

Omni
1965 Broadway
New York, NY 10023-5965
$24, 20, *Ellen Datlow*

Ontario Review
9 Honey Brook Drive

Princeton, NJ 08540
$12, 8, Raymond J. Smith

Other Voices
University of Illinois at Chicago
Department of English
(M/C 162) Box 4348
Chicago, IL 60680
$20, 30, Sharon Fiffer, Lois Hauselman

Oxalis
Stone Ridge Poetry Society
P.O. Box 3993
Kingston, NY 12401
$18, 12, Shirley Powell

Oxford American
115½ South Lamar
Oxford, MS 38655
$16, 12, Marc Smirnoff

Oxygen
Suite 1010
535 Geary Street
San Francisco, CA 94102
$14, 10, Richard Hack

Paris Review
541 East 72nd Street
New York, NY 10021
$34, 14, George Plimpton

Parting Gifts
3006 Stonecutter Terrace
Greensboro, NC 27405
Robert Bixby

Partisan Review
236 Bay State Road
Boston, MA 02215
$22, 4, William Phillips

Passages North
Kalamazoo College
1200 Academy Street
Kalamazoo, MI 49007
$10, 8, Michael Barrett

Playboy
Playboy Building
919 North Michigan Avenue

Chicago, IL 60611
$24, 23, Alice K. Turner

Ploughshares
Emerson College
100 Beacon Street
Boston, MA 02116
$19, 20, Don Lee

Potpourri
P.O. Box 8278
Prairie Village, KS 66208
$12, 20, Polly W. Swafford

Prairie Fire
423-100 Arthur Street
Winnipeg, Manitoba
R3B 1H3 Canada
$24, 8, Andris Taskans

Prairie Schooner
201 Andrews Hall
University of Nebraska
Lincoln, NE 68588-0334
$20, 20, Hilda Raz

Prism International
Department of Creative Writing
University of British Columbia
Vancouver, British Columbia
V6T 1W5 Canada
$16, 20, Shelly Darjes

Provincetown Arts
650 Commercial Street
Provincetown MA 02657
$9, 4, Christopher Busa

Puerto del Sol
P.O. Box 3E
Department of English
New Mexico State University
Las Cruces, NM 88003
$10, 12, Kevin McIlvoy, Antonya Nelson

Quarry Magazine
P.O. Box 1061
Kingston, Ontario
K7L 4Y5 Canada
$22, 20, Steven Heighton

Quarterly
650 Madison Avenue, Suite 2600
New York, NY 10022
$30, 210, Gordon Lish

RE:AL
School of Liberal Arts
Stephen F. Austin State University
P.O. Box 13007
SFA Station
Nacogdoches, TX 75962
$8, 10, Lee Schultz

Redbook
959 Eighth Avenue
New York, NY 10017
$11.97, 10, Dawn Raffel

River Oak Review
River Oak Arts
P.O. Box 3127
Oak Park, IL 60303
$10, 4, Barbara Croft

River Styx
Big River Association
14 South Euclid
St. Louis, MO 63108
$20, 30, Lee Fournier

Room of One's Own
P.O. Box 46160, Station G
Vancouver, British Columbia
V6R 4G5 Canada
$20, 12, collective editorship

Rosebud
P.O. Box 459
Cambridge, WI 53523
$10, 20, Roderick Clark

Salamander
48 Ackers Avenue
Brookline, MA 02146
$12, 10, Jennifer Barber

Salmagundi
Skidmore College
Saratoga Springs, NY 12866
$15, 4, Robert Boyers

San Jose Studies
c/o English Department
San Jose State University
One Washington Square
San Jose, CA 95192
$12, 5, John Engell, D. Mesher

Santa Monica Review
Center for the Humanities
Santa Monica College
1900 Pico Boulevard
Santa Monica, CA 90405
$12, 16, Jim Krusoe

Saturday Night
184 Front Street E, Suite 400
Toronto, Ontario
M5V 2Z4 Canada
*$26.45, 4, Anne Collins, Dianna
   Simmons*

Seattle Review
Padelford Hall, GN-30
University of Washington
Seattle, WA 98195
$8, 12, Charles Johnson

Sewanee Review
University of the South
Sewanee, TN 37375-4009
$16, 10, George Core

Shenandoah
Washington and Lee University
P.O. Box 722
Lexington, VA 24450
$11, 17, Dabney Stuart

Short Fiction by Women
Box 1276 Stuyvesant Station
New York, NY 10009
$18, 20, Rachel Whalen

Sinister Wisdom
P.O. Box 3252
Berkeley, CA 94703
*$17, 15, Akiba Onada-Sikwoia, Kyos
   Featherdancing*

Sonora Review
Department of English

University of Arizona
Tucson, AZ 85721
$10, 12, Dale Gregory Anderson, Bill Brymer

So to Speak
4400 University Drive
George Mason University
Fairfax, VA 22030-444
$7, 10, Colleen Kearney

South Carolina Review
Department of English
Clemson University
Clemson, SC 29634-1503
$7, 8, Frank Day, Carol Johnston

South Dakota Review
University of South Dakota
P.O. Box 111 University Exchange
Vermillion, SD 57069
$15, 15, John R. Milton

Southern Exposure
P.O. Box 531
Durham, NC 27702
$24, 12, Eric Bates

Southern Humanities Review
9088 Haley Center
Auburn University
Auburn, AL 36849
$15, 5, Dan R. Latimer, R. T. Smith

Southern Review
43 Allen Hall
Louisiana State University
Baton Rouge, LA 70803
$20, 17, James Olney, Dave Smith

Southwest Review
Southern Methodist University
P.O. Box 4374
Dallas, TX 75275
$20, 15, Willard Spiegelman

Stories
Box 1467
Arlington, MA 02174
$18, 12, Amy R. Kaufman

Story
1507 Dana Avenue
Cincinnati, OH 45207
$17, 52, Lois Rosenthal

Story Quarterly
P.O. Box 1416
Northbrook, IL 60065
$12, 20, Margaret Barrett, Anne Brashler, Diane Williams

Sun
107 North Roberson Street
Chapel Hill, NC 27516
$30, 30, Sy Safransky

Sycamore Review
Department of English
Heavilon Hall
Purdue University
West Lafayette, IN 47907
$9, 5, Michael Manley

Tamaqua
Humanities Department
Parkland College
2400 West Bradley Avenue
Champaign, IL 61821
$10, 5, Neil Archer

Tampa Review
P.O. Box 13F
University of Tampa
401 West Kennedy Boulevard
Tampa, FL 33606-1490
$10, 2, Andy Solomon

Thema
Box 74109
Metairie, LA 70053-4109
$16, Virginia Howard

Threepenny Review
P.O. Box 9131
Berkeley, CA 94709
$16, 10, Wendy Lesser

Tikkun
5100 Leona Street
Oakland, CA 94619
$36, 10, Michael Lerner

Trafika
Columbia Post Office
Box 250413
New York, NY 10025-1536
*$35, 27, Michael Lee, Alfredo Sanchez,
  Jeffrey Young*

Treasure House
Suite 3A
1106 Oak Hill Avenue
Hagerstown, MD 21742
$9, 6, J. G. Wofensberger

TriQuarterly
2020 Ridge Avenue
Northwestern University
Evanston, IL 60208
$20, 15, Reginald Gibbons

Turnstile
175 Fifth Avenue, Suite 2348
New York, NY 10010
$12, 24, group editorship

University of Windsor Review
Department of English
University of Windsor
Windsor, Ontario
N9B 3P4 Canada
$19.95, 12, Alistair MacLeod

Urbanite
P.O. Box 4737
Davenport, IA 52808
$13.50, 6, Mark McLaughlin

Urbanus
P.O. Box 192561
San Francisco, CA 94119
$8, 4, Peter Drizhal

Venue
512-9 St. Nicholas Street
Toronto, Ontario
M4Y 1W5 Canada
$26, 4, Jane Francisco

Virginia Quarterly Review
One West Range
Charlottesville, VA 22903
$15, 14, Staige D. Blackford

Voice Literary Supplement
842 Broadway
New York, NY 10003
$17, 12, M. Mark

Wascana Review
English Department
University of Regina
Regina, Saskatchewan
S4S 0A2 Canada
$7, 8, J. Shami

Weber Studies
Weber State College
Ogden, UT 84408
$10, 2, Neila Seshachari

Webster Review
Webster University
470 East Lockwood
Webster Groves, MO 63119
$5, 2, Nancy Schapiro

Wellspring
770 Tonkawa Road
Long Lake, MN 55356
$8, 10, Maureen LaJoy

West Branch
Department of English
Bucknell University
Lewisburg, PA 17837
*$7, 10, Robert Love Taylor,
  Karl Patten*

Western Humanities Review
University of Utah
Salt Lake City, UT 84112
$20, 10, Barry Weller

Whetstone
Barrington Area Arts Council
P.O. Box 1266
Barrington, IL 60011
$6.25, 11, Sandra Berris

Whiskey Island
University Center
Cleveland State University
2121 Euclid Avenue

Cleveland, OH 44115
$6, 10, Kathy Smith

William and Mary Review
College of William and Mary
P.O. Box 8795
Williamsburg, VA 23187
$5, 4, Emily Chang, Allan Mitchell

Willow Springs
MS-1
Eastern Washington University
Cheney, WA 99004
$8, 8, Heather Keast

Wind
RFD Route 1
P.O. Box 809K
Pikeville, KY 41501
$7, 20, Quentin R. Howard

Witness
Oakland Community College
Orchard Ridge Campus
27055 Orchard Lake Road
Farmington Hills, MI 48334
$12, 24, Peter Stine

Worcester Review
6 Chatham Street
Worcester, MA 01690
$10, 8, Rodger Martin

Writ
Innis College
University of Toronto
2 Sussex Avenue

Toronto, Ontario
M5S 1J5 Canada
$8, 7, Roger Greenwald

Writers Forum
University of Colorado
P.O. Box 7150
Colorado Springs, CO 80933-7150
$8.95, 15, Alexander Blackburn

Xavier Review
Xavier University
Box 110C
New Orleans, LA 70125
$10, Thomas Bonner, Jr.

Yale Review
1902A Yale Station
New Haven, CT 06520
$20, 12, J. D. McClatchy

Yankee
Yankee Publishing, Inc.
Dublin, NH 03444
$22, 4, Judson D. Hale, Sr.

Yellow Silk
P.O. Box 6374
Albany, CA 94706
$30, 10, Lily Pond

ZYZZYVA
41 Sutter Street, Suite 1400
San Francisco, CA 94104
$28, 12, Howard Junker